A FRIEND OF CÆSAR

THE MACMILLAN COMPANY
NEW YORK • CHICAGO
DALLAS • ATLANTA • SAN FRANCISCO
LONDON • MANILA
IN CANADA
BRETT-MACMILLAN LTD.
GALT, ONTARIO

A FRIEND OF CÆSAR

A TALE OF THE FALL OF THE ROMAN REPUBLIC

Time, 50–47 B.C.

BY

WILLIAM STEARNS DAVIS

"Others better may mould the life-breathing brass of the image,
 And living features, I ween, draw from the marble, and better
 Argue their cause in the court ; may mete out the span of the heavens,
 Mark out the bounds of the poles, and name all the stars in their turnings.
 Thine 'tis the peoples to rule with dominion — this, Roman, remember ! —
 These for thee are the arts, to hand down the laws of the treaty,
 The weak in mercy to spare, to fling from their high seats the haughty."

— Vergil, *Æn.* vi. 847-853.

New York
THE MACMILLAN COMPANY
COLLIER-MACMILLAN LIMITED, LONDON

Set up and electrotyped.   Published May, 1900.
Twenty-third Printing 1964

The Macmillan Company, New York
Collier-Macmillan Canada Ltd., Toronto, Ontario

To My Father

WILLIAM VAIL WILSON DAVIS

WHO HAS TAUGHT ME MORE

THAN ALL MY BOOKS

PREFACE

IF this book serves to show that Classical Life presented many phases akin to our own, it will not have been written in vain.

After the book was planned and in part written, it was discovered that Archdeacon Farrar had in his story of "Darkness and Dawn" a scene, "Onesimus and the Vestal," which corresponds very closely to the scene, "Agias and the Vestal," in this book; but the latter incident was too characteristically Roman not to risk repetition. If it is asked why such a book as this is desirable after those noble fictions, "Darkness and Dawn" and "Quo Vadis," the reply must be that these books necessarily take and interpret the Christian point of view. And they do well; but the Pagan point of view still needs its interpretation, at least as a help to an easy apprehension of the life and literature of the great age of the Fall of the Roman Republic. This is the aim of "A Friend of Cæsar." The Age of Cæsar prepared the way for the Age of Nero, when Christianity could find a world in a state of such culture, unity, and social stability that it could win an adequate and abiding triumph.

Great care has been taken to keep to strict historical probability; but in one scene, the "Expulsion of the Tribunes," there is such a confusion of accounts in the authorities themselves that I have taken some slight liberties.

W. S. D.

HARVARD UNIVERSITY,
 January 16, 1900.

CONTENTS

A FRIEND OF CÆSAR

A young Roman nobleman finds romance during Caesar's conquests and the fall of the Republic.

A FRIEND OF CÆSAR

CHAPTER I

I

PRÆNESTE

It was the Roman month of September, seven hundred and four years after Romulus — so tradition ran — founded the little village by the Tiber which was to become "Mother of Nations," "Centre of the World," "Imperial Rome." To state the time according to modern standards it was July, fifty years before the beginning of the Christian Era. The fierce Italian sun was pouring down over the tilled fields and stretches of woodland and grazing country that made up the landscape, and the atmosphere was almost aglow with the heat. The dust lay thick on the pavement of the highway, and rose in dense, stifling clouds, as a mule, laden with farm produce and driven by a burly countryman, trudged reluctantly along.

Yet, though the scene suggested the heat of midsummer, it was far from being unrefreshing, especially to the eyes of one newly come. For this spot was near "cool Præneste," one of the favourite resorts of Latium to the wealthy, invalid, or indolent of Rome, who shunned the excessive heat of the capital. And they were wise in their choice; for Præneste, with its citadel, which rose twelve hundred feet over the adjoining country, commanded in its ample sweep both the views and the

B   1

breezes of the whole wide-spreading Campagna. Here, clustering round the hill on which stood the far-famed "Temple of Fortune," lay the old Latin town of the Prænestians; a little farther westward was the settlement founded some thirty odd years before by Sulla as a colony. Farther out, and stretching off into the open country, lay the farmhouses and villas, gardens and orchards, where splendid nuts and roses, and also wine, grew in abundant measure.

A little stream ran close to the highway, and here an irrigating machine[1] was raising water for the fields. Two men stood on the treadmill beside the large-bucketed wheel, and as they continued their endless walk the water dashed up into the trough and went splashing down the ditches into the thirsty gardens. The workers were tall, bronze-skinned Libyans, who were stripped to the waist, showing their splendid chests and rippling muscles. Beside the trough had just come two women, by their coarse and unpretentious dress evidently slaves, bearing large earthen water-pots which they were about to fill. One of the women was old, and bore on her face all the marks which a life of hard manual toil usually leaves behind it; the other young, with a clear, smooth complexion and a rather delicate Greek profile. The Libyans stopped their monotonous trudge, evidently glad to have some excuse for a respite from their exertions.

"Ah, ha! Chloë," cried one of them, "how would you like it, with your pretty little feet, to be plodding at this mill all the day? Thank the Gods, the sun will set before a great while. The day has been hot as the lap of an image of Moloch!"[2]

---

[1] Water columbarium.

[2] The Phœnician god, also worshipped in North Africa, in whose idol was built a fire to consume human sacrifices.

"Well, Hasdrubal," said Chloë, the younger woman, with a pert toss of her head, "if my feet were as large as yours, and my skin as black and thick, I should not care to complain if I had to work a little now and then."

"Oh! of course," retorted Hasdrubal, a little nettled. "Your ladyship is too refined, too handsome, to reflect that people with black skins as well as white may get heated and weary. Wait five and twenty years, till your cheeks are a bit withered, and see if Master Drusus doesn't give you enough to make you tired from morning till night."

"You rude fellow," cried Chloë, pouting with vexation, "I will not speak to you again. If Master Drusus were here, I would complain of you to him. I have heard that he is not the kind of a master to let a poor maid of his be insulted."

"Oh, be still, you hussy!" said the elder woman, who felt that a life of labour had spoiled what might have been quite the equal of Chloë's good looks. "What do you know of Master Drusus? He has been in Athens ever since you were bought. I'll make Mamercus, the steward, believe you ought to be whipped."

What tart answer Chloë might have had on the end of her tongue will never be known; for at this moment Mago, the other Libyan, glanced up the road, and cried: —

"Well, mistress, perhaps you will see our master very soon. He was due this afternoon or next day from Puteoli, and what is that great cloud of dust I see off there in the distance? Can't you make out carriages and horsemen in the midst of it, Hasdrubal?"

Certainly there was a little cavalcade coming up the high-way. Now it was a mere blotch moving in the sun and dust; then clearer; and then out of the cloud of light, flying sand came the clatter of hoofs on the pavement, the whir of wheels, and ahead of the rest of the party two dark Numidian outriders in bright red mantles appeared, pricking along their white African steeds. Chloë clapped her little hands, steadied her water-pot, and sprang up on the staging of the treadmill beside Mago.

"It is he!" she cried. "It must be Master Drusus coming back from Athens!" She was a bit excited, for an event like the arrival of a new master was a great occurrence in the monotonous life of a country slave.

The cortège was still a good way off.

"What is Master Drusus like?" asked Chloë. "Will he be kind, or will he be always whipping like Mamercus?"

"He was not in charge of the estate," replied Laïs, the older woman, "when he went away to study at Athens [1] a few years ago. But he was always kind as a lad. Cappadox, his old body-servant, worshipped him. I hope he will take the charge of the farm out of the steward's hands."

"Here he comes!" cried Hasdrubal. "I can see him in the nearest carriage." And then all four broke out with their salutation, " Salve ! Salve, Domine ! " [2] " Good health to your lordship!"

A little way behind the outriders rolled a comfortable, four-wheeled, covered carriage,[3] ornamented with handsome embossed plate-work of bronze. Two sleek, jet-black steeds were whirling it swiftly onward. Behind, a couple of equally speedy grey mules were drawing an open wagon loaded with baggage, and containing two smart-looking slave-boys. But all four persons at the treadmill had fixed their eyes on the

---

[1] A few years at the philosophy schools of that famous city were almost as common to Roman students and men of culture as " studying in Germany " to their American successors.

[2] Master, " Lord " of slaves and freedmen.   [3] Rheda.

other conveyance. Besides a sturdy driver, whose ponderous hands seemed too powerful to handle the fine leather reins, there were sitting within an elderly, decently dressed man, and at his side another much younger. The former personage was Pausanias, the freedman and travelling companion [1] of his friend and patron, Quintus Livius Drusus, the "Master Drusus" of whom the slaves had been speaking. Chloë's sharp eyes scanned her strange owner very keenly, and the impression he created was not in the least unfavourable. Drusus was apparently of about two and twenty. As he was sitting, he appeared a trifle short in stature, with a thick frame, solid shoulders, long arms, and large hands. His face was distinctively Roman. The features were a little irregular, though not to an unpleasant extent. The profile was aquiline. His eyes were brown and piercing, turning perpetually this way and that, to grasp every detail of the scene around. His dark, reddish hair was clipped close, and his chin was smooth shaven and decidedly firm — stern, even, the face might have been called, except for the relief afforded by a delicately curved mouth — not weak, but affable and ingenuous. Drusus wore a dark travelling cloak,[2] and from underneath it peeped his tunic, with its stripe of narrow purple — the badge of the Roman equestrian order.[3] On his finger was another emblem of nobility — a large, plain, gold ring, conspicuous among several other rings with costly settings.

"*Salve ! Salve, Domine !*" cried the slaves a second time, as the carriage drew near. The young master pushed back the blue woollen curtains in order to gain a better view, then motioned to the driver to stop.

---

[1] Most wealthy Romans had such a *major domo*, whose position was often one of honour and trust.

[2] *Pænula.*   [3] The second order of the Roman nobility.

"Are you slaves of mine?" was his question. The tone was interested and kindly, and Mago saluted profoundly, and replied: —

"We are the slaves of the most noble Quintus Livius Drusus, who owns this estate."

"I am he," replied the young man, smiling. "The day is hot. It grows late. You have toiled enough. Go you all and rest. Here, Pausanias, give them each a philippus,[1] with which to remember my home-coming!"

"*Eu! Eu! Io!*[2] *Domine!*" cried the slaves, giving vent to their delight. And Chloë whispered to Laïs: "You were right. The new master will be kind. There will not be so many whippings."

But while Pausanias was fumbling in the money-bags, a new instance of the generosity of Drusus was presented. Down a by-path in the field filed a sorrowful company; a long row of slaves in fetters, bound together by a band and chain round the waist of each. They were a disreputable enough gang of unkempt, unshaven, half-clothed wretches: Gauls and Germans with fair hair and giant physiques; dark-haired Syrians; black-skinned Africans, — all panting and groaning, clanking their chains, and cursing softly at the two sullen overseers, who, with heavy-loaded whips, were literally driving them down into the road.

Again Drusus spoke.

"Whose slaves are these? Mine?"

"They are your lordship's," said the foremost overseer, who had just recognized his newly come employer.

"Why are they in chains?" asked Drusus.

---

[1] A Greek gold piece worth about $3.60 at the time of the story. At this time Rome coined little gold.

[2] Good! Good! Hurrah!

"Mamercus found them refractory," replied the guard, "and ordered them to be kept in the underground prison,[1] and to work in the chain gang."

The young man made a motion of disgust.

"Bah!" he remarked, "the whole *familia*[2] will be in fetters if Mamercus has his way much longer. Knock off those chains. Tell the wretches they are to remain unshackled only so long as they behave. Give them three skins to-night from which to drink their master's health. Drive on, Cappadox!"

And before the fettered slaves could comprehend their release from confinement, and break out into a chorus of barbarous and uncouth thanksgivings and blessings, the carriage had vanished from sight down the turn of the road.

II

Who was Quintus Livius Drusus? Doubtless he would have felt highly insulted if his family history had not been fairly well known to every respectable person around Præneste and to a very large and select circle at Rome. When a man could take Livius[3] for his gentile name, and Drusus for his cognomen, he had a right to hold his head high, and regard himself as one of the noblest and best of the imperial city. But of course the Drusian house had a number of branches, and the history of Quintus's direct family was this. He was the grandson of that Marcus Livius Drusus[4] who, though an

---

[1] *Ergastulum.*   [2] Slave household.

[3] Every Roman had a *prænomen*, or "Christian name"; also a gentile name of the gens or clan to which he belonged; and commonly in addition a cognomen, usually an epithet descriptive of some personal peculiarity of an ancestor, which had fastened itself upon the immediate descendants of that ancestor. The *Livii Drusi* were among the noblest of the Roman houses.

[4] Died in 91 B.C.

aristocrat of the aristocrats, had dared to believe that the oligarchs were too strong, the Roman Commons without character, and that the Italian freemen were suffering from wrongs inflicted by both of the parties at the capital. For his efforts to right the abuses, he had met with a reward very common to statesmen of his day, a dagger-thrust from the hand of an undiscovered assassin. He had left a son, Sextus, a man of culture and talent, who remembered his father's fate, and walked for a time warily in politics. Sextus had married twice. Once to a very noble lady of the Fabian gens, the mother of his son Quintus. Then some years after her death he took in marriage a reigning beauty, a certain Valeria, who soon developed such extravagance and frivolity, that, soon after she bore him a daughter, he was forced " to send her a messenger "; in other words, to divorce her. The daughter had been put under the guardianship of Sextus's sister-in-law Fabia, one of the Vestal virgins at Rome. Sextus himself had accepted an appointment to a tribuneship in a legion of Cæsar in Gaul. When he departed for the wars he took with him as fellow officer a life-long friend, Caius Cornelius Lentulus; and ere leaving for the campaign the two had formed a compact quite in keeping with the stern Roman spirit that made the child the slave of the father: Young Quintus Drusus should marry Cornelia, Lentulus's only child, as soon as the two came to a proper age. And so the friends went away to win glory in Gaul; to perish side by side, when Sabinus's ill-fated legion was cut off by the Eburones.[1]

The son and the daughter remained. Quintus Drusus had had kindly guardians; he had been sent for four years to the " University " at Athens; had studied rhetoric and philosophy; and now he was back with his career before him, — master of

[1] In 54 B.C.

himself, of a goodly fortune, of a noble inheritance of high-born ancestry. And he was to marry Cornelia. No thought of thwarting his father's mandate crossed his mind; he was bound by the decree of the dead. He had not seen his betrothed for four years. He remembered her as a bright-eyed, merry little girl, who had an arch way of making all to mind her. But he remembered too, that her mother was a vapid lady of fashion, that her uncle and guardian was Lucius Cornelius Lentulus Crus, Consul-elect,[1] a man of little refinement or character. And four years were long enough to mar a young girl's life. What would she be like? What had time made of her? The curiosity — we will not call it passion — was overpowering. Pure "love" was seldom recognized as such by the age. When the carriage reached a spot where two roads forked, leading to adjacent estates, Drusus alighted.

"Is her ladyship Cornelia at the villa of the Lentuli?" was his demand of a gardener who was trimming a hedge along the way.

"Ah! Master Drusus," cried the fellow, dropping his sickle in delight. "Joy to see you! Yes, she is in the grove by the villa; by the great cypress you know so well. But how you have changed, sir —"

But Drusus was off. The path was familiar. Through the trees he caught glimpses of the stately mazes of colonnades of the Lentulan villa, surrounded by its artificially arranged gardens, and its wide stretches of lawn and orchard. The grove had been his playground. Here was the oak under which Cornelia and he had gathered acorns. The remnants of the little brush house they had built still survived. His step quickened. He heard the rush of the little stream that wound

[1] The two Roman consuls were magistrates of the highest rank, and were chosen each year by the people.

through the grove. Then he saw ahead of him a fern thicket,
and the brook flashing its water beyond. In his recollection a bridge had here crossed the streamlet. It had been
removed. Just across, swayed the huge cypress. Drusus
stepped forward. At last! He pushed carefully through the
thicket, making only a little noise, and glanced across the
brook.

There were ferns all around the cypress. Ivies twined
about its trunk. On the bank the green turf looked dry, but
cool. Just under the tree the brook broke into a miniature
cascade, and went rippling down in a score of pygmy, sparkling waterfalls. On a tiny promontory a marble nymph, a
fine bit of Greek sculpture, was pouring, without respite, from
a water-urn into the gurgling flood. But Drusus did not gaze
at the nymph. Close beside the image, half lying, half sitting,
in an abandon only to be produced by a belief that she was
quite alone, rested a young woman. It was Cornelia.

Drusus had made no disturbance, and the object on which
he fastened his eyes had not been in the least stirred out of
a rather deep reverie. He stood for a while half bashful,
half contemplative. Cornelia had taken off her shoes and
let her little white feet trail down into the water. She wore
only her white tunic, and had pushed it back so that her
arms were almost bare. At the moment she was resting
lazily on one elbow, and gazing abstractedly up at the
moving ocean of green overhead. She was only sixteen; but
in the warm Italian clime that age had brought her to
maturity. No one would have said that she was beautiful,
from the point of view of mere softly sensuous Greek beauty.
Rather, she was handsome, as became the daughter of Cornelii and Claudii. She was tall; her hair, which was bound
in a plain knot on the back of her head, was dark — almost

black; her eyes were large, grey, lustrous, and on occasion could be proud and angry. Yet with it all she was pretty — pretty, said Drusus to himself, as any girl he had seen in Athens. For there were coy dimples in her delicate little chin, her finely chiselled features were not angular, while her cheeks were aglow with a healthy colour that needed no rouge to heighten. In short, Cornelia, like Drusus, was a Roman; and Drusus saw that she was a Roman, and was glad.

Presently something broke the reverie. Cornelia's eyes dropped from the treetops, and lighted up with attention. One glance across the brook into the fern thicket; then one irrepressible feminine scream; and then : —

"Cornelia!"   "Quintus!"

Drusus sprang forward, but almost fell into the brooklet. The bridge was gone. Cornelia had started up, and tried to cover her arms and shake her tunic over her feet. Her cheeks were all smiles and blushes. But Drusus's situation was both pathetic and ludicrous. He had his fiancée almost in his arms, and yet the stream stopped him. Instantly Cornelia was in laughter.

"Oh! My second Leander," she cried, "will you be brave, and swim again from Abydos to Sestos to meet your Hero?"

"Better!" replied Drusus, now nettled; "see!" And though the leap was a long one he cleared it, and landed close by the marble nymph.

Drusus had not exactly mapped out for himself the method of approaching the young woman who had been his child play-mate. Cornelia, however, solved all his perplexity. Changing suddenly from laughter into what were almost tears, she flung her arms around his neck, and kissed him again and again.

"Oh, Quintus! Quintus!" she cried, nearly sobbing, "*I am so glad you have come!*"

"And I am glad," said the young man, perhaps with a tremor in his voice.

"I never knew how I wanted you, until you are here," she continued; "I didn't look for you to-day. I supposed you would come from Puteoli to-morrow. Oh! Quintus, you must be very kind to me. Perhaps I am very stupid. But I am tired, tired."

Drusus looked at her in a bit of astonishment.

"Tired! I can't see that you look fatigued."

"Not in body," went on Cornelia, still holding on to him. "But here, sit down on the grass. Let me hold your hands. You do not mind. I want to talk with you. No, don't interrupt. I must tell you. I have been here in Præneste only a week. I wanted to get away from Baiæ.[1] I was afraid to stay there with my mother."

"Afraid to stay at that lovely seashore house with your mother!" exclaimed Drusus, by no means unwilling to sit as entreated, but rather bewildered in mind.

"I was afraid of Lucius Ahenobarbus, the consular[2] Domitius's second son. _I don't like him ! there !_" and Cornelia's grey eyes lit up with menacing fire.

"Afraid of Lucius Ahenobarbus!" laughed Drusus. "Well, I don't think I call him a very dear friend. But why should he trouble you ? "

"It was ever since last spring, when I was in the new theatre[3] seeing the play, that he came around, thrust himself upon me, and tried to pay attentions. Then he has kept them up ever since; he followed us to Baiæ; and the worst of it is, my mother and uncle rather favour him. So I had Stephanus, my

---

[1] The famous watering-place on the Bay of Naples.
[2] An ex-consul was known by this title.
[3] Built by Pompeius the Great, in 55-54 B.C.

friend the physician, say that sea air was not good for me, and I was sent here. My mother and uncle will come in a few days, but not that fellow Lucius, I hope. I was so tired try· ing to keep him off."

"I will take care of the knave," said Drusus, smiling. "So this is the trouble? I wonder that your mother should have anything to do with such a fellow. I hear in letters that he goes with a disreputable gang. He is a boon companion with Marcus Læca, the old Catilinian,[1] who is a smooth-headed villain, and to use a phrase of my father's good friend Cicero —'has his head and eyebrows always shaved, that he may not be said to have one hair of an honest man about him.' But he will have to reckon with me now. Now it is my turn to talk. Your long story has been very short. Nor is mine long. My old uncle Publius Vibulanus is dead. I never knew him well enough to be able to mourn him bitterly. Enough, he died at ninety; and just as I arrive at Puteoli comes a message that I am his sole heir. His freedmen knew I was coming, embalmed the body, and wait for me to go to Rome to-morrow to give the funeral oration and light the pyre. He has left a fortune fit to compare with that of Crassus[2] — real estate, investments, a lovely villa at Tusculum. And now I — no, *we* — are wealthy beyond avarice. Shall we not thank the Gods?"

"I thank them for nothing," was her answer; then more shyly, "except for your own coming; for, Quintus, you — you — will marry me before very long?"

"What hinders?" cried the other, in the best of spirits. "To-morrow I go to Rome; then back again! And then all

---

[1] A member of the band who with Catiline conspired in 63 B.C. to overthrow the Roman government.

[2] The Roman millionaire who had just been slain in Parthia.

Præneste will flock to our marriage train. No, pout no more over Lucius Ahenobarbus. He shan't pay disagreeable attentions. And now over to the old villa: for Mamercus is eating his heart out to see me!"

And away they went arm in arm.

Drusus's head was in the air. He had resolved to marry Cornelia, cost what it might to his desires. He knew now that he was affianced to the one maiden in the world quite after his own heart.

III

The paternal villa of Drusus lay on the lower part of the slope of the Præneste citadel, facing the east. It was a genuine country and farming estate — not a mere refuge from the city heat and hubbub. The Drusi had dwelt on it for generations, and Quintus had spent his boyhood upon it. The whole mass of farm land was in the very pink of cultivation. There were lines of stately old elms enclosing the estate; and within, in regular sequence, lay vineyards producing the rather poor Præneste wine, olive orchards, groves of walnut trees, and many other fruits. Returning to the point where he had left the carriage, Drusus led Cornelia up a broad avenue flanked by noble planes and cypresses. Before them soon stood, or rather stretched, the country house. It was a large grey stone building, added to, from time to time, by successive owners. Only in front did it show signs of modern taste and elegance. Here ran a colonnade of twelve red porphyry pillars, with Corinthian capitals. The part of the house reserved for the master lay behind this entrance way. Back of it rambled the structure used by the farm steward, and the slaves and cattle. The whole house was low — in fact practically one-storied;

and the effect produced was perhaps substantial, but hardly imposing.

Up the broad avenue went the two young people ; too busy with their own gay chatter to notice at a distance how figures were running in and out amid the colonnade, and how the pillars were festooned with flowers. But as they drew nearer a throng was evident. The whole farm establishment — men, women, and children — had assembled, garlanded and gayly dressed, to greet the young master. Perhaps five hundred persons — nearly all slaves — had been employed on the huge estate, and they were all at hand. As Drusus came up the avenue, a general shout of welcome greeted him.

"*Ave ! Ave ! Domine !*" and there were some shouts as Cornelia was seen of, "*Ave ! Domina !*"

"*Domina*[1] here very soon," said Drusus, smiling to the young lady; and disengaging himself from her, he advanced to greet personally a tall, ponderous figure, with white, flowing hair, a huge white beard, and a left arm that had been severed at the wrist, who came forward with a swinging military stride that seemed to belie his evident years.

"All hail, dearest Mamercus!" exclaimed the young man, running up to the burly object. "Here is the little boy you used to scold, fondle, and tell stories to, back safe and sound to hear the old tales and to listen to some more admonitions."

The veteran made a hurried motion with his remaining hand, as if to brush something away from his eyes, and his deep voice seemed a trifle husky when he replied, speaking slowly : —

"*Mehercle !*[2] All the Gods be praised! The noble Sextus living again in the form of his son! Ah! This makes my

---

[1] *Domina*, mistress.   [2] By Hercules.

old heart glad;" and he held out his hand to Drusus. But the young man dashed it away, and flinging his arms around Mamercus's neck, kissed him on both cheeks. Then when this warm greeting was over, Drusus had to salute Titus Mamercus, a solid, stocky, honest-faced country lad of eighteen, the son of the veteran; and after Titus — since the Mamerci and Drusi were remotely related and the *jus oscului* [1] — less **legally,** the "right of kissing" — existed between them, he felt called upon to press the cheek of Æmilia, Mamercus's pretty daughter, of about her brother's age. Cornelia seemed a little discomposed at this, and perhaps so gave her lover a trifling delight. But next he had to shake all the freedmen by the hand, also the older and better known slaves; and to say something in reply to their congratulations. The mass of the slaves he could not know personally; but to the assembled company he spoke a few words, with that quiet dignity which belongs to those who are the heirs of generations of lordly ancestors.

"This day I assume control of my estate. All past offences are forgiven. I remit any punishments, however justly imposed. To those who are my faithful servants and clients I will prove a kind and reasonable master. Let none in the future be mischievous or idle; for them I cannot spare. But since the season is hot, in honour of my home-coming, for the next ten days I order that no work, beyond that barely needed, be done in the fields. Let the familia enjoy rest, and let them receive as much wine as they may take without being unduly drunken. Geta, Antiochus, and Kebes, who have been in this house many years, shall go with me before the prætor, to be set free."

---

[1] The right of kissing kinsfolk within the sixth degree.

And then, while the slaves still shouted their *aves* and *salves*, Mamercus led Drusus and Cornelia through the old villa, through the atrium where the fountain tinkled, and the smoky, waxen death-masks of Quintus's noble ancestors grinned from the presses on the wall; through the handsomely furnished rooms for the master of the house; out to the barns and storehouses, that stretched away in the rear of the great farm building. Much pride had the veteran when he showed the sleek cattle, the cackling poultry-yard, and the tall stacks of hay; only he growled bitterly over what he termed the ill-timed leniency of his young patron in releasing the slaves in the chain-gang.

"Oh, such times!" he muttered in his beard; "here's this young upstart coming home, and teaches me that such dogs as I put in fetters are better set at large! There'll be a slave revolt next, and some night all our throats will be cut. But it's none of my doing."

"Well," said Drusus, smiling, "I've been interested at Athens in learning from philosophy that one owes some kindness even to a slave. But it's always your way, Mamercus, to tell how much better the old times were than the new."

"And I am right," growled the other. "Hasn't a man who fought with Marius, and helped to beat those northern giants, the Cimbri and Teutones, a right to his opinion? The times are evil — evil! No justice in the courts. No patriotism in the Senate. Rascality in every consul and prætor. And the 'Roman People' orators declaim about are only a mob! *Vah!* We need an end to this game of fauns and satyrs!"

"Come," said Drusus, "we are not at such a direful strait yet. There is one man at least who I am convinced is not altogether a knave; and I have determined to throw in my lot with him. Do you guess, Mamercus?"

" Cæsar ? "

Drusus nodded. Mamercus broke out into a shout of approval.

"*Euge!* Unless my son Decimus, who is centurion with him, writes me false, *he* is a man ! "

But Cornelia was distressed of face.

" Quintus," she said very gravely, " do you know that I have often heard that Cæsar is a wicked libertine, who wishes to make himself tyrant ? What have you done ? "

" Nothing rashly," said Drusus, also quite grave ; " but I have counted the matter on both sides — the side of Pompeius and the Senate, and the side of Cæsar — and I have written to Balbus, Cæsar's manager at Rome, that I shall use my tiny influence for the proconsul of the Gauls."

Cornelia seemed greatly affected ; she clasped and unclasped her hands, pressed them to her brows ; then when she let them fall, she was again smiling.

" Quintus," she said, putting her arm around him, " Quintus, I am only a silly little girl. I do not know anything about politics. You are wiser than I, and I can trust you. But please don't quarrel with my uncle Lentulus about your decision. He would be terribly angry."

Quintus smiled in turn, and kissing her, said : " Can you trust me ? I hope so. And be assured I will do all I may, not to quarrel with your uncle. And now away with all this silly serious talk ! What a pity for Mamercus to have been so gloomy as to introduce it ! What a pity I must go to Rome to-morrow, and leave this dear old place ! But then, I have to see my aunt Fabia, and little Livia, the sister I haven't met since she was a baby. And while I am in Rome I will do something else — can you guess ? " Cornelia shook her head. "Carpenters, painters, masons ! I will send them out to make this old villa fresh and pretty for some one who, I hope, will come here to live in about a month. No, don't run away," for Cornelia was trying to hide her flushed face by flight; "I have something else to get — a present for your own dear self. What shall it be? I am rich; cost does not matter."

Cornelia pursed her lips in thought.

"Well," she remarked, "if you could bring me out a pretty boy, not too old or too young, one that was honest and quick-witted, he would be very convenient to carry messages to you, and to do any little business for me."

Cornelia asked for a slave-boy just as she might have asked for a new pony, with that indifference to the question of humanity which indicated that the demarcation between a slave and an animal was very slight in her mind.

"Oh! that is nothing," said Drusus; "you shall have the handsomest and cleverest in all Rome. And if Mamercus complains that I am extravagant in remodelling the house, let him remember that his wonderful Cæsar, when a young man, head over ears in debt, built an expensive villa at Aricia, and then pulled it down to the foundations and rebuilt on an improved plan. Farewell, Sir Veteran, I will take Cornelia home, and then come back for that dinner which I know the cook has made ready with his best art."

Arm in arm the young people went away down the avenue of shade trees, dim in the gathering twilight. Mamercus stood gazing after them.

"What a pity! What a pity!" he repeated to himself, "that Sextus and Caius are not alive; how they would have rejoiced in their children! Why do the fates order things as they do? Only let them be kind enough to let me live until I hold another little Drusus on my knee, and tell him of the

great battles! But the Gods forbid, Lentulus should find
out speedily that his lordship has gone over to Cæsar; or
there will be trouble enough for both his lordship and my
lady. The consul-elect is a stubborn, bitter man. He would
be terribly offended to give his niece in marriage to a political
enemy. But it may all turn out well. Who knows?" And
he went into the house.

CHAPTER II

THE UPPER WALKS OF SOCIETY

I

IT was very early in the morning. From the streets, far below, a dull rumbling was drifting in at the small, dim windows. On the couch, behind some faded curtains, a man turned and yawned, grunted and rubbed his eyes. The noise of the heavy timber, stone, and merchandise wagons hastening out of the city before daybreak,[1] jarred the room, and made sleep almost impossible. The person awakened swore quietly to himself in Greek.

"*Heracles!* Was ever one in such a city! What malevolent spirit brought me here? Throat-cutting on the streets at night; highwaymen in every foul alley; unsafe to stir at evening without an armed band! No police worth mentioning; freshets every now and then; fires every day or else a building tumbles down. And then they must wake me up at an unearthly hour in the morning. Curses on me for ever coming near the place!" And the speaker rolled over on the bed, and shook himself, preparatory to getting up.

"Bah! Can these Roman dogs never learn that power is to be used, not abused? Why don't they spend some of their revenues to level these seven hills that shut off the light, and straighten and widen their abominable, ill-paved streets, and

[1] No teaming was allowed in Rome by day.

keep houses from piling up as if to storm Olympus? Pshaw, I had better stop croaking, and be up and about."

The speaker sat up in bed, and clapped his hands. Into the ill-lighted and unpretentiously furnished room came a tall, bony, ebon-skinned old Ethiopian, very scantily attired, who awaited the wishes of his master.

"Come, Sesostris," said the latter, "get out my best *himation*[1]—the one with the azure tint. Give me a clean *chiton*,[2] and help me dress."

And while the servant bustled briskly about his work, Pratinas, for such was his lord's name, continued his monologue, ignoring the presence of his attendant. "Not so bad with me after all. Six years ago to-day it was I came to Rome, with barely an obol of ready money, to make my fortune by my wits. Zeus! But I can't but say I've succeeded. A thousand sesterces here and five hundred there, and now and then a better stroke of fortune — politics, intrigues, gambling; all to the same end. And now? — oh, yes, my 'friends' would say I am very respectable, but quite poor — but they don't know how I have economized, and how my account stands with Sosthenes the banker at Alexandria. My old acquaintance with Lucius Domitius was of some use. A few more months of this life and I am away from this beastly Rome, to enjoy myself among civilized people."

Pratinas went over to a large wooden chest with iron clasps, unlocked it, and gazed for a moment inside with evident satisfaction. "There are six good talents in there," he remarked to himself, "and then there is Artemisia."

He had barely concluded this last, hardly intelligible assertion, when the curtain of the room was pushed aside, and in came a short, plump, rosy-faced little maiden of twelve, with a

---

[1] Greek outer mantle.   [2] Greek under garment.

clearly chiselled Greek profile and lips as red as a cherry. Her white chiton was mussed and a trifle soiled; and her thick black hair was tied back in a low knot, so as to cover what were two very shapely little ears. All in all, she presented a very pretty picture, as the sunlight streamed over her, when she drew back the hangings at the window.

"Good morning, Uncle Pratinas," she said sweetly.

"Good morning, Artemisia, my dear," replied the other, giving her round neck a kiss, and a playful pinch. "You will practise on your lyre, and let Sesostris teach you to sing. You know we shall go back to Alexandria very soon; and it is pleasant there to have some accomplishments."

"And must you go out so early, uncle?" said the girl. "Can't you stay with me any part of the day? Sometimes I get very lonely."

"Ah! my dear," said Pratinas, smoothly, "if I could do what I wished, I would never leave you. But business cannot wait. I must go and see the noble Lucius Calatinus on some very important political matters, which you could not understand. Now run away like a good girl, and don't become doleful."

Artemisia left the room, and Pratinas busied himself about the fine touches of his toilet. When he held the silver mirror up to his face, he remarked to himself that he was not an unhandsome man. "If I did not have to play the philosopher, and wear this thick, hot beard,[1] I would not be ashamed to show my head anywhere." Then while he perfumed himself with oil of saffron out of a little onyx bottle, he went on: —

"What dogs and gluttons these Romans are! They have no real taste for art, for beauty. They cannot even conduct a

[1] At an age when respectable men were almost invariably smooth shaven, the philosophers wore flowing beards, as a sort of professional badge.

murder, save in a bungling way. They have to call in us Hellenes to help them. Ha! ha! this is the vengeance for Hellas, for the sack and razing of Corinth and all the other atrocities! Rome can conquer with the sword; but we Greeks, though conquered, can, unarmed, conquer Rome. How these Italians can waste their money! Villas, statues, pretty slaves, costly vases, and tables of mottled cypress,[1] oysters worth their weight in gold, and I know not what else! And I, poor Pratinas, the Greek, who lives in an upper floor of a Subura house at only two thousand sesterces rental, find in these noble Roman lords only so much plunder. Ha! ha! Hellas, thou art avenged!"

And gathering his mantle about him, he went down the several flights of very rickety stairs, and found himself in the buzzing street.

II

The Romans hugged a fond belief that houses shut out from sunlight and air were extremely healthy. If such were the fact, there should have been no sickness in a great part of the capital. The street in which Pratinas found himself was so dark, that he was fain to wait till his eyes accommodated themselves to the change. The street was no wider than an alley, yet packed with booths and hucksters, — sellers of boiled peas and hot sausage, and fifty other wares. On the worthy Hellene pressed, while rough German slaves or swarthy Africans jostled against him; the din of scholars declaiming in an adjoining school deafened him; a hundred unhappy odors made him wince. Then, as he fought his way, the streets grew a trifle wider; as he approached the Forum the shops became more pretentious; at last he reached his destina-

---

[1] A "fad" of this time. Such tables often cost $20,000.

tion in the aristocratic quarter of the Palatine, and paused before a new and ostentatious mansion, in whose vestibule was swarming a great bevy of clients, all come in the official calling costume — a ponderous toga — to pay their respects to the great man. But as the inner door was pushed aside by the vigilant keeper, all the rest of the crowd were kept out till Pratinas could pass within.

The atrium of the house was a splendid sight, with its veined marble pillars, mosaic floor, bubbling fountain, choice frescoes, and expensive furniture upholstered in Tyrian purple. A little in the rear of this gorgeous room was seated in a high armchair the individual who boasted himself the lord of this establishment, Lucius Atilius Calatinus. He was a large, coarse man, with a rough, bull-dog face and straight red hair. He had been drinking heavily the night before, and his small bluish eyes had wide dark circles beneath them, and his breath showed strongly the garlic with which he had seasoned the bread and grapes of his early lunch. He was evidently very glad to see his Greek visitor, and drove the six large, heavily gemmed rings which he wore on one of his fat fingers, almost into the other's hand when he shook it.

" Well met, Pratinas ! " was his salutation. " Tell me, is that little affair of yours settled ? Have you stopped the mouth of that beastly fellow, Postumus Pyrgensis, who said that I was a base upstart, with no claim to my gentile name, and a bad record as a tax farmer in Spain, and therefore should not be elected tribune [1] ? "

" I have stopped him," said Pratinas, with a little cough. " But it was expensive. He stuck out for ten thousand sesterces."

[1] The ten tribunes had power to convene the people and Senate, propose laws and " veto " the actions of other magistrates.

"Oh, cheaply off," said Calatinus, laughing. "I will give you my cheque on Flaccus the banker. But I want to know about the other matter. Can you make sure of the votes of the Suburana tribe? Have you seen Autronius?"

"I have seen him," said Pratinas, dryly.

"And he said?"

"Twenty thousand sesterces for him to deposit with trustees[1] until the election is over. Then he as go-between[2] will make sure of a majority of the tribesmen, and distribute to them the money if all goes well at the *comitia*.[3] It was the best bargain I could make; for Autronius really controls the tribe, and some one might outbid us."

"All right," broke out Calatinus with a laugh, "another cheque on Flaccus."

"One thing else," said Pratinas; "I must have a little money to shut up any complaints that those ridiculous anti-bribery Licinian and Pompeian Laws are being broken. Then there is my fee."

"Oh, yes," replied the other, not to be daunted in his good humour, "I'll give you fifty thousand in all. Now I must see this rabble."

And the mob of clients swept up to the armchair, grasping after the great man's hand, and raining on him their *aves*, while some daring mortals tried to thrust in a kiss.

Pratinas drew back and watched the crowd with a smile half cynical, half amused. Some of the visitors were regular hangers-on, who perhaps expected an invitation to dine; some were seekers of patronage; some had an eye to political preferment; a few were real acquaintances of Calatinus or came on some legitimate business. Pratinas observed three friends waiting to speak with Calatinus, and was soon in conversation.

[1] *Sequestres.*   [2] *Interpres.*   [3] Assembly of the Roman tribes for election

The first of the trio was known as Publius Gabinius, who was by far the oldest. Coarse-featured, with broken complexion, it needed but a glance to proclaim him as gifted with no other distinctions than those of a hard drinker, fast liver, and the owner of an attenuated conscience. Servius Flaccus, the second, was of a different type. He was languid; spirited only when he railed at a slave who brushed against his immaculate toga. The frills on his robes made him almost feminine; and he spoke, even in invective, in a soft, lisping voice. Around him floated the aroma of countless rare unguents, that made his coming known afar off. His only aim in life was evidently to get through it with as little exertion of brain or muscle as was possible. The third friend was unlike the others. Lucius Domitius Ahenobarbus clearly amounted to more than either of his companions. A constant worship of three very popular gods of the day — Women, Wine, and Gaming — with the other excitements of a dissipated life, had ruined a fine fair complexion. As it was, he had the profile of a handsome, affable man; only the mouth was hard and sensual, and his skin was faded and broken. He wore a little brown beard carefully trimmed around his well-oiled chin after the manner of Roman men of fashion; and his dark hair was crimped in regular steps or gradations, parting in the middle and arranged on both sides like a girl's.[1]

"Good morning, Pratinas!" said Lucius, warmly, taking the Greek's hand. "How glad we are to find you here. I wanted to ask you around to Marcus Læca's to-night; we think he will give something of a feast, and you must see my latest sweetheart — Clyte! She is a little pearl. I have had her head cut in intaglio on this onyx; is she not pretty?"

"Very pretty," said Pratinas, looking at the engraving on

[1] Suet., "Nero," 51.

the ring. "But perhaps it is not right for me, a grave phi
losopher, to go to your banquet."

"How (h)absurd! (H)of c(h)ourse you c(h)an!" lisped
Flaccus, who affected Greek so far as to aspirate every word
beginning with a vowel, and to change every *c* into a *ch*.

"Well," said Pratinas, laughing, for he was a dearly loved
favourite of all these gilded youth, "I will see! And now
Gabinius is inviting Calatinus also, and we are dispersing for
the morning."

"Alas," groaned Ahenobarbus, "I must go to the Forum
to plead with that wretch Phormio, the broker, to arrange a
new loan."

"And I to the Forum, also," added Calatinus, coming up,
"to continue this pest of a canvass for votes."

The clients fell into line behind Calatinus like a file of
soldiers, but before Pratinas could start away with the other
friends, a slave-boy came running out from the inner house,
to say that "the Lady Valeria would be glad of his company
in her boudoir." The Greek bowed his farewells, then followed the boy back through the court of the peristylium.[1]

III

The dressing room occupied by Valeria — once wife of
Sextus Drusus and now living with Calatinus as her third
husband in about four years — was fitted up with every luxury which money, and a taste which carried refinement to
an extreme point, could accomplish. The walls were bright
with splendid mythological scenes by really good artists; the
furniture itself was plated with silver; the rugs were magnificent. The mistress of this palatial abode was sitting in a

[1] An inner private court back of the atrium.

low easy-chair, holding before her a fairly large silver mirror. She wore a loose gown of silken texture, edged to an ostentatious extent with purple. Around her hovered Arsinoë and Semiramis, two handsome Greek slave-girls, who were far better looking than their owner, inasmuch as their complexions had never been ruined by paints and ointments. They were expert hairdressers, and Valeria had paid twenty-five thousand sesterces for each of them, on the strength of their proficiency in that art, and because they were said to speak with a pure Attic Greek accent. At the moment they were busy stripping off from the lady's face a thick layer of dried enamel that had been put on the night before.

Had Valeria been willing, she might have feared no comparison with her maids; for from a merely sensuous standpoint, she would have been reckoned very beautiful. She had by nature large brown eyes, luxuriant brown hair, and what had been a clear brunette skin, and well-rounded and regular features. But her lips were curled in hard, haughty lines, her long eyelashes drooped as though she took little interest in life; and, worse than all, to satisfy the demands of fashion, she had bleached her hair to a German blonde, by a process ineffective and injurious. The lady was just fuming to herself over a gray hair Arsinoë had discovered, and Arsinoë went around in evident fear lest Valeria should vent her vexation on her innocent ministers.

Over in one corner of the room, on a low divan, was sitting a strange-looking personage. A gaunt, elderly man clothed in a very dingy Greek himation, with shaggy grey hair, and an enormous beard that tumbled far down his breast. This personage was Pisander, Valeria's "house-philosopher," who was expected to be always at her elbow pouring into her ears a rain of learned lore. For this worthy lady (and two thou-

sand years later would she not be attending lectures on Dante
or Browning?) was devoted to philosophy, and loved to hear
the Stoics [1] and Epicureans expound their varying systems of
the cosmos. At this moment she was feasting her soul on
Plato. Pisander was reading from the "Phaidros," "They
might have seen beauty shining in brightness, when the happy
band, following in the train of Zeus (as we philosophers did;
or with the other gods, as others did), saw a vision, and were
initiated into most blessed mysteries, which we celebrated in
our state of innocence; and having no feeling of evils yet to
come; beholding apparitions, innocent and simple and calm
and happy as in a mystery; shining in pure light; pure ourselves, and not yet enchained in that living tomb which we
carry about, now that we are imprisoned in the body . . . "

"Pratinas, to see her ladyship!" bawled a servant-boy [2]
at the doorway, very unceremoniously interrupting the good
man and his learnedly sublime lore. And Pratinas, with
the softest and sweetest of his Greek smiles, entered the
room.

"Your ladyship does me the honour," he began, with an
extremely deferential salutation.

"Oh, my dear Pratinas," cried Valeria, in a language she
called Greek, seizing his hand and almost embracing him,
"how delighted I am to see you! We haven't met since —
since yesterday morning. I did so want to have a good talk
with you about Plato's theory of the separate existence of
ideas. But first I must ask you, have you heard whether the
report is true that Terentia, Caius Glabrio's wife, has run off
with a gladiator?"

[1] The opponents of the Epicureans; they nobly antagonized the mere pursuit of pleasure held out as the one end of life by the Epicurean, and glorified
duty.   [2] *Cubicularius.*

"So Gabinius, I believe," replied Pratinas, "just told me. And I heard something else. A great secret. You must not tell."

"Oh! I am dying to know," smirked Valeria.

"Well," said the Greek, confidentially, "Publius Silanus has divorced his wife, Crispia. 'She went too much,' he says, 'with young Purpureo.'"

"You do not say so!" exclaimed the lady. "I always knew that would happen! Now tell me, don't you think this perfume of iris is delicate? It's in that little glass scent bottle; break the neck.[1] I shall use it in a minute. I have just had some bottles sent up from Capua. Roman perfumes are so vulgar!"

"I fear," said Pratinas, doing as bidden, and testing the essence with evident satisfaction, "that I have interrupted your philosophical studies." And he glanced at Pisander, who was sitting lonesome and offended in his corner.

"Oh! not in the least," ran on Valeria; "but though I know you are Epicurean, surely you enjoy Plato?"

"Certainly," said Pratinas, with dramatic dignity, "I suck the sweets from the flowers left us by all the wise and good. Epicurean though I am, your ladyship must permit me to lend you a copy of an essay I have with me, by that great philosopher, the Stoic Chrysippos,[2] although I cannot agree with all his teachings; and this copy of Panaitios, the Eclectic's great *Treatise on Duty*, which cannot fail to edify your ladyship." And he held out the two rolls.

"A thousand thanks," said Valeria, languidly, "hand them to Pisander. I will have him read them. A little more white lead, Arsinoë, I am too tanned; make me paler. Just

[1] To let out the ointment. Capua was a famed emporium for perfumes and like wares.   [2] Born 180 B.C.

run over the veins of my temples with a touch of blue paint Now a tint of antimony on my eyelids."

"Your ladyship seems in wonderfully good spirits this morning," insinuated Pratinas.

"Yes," said Valeria, with a sigh, "I endure the woes of life as should one who is consoled by philosophy."

"Shall I continue the Plato?" edged in poor Pisander, who was raging inwardly to think that Pratinas should dare to assume the name of a "lover of learning."

"When you are needed, I can tell you," snapped Valeria, sharply, at the feeble remonstrance. "Now, Semiramis, you may arrange my hair."

The girl looked puzzled. To tell the truth, Valeria was speaking in a tongue that was a babel of Greek and Latin, although she fondly imagined it to be the former, and Semiramis could hardly understand her.

"If your ladyship will speak in Latin," faltered the maid.

"Speak in Latin! Speak in Latin!" flared up Valeria. "Am I deceived? Are you not Greeks? Are you some ignorant Italian wenches who can't speak anything but their native jargon? Bah! You've misplaced a curl. Take that!" And she struck the girl across the palms, with the flat of her silver mirror. Semiramis shivered and flushed, but said nothing.

"Do I not have a perfect Greek pronunciation?" said the lady, turning to Pratinas. "It is impossible to carry on a polite conversation in Latin."

"I can assure your ladyship," said the Hellene, with still another bland smile, "that your pronunciation is something exceedingly remarkable."

Valeria was pacified, and lay back submitting to her hairdressers[1], while Pratinas, who knew what kind of

---

[1] *Ornatrices.*

"philosophy" appealed most to his fair patroness, read with a delicate yet altogether admirable voice, a number of scraps of erotic verse that he said friends had just sent on from Alexandria.

"Oh! the shame to call himself a philosopher," groaned the neglected Pisander to himself. "If I believed in the old gods, I would invoke the Furies upon him."

But Valeria was now in the best of spirits. "By the two Goddesses,"[1] she swore, "what charming sentiments you Greeks can express. Now I think I look presentable, and can go around and see Papiria, and learn about that dreadful Silanus affair. Tell Agias to bring in the cinnamon ointment. I will try that for a change. It is in the murrhine[2] vase in the other room."

Iasus the serving-boy stepped into the next apartment, and gave the order to one of his fellow slaves. A minute later there was a crash. Arsinoë, who was without, screamed, and Semiramis, who thrust her head out the door, drew it back with a look of dismay.

"What has happened?" cried Valeria, startled and angry.

Into the room came Arsinoë, Iasus, and a second slave-boy, a well-favoured, intelligent looking young Greek of about seventeen. His ruddy cheeks had turned very pale, as had those of Iasus.

"What has happened?" thundered Valeria, in a tone that showed that a sorry scene was impending.

The slaves fell on their knees; cowered, in fact, on the rugs at the lady's feet.

"*A! A! A!* Lady! Mercy!" they all began in a breath "The murrhina vase! It is broken!"

---

[1] Demeter and Persephone, a Greek woman's oath.
[2] A costly substance, probably porcelain agate.

"Who broke it?" cried their mistress, casting lightning glances from one to another.

Now the truth had been, that while Agias was coming through a door covered with a curtain, carrying the vase, Iasus had carelessly blundered against him and caused the catastrophe. But there had been no other witnesses to the accident; and when Iasus saw that his mistress's anger would promptly descend on somebody, he had not the moral courage to take the consequences of his carelessness. What amounted to a frightful crime was committed in an instant.

"Agias stumbled and dropped the vase," said Iasus, telling the truth, but not the whole truth.

"Send for Alfidius the *lorarius*,"[1] raged Valeria, who, with the promptness that characterizes a certain class of women, jumped at a conclusion and remained henceforth obstinate. "This shall not happen again! Oh! my vase! my vase! I shall never get another one like it! It was one of the spoils of Mithridates, and"—here her eye fell on Agias, cringing and protesting his innocence in a fearful agony.

"Stand up, boy! Stop whining! Of course you broke the vase. Who else had it? I will make you a lesson to all the slaves in my house. They need one badly. I will get another serving-boy who will be more careful."

Agias was deathly pale; the beads of sweat stood out on his forehead; he grasped convulsively at the hem of his mistress's robe, and murmured wildly of "mercy! mercy!" Pratinas stood back with his imperturbable smile on his face; and if he felt the least pity for his fellow-countryman, he did not show it.

"Alfidius awaits the mistress," announced Semiramis, with trembling lips.

[1] Whipper; many Roman houses had such a functionary, and he does not seem to have lacked employment.

Into the room came a brutish, hard-featured, shock-headed man, with a large scar, caused by branding, on his forehead. He carried a short rope and scourge,[1] — a whip with a short handle to which were attached three long lashes, set at intervals with heavy bits of bronze. He cast one glance over the little group in the room, and his dull piglike eyes seemed to light up with a fierce glee, as he comprehended the situation.

"What does your ladyship wish?" he growled.

"Take this wretched boy," cried Valeria, spurning Agias with her foot; "take him away. Make an example of him. Take him out beyond the Porta Esquilina and whip him to death. Let me never see him again."

Pisander sprang up in his corner, quivering with righteous wrath.

"What is this?" he cried. "The lad is not guilty of any real crime. It would be absurd to punish a horse for an action like his, and a slave is as good as a horse. What philosopher could endure to see such an outrage?"

Valeria was too excited to hear him. Pratinas coolly took the perturbed philosopher round the waist, and by sheer force seated him in a chair.

"My friend," he said calmly, "you can only lose your place by interfering; the boy is food for the crows already. Philosophy should teach you to regard little affairs like this unmoved."

Before Pisander could remonstrate further Alfidius had caught up Agias as if he had been an infant, and carried him, while moaning and pleading, out of the room. Iasus was still trembling. He was not a knave — simply unheroic, and he knew that he had committed the basest of actions. Semiramis and Arsinoë were both very pale, but spoke never a word. Arsinoë looked pityingly after the poor boy, for she had grown

[1] *Flagellum.*

very fond of his bright words and obliging manners. For some minutes there was, in fact, perfect silence in the boudoir.

Alfidius carried his victim out into the slaves' quarters in the rear of the house; there he bound his hands and called in the aid of an assistant to help him execute his mistress's stern mandate.

Agias had been born for far better things than to be a slave. His father had been a cultured Alexandrine Greek, a banker, and had given his young son the beginnings of a good education. But the rascality of a business partner had sent the father to the grave bankrupt, the son to the slave-market to satisfy the creditors. And now Alfidius and his myrmidon bound their captive to a furca, a wooden yoke passing down the back of the neck and down each arm. The rude thongs cut the flesh cruelly, and the wretches laughed to see how the delicate boy writhed and faltered under the pain and the load.

"Ah, ha! my fine *Furcifer*,"[1] cried Alfidius, when this work was completed. "How do you find yourself?"

"Do you mock at me, you *three letter man*?" retorted Agias in grim despair, referring cuttingly to FVR[2] branded on Alfidius's forehead.

"So you sing, my pretty bird," laughed the executioner. "I think you will croak sorrowfully enough before long. Call me *man of letters* if you will; to-night the dogs tear that soft skin of yours, while my hide is sound. Now off for the Porta Esquilina! Trot along with you!" and he swung his lash over the wretched boy's shoulders.

Agias was led out into the street. He was too pained and numbed to groan, resist, or even think and fear. The thongs might well have been said to press his mind as much as his skin.

[1] Furca-bearer, a coarse epithet.
[2] Thief. Branding was a common punishment for slaves

CHAPTER III

THE PRIVILEGE OF A VESTAL

I

Drusus started long before daybreak on his journey to Rome; with him went Cappadox, his ever faithful body-servant, and Pausanias, the amiable and cultivated freedman who had been at his elbow ever since he had visited Athens. For a while the young master dozed in his carriage; but, as they whirled over mile after mile of the Campagna, the sun arose; then, when sleep left him, the Roman was all alive to the patriotic reminiscences each scene suggested. Yonder to the far south lay Alba, the old home of the Latins, and a little southward too was the Lake of Regillus, where tradition had it the free Romans won their first victory, and founded the greatness of the Republic. Along the line of the Anio, a few miles north, had marched Hannibal on his mad dash against Rome to save the doomed Capua. And these pictures of brave days, and many another vision like them, welled up in Drusus's mind, and the remembrance of the marble temples of the Greek cities faded from his memory; for, as he told himself, Rome was built of nobler stuff than marble; — she was built of the deeds of men strong and brave, and masters of every hostile fate. And he rejoiced that he could be a Roman, and share in his country's deathless fame, perhaps could win for her new honour, — could be consul, triumphator, and lead his applauding legions up to the temple of Capitoline Jove—another national glory added to so many.

So the vision of the great city of tall ugly tenement houses, basking on her "Seven Hills," which only on their summits showed the nobler temples or the dwellings of the great patricians, broke upon him. And it was with eyes a-sparkle with enthusiasm, and a light heart, that he reached the Porta Esquilina, left the carriage for a litter borne by four stout Syrians sent out from the house of his late uncle, and was carried soon into the hubbub of the city streets.

Everywhere was the same crowd; shopping parties were pressing in and out the stores, outrunners and foot-boys were continually colliding. Drusus's escort could barely win a slow progress for their master. Once on the Sacred Way the advance was more rapid; although even this famous street was barely twenty-two feet wide from house wall to house wall. Here was the "Lombard" or "Wall Street" of antiquity. Here were the offices of the great banking houses and syndicates that held the world in fee. Here centred those busy equites, the capitalists, whose transactions ran out even beyond the lands covered by the eagles, so that while Gaul was yet unconquered, Cicero could boast, "not a sesterce in Gaul changes hands without being entered in a Roman ledger." And here were brokers whose clients were kings, and who by their "influence" almost made peace or war, like modern Rothschilds.

Thither Drusus's litter carried him, for he knew that his first act on coming to Rome to take possession of his uncle's property should be to consult without delay his agent and financial and legal adviser, lest any loophole be left for a disappointed fortune-hunter to contest the will. The bearers put him down before the important firm of Flaccus and Sophus

Out from the open, windowless office ran the senior partner, Sextus Fulvius Flaccus, a stout, comfortable, rosy-faced old eques, who had half Rome as his financial clients, the other half in his debt. Many were his congratulations upon Drusus's manly growth, and many more upon the windfall of Vibulanus's fortune, which, as he declared, was too securely conveyed to the young man to be open to any legal attack.

But when Drusus intimated that he expected soon to invite the good man to his marriage feast, Flaccus shook his head.

"You will never get a sesterce of Cornelia's dowry," he declared. Her uncle Lentulus Crus is head over ears in debt. Nothing can save him, unless — "

"I don't understand you," said the other.

"Well," continued Flaccus, "to be frank; unless there is nothing short of a revolution."

"Will it come to that?" demanded Drusus.

"Can't say," replied Flaccus, as if himself perplexed. "Everybody declares Cæsar and Pompeius are dreadfully alienated. Pompeius is joining the Senate. Half the great men of Rome are in debt, as I have cause to know, and unless we have an overturn, with 'clean accounts' as a result, more than one noble lord is ruined. I am calling in all my loans, turning everything into cash. Credit is bad — bad. Cæsar paid Curio's debts — sixty millions of sesterces.[1] That's why Curio is a Cæsarian now. Oh! money is the cause of all these vile political changes! Trouble is coming! Sulla's old throat cuttings will be nothing to it! But don't marry Lentulus's niece!"

"Well," said Drusus, when the business was done, and he turned to go, "I want Cornelia, not her dowry."

[1] I.e. $2,400,000; a sesterce was about 4 cents.

"Strange fellow," muttered Flaccus, while Drusus started off in his litter. "I always consider the dowry the principal part of a marriage."

II

Drusus regained his litter, and ordered his bearers to take him to the house of the Vestals, — back of the Temple of Vesta, — where he wished to see his aunt Fabia and Livia, his little half-sister. The Temple itself — a small, round structure, with columns, a conical roof which was fringed about with dragons and surmounted by a statue — still showed signs of the fire, which, in 210 B.C., would have destroyed it but for thirteen slaves, who won their liberty by checking the blaze. Tradition had it that here the holy Numa had built the hut which contained the hearth-fire of Rome, — the divine spark which now shed its radiance over the nations. Back of the Temple was the House of the Vestals, a structure with a plain exterior, differing little from the ordinary private dwellings. Here Drusus had his litter set down for a second time, and notified the porter that he would be glad to see his aunt and sister. The young man was ushered into a spacious, handsomely furnished and decorated atrium, where were arranged lines of statues of the various *maximæ*[1] of the little religious order. A shy young girl with a white dress and fillet, who was reading in the apartment, slipped noiselessly out, as the young man entered; for the novices were kept under strict control, with few liberties, until their elder sisters could trust them in male society. Then there was a rustle of robes and ribbons, and in came a tall, stately lady, also in pure white, and a little girl of about five, who shrank coyly back when Drusus called her his "Liviola"[2]

[1] Senior Vestals. [2] A diminutive of endearment.

and tried to catch her in his arms. But the lady embraced him, and kissed him, and asked a thousand things about him, as tenderly as if she had been his mother.

Fabia the Vestal was now about thirty-seven years of age. One and thirty years before had the Pontifex Maximus chosen her out — a little girl — to become the priestess of Vesta, the hearth-goddess, the home-goddess of Pagan Rome. Fabia had dwelt almost all her life in the house of the Vestals. Her very existence had become identified with the little sisterhood, which she and her five associates composed. It was a rather isolated yet singularly pure and peaceful life which she had led. Revolutions might rock the city and Empire; Marians and Sullians contend; Catilina plot ruin and destruction; Clodius and his ruffians terrorize the streets; but the fire of the great hearth-goddess was never scattered, nor were its gentle ministers molested. Fabia had thus grown to mature womanhood. Ten years she had spent in learning the Temple ritual, ten years in performing the actual duties of the sacred fire and its cultus, ten years in teaching the young novices. And now she was free, if she chose, to leave the Temple service, and even to marry. But Fabia had no intention of taking a step which would tear her from the circle in which she was dearly loved, and which, though permitted by law, would be publicly deplored as an evil omen.

The Vestal's pure simple life had left its impress on her features. Peace and innocent delight in innocent things shone through her dark eyes and soft, well-rounded face. Her light brown hair was covered and confined by a fillet of white wool.[1] She wore a stola and outer garment of stainless white linen — the perfectly plain badge of her chaste and holy office; while on her small feet were dainty sandals, bound on by thongs of

[1] *Infula.*

whitened leather. Everything about her dress and features betokened the priestess of a gentle religion.

When questions and repeated salutations were over, and Livia had ceased to be too afraid of her quite strange brother, Fabia asked what she could do for her nephew. As one of the senior Vestals, her time was quite her own. "Would he like to have her go out with him to visit friends, or go shopping? Or could she do anything to aid him about ordering frescoers and carpenters for the old Præneste villa?"

This last was precisely what Drusus had had in mind. And so forth aunt and nephew sallied. Some of the streets they visited were so narrow that they had to send back even their litters; but everywhere the crowds bowed such deference and respect to the Vestal's white robes that their progress was easy. Drusus soon had given his orders to cabinet-makers and selected the frescoer's designs. It remained to purchase Cornelia's slave-boy. He wanted not merely an attractive serving-lad, but one whose intelligence and probity could be relied upon; and in the dealers' stalls not one of the dark orientals, although all had around their necks tablets with long lists of encomiums, promised conscience or character. Drusus visited several very choice boys that were exhibited in separate rooms, at fancy prices, but none of these pretty Greeks or Asiatics seemed promising.

Deeply disgusted, he led Fabia away from the slave-market. "I will try to-morrow," he said, vexed at his defeat. "I need a new toga. Let us go to the shop on the Clivus Suburanus; there used to be a good woollen merchant, Lucius Marius, on the way to the Porta Esquilina."

Accordingly the two went on in the direction indicated; but at the spot where the Clivus Suburanus was cut by the Vicus Longus, there was so dense a crowd and so loud a hubbub, that their attendants could not clear a way. For a time it was impossible to see what was the matter. Street gamins were howling, and idle slaves and hucksters were pouring forth volleys of taunts and derision at some luckless wight.

"Away with them! the whip-scoundrel! *Verbero!*"[1] yelled a lusty produce-vender. "Lash him again! Tan his hide for him! Don't you enjoy it? Not accustomed to such rough handling, eh! my pretty sparrow?"

Fabia without the least hesitation thrust herself into the dirty-robed, foul-mouthed crowd. At sight of the Vestal's white dress and fillets the pack gave way before her, as a swarm of gnats at the wave of a hand. Drusus strode at her heels.

It was a sorry enough sight that met them — though not uncommon in the age and place. Some wretched slave-boy, a slight, delicate fellow, had been bound to the bars of a furca, and was being driven by two brutal executioners to the place of doom outside the gates. At the street-crossing he had sunk down, and all the blows of the driver's scourge could not compel him to arise. He lay in the dust, writhing and moaning, with the great welts showing on his bare back, where the brass knots of the lash had stripped away the cloth.

"Release this boy! Cease to beat him!" cried Fabia, with a commanding mien, that made the crowd shrink further back; while the two executioners looked stupid and sheepish, but did nothing.

"Release this boy!" commanded the Vestal. "Dare you hesitate? Do you wish to undo yourselves by defying me?"

"Mercy, august lady," cried Alfidius, — for the chief executioner was he, — with a supplicatory gesture. "If our mistress knows that her commands are unexecuted, it is we, who are but slaves, that must suffer!"

---

[1] A coarse epithet.

"Who is your mistress ? " demanded **Fabia**.

"Valeria, wife of Lucius Calatinus."

"Livia's precious mother!" whispered Drusus. "**I can**
imagine her doing a thing like this." Then aloud, "**What**
has the boy done ? "

"He dropped a murrhine vase," was the answer.

"And so he must be beaten to death ! " exclaimed the young
man, who, despite the general theory that most slaves were on
a par with cattle, had much of the milk of human kindness in
his nature. " *Phui !* What brutality! You must insist on
your rights, aunt. Make them let him go."

Sulkily enough the executioners unbound the heavy furca.
Agias staggered to his feet, too dazed really to know what
deliverance had befallen him.

"Why don't you thank the Vestal ? " said Alfidius. "She
has made us release you — you ungrateful dog ! "

"Released ? Saved ? " gasped Agias, and he reeled as
though his head were in a whirl. Then, as if recollecting
his faculties, he fell down at Fabia's feet, and kissed the hem
of her robe.

"The gods save us all now," muttered Alfidius. "Valeria
will swear that we schemed to have the boy released. We
shall never dare to face her again ! "

"Oh ! do not send me back to that cruel woman!" moaned
Agias. "Better die now, than go back to her and incur her
anger again ! Kill me, but do not send me back ! "

And he broke down again in inward agony.

Drusus had been surveying the boy, and saw that though
he was now in a pitiable enough state, he had been good-look‑
ing ; and that though his back had been cruelly marred, his
face had not been cut with the lashes. Perhaps the very fact
that Agias had been the victim of Valeria, and the high con‑

tempt in which the young Drusian held his divorced step-
mother, made him instinctively take the outraged boy's part.

"See here," began Drusus, "were you to be whipped by
orders of Calatinus?"

"No," moaned Agias; "Valeria gave the orders. My master was out."

"Ha!" remarked Drusus to his aunt, "won't the good man
be pleased to know how his wife has killed a valuable slave in
one of her tantrums?" Then aloud. "If I can buy you of
Calatinus, and give you to the Lady Cornelia, niece of Lentulus, the consul-elect, will you serve her faithfully, will you
make her wish the law of your life?"

"I will die for her!" cried Agias his despair mingled with
a ray of hope.

"Where is your master?"

"At the Forum, I think, soliciting votes," replied the boy.

"Well then, follow me," said Drusus, "our road leads back
to the Forum. We may meet him. If I can arrange with
him, your executioners have nothing to fear from Valeria.
Come along."

Agias followed, with his head again in a whirl.

III

The little company worked its way back to the Forum, not,
as now, a half-excavated ruin, the gazing-stock for excursion-
ists, a commonplace whereby to sum up departed greatness:
the splendid buildings of the Empire had not yet arisen, but
the structures of the age were not unimposing. Here, in plain
view, was the Capitoline Hill, crowned by the Temple of
Jupiter Capitolinus and the Arx. Here was the site of the
Senate House, the Curia (then burned), in which the men who
had made Rome mistress of the world had taken counsel

Every stone, every basilica, had its history for Drusus — though, be it said, at the moment the noble past was little in his mind And the historic enclosure was all swarming, beyond other places, with the dirty, bustling crowd, shoppers, hucksters, idlers. Drusus and his company searched for Calatinus along the upper side of the Forum, past the Rostra, the Comitium,[1] and the Temple of Saturn. Then they were almost caught in the dense throng that was pouring into the plaza from the busy commercial thoroughfares of the Vicus Jugarius, or the Vicus Tuscus. But just as the party had almost completed their circuit of the square, and Drusus was beginning to believe that his benevolent intentions were leading him on a bootless errand, a man in a conspicuously white toga rushed out upon him from the steps of the Temple of Castor, embraced him violently, and imprinted a firm, garlic-flavoured kiss on both cheeks; crying at the same time heartily: —

"Oh, my dear Publius Dorso, I am so glad to meet you! How are all your affairs up in Fidenæ?"

Drusus recoiled in some disgust, and began rub'ing his outraged cheeks.

"Dorso? Dorso? There is surely some mistake, my good man. I am known as Quintus Drusus of Præneste."

Before he had gotten further, his assailant was pounding and shaking a frightened-looking slave-lad who had stood at his elbow.

"The gods blast you, you worthless *nomenclator!*[2] You have forgotten the worthy gentleman's name, and have made me play the fool! You may have lost me votes! All Rome

---

[1] *Comitium*, assembly-place round the Rostra.
[2] Great men, and candidates for office who wished to "know" everybody, kept smart slaves at their elbow to whisper strangers' names in their ears. Sometimes the slaves themselves were at fault.

will hear of this! I shall be a common laughing-stock! *Hei! vah!* But I'll teach you to behave!" And he shook the wretched boy until the latter's teeth rattled.

At this instant a young man of faultless toilet, whom we have already recognized as Lucius Ahenobarbus, pushed into the little knot as a peacemaker.

"Most excellent Calatinus," said he, half suppressing his laughter at the candidate's fury, the nomenclator's anguish, and Drusus's vexed confusion, "allow me to introduce to you a son of Sextus Drusus, who was an old friend of my father's. This is Quintus Drusus, if in a few years I have not forgotten his face; and this, my dear Quintus, is my good friend Lucius Calatinus, who would be glad of your vote and influence to help on his candidacy as tribune."

The atmosphere was cleared instantly. Calatinus forgot his anger, in order to apologize in the most obsequious manner for his headlong salutation. Drusus, pleased to find the man he had been seeking, forgave the vile scent of the garlic, and graciously accepted the explanation. Then the way was open to ask Calatinus whether he was willing to dispose of Agias. The crestfallen candidate was only too happy to do something to put himself right with the person he had offended. Loudly he cursed his wife's temper, that would have wasted a slave worth a "hundred thousand sesterces" to gratify a mere burst of passion.

"Yes, he was willing to sell the boy to accommodate his excellency, Quintus Drusus," said Calatinus, "although he was a valuable slave. Still, in honesty he had to admit that Agias had some mischievous points. Calatinus had boxed his ears only the day before for licking the pastry. But, since his wife disliked the fellow, he would be constrained to sell him, if a purchaser would take him."

The result of the conference was that Drusus, who had inherited that keen eye for business which went with most of his race, purchased Agias for thirty thousand sesterces, considerably less than the boy would have brought in the market.

While Drusus was handing over a money order payable with Flaccus, Lucius Ahenobarbus again came forward, with all seeming friendliness.

"My dear Quintus," said he, "Marcus Læca has commissioned me to find a ninth guest to fill his *triclinium* [1] this evening. We should be delighted if you would join us. I don't know what the good Marcus will offer us to-night, but you can be sure of a slice of peacock [2] and a few other nice bits."

"I am very grateful," replied Drusus, who felt all the while that Lucius Ahenobarbus was the last man in the world with whom he cared to spend an evening's carousing; "but," and here he concocted a white lie, "an old friend I met in Athens has already invited me to spend the night, and I cannot well refuse him. I thank you for your invitation."

Lucius muttered some polite and conventional terms of regret, and fell back to join Servius Flaccus and Gabinius, who were near him.

"I invited him and he refused," he said half scornfully, half bitterly. "That little minx, Cornelia, has been complaining of me to him, I am sure. The gods ruin him! If he wishes to become my enemy, he'll have good cause to fear my bite."

"You say he's from Præneste," said Gabinius, "and yet can he speak decent Latin? Doesn't he say '*conia*' for '*ciconia*,' and '*tammodo*' for '*tantummodo*'? I wonder you invite such a boor."

---

[1] Dining room with couch seats for nine, the regular size.
[2] The *ne plus ultra* of Roman gastronomy at the time.

"Oh! he can speak good enough Latin," said Lucius. "But I invited him because he is rich; and it might be worth our while to make him gamble."

"Rich!" lisped Servius Flaccus. "Rich (h)as my (h)uncle the broker? That silly straightlac(h)ed fellow, who's (h)a C(h)ato, (h)or worse? For shame!"

"Well," said Lucius, "old Crassus used to say that no one who couldn't pay out of his own purse for an army was rich. But though Drusus cannot do quite that, he has enough sesterces to make happy men of most of us, if his fortune were mine or yours."

"(H)its (h)an (h)outrage for him to have (h)it," cried Servius Flaccus.

"It's worse than an outrage," replied Ahenobarbus; "it's a sheer blunder of the Fates. Remind me to tell you about Drusus and his fortune, before I have drunk too much to-night."

* * * * * * * * * *

Agias went away rejoicing with his new master. Drusus owned an apartment house on the Vicus Longus, and there had a furnished suite of rooms. He gave Agias into the charge of the porter,[1] and ordered him to dress the boy's wounds. Cappadox waited on his master when he lunched.

"Master Quintus," said he, with the familiar air of a privileged servant, "did you see that knavish-looking Gabinius following Madame Fabia all the way back to the Temple of Vesta?"

"No," said Drusus; "what do you mean, you silly fellow?"

"Oh, nothing," said Cappadox, humbly. "I only thought it a little queer."

"Perhaps so," said his master, carelessly.

[1] Porter — *Insularius.*

CHAPTER IV

LUCIUS AHENOBARBUS AIRS HIS GRIEVANCE

I

THE pomp and gluttony of Roman banquets have been too often described to need repetition here; neither would we be edified by learning all the orgies that Marcus Læca (an old Catilinian conspirator) and his eight guests indulged in that night: only after the dinner had been cleared, and before the Gadesian[1] dancing girls were called in, the dice began to rattle, and speedily all were engrossed in drink and play.

Lucius Ahenobarbus soon lost so heavily that he was cursing every god that presided over the noble game.

"I am ruined next Ides," he groaned. "Phormio the broker has only continued my loan at four per cent a month. All my villas and furniture are mortgaged, and will be sold at auction. *Mehercle*, destruction stares me in the face!"

"Well, well, my dear fellow," said Pratinas, who, having won the stakes, was in a mood to be sympathetic, "we must really see what can be done to remedy matters."

"I can see nothing!" was his answer.

"Won't your father come to the rescue?" put in Gabinius, between deep pulls on a beaker.

"My father!" snapped Ahenobarbus. "Never a sesterce will I get out of him! He's as good as turned me adrift, and

[1] From Cadiz, Spain.

50

Cato my uncle is always giving him bad reports of me, like the hypocritical Stoic that Cato is."

"By the bye," began Gabinius again, putting down the wine-cup, "you hinted to-day that you had been cheated out of a fortune, after a manner. Something about that Drusus of Præneste, if I recollect. What's the story?"

Lucius settled down on his elbow, readjusted the cushions on the banqueting couch, and then began, interrupted by many a hiccough because of his potations.

"It is quite a story, but I won't bore you with details. It has quite as much to do with Cornelia, Lentulus Crus's pretty niece, as with Drusus himself. Here it is in short. Sextus Drusus and Caius Lentulus were such good friends that, as you know, they betrothed their son and daughter when the latter were mere children. To make the compact doubly strong, Sextus Drusus inserted in his will a clause like this: 'Let my son Quintus enjoy the use of my estate and its income, until he become twenty-five and cease to be under the care of Flaccus his *tutor*.[1] If he die before that time, let his property go to Cornelia, the daughter of Caius Lentulus, except;' and here Sextus left a small legacy for his own young daughter, Livia. You see Drusus can make no will until he is five-and-twenty. But then comes another provision. 'If Cornelia shall marry any person save my son, my son shall at once be free to dispose of my estates.' So Cornelia is laid under a sort of obligation also to marry Quintus. The whole aim of the will is to make it very hard for the young people to fail to wed as their fathers wished."

"True," said Gabinius; "but how such an arrangement can affect you and your affairs, I really cannot understand."

"That is so," continued Ahenobarbus, "but here is the

---

[1] Commercial adviser required for young men under five-and-twenty.

other side of the matter. Caius Lentulus was a firm friend of Sextus Drusus; he also was very close and dear to my father. Caius desired that Cornelia wed young Drusus, and so enjoined her in his will; but out of compliment to my father, put in a clause which was something like this: 'If Quintus Drusus die before he marry Cornelia, or refuse to marry Cornelia at the proper time, then let Cornelia and all her property be given to Lucius, the second son of my dearly loved friend, Lucius Domitius Ahenobarbus.' Now I think you will begin to see why Quintus Drusus's affairs interest me a little. If he refuse to marry Cornelia before he be five-and-twenty, she falls to me. But I understand that Lentulus, her uncle, is badly in debt, and her dowry won't be much. But if Drusus is not married to her, and die before he is twenty-five, *his property is hers and she is mine.* Do you understand why I have a little grudge against him?"

"For what?" cried Læca, with breathless interest.

"For living!" sighed Ahenobarbus, hopelessly.

The handsome face of Pratinas was a study. His nostrils dilated; his lips quivered; his eyes were bright and keen with what evidently passed in his mind for a great discovery.

"Eureka!" cried the Greek, clapping his hands. "My dear Lucius, let me congratulate you! You are saved!"

"What?" exclaimed the young man, starting up.

"You are saved!" repeated Pratinas, all animation "Drusus's sesterces shall be yours! Every one of them!"

Lucius Ahenobarbus was a debauchee, a mere creature of pleasure, without principle or character; but even he had a revulsion of spirit at the hardly masked proposal of the enthusiastic Greek. He flushed in spite of the wine, then turned pale, then stammered, "Don't mention such a thing, Pratinas. I was never Drusus's enemy. I dare not dream of such a move. The Gods forefend!"

"The Gods?" repeated Pratinas, with a cynical intonation. "Do you believe there are any?"

"Do you?" retorted Lucius, feeling all the time that a deadly temptation had hold of him, which he could by no means resist.

"Why?" said the Greek. "Your Latin Ennius states my view, in some of your rather rough and blundering native tetrameters. He says:—

"'There's a race of gods in heaven; so I've said and still will say.
But I deem that we poor mortals do not come beneath their sway.
Otherwise the good would triumph, whereas evil reigns to-day.'"

"And you advise?" said Ahenobarbus, leaning forward with pent-up excitement.

"I advise?" replied Pratinas; "I am only a poor ignorant Hellene, and who am I, to give advice to Lucius Domitius Ahenobarbus, a most noble member of the most noble of nations!"

If Pratinas had said: "My dear Lucius, you are a thick-headed, old-fashioned, superstitious Roman, whom I, in my superior wisdom, utterly despise," he would have produced about the same effect upon young Ahenobarbus.

But Lucius still fluttered vainly,—a very weak conscience whispering that Drusus had never done him any harm; that murder was a dangerous game, and that although his past life had been bad enough, he had never made any one—unless it were a luckless slave or two—the victim of bloodthirsty passion or rascality.

"Don't propose it," he groaned. "I don't dare to think of such a thing! What disgrace and trouble, if it should all come out!"

"Come, come, Ahenobarbus," thrust in Marcus Læca, who had been educated in Catilina's school for polite villains and

.ut-throats. "Pratinas is only proposing what, if you were a man of spirit, would have been done long ago. You can't complain of Fortune, when she's put a handsome estate in your hands for the asking."

"My admirable fellow," said Pratinas, benevolently, "I highly applaud your scruples. But, permit me to say it, I must ask you to defer to me as being a philosopher. Let us look at the matter in a rational way. We have gotten over any bogies which our ancesters had about Hades, or the punishments of the wicked. In fact, what we know — as good Epicureans — is that, as Democritus of Abdera[1] early taught, this world of ours is composed of a vast number of infinitely small and indivisible atoms, which have by some strange hap come to take the forms we see in the world of life and matter. Now the soul of man is also of atoms, only they are finer and more subtile. At death these atoms are dissolved, and so far as that man is concerned, all is over with him. The atoms may recombine, or join with others, but never form anew that same man. Hence we may fairly conclude that this life is everything and death ends all. Do you follow, and see to what I am leading?"

"I think so," said the wretched Lucius, feeling himself like a bird caught in a snare, yet not exactly grasping the direct bearing of all this learned exposition.

"My application is this," went on Pratinas, glibly. "Life is all — all either for pleasure or pain. Therefore every man has a right to extract all the sweetness he can out of it. But suppose a man deliberately makes himself gloomy, extracts no joy from life; lets himself be overborne by care and sorrow, — is not such a man better dead than living? Is not a dreamless sleep preferable to misery or even cold asceticism? And

[1] Born about 470 B.C.

how much more does this all apply when we see a man who makes himself unhappy, preventing by his very act of existence the happiness of another more equably tempered mortal! Now I believe this is the present case. Drusus, I understand, is leading a spare, joyless, workaday sort of existence, which is, or by every human law should be, to him a burden. So long as he lives, he prevents you from enjoying the means of acquiring pleasure. Now I have Socrates of imperishable memory on my side, when I assert that death under any circumstances is either no loss or a very great gain. Considering then the facts of the case in its philosophic and rational bearings, I may say this: Not merely would it be no wrong to remove Drusus from a world in which he is evidently out of place, but I even conceive such an act to rise to the rank of a truly meritorious deed."

Lucius Ahenobarbus was conquered. He could not resist the inexorable logic of this train of reasoning, all the premises of which he fully accepted. Perhaps, we should add, he was not very unwilling to have his wine-befuddled intellect satisfied, and his conscience stilled. He turned down a huge beaker of liquor, and coughed forth: —

"Right as usual, Pratinas! By all the gods, but I believ' you can save me!"

"Yes; as soon as Drusus is dead," insinuated the Greek who was already computing his bill for brokerage in this little affair, "you can raise plenty of loans, on the strength of your coming marriage with Cornelia."

"But how will you manage it?" put in the alert Gabinius. "There mustn't be any clumsy bungling."

"Rest assured," said Pratinas, with a grave dignity, perhaps the result of his drinking, "that in my affairs I leave no room for bungling "

"And your plan is —" asked Lucius.

"Till to-morrow, friend," said the Greek; "meet me at the Temple of Saturn, just before dusk. Then I'll be ready."

II

Lucius Ahenobarbus's servants escorted their tipsy master home to his lodgings in a fashionable apartment house on the Esquiline. When he awoke, it was late the next day, and head and wits were both sadly the worse for the recent entertainment. Finally a bath and a luncheon cleared his brain, and he realized his position. He was on the brink of concocting a deliberate murder. Drusus had never wronged him; the crime would be unprovoked; avarice would be its only justification. Ahenobarbus had done many things which a far laxer code of ethics than that of to-day would frown upon; but, as said, he had never committed murder — at least had only had crucified those luckless slaves, who did not count. He roused with a start, as from a dream. What if Pratinas were wrong? What if there were really gods, and furies, and punishments for the wicked after death? And then came the other side of the shield: a great fortune his; all his debts paid off; unlimited chances for self-enjoyment; last, but not least, Cornelia his. She had slighted him, and turned her back upon all his advances; and now what perfect revenge! Lucius was more in love with Cornelia than he admitted even to himself. He would even give up Clyte, if he could possess her. And so the mental battle went on all day; and the prick of conscience, the fears of superstition, and the lingerings of religion ever grew fainter. Near nightfall he was at his post, at the Temple of Saturn. Pratinas was awaiting him. The Greek had only a few words of greeting, and the curt injunction: —

"Draw your cloak up to shield your face, and follow me." Then they passed out from the Forum, forced their way through the crowded streets, and soon were through the *Porta Ratumena*, outside the walls, and struck out across the Campus Martius, upon the Via Flaminia. It was rapidly darkening. The houses grew fewer and fewer. At a little distance the dim structures of the Portico and Theatre of Pompeius could be seen, looming up to an exaggerated size in the evening haze. A grey fog was drifting up from the Tiber, and out of a rift in a heavy cloud-bank a beam of the imprisoned moon was struggling. Along the road were peasants with their carts and asses hastening home. Over on the Pincian Mount the dark green masses of the splendid gardens of Pompeius and of Lucullus were just visible. The air was filled with the croak of frogs and the chirp of crickets, and from the river came the creak of the sculls and paddles of a cumbrous barge that was working its way down the Tiber.

Ahenobarbus felt awed and uncomfortable. Pratinas, with his mantle wrapped tightly around his head, continued at a rapid pace. Lucius had left his attendants at home, and now began to recall gruesome tales of highwaymen and bandits frequenting this region after dark. His fears were not allayed by noticing that underneath his himation Pratinas occasionally let the hilt of a short sword peep forth. Still the Greek kept on, never turning to glance at a filthy, half-clad beggar, who whined after them for an alms, and who did not so much as throw a kiss after the young Roman when the latter tossed forth a denarius,[1] but snatched up the coin, muttered at its being no more, and vanished into the gathering gloom.

"Where are you leading me?" asked Ahenobarbus, a second

[1] Four sesterces, 16 cents.

time, after all his efforts to communicate with the usually fluent Greek met with only monosyllables.

"To the *lanista*[1] Dumnorix," replied Pratinas, quickening an already rapid pace.

"And his barracks are — ? "

"By the river, near the Mulvian bridge."

At length a pile of low square buildings was barely visible in the haze. It was close to the Tiber, and the rush of the water against the piling of the bridge was distinctly audible. As the two drew near to a closed gateway, a number of mongrel dogs began to snap and bark around them. From within the building came the roar of coarse hilarity and coarser jests. As Pratinas approached the solidly barred doorway, a grating was pushed aside and a rude voice demanded : —

"Your business ? What are you doing here ? "

"Is Dumnorix sober ? " replied Pratinas, nothing daunted. "If so, tell him to come and speak with me. I have something for his advantage."

Either Pratinas was well known at the gladiators' school, or something in his speech procured favour. There was a rattling of chains and bolts, and the door swung open. A man of unusual height and ponderous proportions appeared in the opening. That was all which could be seen in the semi-darkness.

"You are Pratinas ? " he asked, speaking Latin with a northern accent. The Hellene nodded, and replied softly : "Yes. No noise. Tell Dumnorix to come quietly."

The two stepped in on to the flags of a courtyard, and the doorkeeper, after rebolting, vanished into the building. Ahenobarbus could only see that he was standing in a large stone-paved court, perhaps one hundred and forty feet wide and considerably longer. A colonnade of low whitewashed pil

[1] Keeper of a school of gladiators.

lars ran all about: and behind them stretched rows of small rooms and a few larger apartments. There were *tyros* practising with wooden swords in one of the rooms, whence a light streamed, and a knot of older gladiators was urging them on, mocking, praising, and criticising their efforts. Now and then a burly gladiator would stroll across the court; but the young noble and his escort remained hidden in shadow.

Presently a door opened at the other end of the courtyard, and some one with a lantern began to come toward the entrance. Long before the stranger was near, Ahenobarbus thought he was rising like a giant out of the darkness; and when at last Dumnorix — for it was he — was close at hand, both Roman and Greek seemed veritable dwarfs beside him.

Dumnorix — so far as he could be seen in the lantern light — was a splendid specimen of a northern giant. He was at least six feet five inches in height, and broad proportionately. His fair straight hair tumbled in disorder over his shoulders, and his prodigiously long mustaches seemed, to the awed Ahenobarbus, almost to curl down to his neck. His breath came in hot pants like a winded horse, and when he spoke, it was in short Latin monosyllables, interlarded with outlandish Gallic oaths. He wore cloth trousers with bright stripes of red and orange; a short-sleeved cloak of dark stuff, falling down to the thigh; and over the cloak, covering back and shoulders, another sleeveless mantle, clasped under the chin with a huge golden buckle. At his right thigh hung, from a silver set girdle, by weighty bronze chains, a heavy sabre, of which the steel scabbard banged noisily as its owner advanced.

"Holla! Pratinas," cried the Gaul, as he came close. "By the holy oak! but I'm glad to see you! Come to my room. Have a flagon of our good northern mead."

"Hist," said the Greek, cautiously. "Not so boisterous.

Better stay here in the dark. I can't tell who of your men may hear us."

"As you say," said Dumnorix, setting down the light at a little distance and coming closer.

"You remember that little affair of last year," said Pratinas. continuing;—"how you helped me get rid of a witness in a very troublesome law case?"

"Ha! ha!" chuckled the giant, "I wish I had the sesterces I won then, in my coffer now."

"Well," replied Pratinas, "I don't need to tell you what I and my noble friend here — Lucius Domitius Ahenobarbus — have come for. A little more business along the same line. Are you our man?"

"I should say so," answered Dumnorix, with a grin worthy of a baboon. "Only make it worth my while."

"Now," said Pratinas, sinking his voice still lower, "this affair of ours will pay you well; but it is more delicate than the other. A blunder will spoil it all. You must do your best; and we will do the fair thing by you."

"Go on," said the Gaul, folding his huge paws on his breast.

"Have you ever been in Præneste?" questioned Pratinas.

"I matched two *mirmillones* [1] of mine there against two *threces* [2] of another lanista, and my dogs won the prize; but I can't say that I am acquainted with the place," answered the other.

"You should find out, then," said Pratinas, "for here lies your work." And then he proceeded, with occasional prompting from the better-informed Ahenobarbus, to point out the location of Drusus's estate, and the character and habits of the man whom Dumnorix was cheerfully proposing to put out of the way. Dumnorix assented and bade him go on, with hoarse

---

[1] Gladiators equipped as Gaulish warriors.   [2] Buckler men.

grunts; and when the Greek had concluded, growled out in his barbarous Latin : —

"But why all this pother? Why not let me send a knave or two and knock the fellow some dark night in the head? It will save us both time and trouble."

"My excellent master of the gladiators," said Pratinas, as smoothly as ever, "you must not take it ill, if I tell you that to have a taking off such as you propose would be a very bad thing both for you and the most noble Ahenobarbus. This Drusus is not a helpless wight, without friends, waiting to become the fair prey of any dagger man.[1] He has friends, I have learned, who, if he were to be disposed of in such a rude and bungling manner, would not fail to probe deeply into the whole thing. Flaccus the great banker, notably, would spare no pains to bring the responsibility of the matter home, not merely to the poor wretch who struck the blow, but the persons who placed the weapon in his hands. All of which would be very awkward for Ahenobarbus. No, your rough-and-ready plan won't in the least work."

"Well," replied Dumnorix, testily, "I'm a man of shallow wits and hard blows. If I had been of keener mind, the gods know, I would have been a free chief among the Nervii, instead of making sport for these straw-limbed Romans. If what I propose won't answer, what can be done? "

"A great deal," said Pratinas, who knew perfectly how to cringe low, yet preserve his ascendency; "first of all, it is very necessary that the murderers of the amiable Drusus should receive a meet reward for their crime — that justice should be speedy and severe."

"Man!" cried Dumnorix, griping the Greek's arm in his tremendous clutch. "What are you asking?"

[1] *Sicarius.*

"By Zeus!" burst out Pratinas, rubbing his crushed mem
ber. "What a grip is yours! Don't be alarmed. Surely you
would be as willing to have one or **two of** your newest *tiroa*
hung on a cross, as stabbed on the arena — especially when **it**
will pay a great deal better?"

"I don't follow you," said the Gaul, though a little reassured.

"Simply this," said Pratinas, who evidently felt that he was
coming to the revealing of an especially brilliant piece of
finesse. "My general proposal is this. Let you and your
company march through Præneste, — of course carefully tim-
ing your march so as to find the innocent and unfortunate
Drusus at his farm. You will have a very disorderly band
of gladiators, and they begin to attack Drusus's orchard, and
maltreat his slaves. You try to stop them, — without avail.
Finally, in a most unfortunate and outrageous outbreak they
slay the master of the house. The tumult is quelled. The
heirs proceed against you. You can only hand over the murderers for crucifixion, and offer to pay any money damages
that may be imposed. A heavy fine is laid upon you, as
being responsible for the killing of Drusus by your slaves.
You pay the damages. Ahenobarbus marries Cornelia and
enters upon the estate. The world says that all that can be
done to atone for Drusus's murder has been done. All of the
guilty are punished. The dead cannot be recalled. The matter is at an end. Ahenobarbus has what he wished for; you
have all the money you paid in damages quietly refunded;
also the cost of the poor rascals crucified, and a fair sum over
and above for your trouble."

"By the god Belew!"[1] cried the enthusiastic Dumnorix,
"What a clever plan! How the world will be cheated! Ha!
ha! How sharp you little Greeks must be. Only I must

---

[1] The Gallic sun-god.

have fair return for my work, and an oath that the business shall never be coming to the point of giving my eyes to the crows. I can't risk my life in anything but a square fight."

"Well," said Pratinas, after a few words with his companion, "how will this proposition suit you? All expenses, before and after the affair itself, of course refunded; one hundred thousand sesterces clear gain for doing the deed, twenty-five thousand sesterces for every poor fellow we have to nail up to satisfy the law, and you to be guaranteed against any evil consequence. Is this sufficient?"

"I think so," growled Dumnorix, in his mustaches, "but I must have the oath."

"The oath?" said Pratinas, "oh, certainly!" and the Greek raised his hands toward heaven, and muttered some words to the effect that "if he and his friend did not fulfil their oath, let Zeus, the regarder of oaths, destroy them," etc., etc. — an imprecation which certainly, so far as words went, was strong enough to bind the most graceless. Then he proceeded to arrange with Dumnorix how the latter should wait until it was known Drusus had gone back to Præneste, and was likely to stay there for some time; as to how many gladiators the lanista was to have ready. Dumnorix complained that the rather recent law against keeping gladiators at Rome prevented him from assembling in his school any considerable number. But out of his heterogeneous collection of Gauls, Germans, Spaniards, Greeks, and Asiatics he would find enough who could be used for the purpose without letting them know the full intent with which they were launched against Drusus. At all events, if their testimony was taken, it would have to be as slaves on the rack; and if they accused their master of instigating them to riot, it was what any person would expect of such degraded and lying wretches. So, after promising to come again with final word and some bags of earnest-money, Pratinas parted with the lanista, and he and Lucius Aheno-barbus found themselves again in the now entirely darkened Campus Martius. Lucius again feared brigands, but they fell in with no unpleasant nocturnal wayfarers, and reached the city without incident. Ahenobarbus seemed to himself to be treading on air — Cornelia, villas, Drusus's money — these were dancing in his head in a delightful confusion. He had abandoned himself completely to the sway of Pratinas; the Greek was omniscient, was invincible, was a greater than Odysseus. Ahenobarbus hardly dared to think for himself as to the plan which his friend had arranged for him. One observation, however, he made before they parted.

"You swore that Dumnorix should get into no trouble. May it not prove expensive to keep him out of difficulty?"

"My dear Lucius," replied Pratinas, "in cases of that kind there is a line from the Hippolytus of the immortal trage-dian Euripides, which indicates the correct attitude for a phi-losopher and a man of discretion to assume. It runs thus, —

"'My tongue an oath took, but my mind's unsworn.'

Not an inelegant sentiment, as you must see."

III

We left the excellent man of learning, Pisander, in no happy frame of mind, after Agias had been dragged away, presumably to speedy doom. And indeed for many days the shadow of Valeria's crime, for it was nothing else, plunged him in deep melancholy. Pisander was not a fool, only amongst his many good qualities he did not possess that of being able to make a success in life. He had been tutor to a young Asiatic prince, and had lost his position by a local revolution; then he had drifted to Alexandria, and finally Rome, where he had struggled first to teach philosophy, and found no pupils to listen to his lectures; then to conduct an elementary school, but his scholars' parents were backward in paying even the modest fees he charged. Finally, in sheer despair, to keep from starving, he accepted the position as Valeria's "house-philosopher."

His condition was infinitely unsatisfactory for a variety of reasons. The good lady wished him to be at her elbow, ready to read from the philosophers or have on hand a talk on ethics or metaphysics to deliver extempore. Besides, though not a slave or freedman, he fared in the household much worse sometimes than they. A slave stole the dainties, and drained a beaker of costly wine on the sly. Pisander, like Thales, who was so intent looking at the stars that he fell into a well, "was so eager to know what was going on in heaven that he could not see what was before his feet." [1] And consequently the poor pedant dined on the remnants left after his employer and her husband had cleared the board; and had rancid oil and sour wine given him, when they enjoyed the best. The slaves had snubbed him and made fun of him; the freedmen regarded him with absolute disdain; Valeria's regular visitors treated him as a nonentity. Besides, all his standards of ethical righteousness were outraged by the round of life which he was compelled daily to witness. The worthy man would long before have ceased from a vassalage so disgraceful, had he possessed any other means of support. Once he meditated suicide, but was scared out of it by the thought that his bones would moulder in those huge pits on the Esquiline — far from friend or native land — where artisans, slaves, and cattle, creatures alike without means of decent burial, were

---

[1] See Plato's "Theætetus," 174.

F

left under circumstances unspeakably revolting to moulder away to dust.

The day of Agias's misfortune, Pisander sat in his corner of the boudoir, after Valeria had left it, in a very unphilosophical rage, gnawing his beard and cursing inwardly his mistress, Pratinas, and the world in general.

Arsinoë with a pale, strained face was moving about, replacing the bottles of cosmetics and perfumery in cabinets and caskets. Pisander had been kind to Arsinoë, and had taught her to read; and there was a fairly firm friendship between the slave and the luckless man, who felt himself degraded by an equal bondage.

"Poor Agias," muttered Pisander.

"Poor Agias," repeated Arsinoë, mournfully; then in some scorn, "Come, Master Pisander, now is the time to console yourself with your philosophy. Call out everything, — your Zeno, or Parmenides, or Heraclitus, or others of the thousand nobodies I've heard you praise to Valeria, — and make thereby my heart a jot the less sore, or Agias's death the less bitter! Don't sit there and snap at your beard, if your philosophy is good for anything! People used to pray to the gods in trouble, but you philosophers turn the gods into mists or thin air. You are a man! You are free! Do something! Say something!"

"But what can I do?" groaned Pisander, bursting into tears, and wishing for the instant Epicureans, Stoics, Eclectics, Peripatetics, and every other school of learning in the nethermost Hades.

"*Phui!* Fudge!" cried Arsinoë. "What is life made for then, if a man who has spent all his days studying it is as good as helpless! Look at me! Have I not hands, feet, a head, and wits? Am I not as well informed and naturally capable as three fine ladies out of every four? Would I not look as handsome as they, if I had a chance to wear their dresses and jewels? Have I any blemish, any defect, that makes me cease to be a woman, and become a thing? Bah, master *Pisander!* I am only a slave, but I will talk. Why does my blood boil at the fate of Agias, if it was not meant that it should heat up for some end? And yet I am as much a piece of property of that woman whom I hate, as this chair or casket. I have a right to no hope, no ambition, no desire, no reward. I can only aspire to live without brutal treatment. That would be a sort of Elysium. If I was brave enough, I would kill myself, and go to sleep and forget it all. But I am weak and cowardly, and so — here I am."

Pisander only groaned and went away to his room to turn over his Aristotle, and wonder why nothing in the "Nicomachean Ethics" or any other learned treatise contained the least word that made him contented over the fate of Agias or his own unhappy situation. Arsinoë and Semiramis, when he went from them, cried, and cried again, in pity and helpless grief at their whole situation. And so a considerable number of days passed. Calatinus could have given joy to the hearts of several in his household if he had simply remembered that Agias had not been scourged to death, but sold. But Calatinus feared, now that he was well out of the matter, to stir up an angry scene with his wife, by hinting that Agias had not been punished according to her orders. Alfidius, too, and the other slaves with him, imagined that his mistress would blame them if they admitted that Agias was alive. So the household gathered, by the silence of all concerned, that the bright Greek boy had long since passed beyond power of human torment. Pisander recovered part of his equanimity, and Arsinoë and Semiramis began to see life a shade less darkened.

Pratinas occasionally repeated his morning calls upon Valeria. He seemed much engrossed with business, but was always the same suave, elegant, accomplished personage that had endeared him to that lady's heart. One morning he came in, in unusually good spirits. "Congratulate me," he exclaimed, after saluting Valeria; "I have disposed of a very delicate piece of work, and my mind can take a little rest. At least I have roughly chiselled out the matter, as a sculptor would say, and can now wait a bit before finishing. Ah! what elegant study is this which is engrossing your ladyship this morning?"

"Pisander is reading from the works of Gorgias of Leontini," said Valeria, languidly.

"To be sure," went on Pratinas; "I have always had the greatest respect for the three nihilistic propositions of that philosopher. To read him one is half convinced of the affirmation that nothing exists; that if anything existed, the fact could not be known, and that if the fact were known, it could not be communicated; although of course, my dear madam, there are very grave objections to accepting such views in their fulness."

"Of course," echoed Valeria. "Pisander, read Pratinas that little poem of Archilochus, whose sentiment I so much admired, when I happened on it yesterday."

Pisander fumbled among his rolls, then read, perhaps throwing a bit of sarcasm into his tone: —

> "Gyges'[1] wealth and honours great
>   Come not nigh to me!
> Heavenly pow'r, or tyrant's state,
>   I'll not envy thee.
> Swift let any sordid prize
> Fade and vanish from my eyes!"

[1] A Lydian king whose wealth was placed on a par with that of the better known Crœsus.

"Your ladyship," said Pratinas, appearing entranced by the lines, "is ever in search of the pearls of refined expression!"

"I wish," said Valeria, whose mind ran from Gorgias to Archilochus, and then back to quite foreign matters, with lightning rapidity, "you would tell Kallias, the sculptor, that the head-dress on my statue in the atrium must be changed. I don't arrange my hair that way any longer. He must put on a new head-dress without delay."[1]

"Certainly," assented the Greek.

"And now," said the lady, half entreating, half insinuating, "*you must* tell me what has made you so abstracted lately; that business you mentioned, which compelled you to restrict your calls."

"My dear Valeria," said Pratinas, casting a glance over at Pisander in his corner, "I dislike mysteries; but perhaps there are some things which I had better not reveal to any one. Don't be offended, but—"

"I am offended," exclaimed the lady, striking her lap with her hands, "and I accept no '*buts.*' I will be as silent about all your affairs as about the mysteries of the *Bona Dea.*[2]"

"I believe I can be confident you will not betray me," said Pratinas, who in fact considered precautions that were necessary to take among so blundering and thick-witted people as the Latins, almost superfluous. He muttered to himself, "I wouldn't dare to do this in Alexandria,—prate of a murder,—" and then glanced again toward Pisander.

"Pisander," said Valeria, sharply, noting Pratinas's disquietude, "go out of the room. I don't need you at present."

Pisander, unlike many contemporaries, was affected by a sensitive conscience. But if there was one man whom he de-

---

[1] Such alterations were actually made in Rome.
[2] To whose mysteries only women were admitted.

spised to the bottom of his soul, it was Pratinas. Pratinas
had lorded it over him and patronized him, in a way which
drove the mild-tempered man of learning to desperation. The
spirit of evil entered into the heart of Pisander as he left the
room. The average chatter of Pratinas and Valeria had been
gall and wormwood to him, and he had been glad enough to
evade it; but here was Pratinas with a secret which he clearly
did not wish Pisander to know. And Pisander, prompted
by most unphilosophical motives, resolved within himself to
play the eavesdropper. The boudoir was approached by three
doors, one from the peristylium, one from Valeria's private
sleeping chamber, one from the servants' quarters. Pisander
went out through the first, and going through other rooms to
the third, took his station by that entrance. He met Arsinoë,
and took the friendly maid into his plot, by stationing her
on guard to prevent the other servants from interfering with
him. Then applying his ear to the large keyhole of the
door, he could understand all that was passing in the boudoir.
What Pratinas was saying it is hardly necessary to repeat.
The Greek was relating with infinite zest, and to Valeria's
intense delight and amusement, the story of the two wills
which placed Drusus's estate and the hand of Cornelia within
reach of Lucius Ahenobarbus; of the manner in which this
last young man had been induced to take steps to make way
with an unfortunate rival. Finally, in a low, half-audible
tone, he told of the provisional arrangements with Dumnorix,
and how very soon the plan was to be put in execution.

"And you must be sure and tell me," cried Valeria, clapping
her hands when Pratinas concluded, "what the details of the
affair all are, and when and how you succeed. Poor Quintus
Drusus! I am really sorry for him. But when one doesn't
make use of what Fortune has given him, there is nothing
else to do!"

"Yes," said Pratinas, sententiously. "He who fails to realize what is for him the highest good, forfeits, thereby, the right to life itself."

Pisander slipped away from the keyhole, with a white face, and panting for breath. Briefly, he repeated what he had gathered to Arsinoë, then blurted out:—

"I will go in and meet that well-oiled villain face to face. By Zeus! I will make him feel the depths of an honest man's scorn and indignation!"

"You will be a fool," replied Arsinoë, quietly, "if you do. Valeria would instantly dismiss you from her service."

"I will go at once to Drusus," asserted Pisander.

"Drusus may or may not be convinced that what you say is true," answered the girl; "but he, I gather from what you repeat, has just gone back to Præneste. Before you could reach Præneste, you are a dead man."

"How so?" demanded the excited philosopher, brandishing his fists. "I am as strong as Pratinas."

"How little wisdom," commented Arsinoë, "you do gather from your books! Can't you see Pratinas is a reckless scoundrel — with every gladiator in Dumnorix's school at his call if needs be — who would stop at nothing to silence promptly the mouth of a dangerous witness? This isn't worse than many another case. Don't share the ruin of a man who is an utter stranger! We have troubles enough of our own."

And with this consolation Arsinoë left him, again consumed with impotent rage.

"Villain," fumed Pisander to himself, "if I could only place my fingers round your neck! But what can I do? What can I do? I am helpless, friendless, penniless! And I can only tear out my heart, and pretend to play the philosopher. I, a philosopher! If I were a true one. I would have had the courage to kill myself before this."

And in this mental state he continued, till he learned that Pratinas had taken his farewell, and that Calatinus wished him — since all the slaves seemed busy, and the poor house philosopher was often sent on menial errands — to go to the *Forum Boarium*,[1] and bring back some ribs of beef for a dinner that evening. Pisander went as bidden, tugging a large basket, and trying to muster up courage to continue his walk to the Fabrician Bridge, and plunge into the Tiber. In classic days suicide was a commendable act under a great many circumstances, and Pisander was perfectly serious and sincere in his belief that he and the world had been companions too long for the good of either. But the jar and din of the streets certainly served to make connected philosophical meditation upon the futility and unimportance of human existence decidedly unfruitful. By the time he reached the cattle-market the noise of this strange place drove all suicidal intentions from him. Butchers were slaughtering kine; drovers were driving oxen off of barges that had come down the Tiber; sheep and goats were bleating — everywhere around the stalls, booths, shops, and pens was the bustle of an enormous traffic. Pisander picked his way through the crowd, searching for the butcher to whom he had been especially sent. He had gone as far as the ancient shrine of Mater Matuta, which found place in these seemingly unhallowed precincts, when, as he gazed into the throng before him, his hair stood as it were on end, his voice choked in his throat, and cold sweat broke out over him. The next moment his hand was seized by another, young and hearty, and he was gasping forth the name of Agias.

[1] Cattle-market

CHAPTER V

A VERY OLD PROBLEM

I

Drusus had at last finished the business which centred around the death of his uncle, old Publius Vibulanus. He had walked behind the bier, in company with the other relatives of the deceased — all very distant, saving himself. On the day, too, of the funeral, he had been obliged to make his first public oration — a eulogy delivered in the Forum from the Rostra — in which Drusus tried to pay a graceful but not fulsome tribute to the old eques, who had never distinguished himself in any way, except the making of money. The many clients of Vibulanus, who now looked upon the young man as their patron, had raised a prodigious din of applause during the oration, and Quintus was flattered to feel that he had not studied rhetoric in vain. Finally, as next of kin, he had to apply the torch to the funeral pyre, and preside over the funeral feast, held by custom nine days after the actual burning, and over the contests of gladiators which took place at this festivity. Meanwhile Sextus Flaccus had been attending to the legal business connected with the transfer of the dead man's estate to his heir. All this took time — time which Drusus longed to be spending with Cornelia in shady and breezy Præneste, miles from unhealthy, half-parched Rome.

Drusus had sent Agias ahead to Cornelia, as soon as the poor boy had recovered in the least from his brutal scourging. The lad had parted from his deliverer with the most extravagant demonstrations of gratitude, which Quintus had said he could fully repay by implicit devotion to Cornelia. How that young lady had been pleased with her present, Drusus could not tell; although he had sent along a letter explaining the circumstances of the case. But Quintus had other things on his mind than Agias and his fortunes, on the morning when at last he turned his face away from the sultry capital, and found his carriage whirling him once more over the Campagna.

Drusus had by personal experience learned the bitterness of the political struggle in which he had elected to take part. The Cæsarians at Rome (Balbus, Antonius, and Curio) had welcomed him to their number, for young as he was, his wealth and the prestige of the Livian name were not to be despised. And Drusus saw how, as in his younger days he had not realized, the whole fabric of the state was in an evil way, and rapidly approaching its mending or ending. The Roman Republic had exported legions; she had imported slaves, who heaped up vast riches for their masters, while their competition reduced the free peasantry to starvation. And now a splendid aristocracy claimed to rule a subject world, while the "Roman people" that had conquered that world were a degenerate mob, whose suffrages in the elections were purchasable — almost openly — by the highest bidder. The way was not clear before Drusus; he only saw, with his blind, Pagan vision, that no real liberty existed under present conditions; that Pompeius and his allies, the Senate party, were trying to perpetuate the aristocracy in power, and that Cæsar, the absent proconsul of the Gauls, stood, at least, for a sweeping reform. And so the young man made his decision and waited the march of events.

But once at Præneste all these forebodings were thrust into

the background. The builders and frescoers had done their work well in his villa. A new colonnade was being erected. Coloured mosaic floors were being laid. The walls of the rooms were all a-dance with bright Cupids and Bacchantes — cheerful apartments for their prospective mistress. But it was over to the country-house of the Lentuli that Drusus made small delay to hasten, there to be in bliss in company with Cornelia.

"And how," he asked, after the young lady had talked of a dozen innocent nothings, "do you like Agias, the boy I sent you?"

"I can never thank you enough — at least if he is always as clever and witty as he has been since I have had him," was the reply. "I was vexed at first to have a servant with such dreadful scars all over him; but he is more presentable now And he has a very droll way of saying bright things. What fun he has made of Livia's dear mother, his former mistress! I shall have to give up reading any wise authors, if it will make me grow like Valeria. Then, too, Agias has won my favour, if in no other way, by getting a thick grass stem out of the throat of my dear little pet sparrow, that was almost choking to death. I am so grateful to you for him!"

"I am very glad you are fond of him," said Drusus. "Has your uncle come back from Rome yet? I did not meet him while there. I was busy; and besides, to speak honestly, I have a little hesitation in seeing him, since the political situation is so tense."

"He returns to-night, I believe," replied Cornelia. Then as if a bit apprehensive, "Tell me about the world, Drusus; I don't care to be one of those fine ladies of the sort of Clodia,[1] who are all in the whirl of politics, and do everything a man

---

[1] She was a sister of Clodius, a famous demagogue, and was a brilliant though abandoned woman.

does except to speak in the Senate; but I like to know what is going on. There isn't going to be a riot, I hope, as there was two years ago, when no consuls were elected, and Pompeius had to become sole magistrate?"

"There have been no tumults so far," said Drusus, who did not care to unfold all his fears and expectations.

"Yet things are in a very bad way, I hear," said Cornelia "Can't Cæsar and my uncle's party agree?"

"I'm afraid not," replied Drusus, shaking his head. "Cæsar wishes to be consul a second time. Pompeius and he were friends when at Lucca six years ago this was agreed on. Cæsar was then promised that he should have his Gallic proconsulship up to the hour when he should be consul, and besides Pompeius promised to have permission granted Cæsar to be elected consul, without appearing as a candidate in Rome; so at no moment was Cæsar to be without office,[1] and consequently he was not to be liable to prosecution from his enemies. All this was secured to Cæsar by the laws, — laws which Pompeius aided to have enacted. But now Crassus the third triumvir is dead; Julia, Cæsar's daughter and Pompeius's wife, whom both dearly loved, is dead. And Pompeius has been persuaded by your uncle and his friends to break with Cæsar and repudiate his promise. Cæsar and Pompeius have long been so powerful together that none could shake their authority; but if one falls away and combines with the common enemy, what but trouble is to be expected?"

"The enemy! the enemy!" repeated Cornelia, looking down, and sighing. "Quintus, these feuds are a dreadful thing. Can't you," and here she threw a bit of pathetic entreaty into her voice, "join with my uncle's party, and be his friend? I hate

[1] Without the *imperium* — so long as a Roman official held this he was above prosecution.

'o think of having my husoand at variance with the man who stands in place of my father."

Drusus took her face between his hands, and looked straight at her. They were standing within the colonnade of the villa of the Lentuli, and the sunlight streaming between the pillars fell directly upon Cornelia's troubled face, and made a sort of halo around her.

" My dearest, delectissima," said Quintus, earnestly, " I could not honourably take your hand in marriage, if I had not done that which my conscience, if not my reason, tells me is the only right thing to do. It grieves me to hurt you; but we are not fickle Greeks, nor servile Easterns; but Romans born to rule, and because born to rule, born to count nothing dear that will tend to advance the strength and prosperity not of self, but of the state. You would not love me if I said I cared more for keeping a pang from your dear heart, than for the performance of that which our ancestors counted the one end of life — duty to the commonwealth."

Cornelia threw her arms around him.

" You are the noblest man on the whole earth ! " she cried with bright enthusiasm. " Of course I would not love you if you did what you believed to be wrong ! My uncle may scold, may storm. I shan't care for all his anger, for you *must be* right."

" Ah! delectissima," cried Drusus, feeling at the moment as if he were capable of refuting senates and confounding kings, " we will not look at too gloomy a side of the picture. Pompeius and Cæsar will be reconciled. Your uncle's party will see that it is best to allow the proconsul an election as promised. We will have wise laws and moderate reforms. All will come out aright. And we — we two — will go along through life as softly and as merrily as now we stroll up and down in the cool shade of these columns; and I will turn philosopher and evolve a new system that will forever send Plato and Zeno, Epicurus and Timon, to the most remote and spider-spun cupboard of the most old-fashioned library, and you shall be a poetess, a Sappho, an Erinna, who shall tinkle in Latin metres sweeter than they ever sing in Aiolic. And so we will fleet the time as though we were Zeus and Hera on Olympus."

"Zeus and Hera!" repeated Cornelia, laughing. "You silly Græcule.[1] You may talk about that misbehaved pair, who were anything but harmonious and loving, if Homer tells truly. I prefer our own Juppiter and our Juno of the Aventine. *They* are a staid and home-keeping couple, worth imitating, if we are to imitate any celestials. But nothing Greek for me."

"Intolerant, intolerant," retorted Drusus, "we are all Greek, we Romans of to-day — what is left of old Latium but her half-discarded language, her laws worse than discarded, perverted, her good pilum[2] which has not quite lost its cunning, and her — "

"Men," interrupted Cornelia, "such as you!"

"And women," continued Drusus, "such as you! Ah! There is something left of Rome after all. We are not altogether fallen, unworthy of our ancestors. Why shall we not be merry? A Greek would say that it was always darkest before Eōs leaves the couch of Tithonus,[3] and who knows that our Helios is not soon to dawn and be a long, long time ere his setting? I feel like throwing formality to the winds, crying 'Iacchos evoë,' and dancing like a bacchanal, and singing in tipsy delight, —

[1] Contemptuous diminutive for Greek.

[2] The heavy short javelin carried by the Roman legionary, only about six feet long. In practised hands it was a terrible weapon, and won many a Roman victory.

[3] The "rosy-fingered Dawn" of Homer; Tithonos was her consort.

> " ' Oh, when through the long night,
> With fleet foot glancing white,
> Shall I go dancing in my revelry,
> My neck cast back, and bare
> Unto the dewy air,
> Like sportive faun in the green meadow's glee ? ' [1]

as old Euripides sings in his ' Bacchæ.' Yes, the Hellenes were right when they put nymphs in the forest and in the deep. Only our blind practical Latin eyes will not see them. We will forget that we are Romans; we will build for ourselves some cosey little Phæacia up in the Sabine hills beside some lake; and there my Sappho shall also be my Nausicaä to shine fair as a goddess upon her distressed and shipwrecked Odysseus."

"Yes," said Cornelia, smiling, "a delightful idyl; but Odysseus would not stay with Nausicaä."

"I was wrong," replied Drusus, as they walked arm in arm out from the portico, and down the broad avenue of stately shade trees. "You shall be the faithful Penelope, who receives back her lord in happiness after many trials. Your clever Agias can act as Telemachus for us."

"But the suitors whom Odysseus must slay ? " asked Cornelia, entering into the fun.

"Oh, for them," said Drusus, lightly, "we need not search far. Who other than Ahenobarbus ? "

II

Rather late in the afternoon, a few days subsequently, the most noble Lucius Cornelius Lentulus Crus, consul-designate, and one of the most prominent politicians of his time and nation, arrived at Præneste; having hurried away from Rome

---

[1] Milman, translator.

to escape for a little while the summer heats which made the capital anything but a pleasant place for residence. Drusus's travelling cortège would have seemed small enough compared with the hedge of outriders, footmen, and body-servants that surrounded the great man. But notwithstanding his prospective dignities, and his present importance, Lentulus Crus was hardly an imposing personality. He was a bald-pated, florid individual, with rough features, a low, flat forehead, and coarse lips. He was dressed very fashionably, and was perfumed and beringed to an extent that would have been derided anywhere save in the most select circles of Rome. He was stout, and when he alighted from his carriage, he moved away with a somewhat waddling gait, and lifted up a rasping, high-pitched voice in unsonorous complaint against a slave who let fall a parcel of baggage.

Clearly the master of the house had returned, and all the familia and freedmen bustled about their various tasks with the unusual promptitude and diligence which is the outcome of a healthy fear of retribution for slackness. Lentulus went into the atrium, and there had an angry conference with the local land-steward, over some accounts which the latter presented. In fact, so ill was the humour of the noble lord, that Cornelia avoided going out from her room to meet him, and pretended to be so engrossed in her Ennius that she did not hear he had come.

This pretence, however, could not last long. Lentulus called out in a surly tone to know where his niece was, and the latter was fain to present herself. It could not be said that the meeting between Cornelia and her uncle was extremely affectionate. The interchange of kisses was painfully formal, and then Lentulus demanded somewhat abruptly: —

"How have you been spending your time? With that young ne'er-do-weel son of Sextus Drusus?"

"Quintus was here this morning," said Cornelia, feeling a little reproachful at the manner in which her uncle had spoken of her lover.

"Just back from Rome, I presume?" said Lentulus, icily, "and he must fly over to the cote of his little dove and see that she hasn't flitted away? He'd better have a care in his doings. He'll have something more serious on hand than love-making before long."

"I don't understand you, uncle," said Cornelia, turning rather red; "Quintus has never done anything for which he has cause to fear."

"Oh, he hasn't, eh?" retorted Lentulus. "*Mehercle!* what donkeys you women are! You may go, I want to see your mother."

"She is in her own room," said Cornelia, turning her back; "I wish you would not speak to me in that way again."

Lentulus wandered through the mazes of courts, colonnades, and the magnificently decorated and finished rooms of the villa, until he came to the chamber of Claudia, his sister-in-law. Claudia was a woman of the same fashionable type as Valeria, good-looking, ostentatious, proud, selfish, devoid of any aim in life save the securing of the most vapid pleasure. At the moment, she was stretched out on a thickly cushioned couch. She had thrown on a loose dress of silken texture. A negress was waving over her head a huge fan of long white feathers. A second negress was busy mixing in an *Authepsa*, — a sort of silver urn, heated by charcoal, — a quantity of spices, herbs, and water, which the lady was to take as soon as it was sufficiently steeped. Claudia had been enjoying an unusually gay round of excitement while at Baiæ, and she had but just come up to Præneste, to recover herself

G

after the exertions of a score of fashionable suppers, excursions on the Lucrine Lake, and the attendant exhausting amusements. When her brother-in-law entered the room, she raised her carefully tinted eyebrows, and observed with great languor: —

"So you have gotten away from Rome, at last, my Lucius?"

"For a few days," replied Lentulus, in no very affable tone; "the heat and din of the city will drive me mad! And I have had no end of troublesome business. The senators are all fools or slaves of Cæsar. That treacherous rascal, Curio, is blocking all our efforts. Even Pompeius is half-hearted in the cause. It wouldn't take much to make him go back to Cæsar, and then where would we be?"

"Where would we be?" said Claudia, half conscious of what she said, turning over wearily. "Don't talk politics, my dear brother. They are distressingly dull. My head aches at the very word." And she held out her hand and took the golden cup of hot drink which the negress offered her.

"Aye," replied Lentulus, not in the least subdued, "where *will* we be, if Pompeius and Cæsar become friends? If there is no war, no proscription, no chance to make a sesterce in a hurry!"

"My dear brother," said Claudia, still more languidly, and yawning at length, as she handed back the cup, "have I not said that the mere mention of politics makes my head ache?"

"Then let it," said the other, brutally; "I must have some plain words with you." And he pointed toward the door. The two serving-maids took the hint, and retired.

Claudia settled her head back on the pillows, and folded her hands as if to resign herself to a very dull tête-à-tête.

"Have you any new debts?" demanded Lentulus.

"What a tiresome question," murmured the lady. "No—no—yes; I owe Pomponius the fancier—I don't quite know how much—for my last Maltese lap dog."

"Thank the gods that is all," went on her brother-in-law. "Now listen to me. I have been living beyond my means. Last year the canvass to get on the board of guardians of the Sibylline Books—in which that graceless son-in-law of Cicero's, Publius Dolabella, defeated me—cost a deal of money. This year I have the consulship. But it has taken every denarius I own, and more too. All my estates are involved, so that it will require years to redeem them, in the ordinary way."

"How extremely unfortunate!" sighed Claudia, looking dreadfully bored.

"If that was all I had to tell you," snapped back Lentulus, "I would not have disturbed your ladyship's repose. But you must be so indulgent as to listen."

"Well?" said Claudia, yawning again and settling herself.

"Your late husband left some little property," began the other.

"Yes, to be sure; oh! my poor Caius!" and Claudia began to sob and wipe away the tears.

"And this property I have involved," continued Lentulus, driving straight ahead and never heeding the widow's display of emotions. "It will be impossible for me to clear away the encumbrances for some little time."

Claudia was excited now. She sprang up from her cushions and cried, or rather screamed:—

"Brute! Robber of orphans and widows! Heartless wretch! Have you pledged the slender fortune Caius left me, and the dowry of my poor dear Cornelia?" And her voice sank into hoarseness, and she began to sob once more.

Lentulus regarded her with vexation and contempt. "*Meher*

tle! what a fuss you are making! The deed is done, and there's no helping it. I came here, not to offer excuses, but to state the facts. You may call me what you please; I *had to do it*, or lose the consulship. Now look the matter in the face. You must contract no more debts; I can't discharge the old ones. Live as reasonably as you can."

"And no more nice dinners? No more visits to Baiæ?" groaned the lady, rocking to and fro.

"Yes, yes," broke in her brother-in-law, sharply, "I can still raise enough to meet all ordinary expenses. If I let down in my household, my creditors would see I was pinched, and begin to pluck me. I can weather the storm. But look here: Cornelia must have an end with that young Drusus. I can never pay her dowry, and would not have him for a nephew-in-law if I could."

"Cornelia break off with Drusus?" and Claudia stopped whimpering, and sat staring at Lentulus with astonished eyes. To tell the truth she had always liked the young Livian, and thought her daughter was destined for a most advantageous match.

"Certainly, my dear Claudia," said the consul-elect, half relieved to change what had been a very awkward subject; "I can assure you that Quintus is far from being a proper and worthy man for a husband for your daughter. I have heard very evil reports of him while in the city. He has cast in his lot with that gang of knavish Cæsarians centring around Marcus Antonius, Cælius, and that Caius Sallustius [1] whom our excellent censors have just ejected from the Senate, because of his evil living and Cæsarian tendencies. Do I need to say more of him? A worthless, abandoned, shameless profligate!"

Claudia had a little sense of humour; and when Lentulus was

---

[1] Sallust, the well-known historian.

working himself up into a righteous rage over the alleged misdoings of Drusus, she interrupted —

"You do well to say so, my dear Lucius; for all men know that your life is as morally severe as your good friend Cato's."

Lentulus was silent for a moment, and bit his lip; then recommenced : —

"What I meant to say was this. Quintus Drusus and I are enemies; and I will not give him my niece in marriage. If we were friends, I would not be able to pay the dowry. You can complain if you please; but you can't alter my inclinations or my inability to carry out the marriage agreement."

Though Claudia in many respects was an empty woman of the world, she had in a way a desire to promote her daughter's happiness, and, as has been said, she had been extremely fond of Drusus. So she replied diplomatically that Quintus was probably willing to wait a reasonable time for the dowry; and that even if he had held communication with the Cæsarians, he was little more than a boy and could be shaken out of any unfortunate political opinions.

"I will be reasonable," said Lentulus, after pacing up and down for a few minutes. "I was told of his folly by Caius Calvus.[1] Calvus is as a rule accurate in his information. He said he met Drusus in company with Balbus and Curio. But there may have been some mistake. And the lad, as you declare, may be willing to cut loose from a bad course. If he really cares for Cornelia, he will be moderate in his demands for the dowry. Your suggestion is worth taking, Claudia. Let us send for him, and let him know the only terms on which he can have my niece."

Lentulus clapped his hands, and a serving-boy came in for orders.

[1] A distinguished poet and orator — a friend of Catullus.

"Go to the villa of Quintus Drusus," commanded the master, "and tell him that I would see him at once on business of weight."

Claudia arose, and let her maids throw over her a long white *stola*,[1] with deep flounces and an elaborate embroidery of sea-nymphs and marine monsters. Lentulus went out into the atrium and walked up and down, biting his nails, and trying to think out the arguments by which he would confute the political heresies of Drusus. Lentulus was too good a politician not to know that the young man would be a valuable catch for the party that secured him; and the consul-elect was determined, not so much to spare breaking the heart of his niece, but to rob the enemy of a valuable adherent. Cornelia had gone back to her book; but when she saw the boy go down the path, evidently on an errand to the villa of the Drusi, she rolled up the volume, and went into the atrium.

"You have sent after Quintus, uncle?" she asked.

"I have," was the reply; "I expect him shortly."

"What is the matter?" continued Cornelia, growing apprehensive.

"I wish to make the arrangements for your wedding," replied Lentulus, continuing his pacing to and fro.

"Oh, I am so glad!" cried Cornelia, cheerily. "I am so pleased vou wish to make everything agreeable for Quintus and for me!"

"I hope so," was the rather gloomy response.

Presently Drusus was seen coming up the shaded path at a very brisk stride. He had been playing at fencing with old Mamercus, and his face was all aglow with a healthy colour; there was a bright light in his eye. When he saw Cornelia in

---

[1] A long tunic worn by Roman ladies.

the doorway he gave a laugh and broke into a run, which brought him up to her panting and merry.

Then as he saw Lentulus he paused, half ashamed of his display of boyish ardour, and yet, with a smile and a gracious salutation, asked the older man if he was enjoying good health. and congratulated him on his election.

The consul-designate was a little disarmed by this straightforward mode of procedure. He dropped unuttered the elaborate exordium he had been preparing on the tendency of young men to be led astray by speciously pleading schemers, and found himself replying mildly to questions about himself and various old friends of his, whom Drusus had known as a boy before he went to Athens. But finally the young man interrupted this pacific discourse with the query : —

"And, most noble Lentulus, what is the business on which you sent for me ? So far as I am able, the uncle of Cornelia has but to command."

Lentulus glanced at Claudia, as if expecting her to open a delicate subject; but that excellent lady only fingered her *palla*,[1] and gave vent to a slight cough. Cornelia, whose fears had all passed away, stood beside Drusus, with one arm resting on his shoulder, glancing pertly from one man to the other. Lentulus began : —

"I am very sorry to tell you, Quintus, that I fear your wedding with Cornelia cannot be celebrated as soon as you hoped."

"Must be postponed!" exclaimed the young man, in alarm ; and Cornelia dropped her arm and stared at her uncle in dismay.

"I fear so," said Lentulus, dryly. "I have done my best to husband the fortune Caius left his daughter; but, as per

[1] A shawl worn over the stola.

haps you know, I invested a very large part of it in the tax farming syndicate for farther Spain. The speculation seemed safe, but local wars have so reduced the profits that they amount to nothing, and it will be some time before the principal is set free. Of course, in ordinary times I would make up the sum from my own means, but I have had very heavy expenses lately; consequently, I fear you cannot marry Cornelia until I am in a position to pay over her dowry."

Drusus burst out into a hearty, boyish laugh.

"My dear uncle," cried he, "for do let me call you so, I would have you know that when I take Cornelia I have dowry sufficient. Thanks to old Vibulanus's will, I may call myself passing wealthy. As far as I am concerned, you may pay over the marriage portion to my heirs, if so you wish."

Lentulus seemed considerably relieved. Claudia broke out with loud ejaculations to the effect that Drusus, she always knew, was a generous, affectionate fellow, and she loved him dearly. Cornelia, however, looked disturbed, and presently exclaimed: —

"It isn't right, Quintus, that I should come into your house with not a sesterce in my own name, as if you had married some low farmer's daughter."

"*Phy!* pish!" replied Drusus. "You always scold the Greeks, my good mistress, and yet, like them, you hold that a marriage between people of unequal means is unhappy. A penny for your scruples! I have more money to-day than I know what to do with. Besides, if it will make you happier, your uncle can doubtless pay over the dowry before a great while."

"It's certainly very kind of you, Quintus," said Lentulus (who had quite made up his mind that if the young man could wait for what was a very tidy fortune, through sheer affection for Cornelia, he would be pliable enough in the political matter), "not to press me in this affair. Rest assured, neither you nor my niece will be the losers in the end. But there's one other thing I would like to ask you about. From what Calvus told me in Rome, Curio and certain other still worse *Populares*[1] were trying to induce you to join their abominable faction. I trust you gave those men no encouragement?"

Drusus was evidently confused. He was wishing strongly that Cornelia was away, and he could talk to her uncle with less constraint. He felt that he was treading on very dangerous ground.

"It is true," said he, trying painfully to answer as if the words cost him no thought. "Antonius had met many of my father's old comrades in Gaul, and they had sent a number of kind messages to me. Then, too, Balbus invited me to a dinner-party and there I met Curio, and a very pleasant time we had. I cannot recall that they made any special efforts to enlist me as a partisan."

In this last, Drusus spoke truly; for he had already thrown in his lot with the Cæsarian cause. But Lentulus knew enough of the case to realize that he was receiving not the whole truth but only a half; and being a man of a sharp temper that was under very imperfect control, threw diplomacy to the winds, and replied vehemently: "Don't attempt to cover up your folly! I know how you have put yourself in the power of those conspirators. Are you planning to turn out another Catilina?"

"My dear sir," expostulated Drusus, doing his best to retain

---

[1] The party in opposition, since the time of Tiberius Gracchus, to the Senate party — Optimates; at this time the *Populares* were practically all Cæsarians.

his outward calm, "I cannot understand of what fault I have become guilty. Is it wrong in Rome to accept a kindly invitation from an old family friend to a dinner? Am I responsible for the persons the host summoned to meet me there?"

Drusus had been simply sparring to ward off the real point at issue; like many persons he would not assert his convictions and motives till fairly brought to bay. But that moment came almost instantly.

"Don't equivocate! *Mehercle!*" cried Lentulus, getting thoroughly angry. "Can't you speak, except to lie and quibble before my face? Have you joined the gang Curio is rallying for Cæsar?"

Drusus was losing his own patience now.

"Yes! And we shall shortly see whether the Republic is to be longer ruined by incompetence and corruption!"

"Uncle! Quintus!" implored Cornelia, forcing herself between them, and casting out of her wide-open eyes on each a look full of distress. "Don't contend! For my sake be friends!"

"For your sake!" raged Lentulus, his florid face growing redder and redder. "I will take care to keep you out of the clutches of a man who deliberately chooses to associate with all that is base and villanous. Until your handsome lover throws over connections with Cæsar and his fellow-conspirators, let him never ask for your hand!"

"Sir," burst in Drusus, flushing with passion, "do you dare to set at naught the will of your brother and its express commands? Dare you withhold from me what is legally my own?"

"Legally?" replied Lentulus, with sharp scorn. "Don't use that word to a consul-elect, who has the whole Senate and

Pompeius behind him. Laws are very dangerous tools for a young man to meddle with in a case like this. You will be wise not to resort to the courts."

"You defy the law!" thundered Drusus, all the blood of his fighting ancestors tingling in his veins. "Do you say that to a Livian; to the heir of eight consuls, two censors, a master of the horse, a dictator, and three triumphators? Shall not *he* obtain justice?"

"And perhaps," said Lentulus, sinking into an attitude of irritating coldness, "you will further press your claim on the ground that your mother was a Fabian, and the Fabii claim the sole right to sacrifice to Hercules on the Great Altar [1] in the Cattle-market by the Flaminian Circus, because they are descended from Hercules and Evander. I think the Cornelian gens can show quite as many death-masks in its atria, and your mock heroics will only stamp you as a very bad tragedian."

"Uncle! Quintus!" implored Cornelia again, the tears beginning to start from her eyes. "Cease this dreadful quarrel. Go away until you can talk calmly."

"Quintus Livius," shouted Lentulus, dropping the "Drusus," a part of the name which was omitted in formal address, "you can choose here and now. Forswear your Cæsarian connections, or consider my niece's betrothal at an end!"

Drusus stood looking in blank dismay from one to the other of the little company. Claudia had started to speak, but closed her lips without uttering a word. Lentulus faced him, hot, flushed, and with a cynical smile of delight, at the infliction of mental torture, playing over his face. Cornelia had dropped down upon a chair, buried her pretty face in her hands, and was sobbing as if her heart would break. It was a moment Drusus would not soon forget. The whole scene in the atrium was

[1] *Ara Maxima.*

stamped upon his memory; the drops of the fountain seemed frozen in mid-air; the rioting satyr on the fresco appeared to be struggling against the limitations of paint and plaster to complete his bound; he saw Cornelia lift her head and begin to address him, but what she said was drowned by the buzzing and swirl which unsteadied the young man's entire faculties. Drusus felt himself turning hot and cold, and in semi-faintness he caught at a pillar, and leaned upon it. He felt numbed mentally and physically. Then, by a mental reaction, his strong, well-balanced nature reasserted itself. His head cleared, his muscles relaxed their feverish tension, he straightened himself and met the cool leer of Lentulus with a glance stern and high; such a glance as many a Livian before him had darted on foe in Senate or field of battle.

"Lucius Cornelius," said he, his voice perfectly under command, "do you propose to defy law and right and refuse me the hand of your niece, unless I do your will?"

Lentulus thought that in this unimpassioned speech he detected the premonitions of a capitulation on the part of Drusus, and with a voice of ill-timed persuasion, replied, "Be reasonable, Drusus; you have everything to gain and nothing to lose by not thwarting my wishes."

"Your wishes!" retorted Drusus, with a menacing step forward. "Your wishes! You are consul-designate. You have the Senate, you have your tool, Pompeius, you have the gangs of gladiators and street ruffians and all the machinery of your political clubs to invoke to defy the law! I grant it; but though you deny me Cornelia, though by your machinations you bring me any other loss or shame, the grandson of the murdered Marcus Drusus will do that which is right in his own eyes, and accept no mandate from you or any man, against his will!"

"Cornelia," cried Claudia, infinitely distressed, "speak to Quintus, reason with him, implore him, pray him not to resist the requests of your uncle."

"Yes, girl!" said Lentulus, savagely, turning livid with sheer rage, "use all your arts on that graceless would-be conspirator now, or see his face no more!"

But Cornelia interposed in a most summary and unexpected manner. Her face was very white; her nails pressed into her smooth arms, her breath came thick and spasmodically, and her eyes flamed with the intense passion of a strong spirit thoroughly aroused.

"Go, Quintus," she cried, with a strained, loud voice, "go, and never see my face again, until my uncle repents of his cruel madness! He is master here; only woe will come from defying him. Do not anger him further; depart."

"Depart?" burst from Drusus.

"Depart!" replied Cornelia, desperately; "if you stay I shall go mad. I shall beg you to yield, — which would be base of me; and if you heard my prayers, it would be more base in you."

"Fool," shouted Lentulus, "don't you know you will be the first I'll mark for slaughter in the next proscription? You, mistress, go to your room, if you cannot keep a civil tongue! And you, sir, get you gone, unless you wish the slaves to cast you out."

"Farewell, Cornelia!" gasped the young man; and he turned his back, and started out into the colonnade.

"Oh, Quintus, return!" shrieked Claudia, wringing her hands. "All the gods blast you!" muttered Lentulus, quivering with fury; then he shouted at the top of his shrill, harsh voice: "My enemies are my enemies. You are warned. Take care!"

"And do you take warning! A Livian never forgets! *Mars*

regat! Let War rule!" cried Drusus, turning at the vestibule, and brandishing a knotted fist. Lentulus stared after him, half furious, half intimidated. But Claudia glanced back into the room from the just emptied doorway, and gave a scream.

"The servants! Help! Water! Cornelia has fainted!"

III

Drusus strode down the long avenue of shade trees. The gardener stared after him, as the young man went by, his face knitted with a scowl of combined pain and fury, with never a word in reply to the rustic's kindly salutation.

"*Papœ!*"[1] muttered the man, "what has befallen Master Quintus? Has he fallen out with her ladyship?"

Drusus kept on, looking neither to the right hand nor to the left, until he found himself past the boundary stone between his own estate and that of the Lentuli. Then he stopped and passed his hand over his forehead. It was damp with an unhealthy sweat. His hands and frame were quivering as if in an ague. He seated himself on a stone bench by the roadway, and tried to collect his faculties.

"Bear up, Drusus; be a Livian, as you boast yourself," he declaimed frantically to himself. "Cornelia shall still be yours! All things are possible to one who is young and strong, with a clear conscience!"

If this self-debate did not actually stimulate cheerfulness, it at least revived the embers of hope; and Drusus found himself trying to look the situation fairly in the face.

"You have thrown away your right to marry the dearest, loveliest, and noblest girl in the world," he reflected bitterly. "You have made an implacable enemy of one of the most

---

[1] "Strange! Marvellous!"

powerful men of the state. In short, your happiness is gone, and perhaps your life is in danger — and for what? A dream of reform which can never be realized? A mad conspiracy to overthrow the commonwealth? Is Cæsar to be saviour or despot? For what have you sacrificed yourself?"

Lentulus, he knew perfectly well, was really above law. No jury would ever convict the leader of the Senate party. Drusus could never contract lawful marriage with Cornelia, so long as her guardian withheld consent. And for one moment he regretted of his determination, of his defiance. Then came reaction. Drusus called up all his innate pride, all the strength of his nobler inspirations.

"I have set my face toward that which is honourable and right," cried Drusus to his own soul; "I will not doubt. Whether there be gods, I cannot tell. But this I know, the wise and good have counted naught dear but virtues; and toward this end I will strive."

And by a strong effort at self-command, he forced himself to arise from the bench and walk back to his own estate, and soon he was pouring the whole story into the sympathetic ears of Mamercus, Pausanias, and other worthy retainers.

The scene that had taken place at the villa of the Lentuli, soon was reported through all the adjacent farms; for several slaves had been the mute witnesses of the angry colloquy, and had not been slow to publish the report. The familia of Drusus was in a tumult of indignation. All the brawny Germans and Africans whom the young master had released from the slave-prison, and had since treated with kindness, listened with no unfavourable ear to the proposal which Titus Mamercus — more valorous than discreet — was laying before them: to arm and attack Lentulus in his own villa, and so avenge their lord in a summary fashion.

But the elder Mamercus dashed the martial ambitions of his son.

"Fool," cried the veteran, emphatically, when the project came to his ears, "do you wish to undo yourself and Quintus too? No power short of Jove could protect you and him, if aught were to befall Lentulus, in the way you propose."

"But what can we do, father?" replied Titus, sorry to see his scheme for vengeance blocked; "shall that despicable tyrant defy law and justice, and refuse to give Mistress Cornelia to Quintus?"

"Silence your folly!" thundered the other, who was himself quite nonplussed over the situation, and felt Titus's bold chatter would goad him into something desperate.

The truth was, neither Pausanias nor any other of Quintus's friends could see any means of coercing the consul-elect into receding from his position. He was practically above law, and could not with safety be attacked in any way. Pausanias could only counsel moderation and patience; perhaps some fortunate chance would alter matters. Drusus spent the evening in a pathetically forced attempt to read his Callimachus. He was weary physically, and intended to retire early. Æmilia, who felt sorry enough for the plight of her rather distant cousin, had tried to console him and divert him with guitar[1] music, and had called in an itinerant piper,[2] but these well-meant efforts at amusement had been dreary failures. Drusus had just bidden his body-servants undress him, when he was informed that Agias had come from the Lentulan villa, and wished to see him.

Agias was full of protestations of delight at beholding his

[1] *Cithara.*

[2] Itinerant pipers have existed in Italy from earliest times; they still survive, albeit in alien lands and with less tuneful instruments.

intercessor and ransomer. Drusus could hardly recognize in the supple-limbed, fair-complexioned, vivacious lad before him, the wretched creature whom Alfidius had driven through the streets. Agias's message was short, but quite long enough to make Drusus's pale cheeks flush with new life, his sunken eyes rekindle, and his languor vanish into energy. Cornelia would be waiting for him by the great cypress in the gardens of the Lentulan villa, as soon as the moon rose.

Drusus prepared himself hurriedly, and refused all the entreaties of Titus to take him along as a body-guard. Time coursed on winged feet, as the young man hastened out into the night, and half ran down the familiar pathway. The day had been only moderately warm for the season, and the night was cool, though not cold. A soft east wind was blowing down from the distant Apennines, and all the trees were rustling gently. Up to the giant arm of a gnarled oak, fluttered an owl, which hooted noisily as the young man hurried beneath. The crickets were chirping. A little way off was a small stream plunging over a dam; from it came a liquid roar; and the little wall of white spray was just visible in the darkness. Out from the orchards drifted the fragrant scent of apple, pear, plum, and quince. Still more sweet was the breeze, as it swept over the wide-stretching rose-beds. Overhead Orion and Arcturus were glittering in that hazy splendour which belongs to the heavens on a summer's night.

Drusus kept on, only half noting the beauty of the darkness. When he entered the groves of the Lentulan villa, almost all light failed him, and but for his intimate knowledge — from boyhood — of the whole locality, he could never have kept the path. Then the moonlight began to stream up in the east, and between the trees and thickets lay the long, yellow bars of brightness, while all else was still in gloom. Drusus pushed on with confidence, and soon the gurgle of the tiny cataract told him that he was near the old cypress. A few steps more, and a figure rose from out the fern thicket. It was Cornelia. Her hair was tumbling loosely over her shoulders; she wore a soft, light-blue dress that covered her arms and her feet. In the moonlight her face and hands appeared as bloodless as white marble.

"I knew you would come, Quintus," she cried. "I couldn't say farewell to you, in the presence of my uncle!"

"My beautiful!" cried Drusus; and he caught her in his arms.

The moments that followed were as bitter-sweet as may be conceivable. Each knew that they had small hope of an honourable realization of their love one for another; that the moment of parting would soon come. But for the instant they were in Elysium, caught out of mortal care and mortal sorrow, and knowing nothing but the pure delight of the other's presence. Then, at last, their talk became less enraptured; the vision of Olympus faded little by little; the stern reality confronted them in all its seriousness.

"Cornelia," said Quintus, at length, "you are still a very young woman. This day's heart-breakings may, perhaps, be long painful to you; but the pangs will grow faint in time. You and I may still cherish fondness in our hearts for each other, but how dare we reasonably hope for more? Evil times are at hand. If your uncle's party prevail in the struggle, my ruin is assured. But not yours. There are many worthy men who would be proud to take in marriage the niece of the next consul; and with one of these you can live happily. Do not try to forget me. I don't ask that. But do not let my misfortune cast a shadow over your dear life. Marry some honourable man. Only think kindly of me sometimes."

They had been sitting beside the brooklet, on the soft green sward. Cornelia had been resting both her hands in Drusus's, but now she drew them back, and sprang to her feet, as if swept away by a gust of anger.

"How dare you!" she cried, "how dare you bid me throw away all that my heart has turned on, and my hopes depended on, and my imagination dreamed of, since our fathers were slain side by side; and more especially since you came back from Athens? Why might not I bid you renounce your adherence to Cæsar's cause, and say, 'There is no need of blasting your career by such a sacrifice; remember Cæsar and his party kindly, wish them well, but do not dwell too much thereon; submit cheerfully to what is inevitable'? Shall I argue thus? Have I argued thus? If you will, abandon me, and wed some other maiden, and many there are, fair, wealthy, noble, who will be glad to be given in marriage to a Livius Drusus. But till you thus repudiate your father's will, no power of gods or of men shall drive me to violate that of mine."

"Cornelia," said Drusus, in a husky voice, "do you know what you are saying? What resistance to threats and unkind treatment your resolve will mean?"

"I both know the future and accept it," answered the maiden firmly, looking fairly into his face.

"Then by all the powers of earth, sky, and Hades!" cried the young man, lifting one arm toward heaven, and throwing the other about his sweetheart, "I will defy Lentulus, defy Pompeius, defy Senate, army, mob, or any other human might. Hitherto I have thought to play the patriot in espousing Cæsar's cause. Now let love and fury fire my ardour. When the party of violence and tyranny falls, then too will fall the power of Lentulus to outrage your right and mine! Ours shall be a triumph of Venus as well as of Mars, and until that time, may you and I endure faithful unto our fathers, ourselves, and one another!"

Hardly had he spoken ere loud voices were heard calling through the grove. Torches were glaring among the trees, and the harsh tones of Lentulus burst out:—

"Take the wretched girl into the house when you find her; but as for her lover, let him not escape!"

"My uncle!" groaned Cornelia, quivering with terror; "one of my maids has betrayed me! Flee! run! He has called out all his slaves; they will kill you!"

"Kill me?" gasped Drusus, incredulously; "commit deliberate murder?"

"Yes," moaned Cornelia; "he dares anything. He is all fury and violence. Escape! Do not throw yourself away in vain!"

The lights flashed nearer; the slaves were shouting and blundering through the bushes.

"Two philippi to the man who strikes Drusus down!" bawled Lentulus.

It was no time for delay and affectionate leave-taking. The young man threw his arms around Cornelia, kissed her once, twice, and then bounded into the thicket. A moment later several of the servants came splashing over the little stream, and found Cornelia alone beside the great cypress, pale and trembling and sobbing. Drusus caught one last sight of her, surrounded by the torches of the pursuers. Then he struck off into the grove, and thanks to his perfect local knowledge easily avoided meeting Lentulus or his slaves. Lentulus he would gladly have confronted alone. What would have followed, the athletic young man could only surmise grimly; but he was unarmed, and for Cornelia's sake he must take no risks. Close to the confines of his own land he met the Mamerci, father and son, and several slaves and freedmen, all armed and anxious to know whether the din that had been raised over at the Lentulan villa betokened any danger to their young master.

Drusus satisfied them that he had suffered no injury. The personal peril through which he had passed brought a reaction of excitement which raised his spirits, and he went to bed in a mood at least tolerably cheerful. If he could not enjoy his love, he had at least something else to live for — vengeance; and he told himself that he had a whole mature lifetime left in which to make Lentulus repent of his folly and tyrannical cruelty. He awoke late the next morn in a calm frame of mind, and was able to receive with outward equanimity the news that early in the morning Lentulus had taken his sister-in-law and niece, and a large part of his household, back to Rome. This was only to have been expected, and Drusus listened to the information without useless comment.

CHAPTER VI

POMPEIUS MAGNUS

IF we had been painting an ideal heroine, gifted with all the virtues which Christian traditions of female perfection throw around such characters, Cornelia would have resigned herself quietly to the inevitable, and exhibited a seraphic serenity amid tribulation. But she was only a grieved, embittered, disappointed, sorely wronged, Pagan maiden, who had received few enough lessons in forbearance and meekness. And now that her natural sweetness of character had received so severe a shock, she vented too often the rage she felt against her uncle upon her helpless servants. Her maid Cassandra — who was the one that had told Lentulus of her mistress's nocturnal meeting with Drusus — soon felt the weight of Cornelia's wrath. The young lady, as soon as Lentulus was out of the way, caused the tell-tale to receive a cruel whipping, which kept the poor slave-girl groaning in her cell for ten days, and did not relieve Cornelia's own distress in the slightest degree. As a matter of fact, Cornelia was perpetually goaded into fresh outbursts of desperation by the tyrannical attitude of her uncle. Lentulus boasted in her presence that he would accomplish Drusus's undoing. "I'll imitate Sulla," he would announce, in mean pleasure at giving his niece pain; "I'll see how many heads I can have set up as he did at the Lacus Servilius. You can go *there*, if you wish to kiss your lover."

But Cornelia's life at Rome was rendered unhappy by many other things besides these occasional brutal stabs from her uncle. Her mother, as has been hinted, was a woman of the world, and had an intense desire to draw her daughter into her own circle of society. Claudia cared for Cornelia in a manner, and believed it was a real kindness to tear the poor girl away from her solitary broodings and plunge her into the whirl of the world of Roman fashion. Claudia had become an intimate of Clodia, the widow of Quintus Metellus, a woman of remarkable gifts and a notoriously profligate character. "The Medēa of the Palatine Hill," Cicero had bitingly styled her. Nearly all the youth of parts and social distinction enjoyed the wild pleasures of Clodia's garden by the Tiber. Catullus the poet, Cælius the brilliant young politician, and many another had figured as lovers of this soulless and enchanting woman. And into Clodia's gilded circle Claudia tried desperately to drag her daughter. The Lentuli had a handsome palace on the Carinæ, one of the most fashionable quarters of the capital; and here there were many gay gatherings and dinner parties. Cornelia was well born enough, by reputation wealthy enough, and in feature handsome enough, to have a goodly proportion of the young men of this coterie her devoted admirers and slaves. Claudia observed her daughter's social triumphs with glee, and did all she could to give Cornelia plenty of this kind of company. Cornelia would not have been a mortal woman if she had not taken a certain amount of pleasure in noticing and exercising her power. The first occasion when she appeared at a formal banquet in the splendid Apollo dinner hall of the Luculli, where the outlay on the feast was fixed by a regular scale at two hundred thousand sesterces, she gathered no little satisfaction by the consciousness that all the young men were

admiring her, and all the women were fuming with jealousy.
But this life was unspeakably wearisome, after the first
novelty had worn away. Cornelia lived in an age when many
of the common proprieties and decencies of our present society
would have been counted prudish, but she could not close her
eyes to the looseness and license that pervaded her mother's
world. Woman had become almost entirely independent of
man in social and economic matters, though the law still kept
its fictions of tutelage. Honourable marriages were growing
fewer and fewer. Divorces were multiplying. The morality
of the time can be judged from the fact that the "immaculate"
Marcus Cato separated from his wife that a friend might marry
her; and when the friend died, married her himself again.
Scandals and love intrigues were common in the highest
circles; noble ladies, and not ballet-dancers [1] merely, thought
it of little account to have their names besmirched. Everything in society was splendid, polished, decorous, cultivated
without; but within, hollow and rotten.

Cornelia grew weary and sick of the excitement, the fashionable chatter, the mongering of low gossips. She loathed
the sight of the effeminate young fops who tried to win
her smiles by presenting themselves for a polite call each
morning, polished and furbelowed, and rubbed sleek and
smooth with Catanian pumice. Her mother disgusted her so
utterly that she began to entertain the most unfilial feeling
toward the worthy woman. Cornelia would not or could not
understand that in such hot weather it was proper to wear
lighter rings than in winter, and that each ring must be set
carefully on a different finger joint to prevent touching.
Cornelia watched her servants, and reached the astonishing
conclusion that these humble creatures were really extracting

[1] *Mimæ.*

more pleasure out of life than herself. Cassandra had recovered from her whipping, and was bustling about her tasks as if nothing had happened. Agias seemed to have a never failing fund of good spirits. He was always ready to tell the funniest stories or retail the latest news. Once or twice he brought his mistress unspeakable delight, by smuggling into the house letters from Drusus, which contained words of love and hope, if no really substantial promises for the future. But this was poor enough comfort. Drusus wrote that he could not for the time see that any good end would be served by coming to Rome, and he would remain for the present in Præneste. He and she must try to wait in patience, until politics took such a turn as would drive Lentulus into a more tractable attitude. Cornelia found the days monotonous and dreary. Her uncle's freedman kept her under constant espionage to prevent a chance meeting with Drusus, and but for Agias she would have been little better than a prisoner, ever in charge of his keepers.

In a way, however, Cornelia found that there was enough stirring in the outside world to lend zest and often venom to the average emptiness of polite conversation. Politics were penetrating deeper and deeper into fashionable society. Cornelia heard how Paulus, the consul, had taken a large present from Cæsar to preserve neutrality; and how Curio, the tribune, had checked Clodius Marcellus, the other consul, when he wished to take steps in the Senate against Cæsar. All that Cornelia heard of that absent statesman was from hostile lips; consequently she had him painted to her as blood-thirsty, treacherous, of flagrant immorality, with his one object to gather a band of kindred spirits to his cause, and become despot. And to hear such reports and yet to keep confident that Drusus was not sacrificing both himself

and her in a worse than unworthy cause — this tested her to
the uttermost.

To add to her troubles, Lucius Ahenobarbus was ever thrusting in his attentions at every party and at the theatre; and
her uncle openly favoured his suit.

"I wish you would be more friendly to him," remarked
Lentulus on one occasion. "I should be glad to have a closer
tie between his family and ours."

"Uncle," said Cornelia, much distressed, "I do not think I
understand what you mean."

"Well," chuckled Lentulus, moving away, "think it over
until you do understand."

Cornelia had been reading in the library when this conversation took place. There was to be another party that evening
at the house of Marcus Favonius, a prominent anti-Cæsarian,
and since it was growing late in the afternoon, it was time to
dress. Cornelia went into her own room, and was summoning
her maids, when a young lady of about her own age, who
affected to be on terms of considerable intimacy, was announced
— Herennia, a daughter of a certain rich old eques, Caius
Pontius, who had kept out of politics and hoarded money,
which his daughter was doing her best to spend.

Herennia was already dressed for the party. Her brown
hair had been piled up in an enormous mass on her head, eked
out by false tresses and puffings, and the whole plentifully
powdered with gold dust. She wore a prodigious number of
gaudily set rings; her neck and ears and girdle were ablaze
with gold and jewels. So far from aiming, as do modern
ladies, to reduce the waist to the slenderest possible proportions, Herennia, who was actually quite thin, had carefully
padded out her form to proper dimensions, and showed this
fact by her constrained motions. She was rouged and painted,

and around her floated an incense of a thousand and one rare perfumes. Her amethystine tunic and palla were of pure silk — then literally worth its weight in gold — and embroidered with an elaborate pattern in which pearls and other gems played a conspicuous part. For all this display of extravagance, Herennia was of only very mediocre beauty; and it was on this account that she was always glad to make uncomfortable flings at her "dear friend" Cornelia, whenever possible.

Herennia seated herself on a divan, and proceeded to plunge into all the flying gossip of the day. Incidentally she managed to hint that Servius Flaccus, her devoted admirer, had told her that the night before Lucius Ahenobarbus and some of his friends had attacked and insulted a lady on her way back from a late dinner.[1]

"The outrageous scapegrace!" cried Cornelia, while her maids hurried along a toilet which, if not as elaborate as Herennia's, took some little time. "I imagined he might do such things! I always detested him!"

"Then you are not so very fond of Lucius Ahenobarbus," said Herennia, raising her carefully painted eyebrows, as if in astonishment. "I am really a little surprised."

"Surprised?" reëchoed Cornelia. "What have I done or said that makes Lucius Ahenobarbus anything more than a very distant, a *very* distant acquaintance?"

"My dear girl," exclaimed Herennia, throwing up her hands, "either you are the best actress, or the most innocent little wight, in Rome! Don't you know all that they say about you?"

"Who — say — what — about — me?" stammered Cornelia, rising in her chair so suddenly, as to disarrange all the work Cassandra had been doing on her hair.

[1] A common diversion for "young men of spirit."

"Why, everybody," said Herennia, smiling with an exasperating deliberation. "And then it has all come out in the
daily gazette."[1]

"Where is it? Read! Let me see," pleaded Cornelia,
agitated and trembling.

"Why, how troubled you are," giggled Herennia. "Yes, I
have my freedman copy down the whole bulletin every day,
as soon as it is posted by the censor's officers; now let me
see," and she produced from under her robe a number of
wooden, wax-covered tablets, strung together: "the last prætor's edict; the will of old Publius Blæsus;" and she ran over
the headings with maddening slowness: "the speech in the
Senate of Curio — what an impudent rascal; the money paid
yesterday into the treasury, — how dull to copy all that
down! — the meteor which fell over in Tibur, and was such a
prodigy; oh, yes, here it is at last; you may as well hear
what all Rome knows now, it's at the end, among the private
affairs. 'Lucius Ahenobarbus, son of Lucius Domitius, the
Consular, and Cornelia, daughter of the late tribune, Caius
Lentulus, are in love. They will be married soon.'"

These two brief sentences, which the mechanical difficulties
under which journalistic enterprise laboured at that day made
it impossible to expand into a modern "article," were quite
sufficient to tell a whole story to Rome. Cornelia realized
instantly that she had been made the victim of some vile
trick, which she doubted not her would-be lover and her
uncle had executed in collusion. She took the tablets from
Herennia's hand, without a word, read the falsehoods once,
twice, thrice. The meaning of the day attached to the terms
used intimated the existence of a low intrigue, quite as much
as any honourable "engagement." If Cornelia did not soon

[1] *Acta Diurna*, prepared officially.

become the lawful wife of Lucius Ahenobarbus, the world would feel justified in piling scandal upon her name. The blow was numbing in its brutality. Instead of crying and execrating the liars, as Herennia fully expected her to do, Cornelia merely handed back the tablets, and said with cold dignity, "I think some very unfortunate mistake has been made. Lucius Ahenobarbus is no friend of mine. Will you be so kind as to leave me with my maids?"

Herennia was overborne by the calm, commanding attitude of the rival she had meant to annoy. When Cornelia became not the radiant *débutante,* but the haughty patrician lady, there was that about her which made her wish a mandate. Herennia, in some confusion, withdrew. When she was gone, Cornelia ordered her maids out of the room, stripped off the golden tiara they had been plaiting into her hair, tore away the rings, bracelets, necklaces, and flung herself upon the pillows of the divan, quivering with sobs. She did not know of a single friend who could help her. All the knowledge that she had imbibed taught her that there was no God either to hear prayer, or succour the wronged. Her name would become a laughing-stock and a hissing, to be put on a par with Clodia's or that of any other frivolous woman, unless she not merely gave up the man she loved, but also threw herself into the arms of the man she utterly hated. The craving for any respite was intense. She was young; but for the moment, at least, life had lost every glamour. If death was an endless sleep, why not welcome it as a blessed release? The idea of suicide had a grasp on the ancient world which it is hard at first to estimate. A healthy reaction might have stirred Cornelia out of her despair, but at that instant the impulse needed to make her commit an irrevocable deed must have been very slight. But while she lay on the pillows, wretched and heart-sick, the voice of Agias was heard without, bidding the maids admit him to their mistress.

"Stay outside. I can't see you now," moaned poor Cornelia, feeling that for once the sight of the good-humoured, vivacious slave-boy would be maddening. But Agias thrust back the curtains and boldly entered. What he said will be told in its due time and place; but the moment he had gone Cornelia was calling in Cassandra, and ordering the maids to dress her with all possible speed for the dinner-party.

"I must be all smiles, all enchantments," she was saying to herself. "I must dissemble. I must win confidences. I must do everything, and anything. I have no right to indulge in grief any longer. Quintus's dear life is at stake!"

II

Lentulus did not go to the banquet of Favonius, to see the unwonted graciousness with which his niece received the advances of Lucius Ahenobarbus. Neither was Favonius himself present at his own entertainment. They, and several others of the high magnates of their party, had been called away by an urgent summons, and spent the evening in secluded conference with no less a personage than Pompeius, or as he dearly loved to be called, "the Magnus," in his splendid palace outside the walls on the Campus Martius. And here the conqueror of Mithridates — a stout, soldierly man of six-and-fifty, whose best quality was a certain sense of financial honesty, and whose worst an extreme susceptibility to the grossest adulation — told them that he had received letters from Labienus, Cæsar's most trusted lieutenant in Gaul, declaring that the proconsul's troops would never fight for him, that Cæsar would never be able to stir hand or foot against the decrees of the Senate, and that he, Labienus, would desert him at the first opportunity.

Cheerful news this to the noble lords, who had for years scented in Cæsar's existence and prosperity destruction to their own oligarchic rule of almost the known world. But when Cato, the most violent anti-Cæsarian of them all, a sharp, wiry man with angular features, and keen black eyes, demanded: —

"And now, Magnus, you will not hesitate to annihilate the enemies of the Republic?" a look of pained indecision flitted across Pompeius's face.

"*Perpol,* gentlemen," he exclaimed, "I would that I were well out of this. Sometimes I think that you are leading me into breaking with Cæsar for some ends of your own. He was my friend before you had a word of praise for me. He loved Julia; so did I." And the Magnus paused a moment, overcome by the thought of his dead wife. "Perhaps the Republic demands his sacrifice, perhaps — " and he cast a glance half of menace upon Lentulus Crus and Cato, "you are the guilty, not he. But I am in grievous doubt."

"Perhaps, Magnus," said Favonius, with half a sneer, "you think your forces inadequate. The two legions at Luceria are just detached from Cæsar. Perhaps you question their fidelity."

"Man," retorted the general, fiercely, bringing his foot down upon the soft rug on the floor, "I have but to stamp upon the ground to call up legions out of Italy; it is not that which I fear!"

The members of the conference looked uneasy; there was still a bare chance that Pompeius would go back to his old friendship with Cæsar.

"Gentlemen," went on the Magnus, "I have called you

here to reach a final decision — peace or war. Let us consult a higher power than human." And he touched a little silver bell that was upon the table close at hand.

Forthwith there was a rustle of curtains, and out of the gloom of the doorway — for the hour was now very late — advanced a tall, gaunt figure, dressed in a plain, sleeveless robe that fell to the feet. The skin was dry, hard, wrinkled by a hundred furrows; the bones of the face were thrust out prominently; on the head was a plain white turban, and a beard quite as white fell down upon the breast. Only from under the turban shone the eyes, which were bright and piercing as coals of fire.

The stranger advanced without a word, till he stood before Pompeius, then knelt and made an elaborate Oriental prostration. The noble Romans, twelve or more of the magnates of the greatest power on the earth, held their breath in uneasy anticipation. Not one of them perhaps really believed in a personal god; but though atheists, they could not forswear their superstition. Piso, the censor, who notoriously feared neither divine nor human law in his reckless life, spat thrice to ward off the effects of the evil eye, if the stranger were a magician.

"Ulamhala," said Pompeius, addressing the newcomer, "arise. Since I have been in the East,[1] I have consulted you and your science of the stars, in every intended step, and your warnings have never failed."

"My lord doth overcommend the wisdom of his slave," replied Ulamhala (for such was his name) in Syriac Greek, with a second deep obeisance.

"Now, therefore," went on Pompeius — and his voice was unsteady with evident excitement and anxiety, — "I have called you hither to declare the warnings of the stars upon

---

[1] "Chaldean" astrologers played an almost incredibly important part among even the highest-class Romans of the period.

the most important step of my life. What lies now at stake, you know full well. Three days ago I bade you consult the heavens, that this night you might be able to declare their message, not merely to me, but to these my friends, who will shape their actions by mine. Have you a response from the planets?"

"I have, lord," and again Ulamhala salaamed.

"Then declare, be it good or ill;" commanded Pompeius, and he gripped the arms of his chair to conceal his anxiety.

The scene was in a way weird enough. The visitors exchanged uneasy glances, and Cato, who broke out in some silly remark to Favonius, in a bold attempt to interrupt the oppressive silence, suddenly found his words growing thick and broken, and he abruptly became silent. Each man present tried to tell himself that Pompeius was a victim of superstition, but every individual felt an inward monition that something portentous was about to be uttered.

The conference had lasted long. The lamps were flickering low. Dark shadows were loitering in every corner of the room. The aroma of flowers from the adjacent gardens floated in at the open windows, and made the hot air drugged and heavy. Ulamhala slowly and noiseless as a cat stepped to the window, and, leaning out over the marble railing, looked up into the violet-black heavens. There was no moon, but a trembling flame on one of the candelabras threw a dull, ruddy glow over his white dress and snowy turban. His face was hid in the gloom, but the others knew, though they could hardly see, that he was pointing upward with his right hand.

"Behold," began the astrologer, "three thousand seven hundred and fifty years since the days of the great Sargon of Agade have we of the race of the Chaldeans studied the stars. One generation of watchers succeeded another, scanning the

8

heavens nightly from our *ziggurats*,[1] and we have learned the laws of the constellations; the laws of Sin the moon, the laws of Samas the sun, the laws of the planets, the laws of the fixed stars. Their motions and their influence on the affairs of men our fathers discovered, and have handed their wisdom down to us."

"But the word of the stars to *us?*" broke in Pompeius, in extreme disquietude, and trying to shake off the spell that held him in mastery.

"Know, lord, that thy slave has not been disobedient unto thy commandment. Look, yonder burneth a bright red planet, called by us Nergal, which ye Westerns call by the name of Mars. Who denieth that when Mars shines in the heavens, war will break forth among men? Know that I have carefully compared the settings, risings, and movements of the planets at this season with their settings, risings, and movements at the time when my lord was born; and also at the time of the birth of his great enemy. I have made use of the tables which my wise predecessors among the Chaldees have prepared; and which I myself, thy slave, copied from those at the Temple of Bel, in Babylon."

"And they say?" breathlessly interrupted Lentulus.

"This is the message from the planets," and Ulamhala's form grew higher, his voice firmer; he raised his long bony arms above his head, and stood in the dull light like a skeleton arisen in all its white grave clothes to convey a warning to the living. "To the Lord Pompeius, this is the warning, and to his enemy,

> "'*He that is highest shall rise yet higher;*
> *He that is second shall utterly fall!*'

I have said."

---

[1] Babylonian temple towers.

And before the noble Romans could command the free play of their senses, the vision at the window had vanished, either out of doors, or behind some doorway or curtain. The company sat gazing uneasily at each other for several minutes. The Magnus was breathing heavily, as though he had passed through a terrible mental ordeal. Cato, the Stoic and ascetic, had his eyes riveted on the carpet, and his face was as stony as an Egyptian Colossus.

Then a coarse forced laugh from Piso broke the spell.

"Capital, Pompeius! You *are* a favourite of the gods!"

"I?" ventured the Magnus, moving his lips slowly.

"Of course," cried several voices at once, catching the cue from Piso. "You are the first in the world, Cæsar the second! You are to rise to new glories, and Cæsar is to utterly fall!"

"The stars have said it, gentlemen," said Pompeius, solemnly; "Cæsar shall meet his fate. Let there be war."

* * * * * * * * * *

Lentulus Crus rode away from the conference, his litter side by side with that of Lucius Domitius Ahenobarbus, the consular, whom we will know as Domitius to distinguish from his son and namesake. Domitius, a handsome, highly polished, vigorous, but none the less unprincipled man, who was just reaching the turn of years, was in high spirits. No oligarch hated Cæsar more violently than he, and the decision of Pompeius was a great personal triumph, the crowning of many years of political intrigue. What Pompeius had said, he had said; and Cæsar, the great foe of the Senate party, was a doomed man.

Lentulus had a question to ask his companion.

"Would you care to consider a marriage alliance between the Lentuli and the Domitii?" was his proposition.

"I should be rejoiced and honoured to have the opportunity," was the reply; and then in another tone **Domitius** added, "Lentulus, do you believe in astrologers?"

"I do not really know," answered the other, uneasily.

"Neither do I," continued Domitius. "But suppose the stars speak truly; and suppose," and here his voice fell, "it is Cæsar who is highest in power, in ability, in good fortune; — what then for Pompeius? for us?"

"Be silent, O prophet of evil!" retorted Lentulus, laughing, but not very naturally.

CHAPTER VII

AGIAS'S ADVENTURE

I

PISANDER's view of life became a score of shades more rosy when he seized the hand of the handsome slave-boy, then embraced him, and began praising the gods for preserving his favourite's life. Then the worthy philosopher recollected that his wisdom taught him there were no gods, and he plunged into a rambling explanation of his position, which would have lasted forever, unless Agias had cut him short with a merry gibe, and told him that he must positively come to a tavern and enjoy at least one beaker of good Massic in memory of old friendship. And Pisander, whose spareness of living arose more from a lack of means than from a philosophic aversion to food and good cheer, was soon seated on a bench in one of the cheap restaurants[1] that abounded in the city, balancing a very large goblet, and receiving a volley of questions which Agias was discharging about Valeria's eccentricities, Calatinus's canvass, Arsinoë, Semiramis, and the rest of the household of which he had been a member.

"But you haven't told me, Agias," finally interrupted the poor philosopher, who had been struggling in turn to satisfy his curiosity, "how you are here, and not — ugh! I hate to think of it — feeding the dogs and the crows."

[1] *Popinæ*.

Agias's face grew grave while he gave the story of his release by the Vestal, and subsequent transfer of ownership.

"What was the name of the young man who purchased you, eh?" interpolated Pisander. "I didn't get it."

"Quintus Livius Drusus," replied Agias.

"Who?" cried the philosopher, starting up.

"Quintus Drusus, of Præneste," repeated the other.

"*Ai! Ai!* In the name of Zeus!" cried Pisander, dropping the beaker, and spilling the wine all over his threadbare himation. "Oh, such a plot! Such a crime! Was ever anything so villanous ever heard of before!"

"My dear Pisander," exclaimed Agias, all amazement, "what *is* the matter? Your speech is as obscure as Cinna's[1] poem called 'Zmyrna,' which I've heard was ten years in being written, and must be very fine, because no one can understand it. No more can I fathom you."

"What a stroke of fortune!" raved the philosopher. "How we will be revenged on that rascal, Pratinas! O Destiny, thy decrees are just!"

Again Agias expostulated, and at last brought out of Pisander a tolerably coherent account of the conversation which he had heard between Valeria and Pratinas. Then, indeed, the merry slave-boy was troubled. Accustomed to a rather limited ambition in life, he had attached himself with implicit devotion to Cornelia; first because his preserver, Drusus, had so enjoined him, and second because each day he grew more drawn to her personally. The peril which yawned before the unfortunate Drusus menaced at the same time the happiness of his mistress and his own welfare, — for if Lucius Ahenobarbus had his way, Agias himself would become the slave of that not very gentle patrician. Cornelia

[1] A poet at that time of some little reputation.

and Drusus had had troubles enough before; but in the present crisis, actual destruction stared Agias's saviour in the face.
The situation was maddening, was sickening. Agias wrung
his hands in anguish. Then came the healthy reaction.
Drusus was still alive and well. He could be warned. The
plot could be thwarted. Pratinas and Ahenobarbus were
not yet beyond the reach of retribution. He — Agias — was
no longer to be a mere foot-boy and lackey; he was to match
his keen Greek wits in subtle intrigue against foemen worthy
of his steel. He would save Drusus's life, would save Cornelia's happiness. If he succeeded, who knew but that his
owner would reward him — would give him freedom. And
with a natural rebound of spirits, Agias's eyes glittered with
expectation and excitement, his cheeks flushed, his form
expanded to a manly height.

"*Euge!* Well done, old friend!" he cried, with the mer-
riment of intense excitement. "No matter if you say you
were only able to hear a small part of what our dear fellow-
Hellene, Pratinas, told Valeria. I have gathered enough to
defeat the plotters. Leave all to me. If you learn anything
new, send word to the house of Lentulus Crus, and ask to see
me. And now I must forsake this pleasant wine untasted, and
hurry away. My mistress will bless you, and perhaps there
will be some reward."

And leaving the bewildered Pisander to wipe the wine
from his dress, Agias had darted out of the tavern, and was
lost in the hurly-burly of the cattle-market.

How Agias had forced his way into Cornelia's presence we
have related. The young Greek had stated his unpleasant
intelligence as diplomatically and guardedly as possible; but
Cornelia had borne this shock — following so soon upon one
sufficiently cruel — grievously enough. After all, she was only

a girl — perhaps more mature for her years than the average maiden of her age of to-day, but almost friendless, hopeless, and beset with many trials. And this new one was almost more than she could bear. We have said that to her suicide had but just before appeared a refuge to be desired; but to have Quintus die, to have him taken out of that life that ought to be so fair for him, no matter how darksome it was for her; to have him never realize her ambition that he become a statesman, warrior, philosopher, in short her ideal hero — this was unbearable! This phase of the question was so overpowering that she forgot to feel rage against Ahenobarbus and his wily ally. Cornelia threw herself down upon the floor, and cried to Agias to slay her quickly. She did not care to live; she could endure no more.

Agias here manifested exquisite tact. Instead of attempting any ordinary means of expostulation, he pleaded with her not to give way to despair; that Drusus was not yet at the mercy of his enemies; that she, if she would, could do an infinite deal to assist him.

"I save Quintus?" questioned Cornelia, with white, quivering lips.

"You can do much, my lady," replied Agias, kindly taking her by the hand, and with gentle pressure forcing her to sit on the divan. "You can do what neither I, nor Pisander, nor any one else can accomplish. You can make Lucius Ahenobarbus betray his own plot. You, and you only, can penetrate the final plans of the conspirators. Therefore be strong, and do not despair."

"I? What can I do?" cried Cornelia, staring at him with sad, tearless eyes.

"Lady Cornelia," said Agias, delicately, "Drusus would never receive back his life if it were to be purchased by any sac rifice of honour on your part. But this is not needed. Lucius Ahenobarbus — forgive my plain speech — worships the ground whereon you tread. A smile from you raises him to Olympus ; a compliment from you makes him feel himself a god ; a soft word from you creates him the peer of Zeus. Lady, I know you hate that man ; but for Master Drusus's sake make Ahenobarbus believe that you are not indifferent to his advances. Slander Drusus before him. Complain of the provisions of your father's will that, despite your uncle's intention, will make it difficult to avoid a hateful marriage. If in the past you have been cold to Ahenobarbus, grow gracious ; but not too rapidly. Finally, at the proper time, do not hesitate to urge him to commit the act we know he is meditating. Then he will make you a full partner of his plot, and Pratinas and he can be permanently thwarted."

"You say that Drusus can be saved by this?" asked Cornelia, steadying herself as she rose from the divan.

"I will warn him at once," replied Agias. "Any premature attempt on his life will certainly fail. But it is not Ahenobarbus that I fear ; it is Pratinas. Pratinas, if baffled once, will only be spurred on to use all his cunning in a second trial. We must enmesh the conspirators so completely that when their stab is parried, not merely will their power to repeat it be gone, but they themselves will be in danger of retribution. And for this, some one must be confederate to their final plan."

"Agias," said Cornelia, quietly, "Quintus said that you would be a faithful servant to him and to myself. I believe he was right. You have asked a great thing of me, Agias. I would not do it unless I believed that you were unlike other slaves. I might imagine that Lucius Ahenobarbus had bribed you to tell me this story, in order that I should put myself in his power. But I trust you. I will do anything you say. For you Hellenes have wits as keen as sharp steel, and I know that you will do all you may to repay your debt to Quintus."

Agias knelt down and kissed the robe of his mistress. "My lady," he said gently, "it is no grievous thing to be a slave of such as you. Believe me; I will not betray my trust. And now if you can let me leave you, I will hurry to Præneste, and for the present our minds may be at rest. For old Mamercus will, I am sure, be able to take good care of Master Drusus for yet awhile."

"Go, and the gods — if there be gods — go with you!" replied Cornelia. Agias kissed her robe a second time, and was gone. His mistress stood in the middle of the empty room. On the wall facing her was a painting of "Aphrodite rising from the Foam," which Drusus had given her. The sensuous smiles on the face of the goddess sickened Cornelia, as she looked upon it. To her, at the moment, laughter was more hideous than any sobbing. Outside the door she heard the gay, witless chatter of the maids and the valets. They were happy — they — slaves, "speaking tools,"— and she with the blood of the Claudii and Cornelii in her veins, a patrician among patricians, the niece of a consul-elect, a woman who was the heiress of states-men and overturners of kingdoms, — *she* was miserable beyond endurance. Cornelia paced up and down the room, wishing she might order the giggling maids to be flogged and their laughter turned into howling. Then she summoned Cassandra.

* * * * * * * * * *

Cornelia had never before tried to play the actress, but that night she flung herself into the game for life and death with all the earnestness of an energetic, intelligent, and spontaneous woman. She had been barely civil to Lucius Ahenobarbus be-fore; to-night the young man began to persuade himself that the object of his affections was really a most adorable coquette, who used a certain brusqueness of speech to add to her witchery. He had heard that there had been some very disagreeable scenes at Præneste, when Lentulus had told his niece that Drusus, on account of his dangerous politics, was unfit to be her husband. But Ahenobarbus was sure that either these accounts were exaggerated, or more likely, Cornelia, like most women, was quick to fall in love and quick to leave an old sweetheart for a new one. Be that as it may, Lucius felt that night on good terms with himself and all the world. Phormio had consented to continue his loans — until his debtor could realize on "certain property." Pratinas had said that Dumnorix would shortly start with a band of gladiators for some local festival at Anagnia, a little beyond Præneste; and on the way back, if nothing went amiss, the prearranged programme could be carried out. Some pretext must be found for keeping Drusus on his estate at the time when Dumnorix would march past it, and that task could be confided to Phaon, Lucius's freedman, a sly fox entirely after his patron's own heart.

Cornelia, to whom the dinner-party at Favonius's house began as a dreary enough tragedy, before long discovered that it was by no means more easy to suck undiluted sorrow than unmixed gladness out of life. It gratified her to imagine the rage and dismay of the young exquisite whose couch was beside her chair,[1] when he should learn how completely he had been duped. Then, too, Lucius Ahenobarbus had a voluble flow of polite small talk, and he knew how to display his accomplishments to full advantage. He had a fair share of wit and humour; and when he fancied that Cornelia was not impervious to his advances, he became more agreeable and more ardent. Once or twice Cornelia frightened herself by laughing without conscious

[1] Women sat at Roman banquets, unless the company was of a questionable character.

forcing. Yet it was an immense relief to her when the banquet was over, and the guests — for Favonius had ordered that none should be given enough wine to be absolutely drunken — called for their sandals and litters and went their ways.

"And you, O Adorable, Calypso, Circe, Nausicaä, Medēa, — what shall I call you? — you will not be angry if I call to see you to-morrow?" said Ahenobarbus, smiling as he parted from Cornelia.

"If you come," was her response, "I shall not perhaps order the slaves to pitch you out heels over head."

"Ah! That is a guarded assent, indeed," laughed Lucius, "but farewell, *pulcherrima!*"[1]

Cornelia that night lay down and sobbed herself to sleep. Her mother had congratulated her on her brilliant social success at the dinner-party, and had praised her for treating Lucius Ahenobarbus as she had.

"You know, my dear," the worthy woman had concluded, "that since it has seemed necessary to break off with Drusus, a marriage with Lucius would be at once recommended by your father's will, and in many ways highly desirable."

II

Only a very few days later Lucius Ahenobarbus received a message bidding him come to see his father at the family palace on the Palatine. Lucius had almost cut himself clear from his relations. He had his own bachelor apartments, and Domitius had been glad to have him out of the way. A sort of fiction existed that he was legally under the *patria potestas*,[2] and

---

[1] Most beautiful.
[2] Sons remained under the legal control of a father until the latter's death unless the tie was dissolved by elaborate ceremonies.

could only have debts and assets on his father's responsibility, but as a matter of fact his parent seldom paid him any attention; and only called on him to report at home when there was a public or family festival, or something very important. Consequently he knew that matters serious were on foot, when he read in his father's note a request to visit Domitius's palace as soon as convenient. Lucius was just starting, in his most spotless toga, — after a prolonged season with his hairdresser, — to pay a morning call on Cornelia, and so he was the more vexed and perturbed.

"Curses on Cato,[1] my old uncle," he muttered, while he waited in the splendid atrium of the house of the Ahenobarbi. "He has been rating my father about my pranks with Gabinius and Læca, and something unpleasant is in store for me."

Domitius presently appeared, and his son soon noticed by the affable yet diplomatic manner of his father, and the gentle warmth of his greeting, that although there was something in the background, it was not necessarily very disagreeable.

"My dear Lucius," began Domitius, after the first civilities were over, and the father and son had strolled into a handsomely appointed library and taken seats on a deeply upholstered couch, "I have, I think, been an indulgent parent. But 1 must tell you, I have heard some very bad stories of late about your manner of life."

"Oh!" replied Lucius, smiling. "As your worthy friend Cicero remarked when defending young Cælius, 'those sorts of reproaches are regularly heaped on every one whose person or appearance in youth is at all gentlemanly.'"

"I will thank you if you will not quote Cicero to me,"

1 Cato Minor's sister Portia was the wife of Lucius Domitius. Cato was also connected with the Drusi through Marcus Livius Drusus, the murdered reformer, who was the maternal uncle of Cato and Portia. Lucius Ahenobarbus and Quintus Drusus were thus third cousins.

replied the elder man, a little tartly. "He will soon be back from Cilicia, and will be prodding and wearying us in the Senate quite enough, with his rhetoric and sophistries. But I must be more precise. I have found out how much you owe Phormio. I thought your dead uncle had left you a moderately large estate for a young man. Where has it gone to? Don't try to conceal it! It's been eaten up and drunk up — spent away for unguents, washed away in your baths, the fish-dealer and the caterer have made way with it, yes, and butchers and cooks, and greengrocers and perfume sellers, and poulterers — not to mention people more scandalous — have made off with it."

Lucius stretched himself out on the divan, caught at a thick, richly embroidered pillow, tossed it over his head on to the floor, yawned, raised himself again upright, and said drawlingly : —

"Y-e-s, it's as you say. I find I spend every sesterce I have, and all I can borrow. But so long as Phormio is accommodating, I don't trouble myself very much about the debts."

"Lucius," said Domitius, sternly, "you are a graceless spendthrift. Of course you must have the sport which all young blood needs. But your extravagance goes beyond all bounds. I call myself a rich man, but to leave you half my fortune, dividing with your older brother Cnæus, who is a far steadier and saner man than you, would be to assure myself that Greek parasites and low women would riot through that part of my estate in a twelvemonth. You must reform, Lucius; you must reform."

This was getting extremely disagreeable in spite of his expectations, and the young man yawned a second time, then answered : —

" Well, I presume Uncle Cato has told you all kinds of
stories; but they aren't at all true.   I really never had a great
deal of money."

" Lucius," went on his father, " you are grown to manhood.
It is time that you steadied in life.   I have let you live by
yourself too long.   You are even too indolent to engage in
politics, or to go into the army.   I have come to a determination.   You must marry the woman I have selected for
you."

Ahenobarbus pricked up his ears.   As a matter of fact, he
had surmised what was coming, but he had no intention of
admitting anything prematurely.

" Really, father," he said, " I hope you won't use your legal
right and force a wife on me.   I have no desire to tie myself
up to a decent married life."

" I hardly think," said Domitius, smiling, " that you will
resist my wishes long.   I have seen Lentulus Crus the consul-
elect, and he and I agree that since your mother's distant kinsman Quintus Drusus of Præneste is an unsuitable husband for
Cornelia, Lentulus's niece, on account of his very dangerous
political tendencies, no happier alliance could bind our families
together than a marriage between Cornelia and yourself."

Lucius yawned a third time and fell back on the couch.

" It's true," he ventured, " I have cared a good deal for Cornelia; and I've thrown over that little Greek Clyte and all the
others for her; but then, to make a girl your sweetheart and to
make her your wife are two very different things.   *Vina
Opimia* is best; but because one drinks a *cyathus*[1] of that,
why should he forego a good fill of Thasian or Cæcuban?   If I
could have but one choice, give me plenty of the good, and I'll
give up my few drops of the best."

[1] About one-twelfth pint.

"Come, come," said Domitius, a little impatiently, "you must positively reform. Besides, while appearances must be kept up, there is no need for leading the life of a Stoic. You won't find Cornelia a hard companion. You have your pleasures and she hers, and you will live harmoniously enough and not the least scandal."

And with this remark Domitius closed the matter, and Lucius was actually delighted at the situation. What his father had said had been true enough; half, nay, nearly all, Rome lived in the manner Domitius had guardedly proposed for his son and intended daughter-in-law. Marriage was becoming more and more a mere formality, something that was kept up as the ancient state Pagan worship was kept up by the remnants of old-time superstition, and as a cloak to hide a multitude of sins. Fifty-nine years before, the consul Metellus Numidicus had declaimed, "Quirites, we would fain be free from all this annoyance (of marriage); but since nature has so brought it about that it is neither possible to live pleasantly with our wives nor by any means to live (as a race) without them, we ought to consider the welfare of the future rather than the mere passing pleasure of the present." And ever since that day Romans had been striving desperately to make the married state as endurable as possible; usually by reducing the importance of lawful wedlock to a minimum.

Of course the announcement of the informal betrothal was soon spread over Rome. The contracting parties were in the very highest life, and everybody declared that the whole affair was a political deal between Lentulus Crus and Domitius. It was commonly reported, too, how Cornelia had broken with Drusus, and every one remarked that if the young man had cared to enforce her father's will in the courts, his claim to her hand and fortune would be valid unless — and here most people exchanged sly winks, for they knew the power of Domitius and Lentulus Crus over a jury.

And how had Cornelia borne it — she at whom Herennia had stared in amazement, when that "dear friend" discovered the friendship the other was displaying to Lucius Ahenobarbus? Cornelia had received the announcement very quietly, one might almost say resignedly. She had one great hope and consolation to support her. They would not force her to marry Lucius Ahenobarbus until Drusus was dead or had reached the age of five-and-twenty. The marriage formula with Ahenobarbus once uttered, while Quintus lived, and by no possibility, save by an open spoliation that would have stirred even calloused Rome, could Lucius touch a sesterce of his intended victim's property. Cornelia's hope now, strangely enough, was in the man she regarded as the most consummate villain in the world, Pratinas. Ahenobarbus might have his debts paid by his father, and forego risk and crime if he did not absolutely need Drusus's fortune; but Pratinas, she knew, must have planned to secure rich pickings of his own, and if Ahenobarbus married permanently, all these were lost; and the Greeks never turned back or let another turn back, when there was a fortune before them. It was a fearful sort of confidence. Drusus had been warned promptly by Agias. Old Mamercus had straightway taken every precaution, and forced his foster son to put himself in a sort of custody, which was sufficiently galling, in addition to the ever present sense of personal danger. The villa at Præneste was guarded quietly by several armed slaves and peasants; not a morsel or drop passed Drusus's lips that had not been tested and tasted by a trusty dependent. The young man was not to go to Rome, despite his infinite yearning to see Cornelia, for every opportunity would be given in the dark city streets for an assassin. In fact, Drusus was virtually a prisoner in his own estates, for only there could he feel reasonably safe from attack.

All these precautions Cornelia knew, for Agias was a master at smuggling letters in and out. She had told Drusus frankly all that had passed, and how that she was acting as she did only for his sake. She asked him to trust her, and he wrote back that no doubt of her fidelity to him had crossed his mind; he was not worthy of such love as she had for him; it did not matter very much if Ahenobarbus did kill him, except that it would give her new grief and pain, and the thought of that he could not bear. Cornelia had replied that if Drusus was murdered, she was woman enough and Roman enough to stab Lucius Ahenobarbus on their marriage night, and then plunge the dagger into her own breast. And there the fearful matter had rested; Cornelia smiled by day, and dazzled all she met by her vivacity, and her aggressive queenliness; and by night cried with tearless sobs, which came out of the depths of her heart. And all the time she waited for Agias to foil the plot, and assure Drusus of his life. Let Quintus once be safe, and then — how could she resist the irresistible pressure that would be brought to bear to force her into a hated marriage, which Ahenobarbus — balked though he might be of a fortune — would no longer care to defer? And when Cornelia thought of this, and when she was alone, she would open a little casket, of which no other had the key, and touch the ivory-carved hilt of a small damascened knife. The blade was very sharp; and there was a sticky gum all along the edge, — a deadly poison; only a very slight scratch put one beyond aid of physician.

The bitterest cup of all was the attitude she felt forced to assume toward Lucius Ahenobarbus. There were limits of familiarity and simulated affection beyond which she could not drive herself to go. Lucius was with her at all hours and in all places. The more she saw of him the more she abhorred his effeminate sensuality and lack of almost every quality that made life worth the living. But she must — she must learn the plot against Drusus, and precisely how and when the trap was to be sprung. And in a measure, at least so far as Lucius was concerned, she succeeded. By continually and openly reviling Quintus, by professing to doubt the legality of a marriage contracted against the terms of her father's will, by all but expressing the wish that her late lover were out of harm's way, she won her point. In a fit of half-drunken confidence Ahenobarbus assured her that she would not be troubled by Drusus for long; that he would soon be unable to annoy her. And then came a great disappointment. When Cornelia asked — and how much the request cost her, only she herself knew — to be let into the plot, Lucius owned that he had left the details in the hands of Pratinas, and did not himself know just how or when the blow was to fall. In Pratinas — whom Cornelia met very seldom — she met with a sphinx, ever smiling, ever gracious, but who, as if regretting the burst of confidence he had allowed Valeria, kept himself closed to the insinuations and half-questions of every one else. The truth was, the lanista Dumnorix was unwilling to do his part of the business until the festival at Anagnia brought him and his band through Præneste, and this festival had been postponed. Consequently, the projected murder had been postponed a few days also. Agias had tried to penetrate into the secrets of Pratinas, but found that judicious intriguer had, as a rule, carefully covered his tracks. He spent a good deal of time and money, which Cornelia gave him, trying to corrupt some of the gladiators of Dumnorix's band and get at the intentions of their master; but he was not able to find that any of these wretches, who took his gold greedily enough, really knew in the least what were the appointments and engagements of the Gallic giant. As a matter of fact, the boy began to feel decidedly discouraged. Pisander had nothing more to tell; and, moreover, the worthy philosopher often gave such contradictory accounts of what he had overheard in Valeria's boudoir, that Agias was at his wit's end when and where to begin.

So passed the rest of the month since Cornelia had been brought from Præneste to Rome.

III

Cornelia began to grow sick at heart. The conviction was stealing over her that she was the victim of a cruel destiny, and it was useless to fight against fate. She had made sacrifices for Drusus's sake that had cost her infinitely. All Rome said that Cornelia returned the love of Lucius Ahenobarbus. And with it all, she knew that she had not succeeded in discovering the real plot of Pratinas, and could not thwart it. She knew that nearly every one placed her, if actually not as vicious as the rest, at least in the same coterie with Clodia, and the wife of Lentulus Spinther the younger Metella, and only a grade better than such a woman as Arbuscula, the reigning actress of the day. There was no defence to offer to the world. Did she not go with her mother to the gay gathering, in the gardens by the Tiber ? Was she not waited on by half the fashionable young aristocrats of Rome ? Was she not affianced to a man who was notoriously a leader of what might to-day be called the "fast set" of the capital ? And from Drusus, poor fellow, she gained not the least consolation. That he loved her as she loved him, she had never cause to doubt. But in his self-renunciation he gave her advice that sprang out of his own sorrow and pessimism. It was no use, ran his letters, for a woman like her to try and battle against the evident decrees of Fortune. He was a man, and must fight his battle or die his death bravely; but she was not called on for this. There was no reason why she should not really enjoy herself, in the way most of the world thought she was enjoying herself. She had better wed Lucius Ahenobarbus, and stoop to the inevitable. Her husband could go his way and she go hers, and none would complain. Perhaps the Epicureans were right, — this life was all, and it was best to suck from it all the sweets one might, and not be disturbed by pricks of conscience. Drusus and Cornelia were not lovers of a modern romance, to entertain fantastic ideas of love and duty, to throw themselves away for a fancy, or tie themselves with vows which militated against almost every worldly advantage. They were both Romans, and by that we mean eminently practical persons, faithful to one another, pure and noble in their affections, but habituated to look a situation in the face and accept the plain consequences. In this spirit Drusus had advised as he did, and Cornelia became discouraged accordingly. Her reason told her to submit to the inevitable. Her heart cried out against it. And so she continued to finger the hilt of the little dagger, and look at its keen poison-smeared edge.

But one day at the end of this dreary period Agias appeared before his mistress with a smiling face.

"Don't raise high hopes, my lady, but trust me. I have struck a path that I'm sure Pratinas will wish I'd never travelled." And that was all he would say, but laid his finger on his lips as though it was a great secret. When he was gone, for Cornelia the sun shone brighter, and the tinkling of the water in the fountain in the peristylium sounded sweeter than before. After all, there had come a gleam of hope.

Cornelia needed the encouragement. That same day when Herennia called to see her, that excellent young lady — for not the least reason in the world — had been full of stories of poisoning and murders, how some years ago a certain Balbutius of Larinum was taken off, it was said, at a wedding feast of a friend for whom the poison had been intended; and then again she had to tell how, at another time, poison had been put in a bit of bread of which the victim partook. The stories were old ones and perhaps nothing more than second-hand scandal, but they were enough to make poor Cornelia miserable; so she was doubly rejoiced when Agias that evening pressed his lips again and smiled and said briefly: "All is going well. We shall have the root of the matter in a few days."

Agias had actually come upon what he was right in considering a great piece of good fortune. He had easily found the tenement in the Subura where Pratinas lodged, but to learn anything there that would be useful was a far more difficult affair. He had hung around the place, however, as much as he dared, making his headquarters at a tavern conveniently near, and tried to learn Pratinas's habits, and whether he ever took any visitors home with him. All this came to little purpose till one morning he observed an old Ethiop, who was tugging a heavy provision basket, stagger up the street, through the nondescript crowd. The old slave was being assailed by a mob of street gamins and low pedlers who saw in the contents of the hamper so much fair plunder. These vagabonds had just thrown the Ethiop down into the mud, and were about to divide their booty, when

Agias, acting on a generous impulse, rushed out from the tavern to the rescue. Nimble, for his age powerful, and armed with a stout staff which he had caught up in the wine-shop to aid him, the young Greek won an easy victory over cowardly antagonists, put all the plunderers to flight, and lifted the old slave out of the mire. The Ethiop was profuse in his thanks.

"And whose slave are you?" demanded Agias, well pleased to be out of the adventure.

"I'm Sesostris, servant of Pratinas the Greek."

Agias pricked up his ears. "And you live —"

"In the top story of this tenement;" and Sesostris tried to pick up the hamper.

"Oh!" laughed his rescuer, "you must let me save you that trouble. I will carry up the basket. Your master is a brute to pile on such loads."

Sesostris again fawned his gratitude, and Agias, with quickened wits and eyes alert, toiled up the dark stairway, and found himself at the top of the building. He had "entered the enemy's country." The Ethiop might not have been open to bribes, but he might be unlocked through friendship, and Agias never needed all his senses more than now. They had reached the topmost flight of stairs, and Sesostris had stopped as if embarrassed whether to invite his deliverer in to enjoy some hospitality, or say him farewell. Then of a sudden from behind the closed door came a clear, sweet, girlish voice, singing, in Greek: —

> "O Aitnē, mother mine: A grotto fair
>   Scooped in the rocks have I, and there I keep
> All that in dreams man pictures! Treasured there
>   Are multitudes of she-goats and of sheep,
>   Swathed in whose wool from top to toe I sleep."

It was an idyl of Theocritus, very well known by Agias, and without the least hesitation he took up the strain, and continued: —

> "The fire boils my pot; with oak or beech
> Is piled, — dry beech logs when the snow lies deep.
> And storm and sunshine, I disdain them each
> As toothless sires a nut, when broth is in their reach." [1]

Agias paused. There was a silence, then a giggle behind the door, and it half opened, and out peered the plump and rosy face of the young girl we have heard Pratinas salute as his niece, Artemisia. The moment she caught sight of the rather manly form of Agias, the door started to close with a slam, but the latter thrust out his foot, blocked the door, and forced an entrance.

"*Eleleu!*" cried Agias, pushing into a small but neatly furnished room. "What have we here? Do the muses sing in Subura? Has Sappho brought hither her college of poetesses from Lesbos?"

"*Ai!*" exclaimed Artemisia, drawing back, "who are you? You're dreadfully rude. I never saw you before."

"Nor I you;" replied Agias, in capital good humour, "but that is no reason why I should take my eyes away from your pretty little face. No, you needn't point your middle finger at me so, to ward off the evil eye. I'm neither Chaldean astrologer, nor Etruscan soothsayer. Come, tell me who you are, and whom you belong to?"

Artemisia did not have the least idea what to say. Agias, partly through youthful love of adventure, partly because he felt that he was playing now for very high stakes and must risk a good deal, had thrown himself on the divan, and was holding Artemisia captive under his keen, genial eyes. She

[1] Calverly's translation

grew redder in face than before, began to speak, then broke off with more confused blushes.

"She means to say," finally ventured Sesostris, "that she is Artemisia, the niece of Pratinas."

"The niece of Pratinas!" exclaimed Agias, settling himself upon the cushions in a manner that indicated his intention to make a prolonged stay ; "and does Pratinas keep his pretty niece shut up in a gloomy tenement, when she has the voice of one of the Graces, and more than their share of beauty! Shame on him; I thought he had better sense than that!"

"Sir," ventured Artemisia, trying desperately to stand on her dignity, "I do not know you. My uncle will be greatly vexed to find you here. Will you go away at once?"

"That I will not," replied Agias, firmly; and he drew from the hamper a baker's bun, and began to munch it, as though laying in provision for a lengthy stay.

Artemisia and Sesostris exchanged glances of dismay.

"What *shall* I do?" said the girl to the Ethiop in a very audible whisper.

"Sing," interrupted Agias. "Let me hear the rest of the Theocritus."

"I don't like to sing those songs," objected Artemisia. "Pratinas makes me, I don't know why."

"Well," said Agias, smiling, "I wouldn't for the world make you sing against your will. Suppose you tell me about yourself. Tell me when your uncle is away, and when I may come and see you again."

"He's away nearly all the time," said Artemisia, very incautiously. "But *who are* you? Why do you want to come and see me?"

"Why do I want to look at a flower? Why do I want to hear the nightingale sing? Why do I like a cup of good wine?" laughed Agias. "Then, fair mistress, you may look for my answer when *you* have answered all of these questions of mine."

"I don't see what you mean," said poor Artemisia, looking dreadfully puzzled.

"I mean," exclaimed the other, "what Sappho meant of the bride, —

"'She like an apple turned red; which reddens far up on the tree-top: —
Upon the topmost of boughs, — the gatherers they have quite missed it.
Yes, they saw it indeed ; but too high to dare try to pluck it.'

Only I, if you don't greatly mind, will be the bold tree-climber and pluck the apple."

"But I do mind," cried Artemisia, all blushes, and springing a little back. Old Sesostris looked alarmed.

"You — you mean the girl no ill?" he faltered.

Agias looked from the innocent little thing over to the Ethiop, snapped his finger, and replied: —

"Ill? I am not a human wolf, making pretty objects like this my prey!" Then, choosing his moment carefully, by a quick turn he confronted Sesostris sternly, and almost thundered: "*You* speak of my doing ill to this maiden? You speak — the slave of Pratinas, who is the leader in every vice and wild prank in Rome! Has the slave as well as the master learned to play the hypocrite? Do you want to be tortured into confessing your part in all your master's crimes when the hour of reckoning comes and he is brought to justice. *A ! A !*" he went on, seeing that Sesostris was rolling the whites of his eyes, and was trembling in every limb. "you know for a certainty how and when Pratinas is to have Quintus Drusus killed! Don't deny it. You will soon be in the meshes. Don't hope to escape. If murder comes to Drusus he may perish, but he has friends who will fearfully avenge his death."

"Mercy! Mercy!" howled the Ethiop, falling on his knees and clutching at the young Greek's robe, "I know very little of the plot. I only know — "

"Don't equivocate," thundered Agias. "If I had known the kind of man you were, I would hardly have saved you from those street ruffians. You don't deserve to live. Well, the crows will soon have you! You Egyptians believe in a judgment of the dead; what defence can you make before the court of Osiris [1] for being privy to a foul murder? You'll come back to earth as a fly, or a toad, or a dung-beetle, to pay the penalty for your sins."

"Mercy," whined Sesostris, who was in a paroxysm of fright. "Indeed I am innocent! I am only a poor slave! I can't help knowing what Pratinas is doing; but how can I prevent him? Don't look at me so! I am innocent — innocent!"

"I can scarce believe you," said Agias, affecting great reluctance to show any leniency. "Doubtless you are steeped in blood. Still, you may save yourself this once. Remember, you are known, and the plans of Pratinas against Drusus are partly known. We know about Dumnorix, and Lucius Ahenobarbus, and — "

"Oh!" cried Sesostris, as though a hot iron had touched him, "I will find out everything, and tell you. Indeed I will. Only do not send me to the rack or crucify me if my master's plans go astray!"

"Well," said Agias, still simulating hesitancy, "I will report to my superiors. Perhaps you are not a willing accomplice of your master. In that case, if he is apprehended, your

---

[1] The Egyptian judge of the dead.

life will doubtless be spared. But we must thwart his plot before it can be carried out. This you must aid us to do. When will Dumnorix start for Præneste?"

Again Sesostris quailed. "I don't know," he faltered, "there has been a postponement. There was a plan that if Drusus came to the city he was to be lured outside the Esquiline gate, as if going to some villa, and murdered in the sand-pits, as have been many people."

"But this plan has been given up? Speak the truth!" sharply demanded Agias.

"Yes; for Drusus will not stir from Præneste. So there the scheme must be executed, as originally arranged."

"And Dumnorix will go soon?"

"I think in a few days. I will find out."

"As you love your own life do so! I will call on each day at this hour. If Pratinas is at home, leave some bright garment outside near the door, that I may not stumble on him. Deceive or betray me, and my masters will take a terrible revenge on you; for you haven't the least idea what is the power of the men Pratinas has for enemies."

Agias turned to depart. Then to Artemisia: —

"And you, my pretty, — when I come again, I will try to stay longer, and make you feel as glad to see Agias, as Agias will be to see Artemisia."

Agias was descending the stairs, when Sesostris called him back with a whisper.

"You are a dreadful youth; but since I am so utterly in your power, hear something that may prove that I am not a knave at heart. You have a fancy to the girl?"

"Certainly I have eyes for her face, and ears for her sweet little voice," said Agias, smiling.

"Then listen," went on the Ethiop: "I care for the dear

more than anything else in the world. She said she was Pratinas's niece. It isn't true. She is a slave-girl he picked up when very little at Delos,[1] as he told me, though I doubt it. He took a fancy to her, and really thought of adopting her. Then his soul became so set on money, that he saw she would fetch a great price when grown; and sell her he will. He still pretends to call her his niece; but that won't be for long. He is teaching her to sing, to add to her value. *A!* But my old heart is almost breaking for her sake. *Mu, mu!*" and Sesostris puffed his groans through his nostrils. "Think of it! He has an idea to sell her to that rich Roman, Lucius Calatinus — and then I don't dare hint what will be her fate."

"Calatinus!" hissed Agias, concentrating volumes of scorn into a word.

"You know him! You hate him!" cried Sesostris. "Then by Ammon-Ra, by Isis, by every god in whom you believe, save my darling from worse than death! Do that, and I will die for you!"

Sesostris's emotion was too genuine to be a mere trap for ensnaring his visitor; and Agias in turn was stirred.

"Old man," he exclaimed, seizing the other's hand, "you and I have suffered much from evil masters. Thank the gods, I am now serving one I love — albeit unfortunate enough! But we have a common right to punish the wrongdoers, and earn a little bit of happiness for ourselves. Come, now! If Artemisia is a slave, she is in no wise above me. Let me save Drusus from Pratinas, and I pledge my word that I will save Artemisia from him and his nefarious schemes,—yes, and you, too. If Artemisia likes me, why then there will be perhaps more to add to the story. Come — I am your friend, and you, mine."

---

[1] At this period the great slave emporium of the world.

Sesostris wrung the other's hand. The honest servant was moved too much to speak. His heart and soul had been bound up in Artemisia.

"May your *Ka*[1] stand before Osiris justified!" he choked. "I have been privy to many a dark action, until I used to try to forget the day when I must answer to the Judge of the Dead for every deed done and word spoken. But I could not stifle my fear for the only dear thing in the world."

Agias went away in a happy frame of mind. He had every confidence that Sesostris would worm out of Pratinas the exact details of the plot, and put the conspirators at the mercy of Drusus and Mamercus.

*   *   *   *   *   *   *   *   *   *

And Agias had felt there was good reason to rejoice in his discovery in more ways than one. Especially was he conscious that there were no lips as red and as merry, no cheeks as rosy, no eyes as dancing, no chatter as sweet, as those of Artemisia. And what is more, he rejoiced to believe that that young lady was not half so shy of him as at first, and was as anxious to see him as he to see her. Thanks to due warnings and precautions, Agias never stumbled on Pratinas, when the latter was at his lodgings. The time he dared to stay was all too short for Artemisia. She was always telling how lonesome she was with only old Sesostris for company, before she knew Agias. Once when the latter was late in his daily visit, he was delighted to find scribbled on the wall, "Artemisia to her Agias: you are real mean." Agias hated to make her erase it lest it fall under Pratinas's eagle eye.

[1] The spiritual double which belonged to every man according to the Egyptian ideas.

But still Sesostris had nothing to tell about the plot against Drusus. Some days passed. Agias began to grow uneasy. Sesostris had represented that he was conversant with everything his master had on foot; but Pratinas might have been more discreet than to unfold all his affairs, even before his servant; and then, too, there was always the possibility that Sesostris was playing fast and loose, and about to betray Agias to his master. So the latter grew disquieted, and found it a little hard to preserve the character of cheerful mystery which he simulated to Cornelia. The long-sought information came at a time when he was really off his guard. Agias had been visiting Artemisia. Sesostris as well as Pratinas had been out; the two young people were amusing themselves trying to teach a pet magpie to speak, when the Ethiop rushed into the room, all in a tremble with anxious excitement.

"*A! A!*" he was ejaculating. "Up, speed, don't delay! There's murder afoot!"

Agias let the bird slip from his hands, and never noticed that it fluttered on its clipped wings around the room, to Artemisia's infinite dismay.

"What? Is the plot hatched?"

"Yes, yes," puffed Sesostris, great beads of perspiration on his honest face. "I was attending Pratinas when he met Lucius Ahenobarbus in the Forum. They veiled their talk, but I readily caught its drift. Dumnorix went yesterday with the pick of his band to Anagnia for some games. To-morrow he will return through Præneste, and the deed will be done. Phaon, Ahenobarbus's freedman, has started already for Præneste to spy out the ground and be ready to direct Dumnorix where, when, and how to find Drusus. Phaon has been spying at Præneste, and is the dangerous man!"

"He has gone?" demanded Agias.

"Gone, early this morning!"

"Then, — the gods reward you for your news, — I am gone too!"

And without another word to Artemisia or the old slave, Agias had rushed out into the street. He had a double game to play — to prevent Phaon from ever reaching Præneste, and then get such help to Drusus as would enable him to beat off Dumnorix and his gang. For Agias felt certain that the hard-hitting Gaul would execute his part of the bargain, whether he met Phaon or not, and afterward look into the consequences of what — unmitigated by the freedman's *finesse* — would take the form of an open clumsy murder. But Phaon had started that morning; and it was now well into the afternoon. Time was dangerously scanty. Cornelia he felt he should inform, but she could do nothing really to help him. He turned his steps toward the Forum and the Atrium Vestæ. He had some difficulty in inducing the porter to summon Fabia, to meet in personal interview a mere slave, but a gratuity won the point; and a minute later he was relating the whole story and the present situation of Drusus to Fabia, with a sincere directness that carried conviction with it. She had known that Drusus had enemies; but now her whole strong nature was stirred at the sense of her nephew's imminent peril.

"If you were a freeman, Agias," were her words, "and could give witness as such, Pratinas and Ahenobarbus — high as the latter is — should know that my influence at the law outweighs theirs. But they shall be thwarted. I will go to Marcellus the consul, and demand that troops be started to Præneste to-night. But you must go after Phaon."

"You will send word to Cornelia?" requested Agias.

"Yes," said Fabia, "but not now: it is useless. Here is an

order on Gallus, who keeps a livery-stable [1] by the Porta Esquilina. He will give you my new white Numidian, that I keep
with him. Ride as you have never ridden before. And here
is money. Twenty gold philippi in this bag. Bribe, do anything. Only save Drusus! Now go!"

"Farewell, lady," cried Agias, "may I redeem the debt of
gratitude I owe you!"

Fabia stood looking after him, as he hastened out from the
quiet atrium into the busy street. Little Livia had cuddled up
beside her aunt.

"Oh, Livia," said Fabia, "I feel as though it were of no use
to live good and pure in this world! Who knows what trouble
may come to me from this day's doings? And why should
they plot against your brother's dear life? But I mustn't talk
so." And she called for her attendants to escort her abroad.

---

[1] Such establishments were common near the gates, and the Vestals often
had their horses at such places.

CHAPTER VIII

"WHEN GREEK MEETS GREEK"

I

CORNELIA had surmised correctly that Pratinas, not Lucius Ahenobarbus, would be the one to bring the plot against Drusus to an issue. Lucius had tried in vain to escape from the snares the wily intriguer had cast about him. His father had told him that if he would settle down and lead a moderately respectable life, Phormio should be paid off. And with this burden off his mind, tor reformation was very easily promised, Lucius had time to consider whether it was worth his while to mix in a deed that none of Pratinas's casuistry could quite convince him was not a foul, unprovoked murder, of an innocent man. The truth was, Ahenobarbus was desperately in love with Cornelia, and had neither time nor desire to mingle in any business not connected with the pursuit of his "tender passion." None of his former sweethearts — and he had had almost as many as he was years old — were comparable in his eyes to her. She belonged to a different world from that of the Spanish dancers, the saucy maidens of Greece, or even the many noble-born Roman women that seemed caught in the eddy of Clodia's fashionable whirlpool. Lucius frankly told himself that he would want to be divorced from Cornelia in five years — it would be tedious to keep company longer with a goddess. But for the present her vivacity, her wit, her bright intelligence,

146

no less than her beauty, charmed him. And he was rejoiced to believe that she was quite as much ensnared by his own attractions. He did not want any unhappy accident to mar the smooth course which was to lead up to the marriage in no distant future. He did not need Drusus's money any longer to save him from bankruptcy. The legacy would be highly desirable, but life would be very pleasant without it. Lucius was almost induced by his inward qualms to tell Pratinas to throw over the whole matter, and inform Dumnorix that his services were not needed.

It was at this juncture that Cornelia committed an error, the full consequences of which were, to her, happily veiled. In her anxiety to discover the plot, she had made Lucius believe that she was really pining for the news of the murder of Drusus. Cornelia had actually learned nothing by a sacrifice that tore her very heart out; but her words and actions did almost irreparable harm to the cause she was trying to aid.

"And you have never given me a kiss," Lucius had said one morning, when he was taking leave of Cornelia in the atrium of the Lentuli. "Will you ever play the siren, and lure me to you? and then devour, as it were, your victim, not with your lips, but with your eyes?"

"*Eho!* Not so bold!" replied Cornelia, drawing back. "How can I give you what you wish, unless I am safe from that awful Polyphemus up in Præneste?"

When Ahenobarbus went away, his thoughts were to the following effect: "I had always thought Cornelia different from most women; but now I can see that, like them all, she hates and hates. To say to her, 'Drusus is dead,' will be a more grateful present than the largest diamond Lucullus brought from the East, from the treasure of King Tigranes."

And it was in such a frame of mind that he met **Pratinas** by appointment at a low tavern on the Vicus Tuscus. The Greek was, as ever, smiling and plausible.

"Congratulations!" was his greeting. "Dumnorix has already started. He has my orders; and now I must borrow your excellent freedman, Phaon, to go to Præneste and spy out, for the last time, the land, and general our army. Let him start early to-morrow morning. The time is ample, and unless some malevolent demon hinder us, there will be no failure. I have had a watch kept over the Drusus estate. An old sentry of a steward, Mamercus, — so I learn, — has been afraid, evidently, of some foul play on the part of the consul-designate, and has stationed a few armed freedmen on guard. Drusus himself keeps very carefully on his own premises. This is all the better for us. Dumnorix will dispose of the freedmen in a hurry, and our man will be in waiting there just for the gladiators. Phaon will visit him — cook up some errand, and inveigle him, if possible, well out in the colonnade in front of the house, before Dumnorix and his band pass by. Then there will be that very deplorable scuffle, and its sad, sad results. Alas, poor Drusus! Another noble Livian gathered to his fathers!"

"I don't feel very merry about it," ventured Lucius. "I don't need Drusus's money as much as I did. If it wasn't for Cornelia, I would drop it all, even now. Sometimes I feel there are avenging Furies — *Diræ*, we Latins call them — haunting me."

Pratinas laughed incredulously. "Surely, my dear fellow," he began, "you don't need to have the old superstitions explained away again, do you?"

"No, no," was his answer; Lucius capitulating another time.

So it came to pass that Pratinas had an interview with Phaon, Lucius's freedman, a sleek, well-oiled Sicilian Greek, who wore his hair very long to cover the holes bored in his ears — the mark of old-time servitude. He was the darling of waiting-maids; the collector of all current scandal; the master spirit in arranging dinners, able to tell a Tuscan from a Lucanian boar by mere taste. He used also to help his patron compose *billets-doux*, and had, by his twistings and scrapings, repeatedly staved off Phormio, Lucius's importunate creditor. As for Phaon's heart, it was so soft and tender that the pricks of conscience, if he ever had any, went straight through, without leaving a trace behind. And when Pratinas now informed him as to his final duties at Præneste, Phaon rubbed his beringed hands and smoothed his carefully scraped chin with ill-concealed satisfaction.

"And a word more in closing," said Pratinas, as he parted with Phaon in the tavern — while Lucius, who had been drinking very heavily, nodded stupidly over his goblet of amber Falernian, in a vain attempt to gulp down eight *cyathi* at once, one measure to each letter in the name of Cornelia — "a word more. Dumnorix is a thick-skulled knave, who is, after all, good for little but blows. I have made an arrangement which will ensure having a careful man at his elbow in time of need. You, of course, will have to do your best to save the unfortunate Quintus from inevitable fate. But I have asked Publius Gabinius to leave for Præneste very early on the morning when Dumnorix passes through that place. Gabinius has a small villa a little beyond the town, and there will be nothing suspicious in a journey to visit one's country house. He will meet Dumnorix, and be at his side when the pinch comes. You see? He is an adventurous fellow, and will help us just for the sake of the mischief. Besides, I believe he has a grudge against the Drusian family as a whole, for he lately tried to pass some familiarities with Fabia the Vestal, Drusus's aunt, and she proved disgustingly prudish."

"And how much will you and I," said Phaon, with a sly smirk, "gain out of this little business, if all goes well? Of course one should help one's patron, but — "

"It is folly to divide the spoils of Troy before Troy is taken," laughed Pratinas. "Don't be alarmed, my good fellow. Your excellent patron will reward us, no doubt, amply." And he muttered to himself: "If I don't bleed that Lucius Ahenobarbus, that Roman donkey, out of two-thirds of his new fortune; if I don't levy blackmail on him without mercy when he's committed himself, and becomes a partner in crime, I'm no fox of a Hellene. I wonder that he is the son of a man like Domitius, who was so shrewd in that old affair with me at Antioch."

*   *   *   *   *   *   *   *   *   *

So it came to pass that the next morning, long before Pratinas and Ahenobarbus met in the Forum and reviewed the steps taken in the words that gave Sesostris the key to the situation, Phaon was driving toward Præneste. Of course a mere freedman, on a journey preferably kept quiet, travelled in not the least state. He rode alone, but had borrowed from his patron two of those small but speedy Gallic horses called mammi, that whirled his gig over the Campagna at a rapid trot. Still there was no great call for haste. He wished to get to Præneste about dark, and there make a few inquiries as to the whereabouts and recent doings of Drusus. Pratinas had had considerable espionage kept up over his intended victim, and the last results of this detective work were to be reported to Phaon by the slaves of Ahenobarbus performing it. Perhaps there would be no real harm in driving straight through to Præneste in the open daylight, but it was better not to show himself until the right time. So it was that, halfway on the road, Phaon turned in to the tavern of the decaying little town of Gabii, gave his team to the hostler, and rested himself by fuming over the squalor and poor cooking of the inn.

II

Agias secured the fast Numidian from the stables of Gallus, and was soon away. His frequent journeys between Rome and Præneste, in service of Cornelia and Drusus, made him a fairly expert rider, and his noble mount went pounding past the milestones at a steady, untiring gallop. The young Hellene was all tingling with excitement and expectation; he would save Drusus; he would send the roses back into his beloved mistress's cheeks; and they would reward him, give him freedom; and then the future would be bright indeed.

But it grew late, fast as the horse bore him. He felt it his duty to press on with all speed to Præneste. He had still a very vague notion of the final form of the conspiracy, especially of the rôle assigned to Phaon. Of one thing he was certain: to intercept Phaon was to deprive Dumnorix of an essential ally; but how to intercept the wily freedman was nothing easy.

As the Numidian swept into Gabii, Agias drew rein, telling himself that the horse would make better speed for a little rest and baiting. The tavern court into which he rode was exceedingly filthy; the whole building was in a state of decay; the odours were indescribable. In the great public-room a carter was trolling a coarse ditty, while through the doorway ran a screaming serving-maid to escape some low familiarity.

A shock-headed boy with a lantern took Agias's bridle, and the Greek alighted; almost under his eyes the dim light fell on a handsome, two-horse gig, standing beside the entrance to the court. Agias gave the vehicle close attention.

"It belongs to a gentleman from Rome, now inside," explained the boy, "one horse went lame, and the veterinary[1] is coming." Agias's eye caught a very peculiar bend in the hollow in the neck-yoke. He had seen that carriage before, on the fashionable boulevards — along the Tiber, in the Campus Martius — the carriage of Lucius Ahenobarbus. Phaon was waiting in the tavern!

"Care for my horse at once," remarked Agias, a little abruptly. "Time presses." And he turned on his heel, and leaving the boy gaping after him, went into the squalid public-room of the tavern.

The landlord of the establishment, a small, red-faced, bustling man, was fussing over some lean thrushes roasting on a spit before the open fire that was roaring on the hearth. The landlady, lazy, muscular, corpulent, and high-voiced, was expostulating with a pedler who was trying to slip out without settling. Four other persons, slaves and peasants, were sitting on two low benches beside a small, circular table, and were busy pouring down the liquor which a young serving-boy brought them in tumbler-shaped cups, or eating greedily at loaves of coarse bread which they snatched from the table. It was so late that little light came into the room from the door and windows. The great fire tossed its red, flickering glow out into the apartment and cast a rosy halo over the hard brown marble pavement of the floor. Upon the dingy walls and rafters hung from pegs flitches of bacon, sausages, and nets of vegetables. Agias stopped in the doorway and

---

[1] *Equarius.*

waited till his eyes were fairly accustomed to the fire-light. Over in a remote corner he saw a lamp gleaming, and there, sprawling on a bench, beside a table of his own, well piled with food and drink, he distinguished in solitary majesty Phaon — too exquisite to mingle with the other guests of the tavern.

The landlord quickly noticed his new customer, and sprang up from the fire. Agias had on a coarse grey woollen cloak over his light tunic, and he drew his hood up so as partly to cover his face as he stepped into the room.

"*Salve!*" was the landlord's salutation. "What hospitality can the Elephant [1] afford you?"

The good host did not think Agias anything more by his dress than a common slave, and saw no need of excessive politeness.

Agias noticed that he was expected to join the other drinkers around the centre table.

"*Eho*, mine host!" cried he, letting the fire give one glint on a gold piece. "Can't you give me a seat at the other end of the room? I don't know these good people, and they won't thank me for thrusting myself on them."

"Certainly, certainly," exclaimed the landlord, all condescension. "There is a gentleman from Rome drinking by himself at that table over there. Perhaps he will not object."

Now was the crisis. Agias had seen Phaon many times with Lucius Ahenobarbus; but he was reasonably certain that the freedman had never degraded himself by taking any notice of the numerous slaves of Lentulus's household. Without waiting for the host to continue, he hastened over to the farther table, and exclaimed with all the effrontery at his command: —

---

[1] Inns were known by such signs.

"*Hem!* Phaon; don't you remember an old friend?"

The freedman for once was completely off his guard. He started up, stared at Agias, and began to mutter excuses for a very short memory.

"Well, well," cried Agias. "You *have* a poor recollection of faces! Don't you remember how Pratinas took you to the Big Eagle restaurant, down on the Vicus Jugarius, on the last Calends, and how you met me there, and what good Lesbian and Chian wine there was? None of your weak, sickening Italian stuff! Surely you remember Cleombrotus, from whom you won four hundred sesterces."

Phaon, who remembered the tavern, a visit, and winning four hundred sesterces at one time or another, tried to make himself believe that he won them from a young man, like the one before him, and that his name was Cleombrotus.

"Um! Yes, of course," he faltered. "I'm very glad to see you. What brings you here?"

"Business, business," complained Agias; "my master's a grain merchant with dealings at Puteoli, and he has sent me thither, to make some payments." Phaon pricked up his ears. "The Via Appia is more direct, but there is less chance of robbers by the Via Prænestina."

"I hope your master can trust you not to lighten his pouch on the way," remarked Phaon.

"Well," chuckled Agias, "he'll have to take his risk. If it's lost on the road, why, highwaymen stripped me. It is one of the fortunes of trade." Phaon was fully convinced that here was a fine chance to do some picking on his own account.

"Doubtless," he began, "you are not in such haste that you cannot enjoy one of those thrushes that sheep of a landlord is roasting for me. *Phui!* What a nasty place to have one's

horse give out in. You will give me at least a little company
to pass the time?"

Agias affected reluctance; then as the host brought up the
birds, savory and hot, on an earthen platter, he gracefully
accepted the invitation. The thrushes and the rest of the bill
of fare, bacon, sweet nut-flavoured oil, bread, and the cheap
wine of the Campagna were not unwelcome, though Phaon
cursed the coarse food roundly. Then, when hunger had
begun to yield, Phaon suggested that Cleombrotus "try to
secure revenge for his losses on the Calends"; and Agias,
nothing loth, replied that he did not wish to risk a great sum;
but if a denarius were worth playing for, there was no objection to venturing a few casts, and "he would ask the host to
bring them the gaming implements."

So the landlord brought dice and dice boxes, and Phaon —
who had come to the conclusion that he had to deal with a
light-headed bumpkin, who represented merely so much fair
plunder — began to play with a careless heart. The landlord
brought more and more flagons of wine, wine that was mixed
with little water and was consequently very heady. But
the game — with some veering of fortune — went the freedman's way. He won a denarius; then another; then a third;
lost a fourth time; won back everything and five denarii more;
and finally his opponent, heated with play, consented to stake
two gold pieces.

"What did you say a minute ago to the landlord?" muttered
Phaon, feeling that the undiluted liquor was getting the best
of him. "This wine is very strong. It makes my head
ache."

"*Phy!*" retorted Agias. "Who complains of good liquor?
I only told the host to set another lamp near us. Shall we
play again?"

"By Zeus!" exclaimed the delighted freedman. "Here I have cast four 'sixes' once more." And again he drained the beaker.

"*Vah!*" sniffed Agias. "Luck will turn at last. Let us play for real stakes. More wine, mine host! I will put down ten philippi. This will be worth winning or losing."

"As you say," gleefully chuckled Phaon, tossing the gold on the table. "Yes, more wine, I say too. One always enjoys play when his temples are all athrob."

Agias quietly reached over, took up his opponent's dice box, and rattled it, and appeared inspecting and fingering the *tali*.[1] "You have won your throws fairly," he said, handing it back. "Now let us invoke the decision of Fortune once more. A libation to the Genius of Good Luck!" And instead of spilling out a few drops only, he canted the flagon too far and spattered the wine on to the floor.

"Heracles!" growled Phaon, "what a poor hazard! I have thrown four 'ones'!"

"And I have all 'fours' and 'sixes,'" cried Agias, in delight, sweeping the money toward him.

"The gods blast my luck," muttered the freedman, "I shall be ruined at this rate." And he poured down more liquor. "I have hardly five philippi left."

"Come," shouted Agias, jumping up; "I make a fair offer. Your five philippi against all my winnings."

Phaon had a dim consciousness that he was getting very drunk, that he ought to start at once for Præneste, and that it was absolutely needful for him to have some money for bribes and gratuities if he was not to jeopardize seriously the success of his undertaking. But Agias stood before him exultant and provoking. The freedman could not be induced to confess to

---

[1] **Four-sided dice.**

himself that he had been badly fleeced by a fellow he expected to plunder. In drunken desperation he pulled out his last gold and threw it on the table.

"Play for that, and all the Furies curse me if I lose," he stormed.

Agias cast two "threes," two "fours."

"I must better that," thundered the freedman, slapping the tali out on to the table.

"'Ones' again," roared Agias; "all four! you have lost!"

Phaon sprang up in a storm of anger, and struck over the dice. "Three of them are 'sixes,'" he raged. "I have won! You got loaded dice from the landlord, just now, when he brought the wine!"

"Not at all, you cheating scoundrel," retorted Agias, who had already scooped in the money, "I have you fairly enough."

"Fair?" shouted Phaon, dashing down the dice again, "they are loaded! Lack-shame! Villain! Whipping-post! Tomb-robber! Gallows-bird! You changed them when you pretended to inspect them! Give me my money, thief, or — " and he took a menacing but unsteady step toward Agias.

The young Greek was ready for the emergency. He knew that Phaon was almost overcome with his wine, and had no dread of the issue. A stroke of his fist sent the freedman reeling back against the wall, all the wind pounded from his chest. "You born blackguard," coughed Phaon, "I won it." Agias was renewing the attack, when the landlord interfered. Seizing both of the gamesters by their cloaks, he pushed them out a side door into the court-yard. "Out with you!" cried the host. "Quarrel without, if you must! This is no place for brawls."

Phaon staggered a step or two out into the dark, then reeled and fell heavily upon the dirty pavement. Agias prodded him with his foot, but he was quite insensible. For the present he was harmless enough.

"My good host," said Agias, to the disquieted landlord, "I did not ask you to give us an unmixed wine and those dice for no purpose. This excellent gentleman here seems sadly in need of a bed, where he must stay for some time. But since I have won every sesterce he owns I must needs pay for his board. Take good care of him, and here are six philippi which are yours on condition that you keep him quiet until to-morrow at this time, and suffer no one coming from Rome to see him, or send him a message. To-morrow evening a messenger from Præneste will come here, and if your guest is still safe in your custody, you shall have six more gold pieces. At that time, doubtless, you can let him go; but don't violate my orders, or — "

"Your excellency pays like a senator," said the landlord, bowing, as he fingered the gold. "Trust me that your wishes shall be obeyed."

"They had better be," hinted Agias. "I am not what I seem by my dress. If you disobey, fear the wrath of a man before whom the world trembles!"

"He must be an agent of Cæsar, or Pompeius," muttered the landlord to himself. And Agias, having seen two serving-boys tugging Phaon's prone weight away to a secluded haymow, called for his refreshed Numidian, clattered out of the filthy court, and rode away into the night, with the stars burning above him.

CHAPTER IX

HOW GABINIUS MET WITH A REBUFF

I

PUBLIUS GABINIUS, the boon comrade of Lucius Aheno-barbus, differed little from many another man of his age in mode of life, or variety of aspirations. He had run through all the fashionable excitements of the day; was tired of horse-racing, peacock dinners, Oriental sweethearts; tired even of dice. And of late he had begun to grow morose, and his friends commenced to think him rather dull company.

But for some days he had found a new object of interest. With Lucius Ahenobarbus he had been at the Circus Flaminius, waiting for the races to begin, when he startled his friend by a clutch on the arm.

"Look!" was Gabinius's exclamation. "Is she not beautiful?"

He pointed to where Fabia, the Vestal, was taking her seat upon a cushion placed for her by a maid, and all the people around were standing, very respectfully, until she was seated. The priestess was clothed in perfect white,—dress, ribbons, fillet—a notable contrast to the brave show of purple, and scarlet, and blue mantles all about her.

"Beautiful? Yes," repeated Lucius, rather carelessly. "But such birds are not for our net."

"Are not?" repeated Gabinius, a little sharply. "What makes you so sure of that?"

"I hardly think that you will find my dear friend Quintu' Drusus's aunt, for so I understand she is," said Ahenobarbus, "very likely to reciprocate your devotion."

"And why not?" reiterated Gabinius, in a vexed tone.

"My dear fellow," answered Lucius, "I won't argue with you. There are plenty of women in Rome quite as handsome as Fabia, and much younger, who will smile on you. Don't meddle in a business that is too dangerous to be profitable."

But Gabinius had been wrought up to a pitch of amorous excitement, from which Ahenobarbus was the last one to move him. For days he had haunted the footsteps of the Vestal; had contrived to thrust himself as near to her in the theatre and circus as possible; had bribed one of the Temple servants to steal for him a small panel painting of Fabia; had, in fact, poured over his last romance all the ardour and passion of an intense, violent, uncontrolled nature. Gabinius was not the kind of a man either to analyze his motives, or express himself in the sobbing lyrics of a Catullus. He was thrilled with a fierce passion, and knew it, and it only. Therefore he merely replied to Lucius Ahenobarbus:—

"I can't help myself. What does Terence say about a like case? 'This indeed can, to some degree, be endured; night, passion, liquor, young blood, urged him on; it's only human nature.'"[1]

And all the afternoon, while the chariots ran, and wager on wager marked the excitement of the cloud of spectators, Gabinius had only eyes for one object, Fabia, who, perfectly unconscious of his state of fascination, sat with flushed cheeks and bright, eager eyes, watching the fortunes of the races, or turned now and then to speak a few words to little Livia, who was at her side. When the games were over, Gabinius strug-

[1] Terence, "Adelphœ." 467 and 471.

gled through the crowd after the Vestal, and kept near to her until she had reached her litter and the eight red-liveried Cappadocian porters bore her away. Gabinius continued to gaze after her until Fabia drew the leather curtains of her conveyance and was hid from sight.

"*Perpol!*" reflected Gabinius. "How utterly enslaved I am!"

* * * * * * * * * *

The following morning Fabia received a letter in a strange hand, asking her to come to a villa outside the Porta Capena, and receive a will from one Titus Denter, who lay dying. The receiving and safe-keeping of wills was a regular duty of Vestals, and Fabia at once summoned her litter, and started out of the city, along the Via Appia, until, far out in the suburbs where the houses were wide apart, she was set down before the country-house indicated. A stupid-appearing slave-boy received her at the gateway. The villa was old, small, and in very indifferent repair. The slave could not seem to explain whether it had been occupied of late, but hastened to declare that his master lay nigh to death. There was no porter in the outer vestibule.[1] The heavy inner door turned slowly on its pivot, by some inside force, and disclosed a small, darkened atrium, only lighted by a clear sunbeam from the opening above, that passed through and illumined a playing fountain. A single attendant stood in the doorway. He was a tall, gaunt man in servile dress, with a rather sickly smile on his sharp yellow face. Fabia alighted from her litter. There was a certain secluded uncanniness about the house, which made her dislike for an instant to enter. The slave in the door silently beckoned for her to come in. The Vestal informed her bearers that she was likely to be absent some little

[1] *Ostium.*

M

time, and they must wait quietly without, and not annoy a dying man with unseemly laughter or loud conversation. Then, without hesitancy, Fabia gathered her priestess's cloak about her, and boldly entered the strange atrium. As she did so, the attendant noiselessly closed the door, and what was further, shot home a bolt.

"There is no need for that," remarked the Vestal, who never before in her life had experienced such an unaccountable sense of disquietude.

"It is my habit always to push the bolt," said the slave, bowing, and leading the way toward the peristylium.

"You are Titus Denter's slave?" asked Fabia. The other nodded. "And your master is a very sick man?"

"Your most noble ladyship shall judge for herself."

"Take me to him at once, if he can see me."

"He is waiting."

The two went through the narrow passageway which led from the outer court of the atrium into the inner court of the peristylium. Fabia was surprised to see that here all the marble work had been carefully washed clean, the little enclosed garden was in beautiful order, and in various corners and behind some of the pillars were bronze and sculptured statues of really choice art. The slave stopped and pointed to a couch upholstered in crimson, beside the fish tank, where tame lampreys were rising for a bit of food.

"Take me to your master!" repeated Fabia, puzzled by the gesture. "I am not weary. You say he waits me?"

"He will be here," replied the servant, with another bow.

"Here?" exclaimed the Vestal, now really alarmed. "Here? He, a man sick unto death?"

"Certainly; here!" broke in a strange voice; and forth from behind a pillar stepped Publius Gabinius, all pomaded

and rouged, dressed only in a gauzy, many-folded scarlet
synthesis.[1]

Fabia gave a scream and sprang back in instinctive alarm.
In the twinkling of an eye it flashed over her that for some
purpose or other she had been trapped. Gabinius she knew
barely by sight; but his reputation had come to her ears, and
fame spoke nothing good of him. Yet even at the moment
when she felt herself in the most imminent personal peril, the
inbred dignity and composed hauteur of the Vestal did not
desert her. At the selfsame instant that she said to herself,
"Can I escape through the atrium before they can stop me?"
recovering from her first surprise, and with never a quiver of
eyelash or a paling of cheek, she was saying aloud, in a tone
cold as ice, "And indeed, most excellent Gabinius, you must
pardon me for being startled; for all that I know of you tells
me that you are likely to find a sombre Vestal sorry enough
company."

Gabinius had been counting coolly on a very noisy scene,
one of a kind he was fairly familiar with — an abundance of
screaming, expostulation, tearing of hair, and other manifes-
tations of feminine agony — to be followed, of course, by
ultimate submission to the will of all-dominant man. He
was not accustomed to have a woman look him fairly in the
eye and speak in tones, not of bootless fury, but of superior
scorn. And his answer was painfully lacking in the ascendant
volubility which would have befitted the occasion.

"Forgive me; pardon; it was of course necessary to resort to
some subterfuge in order — in order to prevent your attendants
from becoming suspicious."

Fabia cast a glance behind her, and saw that before the two
doors leading to the atrium her conductor and another tall

---

[1] The "dinner coat" of the Romans.

slave had placed themselves; but she replied in a tone a little more lofty, if possible, than before: —

"I cannot well, sir, understand you. Are you a friend of Titus Denter, who is sick? I do not see that any subterfuge is necessary when I am to receive the deposit of a will from a dying man. It is a recognized duty of my office."

Gabinius was still more at a loss.

"You should certainly understand, lady," he began, cursing himself for having to resort to circumlocutions, "that this is my own villa, and I have not the pleasure of knowing Titus Denter. I sent the letter because — "

"Because, my worthy sir," interrupted Fabia, not however raising her voice in the least, "you are weary of Greek flute-players for sweethearts or such Roman young ladies as admire either the ointments or the pimples of your face, and consequently seek a little diversion by laying snares for a sacred Vestal."

Gabinius at last found free use for his tongue.

"Oh, lady; Lady Fabia," he cried, stretching out his arms and taking a step nearer, "don't misjudge me so cruelly! I will forsake anything, everything, for you! I have nothing to dream of day or night but your face. You have served your thirty years in the Temple, and can quit its service. Why entertain any superstitious scruple against doing what the law allows? Come with me to Egypt; to Spain; to Parthia; anywhere! Only do not reject me and my entreaties! I will do anything for your sake!"

Critical as was her situation, Fabia could not refrain from a sense of humour, when she saw and heard this creature — the last intimate she would select in the world — pressing his suit with such genuine passion. When she answered, an exasperating smile was on her lips.

"By Castor!" she replied, "the noble Gabinius is not a bad tragedian. If he has nothing further to inform me than that I am favoured by his good graces, I can only decline his proposals with humble firmness, and depart."

"By the immortal gods!" cried Gabinius, feeling that he and not his would-be victim were like to go into a frenzy, "you shan't go! I have you here. And here you shall remain until I have your word that you will quit the Temple service and fly with me to Egypt. If you won't have me as your slave, I'll have you as your master!" And again he advanced.

"What restrains me here?" queried Fabia, sternly, the blood sinking from her cheeks, but by step or by glance quailing not in the least. "Who dare restrain or offer harm to a Vestal of the Roman Republic?"

"I!" shouted Gabinius in mad defiance, with a menacing gesture.

Fabia took a step toward him, and instinctively he fell back.

"You?" she repeated, her black eyes, ablaze with the fire of a holy indignation, searching Gabinius's impure heart through and through. "You, little man? Are you fond of death, and yet lack courage to drink the poison yourself?"

"I dare anything!" cried Gabinius, getting more and more uncontrolled. "This is my house. These are my slaves. The high walls will cut off any screams you may utter in this court. I have you in my power. You have placed yourself in my hands by coming here. Refuse to do as I say, and a charge will be laid against you before the *pontifices*,[1] that you have broken the vow which binds every Vestal. All the appearances will be against you, and you know what will follow then!"

---

[1] College of chief priests.

Fabia grew a shade paler, if it were possible, than before.

"I know," she replied, still very gently, "that an unfaithful Vestal is buried alive in the Campus Sceleratus; but I know, too, that her seducer is beaten to death with rods. Accuse me, or attack me, and whatever be *my* fate, I can say that which will send your black soul down to Tartarus with guilt enough for Minos to punish. Your delicately anointed skin would be sadly bruised by the stripes falling upon it. And now, if these creatures will stand one side, I will leave you."

And Fabia drew her mantle about her, and walked straight past the awestruck slaves into the atrium, where she unbolted the door and passed out. Gabinius stood gazing after her, half-fascinated, half-dazed. Only when the door closed did he burst out to one of the slaves: —

"Timid dog, why did you let her escape?"

"Dominus," whimpered the menial, "why did *you* let her escape?"

"Insolence!" cried Gabinius, seizing a staff, and beating first one, then the other, of his servants indiscriminately; and so he continued to vent his vexation, until Fabia's litter was well inside the Porta Capena.

II

Fabia had thus escaped from the clutches of Gabinius, and the latter was sullen and foiled. But none the less the Vestal was in a tremor of fear for the consequences of her meeting with the libertine. She knew that Gabinius was determined, dexterous, and indefatigable; that he was baffled, but not necessarily driven to throw over his illicit quest. And Fabia realized keenly that going as she had unattended into a strange house, and remaining there some time with no friendly eye to bear witness to her actions, would count terribly against her, if Gabinius was driven to bay. She dared not, as she would gladly have done, appear before the pontifices and demand of them that they mete out due punishment on Gabinius for grossly insulting the sanctity of a Vestal. Her hope was that Gabinius would realize that he could not incriminate her without ruining himself, and that he had been so thoroughly terrified on reflection as to what might be the consequences to himself, if he tried to follow the intrigue, that he would prudently drop it. These considerations hardly served to lighten the gloom which had fallen across Fabia's life. It was not so much the personal peril that saddened her. All her life she had heard the ugly din of the world's wickedness pass harmlessly over her head, like a storm dashing at the doors of some secluded dwelling that shielded its inhabitants from the tempest. But now she had come personally face to face with the demon of impurity; she had felt the fetid touch almost upon herself; and it hurt, it sickened her. Therefore it was that the other Vestals marvelled, asking what change had come over their companion, to quench the mild sunshine of her life; and Fabia held little Livia very long and very closely in her arms, as if it were a solace to feel near her an innocent little thing "unspotted of the world."

All this had happened a very few days before the breathless Agias came to inform Fabia of the plot against her nephew. Perhaps, as with Cornelia, the fact that one near and dear was in peril aided to make the consciousness of her own unhappiness less keen. None could question Fabia's resolute energy. She sent Agias on his way, then hurried off in her litter in quest of Caius Marcellus, the consul. Æmilius Paulus, the other consul, was a nonentity, not worth appealing to, since he had virtually abdicated office upon selling his neutrality to Cæsar. But Marcellus gave her little comfort.

She broke in upon the noble lord, while he was participating in a drunken garden-party in the Gardens of Lucullus. The consul — hardly sober enough to talk coherently — had declared that it was impossible to start any troops that day to Præneste. "To-morrow, when he had time, he would consider the matter." And Fabia realized that the engine of government would be very slow to set in motion in favour of a marked Cæsarian.

But she had another recourse, and hastened her litter down one of the quieter streets of the Subura, where was the modest house occupied by Julius Cæsar before he became Pontifex Maximus. This building was now used by the Cæsarian leaders as a sort of party headquarters. Fabia boldly ordered the porter to summon before her Curio — who she was sure was in the house. Much marvelling at the visit of a Vestal, the slave obeyed, and in a few moments that tribune was in her presence.

Caius Scribonius Curio was probably a very typical man of his age. He was personally of voluptuous habits, fearfully extravagant, endowed with very few scruples and a very weak sense of right and wrong. But he was clear-headed, energetic, a good orator, a clever reasoner, an astute handler of men, courageous, versatile, full of recourse, and on the whole above the commission of any really glaring moral infraction. He was now in his early prime, and he came before Fabia as a man tall, athletic, deep-chested, deep-voiced, with a regular profile, a clear, dark complexion, curly hair carefully dressed, freshly shaven, and in perfect toilet. It was a pleasure, in short, to come in contact with such a vigorous, aggressive personality, be the dark corners of his life what they might.

Curio yielded to no man in his love of Lucrine oysters and good Cæcuban wine. But he had been spending little time on the dining couch that evening. In fact he had at that moment in his hand a set of tablets on which he had been writing.

"*Salve! Domina!*" was his greeting, "what unusual honour is this which brings the most noble Vestal to the trysting spot of us poor Populares."

And, with the courtesy of a gentleman of the world, he offered Fabia an armchair.

"Caius Curio," said the Vestal, wasting very few words, "do you know my nephew, Quintus Drusus of Præneste?"

"It is an honour to acknowledge friendship with such an excellent young man," said Curio, bowing.

"I am glad to hear so. I understand that he has already suffered no slight calamity for adhering to your party."

"*Vah!*" and the tribune shrugged his shoulders. "Doubtless he has had a disagreeable time with the consul-elect, but from all that I can hear, the girl he lost was hardly one to make his life a happy one. It's notorious the way she has displayed her passion for young Lucius Ahenobarbus, and we all know what kind of a man *he* is. But I may presume to remark that your ladyship would hardly come here simply to remind me of this."

"No," replied Fabia, directly, "I have come here to appeal to you to do something for me which Marcellus the consul was too drunk to try to accomplish if he would."

Fabia had struck the right note. Only a few days before Appius Claudius, the censor, had tried to strike Curio's name from the rolls of the Senate. Piso, the other censor, had resisted. There had been an angry debate in the Senate, and Marcellus had inveighed against the Cæsarian tribune, and had joined in a furious war of words. The Senate had voted to allow Curio to keep his seat; and the anti-Cæsarians had paraded in mourning as if the vote were a great calamity.

Curio's eyes lit up with an angry fire.

"Lump of filth! Who was he, to disoblige you!"

"You will understand," said Fabia, still quietly; and then briefly she told of the conspiracy against the life of Drusus, so far as she had gathered it.

"Where did you learn all this," queried Curio, "if I may venture to ask?"

"From Agias, the slave of Cornelia, niece of Lentulus."

"But what is Drusus to her?" demanded the marvelling tribune.

"He is everything to her. She has been trying to win her way into Ahenobarbus's confidence, and learn all of the plot."

A sudden light seemed to break over the face of the politician. He actually smiled with relieved pleasure, and cried, "*Papœ!* Wonderful! I may be the farthest of all the world from Diogenes the Cynic; but a man cannot go through life, unless he has his eyes shut, and not know that there are different kinds of women. I was sorry enough to have to feel that a girl like Cornelia was becoming one of Clodia's coterie. After all, the world isn't so bad as we make it out to be, if it is Curio the profligate who says it."

"But Drusus, my nephew?" exclaimed Fabia. "He is in frightful danger. You know Dumnorix will have a great band of gladiators, and there is no force in Præneste that can be counted on to restrain him."

"My dear lady," said Curio, laughing, "I am praising the happy Genius that brought you here. We Cæsarians are taught by our leaders never to desert a friend in need; and Drusus has been a very good friend to us, especially by using all his influence, very successfully, for our cause among the Prænestians and the people of those parts. When did you say that Dumnorix would pass through the town?"

"Early to-morrow, possibly," replied the Vestal.

"*Phui!* Dismiss all care. I'll find out at once how many gladiators he took with him to Anagnia. Some of his gang will be killed in the games there, and more will be wounded and weak or disabled. I am tribune, and I imagine I ought not to be out of the city over night,[1] but before daybreak to-morrow I will take Antonius and Sallustius and Quintus Cassius; and perhaps I can get Balbus and our other associates to go. We will arm a few slaves and freedmen; and it will be strange indeed if we cannot scatter to the four winds Dumnorix's gladiators, before they have accomplished any mischief."

"The gods reward you!" said Fabia, simply. "I will go back to the Temple, and pray that my nephew be kept from harm; and you also, and your friends who will defend him."

Curio stood in the atrium a long time after the Vestal had left.

"The gods reward you!" he repeated. "So *she* believes in the gods, that there are gods, and that they care for us struggling men. Ah! Caius, Caius Curio; if the mob had murdered you that day you protected Cæsar after he spoke in the Senate in favour of the Catilinarians, where would you be to-day? Whence have you come? Whither do you go? What assurance have you that you can depend on anything, but your own hand and keen wits? What is to become of you, if you are knocked on the head in that adventure to-morrow? And yet that woman believes there are gods! What educated man is there that does? Perhaps we would, if we led the simple lives our fathers did, and that woman lives. Enough of this! I must be over letters to Cæsar at Ravenna till midnight: and then at morn off to gallop till our horses are foundered."

[1] This was the law, that the tribunes might always be ready to render help (*auxilium*) to the distressed.

CHAPTER X

MAMERCUS GUARDS THE DOOR

I

Agias left Phaon in the clutches of the landlord and his subordinates and was reasonably certain that since the freedman had not a farthing left with which to bribe his keepers, he was out of harm's way for the time being. The moon was risen, and guided by its light the young slave flew on toward Præneste without incident. Whatever part of the conspirator's plans depended on Phaon was sure to collapse. For the rest, Agias could only warn Drusus, and have the latter arm his clients and slaves, and call in his friends from the town. With such precautions Dumnorix could hardly venture to risk himself and his men, whatever might be the plot.

Thus satisfied in mind, Agias arrived at the estate of the Drusi, close to Præneste, and demanded admittance, about two hours before midnight. He had some difficulty in stirring up the porter, and when that worthy at last condescended to unbar the front door, the young Greek was surprised and dismayed to hear that the master of the house had gone to visit a farm at Lanuvium, a town some fifteen miles to the south. Agias was thunderstruck; he had not counted on Drusus being absent temporarily. But perhaps his very absence would cause the plot to fail.

"And what time will he return?" asked Agias.

"What time?" replied the porter, with a sudden gleam of intelligence darting up in his lack-lustre eyes. "We expect he will return early to-morrow morning. But the road from Lanuvium is across country and you have to skirt the Alban Mount. He may be rather late in arriving, drives he ever so hard."

"Hercules!" cried the agitated messenger. "My horse is blown, and I don't know the road in the dark. Send, I pray you — by all the gods — to Lanuvium this instant."

"Aye," drawled the porter. "And wherefore at such an hour?"

"It's for life and death!" expostulated Agias.

The porter, who was a thick-set, powerful man, with a bristly black beard, and a low forehead crowned by a heavy shock of dark hair, at this instant thrust out a capacious paw, and seized Agias roughly by the wrist.

"Ha, ha, ha, young cut-throat! I wondered how long this would last on your part! Well, now I must take you to Falto, to get the beginning of your deserts."

"Are you mad, fellow?" bawled Agias, while the porter, grasping him by the one hand, and the dim lamp by the other, dragged him into the house. "Do you know who I am? or what my business is? Do you want to have your master murdered?"

"*Perpol!* Not in the least. That's why I do as I do. Tell your story to Falto. *Eho!* What's that you've got under your cloak?" And he pounced upon a small dagger poor Agias had carried as a precaution against eventualities. "I imagine you are accustomed to use a little knife like this." And the fellow gave a gleeful chuckle.

It was in vain that Agias expostulated and tried to explain. The porter kept him fast as a prisoner, and in a few moments by his shouts had aroused the whole sleeping household, and

stewards, freedmen, and slaves came rushing into the atrium.
Candelabra blazed forth. Torches tossed. Maids screamed.
Many tongues were raised in discordant shout and question.
At last order was in some measure restored. Agias found him
self before a tribunal composed of Falto, the subordinate *villicus*,[1] as chief judge, and two or three freedmen to act in
capacity of assessors. All of this bench were hard, grey-
headed, weazened agriculturists, who looked with no very
lenient eye upon the delicate and handsome young prisoner
before them. Agias had to answer a series of savagely pro-
pounded questions which led he knew not whither, and which
he was almost too bewildered to answer intelligently. The true
state of the case only came over him by degrees. These were
the facts. Drusus had known that there was a conspiracy
against his life, and had taken precautions against poisoning
or being waylaid by a small band of cut-throats such as he
imagined Ahenobarbus might have sent to despatch him. He
had not expected an attack on the scale of Dumnorix's whole
band ; and he had seen no reason why, accompanied by the
trusty Mamerci and Cappadox, he should not visit his Lanu-
vian farm. The whole care of guarding against conspirators
had been left to Marcus Mamercus, and that worthy ex-war-
rior had believed he had taken all needed precautions. He
had warned the porter and the other slaves and freedmen to
be on the lookout for suspicious characters, and had let just
enough of the plot — as it was known to him — leak out, to put
all the household on the *qui vive* to apprehend any would-be
assassin of their beloved young master. But with that fatuity
which often ruins the plans of "mice and men," he had failed
to inform even his subordinate Falto of the likelihood of Agias
arriving from Rome. It had obviously been desirable that it

---

[1] Farm steward.

should not be bruited among the servants that Cornelia and Drusus were still communicating, and when Agias was haled into the atrium, his only identification was by some over-zealous slave, who declared that the prisoner belonged to the familia of Lentulus Crus, the bitter foe of their master.

With senses unduly alert the porter, as soon as he was aroused from his slumbers, had noticed that evening that Agias had come on some unusual business, and that he was obviously confused when he learned that Drusus was not at home. With his suspicions thus quickened, every word the luckless Greek uttered went to incriminate him in the mind of the porter. Agias was certainly an accomplice in the plot against Drusus, sent to the house at an unseasonable hour, on some dark errand. The porter had freely protested this belief to Falto and his court, and to support his indictment produced the captured dagger, the sure sign of a would-be murderer. Besides, a large sum of gold was found on Agias's person; his fast Numidian horse was still steaming before the door — and what honest slave could travel thus, with such a quantity of money?

Agias tried to tell his story, but to no effect; Falto and his fellow-judges dryly remarked to one another that the prisoner was trying to clear himself, by plausibly admitting the existence of the conspiracy, but of course suppressing the real details. Agias reasoned. He was met with obstinate incredulity. He entreated, prayed, implored. The prejudiced rustics mocked at him, and hinted that they cared too much for their patron to believe any tale that such a manifest impostor might tell them. Pausanias, the Mamerci, and Cappadox, the only persons, besides Drusus, who could readily identify him, were away at Lanuvium.

The verdict of guilty was so unanimous that it needed little or no discussion; and Falto pronounced sentence.

"Mago," to the huge African, "take this wretched boy to the slave-prison; fetter him heavily. On your life do not let him escape. Give him bread and water at sunrise. When Master Drusus returns he will doubtless bid us crucify the villain, and in the morning Natta the carpenter shall prepare two beams for the purpose."

Agias comforted himself by reflecting that things would hardly go to that terrible extremity; but it was not reassuring to hear Ligus, the crabbed old cellarer, urge that he be made to confess then and there under the cat. Falto overruled the proposition. "It was late, and Mamercus was the man to extort confession." So Agias found himself thrust into a filthy cell, lighted only by a small chink, near the top of the low stone wall, into which strayed a bit of moonlight. The night he passed wretchedly enough, on a truss of fetid straw; while the tight irons that confined him chafed his wrists and ankles. Needless to add, he cursed roundly all things human and heavenly, before he fell into a brief, troubled sleep. In the morning Mago, who acted as jailer, brought him a pot of water and a saucer of uncooked wheat porridge;[1] and informed him, with a grin, that Natta was making the beams ready. Agias contented himself by asking Mago to tell Drusus about him, as soon as the master returned. "You are very young to wish to die," said the Libyan, grimly. Agias did not argue. Mago left him. By climbing up a rude stool, Agias could peer through the loophole, which by great luck commanded a fairly ample view of the highway. Drusus he naturally expected would come from the south, toward Præneste. And thence every moment he trembled lest Dumnorix's gang should appear in sight. But every distant dust-cloud for a long time resolved itself sooner or later into a shepherd with a flock of unruly

[1] *Puls*, the primitive Italian food.

sheep, or a wagon tugged by a pair of mules and containing a single huge wine-skin. Drusus came not; Dumnorix came not. Agias grew weary of watching, and climbed painfully down from the stool to eat his raw porridge. Hardly had he done so than a loud clatter of hoofs sounded without. With a bound that twisted his confined ankles and wrists sadly, Agias was back at his post. A single rider on a handsome bay horse was coming up from the direction of Rome. As he drew near to the villa, he pulled at his reins, and brought his steed down to a walk. The horseman passed close to the loophole, and there was no mistaking his identity. Agias had often seen that pale, pimpled face, and those long effeminate curls in company with Lucius Ahenobarbus. The rider was Publius Gabinius, and the young Greek did not need to be told that his coming boded no good to Drusus. Gabinius looked carefully at the villa, into the groves surrounding it, and then up and down the highway. Then he touched the spur to his mount, and was gone.

Agias wrung his manacled hands. Drusus would be murdered, Cornelia's happiness undone, and he himself would become the slave of Lucius Ahenobarbus, who, when he had heard Phaon's story, would show little enough of mercy. He cursed the suspicious porter, cursed Falto, cursed every slave and freedman on the estate, cursed Mamercus for not leaving some word about the possibility of his coming from Rome. Agias's imprecations spent themselves in air; and he was none the happier. Would Drusus never come? The time was drifting on. The sun had been up three or more hours. At any instant the gladiators might arrive.

Then again there was a clatter of hoofs, at the very moment when Agias had again remounted to the loophole. There were voices raised in questions and greetings; slave-boys were scampering to and fro to take the horses; Drusus with Pausanias and the Mamerci had returned from Lanuvium. Agias pressed his head out the loophole and screamed to attract attention. His voice could not penetrate the domestic hubbub. Drusus was standing shaking hands with a couple of clients and evidently in a very good humour over some blunt rustic compliment. Mago was nowhere to be seen. Agias glanced up the road toward Præneste. The highway was straight and fairly level, but as it went over a hill-slope some little way off, what was that he saw upon it? — the sun flashing on bright arms, which glinted out from the dust-cloud raised by a considerable number of men marching!

"Drusus! Master Drusus!" Agias threw all his soul into the cry. As if to blast his last hope, Drusus hastily bowed away the salves and aves of the two clients, turned, and went into the villa. Agias groaned in agony. A very few moments would bring Dumnorix to the villa, and the young slave did not doubt that Gabinius was with the lanista to direct the attack. Agias tore at his chains, and cursed again, calling on all the Furies of Tartarus to confound the porter and Falto. Suddenly before the loophole passed a slave damsel of winning face and blithesome manner, humming to herself a rude little ditty, while she balanced a large earthen water-pot on her head. It was Chloë, whom the reader has met in the opening scene of this book, though Agias did not know her name.

"By all the gods, girl!" he cried frantically, "do you want to have your master slaughtered before your very eyes?"

Chloë stopped, a little startled at this voice, almost from under her feet.

"Oh, you, Master Assassin!" she sneered. "Do you want

to repeat those pretty stories of yours, such as I heard you tell last night?"

"Woman," cried Agias, with all the earnestness which agony and fear could throw into face and voice, "go this instant! Tell Master Drusus that Dumnorix and his gang are not a furlong[1] away. They mean to murder him. Say that I, Agias, say so, and he, at least, will believe me. You yourself can see the sun gleaming on their steel as they march down the hill."

Perhaps it was the sight which Agias indicated, perhaps it was his earnest words, perhaps it was his handsome face — Chloë was very susceptible to good looks — but for some cause she put down the pot and was off, as fast as her light heels could carry her, toward the house.

II

Drusus had ridden hard to get back early from Lanuvium and write some letters to Cornelia, for he had expected that Agias would come on that very afternoon, on one of his regular, though private, visits; and he wished to be able to tell Cornelia that, so long a time had elapsed since he had been warned against Ahenobarbus and Pratinas, and as no attempt at all had been made on his life, her fears for him were probably groundless and the plot had been for some cause abandoned. Drusus himself was weary, and was glad to shake off the little knot of clients and retire to his chamber, preparatory for a bath and a change of clothes. He had seen Falto, but the latter deemed it best not to trouble his patron at the time by mentioning the prisoner. Mago, too, concluded that it was best to defer executing his promise. Drusus was just letting Cappadox take off his cloak, when the shrill voice of Chloë

- **About 606⅓ English foot**

was heard outside the door, expostulating with the boy on guard.

"I must see the dominus at once. It's very important."

"Don't you see, you idiot, that you can't while he's dressing?"

"I *must!*" screamed Chloë. And, violating every law of subordination and decorum, she threw open the door.

Cappadox flew to eject her, but Chloë's quick tongue did its work.

"A lad who calls himself Agias is chained in the ergastulum. He says some gladiators are going to attack the house, and will be here in a moment! Oh, I am so frightened!" and the poor girl threw her mantle over her head, and began to whimper and sob.

"Agias!" shouted Drusus, at the top of his voice. "In the ergastulum? *Per deos immortales!* What's this? Mamercus! Falto!"

And the young master rushed out of the room, Cappadox, who like lightning had caught up a sword, following him.

Falto came running from the stables; Mamercus from the garden. Drusus faced his two subordinates, and in an eye's twinkling had taken in the situation. Mamercus, who felt within himself that he, by his oversight, had been the chief blunderer, to vent his vexation smote Falto so sound a cuff that the under villicus sprawled his full length.

"Go to the ergastulum and fetch Agias this instant," cried Drusus, in thundering accents, to the trembling Mago, who had appeared on the scene.

Mago disappeared like magic, but in an instant a din was rising from the front of the house,—cries, blows, clash of steel. Into the peristylium, where the angry young master was standing, rushed the old slave woman, Laïs.

"*Hei! hei!*" she screamed, "they are breaking in! Mon·
sters! a hundred of them! They will kill us all!"

Drusus grew calm in an instant.

"Barricade the doors to the atrium!" he commanded, "while
I can put on my armour. You, Mamercus, are too old for this
kind of work; run and call in the field-hands, the clients, and
the neighbours. Cappadox, Falto, and I can hold the doors
till aid comes."

"I run?" cried the veteran, in hot incredulity, while with
his single hand he tore from its stout leather wall-fastenings
a shield that had been beaten with Punic swords at the
Metaurus.[1] "I run?" he repeated, while a mighty crash told
that the front door had given way, and the attackers were
pouring into the atrium. And the veteran had thrust a venerable helmet over his grizzled locks, and was wielding his shield
with his handless left arm, while a good Spanish short-sword
gleamed in his right hand.

The others had not been idle. Cappadox had barred both
doors leading into the front part of the house. Drusus had
armed, and Falto, — a more loyal soul than whom lived not, —
burning to retrieve his blunder, had sprung to his patron's side,
also in shield and helm.

"They will soon force these doors," said Drusus, quietly,
growing more composed as closer and closer came the actual
danger. "Falto and I will guard the right. Cappadox and
you, Mamercus, if you will stay, must guard the left. Some
aid must come before a great while."

But again the veteran whipped out an angry oath, and
thundered, "You stay, you soft-fingered Quintus! You stay
and face those German giants! Why, you are the very man

---

[1] The great battle won in 207 B.C. over Hasdrubal.

they are after! Leave fighting to an old soldier! Take him away, Cappadox, if you love him!"

"I will never leave!" blazed forth Drusus. "My place is here. A Livian always faces his foes. Here, if needs be, I will die." But before he could protest further, Cappadox had caught him in his powerful arms, and despite his struggles was running with him through the rear of the house.

Pandemonium reigned in the atrium. The gladiators were shivering fine sculptures, ripping up upholstery, swearing in their uncouth Celtic or German dialects, searching everywhere for their victim in the rooms that led off the atrium. A voice in Latin was raising loud remonstrance.

"*Ædepol!* Dumnorix, call off your men! Phaon hasn't led our bird into the net. We shall be ruined if this keeps on! Drusus isn't here!"

"By the Holy Oak, Gabinius," replied another voice, in barbarous Latin, "what I've begun I'll end! I'll find Drusus yet; and we won't leave a soul living to testify against us! You men, break down that door and let us into the rest of the house!"

Mamercus heard a rush down one of the passages leading to the peristylium. The house was almost entirely deserted, except by the shrieking maids. The clients and freedmen and male slaves were almost all in the fields. The veteran, Falto, and Pausanias, who had come in, and who was brave enough, but nothing of a warrior, were the only defenders of the peristylium.

"You two," shouted Mamercus, "guard the other door! Move that heavy chest against it. Pile the couch and cabinet on top. This door I will hold."

There was the blow of a heavy mace on the portal, and the wood sprang out, and the pivots started.

"Leave this alone," roared Mamercus, when his two helpers paused, as if to join him. "Guard your own doorway!"

"Down with it!" bellowed the voice of the leaders without. "Don't let the game escape! Strike again!"

Crash! And the door, beaten from its fastenings by a mighty stroke, tumbled inward on to the mosaic pavement of the peristylium. The light was streaming bright and free into that court, but the passageway from the atrium was shrouded in darkness. Mamercus, sword drawn, stood across the entrance.

"By the god Tarann [1]!" shouted Dumnorix, who from the rear of his followers was directing the attack. "Here is a stout old game-cock! Out of the way, greybeard! We'll spare you for your spirit. Take him, some of you, alive!"

Two gigantic, blond Germans thrust their prodigious bodies through the doorway. Mamercus was no small man, but slight he seemed before these mighty Northerners.

The Germans had intended to seize him in their naked hands, but something made them swing their ponderous long swords and then, two flashes from the short blade in the hand of the veteran, and both the giants were weltering across the threshold, their breasts pierced and torn by the Roman's murderous thrusts.

"*Habet!*" cried Mamercus. "A fair hit! Come on, you scum of the earth; come on, you German and Gallic dogs; do you think I haven't faced the like of you before? Do you think your great bulks and fierce mustaches will make a soldier of Marius quiver? Do you want to taste Roman steel again?"

And then there was a strange sight. A phantasm seemed to have come before every member of that mad, murderous band:

[1] The Gallic thunder-god.

for they saw, as it were, in the single champion before them, a long, swaying line of men of slight stature like him; of men who dashed through their phalanxes and spear hedges; who beat down their chieftains; whom no arrow fire, no sword-play, no stress of numbers, might stop; but who charged home with pilum and short-sword, and defeated the most valorous enemy.

"Ha! Dogs!" taunted Mamercus, "you have seen Romans fight before, else you were not all here, to make sport for our holiday!"

"He is Tyr,[1] the 'one-armed,' who put his left hand in the jaws of Fenris-wolf!" cried a German, shrinking back in dread. "A god is fighting us!"

"Fools!" shouted Gabinius from a distance. "At him, and cut him down!"

"Cut him down!" roared Dumnorix, who had wits enough to realize that every instant's delay gave Drusus time to escape, or collect help.

There was another rush down the passage; but at the narrow doorway the press stopped. Mamercus fought as ten. His shield and sword were everywhere. The Roman was as one inspired; his eyes shone bright and clear; his lips were parted in a grim, fierce smile; he belched forth rude soldier oaths that had been current in the army of fifty years before. Thrusting and parrying, he yielded no step, he sustained no wound. And once, twice, thrice his terrible short-sword found its sheath in the breast of a victim. In impotent rage the gladiators recoiled a second time.

"Storm the other door!" commanded Dumnorix.

The two defenders there had undertaken to pile up furniture against it; but a few blows beat down the entire barrier. Falto and Pausanias stood to their posts stoutly enough; but

[1] A Germanic war-god.

there was no master-swordsman to guard this entrance.   The
first gladiator indeed went down with a pierced neck, but the
next instant Falto was beside him, atoning for his stupid folly,
the whole side of his head cleft away by a stroke from a Gallic
long-sword.

"One rush and we have the old man surrounded," exhorted
Dumnorix, when only Pausanias barred the way.

There was a growl and a bound, and straight at the foremost
attacker flew Argos, Mamercus's great British mastiff, who had
silently slipped on to the scene.   The assailant fell with the
dog's fangs in his throat.   Again the gladiators recoiled, and
before they could return to the charge, back into the peristylium rushed Drusus, escaped from Cappadox, with that
worthy and Mago and Agias, just released, at his heels.

"Here's your man!" cried Gabinius, who still kept dis-
creetly in the rear.

"Freedom and ten *sestertia*[1] to the one who strikes Drusus
down," called Dumnorix, feeling that at last the game was in
his hands.

But Mamercus had made of his young patron an apt pupil.
All the fighting blood of the great Livian house, of the consulars and triumphators, was mantling in Drusus's veins, and
he threw himself into the struggle with the deliberate courage
of an experienced warrior.   His short-sword, too, found its
victims; and across Falto's body soon were piled more.   And
now Drusus was not alone.   For in from the barns and fields
came running first the servants from the stables, armed with
mattocks and muck-forks, and then the farm-hands with their
scythes and reaping hooks.

"We shall never force these doors," exclaimed Gabinius, in
despair, as he saw the defenders augmenting.

[1] About $400.

Dumnorix turned to his men.

"Go, some of you. Enter from behind! Take this rabble from the rear. In fair fight we can soon master it."

A part of the gladiators started to leave the atrium, Gabinius with them. An instant later he had rushed back in blank dismay.

"Horsemen! They are dismounting before the house. There are more than a score of them. We shall be cut to pieces."

"We have more than fifty," retorted Dumnorix, viciously. "I will sacrifice them all, rather than have the attack fail! — " But before he could speak further, to the din of the fighting at the doors of the peristylium was added a second clamour without. And into the atrium, sword in hand, burst Caius Curio, and another young, handsome, aquiline-featured man, dressed in a low-girt tunic, with a loose, coarse mantle above it, — a man known to history as Marcus Antonius, or "Marc Antony"; and at their backs were twenty men in full armour.

The courage of the lanista had failed him. Already Drusus's reinforcements in the peristylium had become so numerous and so well armed that the young chieftain was pushing back the gladiators and rapidly assuming the offensive. Gabinius was the first to take flight. He plunged into one of the rooms off the atrium, and through a side door gained the open. The demoralized and beaten gladiators followed him, like a flock of sheep. Only Dumnorix and two or three of his best men stood at the exit long enough to cover, in some measure, the retreat.

Once outside, the late assailants gained a temporary respite, owing to the fact that the defenders had been disorganized by their very victory.

"We have lost," groaned Gabinius, as the lanista drew his men together in a compact body, before commencing his retreat.

"We are alive," growled Dumnorix.

"We cannot go back to Rome," moaned the other. "We are all identified. No bribe or favour can save us now."

"A robber's life is still left," retorted Dumnorix, "and we must make of it what we can. Some of my men know these parts, where they have been slaves, before coming to my hands. We must strike off for the mountains, if we live to get there."

All that day the country was in a turmoil. The Prænestean senate had met in hasty session, and the *decurions*[1] ordered the entire community under arms to hunt down the disturbers of the peace. Not until nightfall did Dumnorix and a mere remnant of his band find themselves able, under the shadow of the darkness, to shake off the pursuit. Gabinius was still with him. Curio and Antonius had chased them down with their horsemen; many of the gladiators had been slain, many more taken. For the survivors only the life of outlaws remained. The fastnesses of the Apennines were their sole safety; and thither — scarce daring to stop to pillage for victuals — they hurried their weary steps.

III

Lucius Ahenobarbus spent that day in frightful anxiety. One moment he was fingering Drusus's money bags; the next haunted by the murdered man's ghost. When he called on Cornelia, her slaves said she had a headache and would receive no one. Pratinas held aloof. No news all day — the suspense became unendurable. He lived through the following night harassed by waking visions of every conceivable calamity; but toward morning fell asleep, and as was his wont, awoke late. The first friend he met on the street was Calvus, the young poet and orator.

[1] Local municipal magistrates.

"Have you heard the news from Præneste?" began Calvus.

"News? What news?"

"Why, how Dumnorix's gang of gladiators attacked the villa of your distant relative, Quintus Drusus, and were beaten off, while they tried to murder him. A most daring attempt! But you will hear all about it. I have a case at the courts and cannot linger."

And Calvus was gone, leaving Ahenobarbus as though he had been cudgelled into numbness. With a great effort he collected himself. After all, Dumnorix's gladiators were nothing to him. And when later he found that neither Dumnorix, nor Gabinius, nor Phaon had been taken or slain at Præneste, he breathed the easier. No one else except Pratinas, he was certain, knew *why* the lanista had made his attack; and there was no danger of being charged with complicity in the conspiracy. And so he was able to bear the stroke of ill-fortune with some equanimity, and at last rejoice that his dreams would no longer be haunted by the shade of Drusus. He was in no mood to meet Pratinas, and the smooth Greek evidently did not care to meet him. He went around to visit Cornelia again — she was still quite indisposed. So he spent that morning with Servius Flaccus playing draughts, a game at which his opponent was so excessively stupid that Ahenobarbus won at pleasure, and consequently found himself after lunch[1] in a moderately equable humour. Then it was he was agreeably surprised to receive the following note from Cornelia.

"Cornelia to her dearest Lucius, greeting.

I have been very miserable these past two days, but this afternoon will be better. Come and visit me and my uncle, for there are several things I would be glad to say before you both. Farewell."

[1] *Prandium.*

"I think," remarked Lucius to himself, "that the girl wants to have the wedding-day hastened. I know of nothing else to make her desire both Lentulus and myself at once. I want to see her alone. Well, I cannot complain. I'll have Drusus's bride, even if I can't have his money or his life."

And so deliberating, he put on his finest saffron-tinted synthesis, his most elegant set of rings, his newest pair of black shoes,[1] and spent half an hour with his hairdresser; and thus habited he repaired to the house of the Lentuli.

"The Lady Cornelia is in the Corinthian hall," announced the slave who carried in the news of his coming, "and there she awaits you."

Lucius, nothing loth, followed the servant. A moment and he was in the large room. It was empty. The great marble pillars rose cold and magnificent in four stately rows, on all sides of the high-vaulted apartment. On the walls Cupids and blithesome nymphs were careering in fresco. The floor was soft with carpets. A dull scent of burning incense from a little brazier, smoking before a bronze Minerva, in one corner of the room, hung heavy on the air. The sun was shining warm and bright without, but the windows of the hall were small and high and the shutters also were drawn. Everything was cool, still, and dark. Only through a single aperture shot a clear ray of sunlight, and stretched in a radiant bar across the gaudy carpets.

Lucius stumbled, half groping, into a chair, and seated himself. Cornelia had never received him thus before. What was she preparing? Another moment and Lentulus Crus entered the darkened hall.

"*Perpol !* Ahenobarbus," he cried, as he came across his prospective nephew-in-law, "what can Cornelia be wanting of

---

[1] Black shoes were worn as a sort of badge by *equites.*

us both? And in this place? I can't imagine. Ah! Those were strange doings yesterday up in Præneste. I would hardly have put on mourning if Drusus had been ferried over the Styx; but it was a bold way to attack him. I don't know that he has an enemy in the world except myself, and I can bide my time and pay off old scores at leisure. Who could have been back of Dumnorix when he blundered so evidently?"

Ahenobarbus felt that it was hardly possible Lentulus would condemn his plot very severely; but he replied diplomatically:—

"One has always plenty of enemies."

"*Mehercle!* of course," laughed the consul-elect, "what would life be without the pleasure of revenge! But why does my niece keep us waiting? Jupiter, what can she want of us?"

"Uncle, Lucius, I am here." And before them, standing illumined in the panel of sunlight, stood Cornelia. Ahenobarbus had never seen her so beautiful before. She wore a flowing violet-tinted stola, that tumbled in soft, silky flounces down to her ankles, and from beneath it peered the tint of her shapely feet bound to thin sandals by bright red ribbons. Her bare rounded arms were clasped above and below the elbow and at the wrists by circlets shaped as coiled serpents, whose eyes were gleaming rubies. At her white throat was fastened a necklace of interlinked jewel-set gold pendants that shimmered on her half-bare shoulders and breast. In each ear was the lustre of a great pearl. Her thick black hair fell unconfined down her back; across her brow was a frontlet blazing with great diamonds, with one huge sapphire in their midst. As she stood in the sunlight she was as a goddess, an Aphrodite descended from Olympus, to drive men to sweet madness by the ravishing puissance of her charms.

"Cornelia!" cried Lucius, with all the fierce impure admira‑ tion of his nature welling up in his black heart, "you are an immortal! Let me throw my arms about you! Let me kiss you! Kiss your neck but once!" And he took a step forward.

"Be quiet, Lucius," said Cornelia, speaking slowly and with as little passion as a sculptured marble endued with the powers of speech. "We have other things to talk of now. That is why I have called you here; you and my uncle."

"Cornelia!" exclaimed the young man, shrinking back as though a sight of some awful mystery had stricken him with trembling reverence, "why do you look at me so? Why do your eyes fasten on me that way? What are you going to do?"

It was as if he had never spoken. Cornelia continued steadily, looking straight before her.

"Uncle, is it your wish that I become the wife of Lucius Ahenobarbus?"

"You know it is," replied Lentulus, a little uneasily. He could not see where this bit of affection on the part of his niece would end. He had never heard her speak in such a tone before.

"I think, uncle," went on Cornelia, "that before we say any‑ thing further it will be well to read this letter. It was sent to me, but both you and Lucius will find it of some interest." And she held out two or three wax tablets.

Lentulus took them, eager to have done with the by-play. But when he saw on the binding-cords the seal — which, though broken, still showed its impression — he gave a start and exclamation.

"*Perpol!* The seal of Sextus Flaccus, the great capitalist."

"Certainly, why should it not be from him?"

Lentulus stepped nearer to the light, and read; Lucius

standing by and hanging on every word, Cornelia remaining at her previous station rigid as the bronze faun on the pedestal at her elbow. Lentulus read : —

"Sextus Fulvius Flaccus, to the most noble lady Cornelia : — If you are well it is well with me.

Perhaps you have heard how the plots of the conspirators against my dear friend and financial client Quintus Drusus have been frustrated, thanks, next to the god, to the wit and dexterity of Agias, who has been of late your slave. Drusus as soon as he had fairly beaten off the gladiators sent at once for me, to aid him and certain other of his friends in taking the confession of one Phaon, the freedman of Lucius Ahenobarbus, whom Agias had contrived to entrap in Gabii, and hold prisoner until the danger was over. Phaon's confession puts us in complete possession of all the schemes of the plotters; and it will be well for you to inform that worthy young gentleman, Lucius Ahenobarbus, that I only forbear to prosecute him, and Pratinas, who really made him his supple tool, because I am a peaceable man who would not bring scandal upon an old and noble family. If, however, anything should befall Drusus which should indicate that fresh plots against his life were on foot, let Ahenobarbus be assured that I can no more regard him so leniently. I may add that since it was through a marriage with you that Ahenobarbus expected to profit by the murder, I have already advised Drusus that, according to the decisions of several of the most eminent *jurisconsulti*,[1] a property provision such as his father inserted in his will would not be binding, especially in view of the present facts of the case. Drusus has accordingly prepared a new will which, if questioned, I shall defend in the courts with all my power. Farewell."

[1] Expounders of the Roman law.

Lentulus turned and glared with sullen amazement at his niece. That Ahenobarbus should conspire against Drusus seemed the most natural thing in the world. That the news that the conspiracy had failed should come from such a quarter, and through the hands of his own niece, at once terrified and angered him. Lucius was standing gaping, in half horror, half fascination, at Cornelia. Had she not urged him on? Had she not almost expressed her wish for Drusus's blood? The name of Flaccus fell on his heart like a stone; for the great banker never went back when he had taken a stand, and was rich enough to corrupt the most lax and merciful jury. Ahenobarbus felt a trap snap upon him, and yet he had no hope of revenge.

"Cornelia," cried Lentulus, regaining at last the powers of speech, "why was this letter sent to you? What to you is that wretched youth, Quintus Drusus, who escaped a fate he richly deserved? Why do you not condole with your lover on his misfortune? What do you mean by your stony stare, your —"

"I mean," retorted Cornelia, every word coming as a deep pant from her heaving chest, while her fingers clasped and unclasped nervously, and the blood surged to her pallid cheeks, "I mean that I need no longer profess to love what I hate; to cherish what I despise; to fondle what I loathe; to cast soft looks on that which I would pierce with daggers!" And she in turn took a step, quick and menacing, toward her wretched lover, who cowered and shrank back into the shadow of a pillar.

"But you yourself said you hoped I would soon rid you of Drusus," howled Lucius.

"Fool!" hissed the woman, through her clenched teeth. "Didn't you know that all that I said, all that I did, all that I

o

thought, was for this end — how might I save Quintus by learning the plans of the wretch who thirsted for his blood? Do you feel paid, now, for all your labours to secure the wealth of a man whose name should not be uttered beside that of yours?"

"And you do not love me!" screamed Ahenobarbus, springing at her, as if to force his arms around her neck.

"Dog!" and Cornelia smote him so fairly in the face that he shrank back, and pressed his hand to a swelling cheek. "I said I hated and despised you. What I despise, though, is beneath my hate. I would tread on you as on a viper or a desert asp, as a noxious creature that is not fit to live. I have played my game; and though it was not I who won, but Agias who won for me, I am well content. Drusus lives! Lives to see you miserably dead! Lives to grow to glory and honour, to happiness and a noble old age, when the worms have long since finished their work on you!"

"Girl," thundered Lentulus, fiercely, "you are raving! Ahenobarbus is your affianced husband. Rome knows it. I will compel you to marry him. Otherwise you may well blush to think of the stories that vulgar report will fasten around your name."

But Cornelia faced him in turn, and threw her white arms aloft as though calling down some mightier power than human to her aid; and her words came fast: —

"What Rome says is not what my heart says! My heart tells me that I am pure where others are vile; that I keep truth where others are false; that I love honourably where others love dishonourably. I knew the cost of what I would do for Drusus's sake; and, though the vilest slave gibber and point at me, I would hold my head as proudly as did ever a Cornelian or Claudian maiden: for I have done that which my own heart tells me was right; and more than that or less than that, can no true woman do!"

Ahenobarbus felt the room spinning round him. He saw himself ruined in everything that he had held dear. He would be the laughing-stock of Rome; he, the hero of a score of amorous escapades, the darling of as many patrician maidens, jilted by the one woman to whom he had become the abject slave. Courage came from despair.

"Be silent!" he gasped, his face black with fury. "If every word you say were true, yet with all the more reason would I drag you in my marriage procession, and force you to avow yourself my wife. Never have I been balked of woman; and you, too, with all your tragic bathos, shall learn that, if you won't have me for a slave, I'll bow your neck to my yoke."

"I think the very noble Lucius Ahenobarbus," replied Cornelia, in that high pitch of excitement which produces a calm more terrible than any open fury, "will in person be the protagonist in a tragedy very sorry for himself. For I can assure him that if he tries to make good his threat, I shall show myself one of the Danaides, and he will need his funeral feast full soon after the wedding banquet."

"Woman!" and Lentulus, thoroughly exasperated, broke in furiously. "Say another word, and I with my own hands will flog you like a common slave."

Cornelia laughed hysterically.

"Touch me!" she shouted; and in her grasp shone a small bright dagger.

Lentulus fell back. There was something about his niece that warned him to be careful.

"Wretched girl!" he commanded, "put down that dagger."

"I will not," and Cornelia stood resolutely, confronting her

two persecutors; her head thrown back, and the light making
her throat and face shine white as driven snow.

There was very little chivalry among the ancients. Lentulus
deliberately clapped his hands, and two serving-men appeared.

"Take that dagger from the Lady Cornelia!" commanded the
master. The men exchanged sly glances, and advanced to accomplish the disarming.

But before they could catch Cornelia's slender wrists in their
coarse, rough hands, and tear the little weapon from her, there
were cuts and gashes on their own arms; for the struggle if
brief was vicious. Cornelia stood disarmed.

"You see what these mock heroics will lead to," commented
Lentulus, with sarcastic smile, as he observed his order had
been obeyed.

"*You* will see!" was her quick retort.

"*Hei! hei!*" screamed one of the slaves an instant later,
sinking to the floor. "Poison! It's running through my veins!
I shall die!"

"You will die," repeated Cornelia, in ineffable scorn, spurning the wretch with her foot. "Lie there and die! Cease
breathing; sleep! And that creature, Ahenobarbus, yonder,
shall sleep his sleep too, ere he work his will on me! Ha! ha!
Look at my handiwork; the other slave is down!"

"Girl! Murderess!" raged Lentulus. "What is this? You
have slain these men."

"I have slain your slaves," said Cornelia, resolutely folding
her arms; "the poison on the dagger was very swift. You did
excellently well, Lucius, not to come near me." And she picked
up the dagger, which the slave, writhing in agony, had dropped.

"Do you wish to attack me again? *Phy!* I have more resources than this. This venom works too quickly. See, Syrax
s already out of his misery; and his fellow will soon be beyond

reach of woe. When I strike *you*, Lucius Ahenobarbus, you shall die slowly, that I may enjoy your pain. What need have I of this weapon?" And she flung the dagger across the carpet so that it struck on the farther wall. "Pick it up, and come and kill me if you wish! Drusus lives, and in him I live, for him I live, and by him I live. And you — and you are but as evil dreams in the first watch of a night which shall be forgotten either in sweet unending slumbers, or the brightness of the morning. And now I have spoken. Do with me as it lies in your power to do; but remember what power is mine. *Vale!*"

And Cornelia vanished from the darkened hall. The two men heard the click of the door, and turned and gazed blankly into one another's faces.

"The gods defend me, but I shall be yoked to one of the Diræ!" stammered Ahenobarbus.

CHAPTER XI

THE GREAT PROCONSUL

I

THE plot was foiled. Drusus was unquestionably safe. So long as Flaccus had the affidavits of Phaon's confession and the depositions of the captured gladiators stored away in his strong-box, neither Lucius Ahenobarbus nor the ever versatile Pratinas would be likely to risk a new conspiracy — especially as their intended victim had carefully drawn up a will leaving the bulk of his property to Titus Mamercus and Æmilia. Drusus had no near relatives, except Fabia and Livia; unless the Ahenobarbi were to be counted such; and it pleased him to think that if aught befell him the worthy children of his aged defender would acquire opulence.

But after the excitement was over, after Phaon had been brought up from the inn at Gabii to Præneste, and there had the truth wormed out of him by the merciless cross-examination of Curio and Flaccus; after the freedman had been suffered to depart with a warning and threat to his prompters, after the captured gladiators had been crucified along the roadway leading toward Rome, and the wreck left in the atrium of the villa caused by the attack had been cleared away, — after all this, then the reaction came. Drusus, indeed, found that though the sun shone bright, its brightness was not for him. He had friends in plenty; but not such friends as he needed

—as his heart craved. Truth to tell, he was one of those more delicate natures to whom the average pity and the ordinary demonstrations of sympathy come with an offending jar, and open, not heal, long-festering wounds. Curio was kind, but could only hold out the vaguest hopes that, for the present at least, anything would compel the consul-elect to consent to his niece's marriage with a mortal enemy. Flaccus took the same position. The hard-headed man of money thought that Drusus was a visionary, to be so distraught over the loss of a wife — as if the possession of a fortune of thirty odd millions did not make up for every possible calamity. Antonius was still less happy in his efforts at consolation. This dashing young politician, who had been equally at home basking in the eyes of the young Egyptian princess, Cleopatra, eight years before, when he was in the East with Aulus Gabin-ius, or when fighting the Gauls as he had until recently undei his uncle, the great proconsul, — had now been elected Tribune of the Plebs for the coming year; and was looking forward to a prosperous and glorious career in statecraft. He had had many a love intrigue, and made such matters a sort of recrea-tion to the real business of life. Why Drusus — who certainly had very fair worldly prospects before him — should not con-sole himself for one unsuccessful passage of arms with Cupid, by straightway engaging in another, he could not see. He plainly intimated to his friend that there were a great many women, almost if not quite as good looking as Cornelia, who would survey him with friendly eyes if he made but a few advances. And Drusus, wounded and stung, was thrown back on himself; and within himself he found very little comfort.

Although he believed himself safe at last from the wiles of Ahenobarbus and his Greek coadjutors, there was still a great dread which would steal over Drusus lest at any moment a

stroke might fall.   Those were days when children murdered
parents, wives husbands, for whim or passion, and very little
came to punish their guilt.   The scramble for money was
universal.   Drusus looked forth into the world, and saw little
in it that was good.   He had tried to cherish an ideal, and
found fidelity to it more than difficult.   His philosophy
did not assure him that a real deity existed.   Death ended
all.   Was it not better to be done with the sham of life;
to drink the Lethe water, and sink into eternal, dreamless
slumber?   He longed unspeakably to see Cornelia face to face;
to kiss her; to press her in his arms; and the desire grew and
grew.

She was no longer in the capital.   Her uncle had sent her
away — guarded by trusty freedmen — to the villa of the
Lentuli at Baiæ.   The fashionable circles of the great city
had made of her name a three days' scandal, of which the
echo all too often came to Drusus's outraged ears.   His only
comfort was that Ahenobarbus had become the butt and
laughing-stock of every one who knew of his repulse by his
last inamorata.   Then at last Drusus left Præneste for Rome.
Ahenobarbus and Pratinas were as well checked as it was
possible they could be, and there was no real ground to dread
assassination while in the city, if moderate precautions were
taken.   Then too the time was coming when the young man
felt that he could accomplish something definite for the party
for which he had already sacrificed so much.

The events clustering around Dumnorix's unsuccessful attack
had made Drusus a sort of hero in the eyes of the Prænesteans.
They had years before elected his father as their patron, their
legal representative at Rome, and now they pitched upon the
son, proud to have this highly honourable function continued
in the same family.   This election gave Drusus some little

prestige at the capital, and some standing in the courts and politics. When he went to Rome it was not as a mere individual who had to carve out his own career, but as a man of honour in his own country, a representative of a considerable local interest, and the possessor of both a noble pedigree and an ample fortune.

Curio found him plenty to do; wire-pulling, speech-making, private bargaining, — all these were rife, for everybody knew that with the first of January, when Lentulus became consul, the fortunes of Cæsar were to be made or marred irretrievably. There were rumours, always rumours, now of Cæsar, now of Pompeius. The proconsul was going to march on Rome at once, and put all his enemies to the sword. Pompeius was to be proclaimed dictator and exterminate all who adhered to the anti-senatorial party. And into this *mêlée* of factions Drusus threw himself, and found relief and inspiration in the conflict. His innate common-sense, a very considerable talent for oratory which had received a moderate training, his energy, his enthusiasm, his incorruptibility, his straightforwardness, all made him valuable to the Cæsarians, and he soon found himself deep in the counsels of his party, although he was too young to be advanced as a candidate for any public office.

Agias continued with him. He had never formally deeded the boy to Cornelia, and now it was not safe for the lad to be sent to dwell at Baiæ, possibly to fall into the revengeful clutches of Phaon, or Pratinas, or Ahenobarbus. Drusus had rewarded Agias by giving him his freedom; but the boy had nowhere to go, and did not desire to leave Quintus's service; so he continued as a general assistant and understrapper, to carry important letters and verbal messages, and to aid his patron in every case where quick wits or nimble feet were

useful. He went once to Baiæ, and came back with a letter
from Cornelia, in which she said that she was kept actually as
a prisoner in her uncle's villa, and that Lentulus still threatened to force Ahenobarbus upon her; but that she had prepared herself for that final emergency.

The letter came at a moment when Drusus was feeling the
exhilaration of a soldier in battle, and the missive was depress-
ing and maddening. What did it profit if the crowd roared
its plaudits, when he piled execration on the oligarchs from
the Rostra, if all his eloquence could not save Cornelia one
pang? Close on top of this letter came another disquieting
piece of information, although it was only what he had
expected. He learned that Lentulus Crus had marked him
out personally for confiscation of property and death as a
dangerous agitator, as soon as the Senate could decree martial
law. To have even a conditional sentence of death hanging
over one is hard to bear with equanimity. But it was too late
for Drusus to turn back. He had chosen his path; he had
determined on the sacrifice; he would follow it to the end.
And from one source great comfort came to him. His aunt,
Fabia, had always seen in him her hero. With no children
of her own, with very little knowledge of the world, she had
centred all her hopes and ambitions on her sister's son; and
he was not disappointing her. She dreamed of him as consul,
triumphator, and dictator. She told him her hopes. She
applauded his sacrifice. She told him of the worthies of old,
of Camillus, of the Scipios, of Marcellus, the "Sword of
Rome," of Lucius Æmilius Paulus, and a host of others, good
men and true, whose names were graven on the fabric of the
great Republic, and bade him emulate them, and be her perfect Fabian and Livian. And from his aunt Drusus gained
infinite courage. If she was not Cornelia, yet it was a boon

ineffable to be able to hear a pure, loving woman tell him face to face that her heart suffered when he suffered, and that all his hopes and fears were hers.

Finally an interlude came to Quintus's political activity. Curio was becoming uneasy, lest his distant superior should fail to realize the full venom of the Senate party and the determination of his enemies to work his ruin.

"I must go to Ravenna," said the politician to his young associate. "My tribuneship is nearly run out. Antonius and Cassius will take my place in the office. And you, who have done so much for Cæsar, must go also, for he loves to meet and to know all who are his friends."

"To Cæsar I will go," answered Drusus; and of himself he asked, "What manner of man will this prove, whom I am serving? A selfish grasper of power? Or will he be what I seek — a man with an ideal?"

II

Night was falling on the dark masses of the huge Prætorium, the government-house and army barracks of the provincial capital of Ravenna. Outside, sentinels were changing guard; Roman civil officials and provincials were strolling in the cool of the porticos. Laughter, the shout of loungers at play, broke the evening silence. But far in the interior, where there was a secluded suite of rooms, nothing but the tinkle of a water-duct emptying into a cistern broke the stillness, save as some soft-footed attendant stole in and out across the rich, thick carpet.

The room was small; the ceiling low; the frescos not elaborate, but of admirable simplicity and delicacy. The furniture comprised merely a few divans, chairs, and tripods, but all of the choicest wood or brass, and the most excellent upholstery.

One or two carved wooden cupboards for books completed the furnishings.

There were only two persons in the room. One of them,— a handsome young Hellene, evidently a freedman, was sitting on a low chair with an open roll before him. His companion half sat and half lay on a divan near by. This second person was a man of height unusual to Italians of his day; his cheeks were pale and a little sunken; his dark eyes were warm, penetrating; his mouth and chin mobile and even affable, but not a line suggested weakness. The forehead was high, massive, and was exaggerated by a semi-baldness which was only partially concealed by combing the dark, grey-streaked hair forward. He was reclining; if he had arisen he would have displayed a frame at once to be called soldierly, though spare and hardly powerful. To complete the figure it should be added that on one finger he wore a large ring set with a very beautiful seal of an armed Venus; and over his loose but carefully arranged tunic was thrown a short, red mantle, caught together on the left shoulder — the paludamentum, a garment only worn by Roman military officers of the very highest rank.

The general — for so his dress proclaimed him — was playing with a stylus and a waxen tablet, while the young Greek read. Now and then he would bid the latter pause while he made a few notes. The book was Euripides's "Troades."

"Read those lines again," interrupted the general. The voice was marvellously flexile, powerful, and melodious.

And the freedman repeated:—

> "Sow far and wide, plague, famine, and distress;
> Make women widows, children fatherless;
> Break down the altars of the gods, and tread

On quiet graves, the temples of the dead;
Play to life's end this wicked witless game
And you will win what knaves and fools call Fame!" [1]

The freedman waited for his superior to ask him to continue, but the request did not come. The general seemed lost in a reverie; his expressive dark eyes were wandering off in a kind of quiet melancholy, gazing at the glass water-clock at the end of the room, but evidently not in the least seeing it.

"I have heard enough Euripides to-day," at length he remarked. "I must attend to more important matters. You may leave me."

The Greek rolled up the volume, placed it in the cupboard, and left the room with noiseless step. The general had arisen, and was standing beside the open window that looked out into a quiet little court. It was dark. The lamps of the room threw the court-yard into a sombre relief. Overhead, in the dimming, violet arch of the sky, one or two faint stars were beginning to twinkle.

" Play to life's end this wicked witless game
And you will win what knaves and fools call Fame!"

repeated the general, leaning out from the stone work of the window-casing in order to catch the cool air of the court. "Yes, fame, the fame of a Xerxes; perhaps the fame of a Hannibal—no, I wrong the Carthaginian, for he at least struck for his country. And what is it all worth, after all? Does Agamemnon feel that his glory makes the realm of Hades more tolerable? Does not Homer set forth Achilles as a warrior with renown imperishable? And yet, 'Mock me not,' he makes the shade of Achilles say; 'Better to be the hireling of a stranger and serve a man of mean estate, whose living is but small, than be the monarch over all those dead and gone.'"

[1] Translated in the collection "Sales Attici."

The general leaned yet farther out, and looked upward.
"These were the stars that twinkled over the Troy of Priam;
these were the stars that shone on Carthage when she sent
forth her armies and her fleets, and nigh drove the Greeks
from Sicily; and these are the stars which will shine when
Rome is as Troy and Carthage. And I — I am an atom, a
creature of chance, thrown out of the infinite to flash like a
shooting star for a moment across a blackened firmament and
then in the infinite to expire. *Cui bono?* Why should I
care how I live my life, since in a twinkling it will all be as
if it had never been? And if Cato and Domitius and Lentulus Crus have their way with me, what matter? What matter
if a stab in the dark, or open violence, or the sham forms of
justice end this poor comedy? I and all others play. All
comedy is tragedy, and at its merriest is but dolorous stuff.
While the curtain stays down[1] we are sorry actors with the
whole world for our audience, and the hoots mingle full often
with the applause. And when the curtain rises, that which
is good, the painstaking effort, the labour, is quickly forgotten;
the blunders, the false quantities in our lives, are treasured up
to be flung against our names. We play, but we do not know
our parts; we are Œdipus, who has committed unwitting sin,
and yet must reap his reward; we are Prometheus who is to
be chained to the rock forever, for offending the gods; we are
Orestes whom the Eumenides pursue, chasing him down for
his guilt. And all the time we vainly imagine that we are
some victorious hero, some Perseus, especially favoured by the
gods to fare scatheless over land and sea, and bear away the
Medusa's head, and live renowned and happy forever." The
reverie was becoming deeper and deeper; the Roman was beginning no longer to whisper merely to himself, he was half

---

[1] The ancient curtain (*aulæum*) had its roller at the bottom.

declaiming; then of a sudden, by a quick revolution of mind he broke short the thread of his monologue. "*Phui!* Caius, you are ranting as if you were still a youth at Rhodes, and Apollonius Molo were just teaching you rhetoric! Why has no letter come from Curio to-day? I am anxious for him. There may have been a riot. I hadn't expected that those excellent 'Optimates' would begin to murder tribunes quite so soon. The carrier is late!" and the general moved away from the window, and took from a cupboard a package of tablets, which he ran over hastily. "Here are the despatches of yesterday. None to-day. I fear the worst." The brow of the solitary speaker grew darker. "Poor Curio, poor Antonius; if they've dared to murder them, let them tremble. I could forgive a mortal enemy to myself, but not one who had slaughtered a friend."

There were steps in the court below, and voices were raised. In an instant the general's eyes were kindled, his frame on a poise. He sprang to the window, and shouted down the dark court.

"Curio! Do I hear you speaking?"

"*Salve!* Cæsar. It is I!"

"Venus be praised!" and the proconsul, with almost undignified haste, was running out upon the stairs to meet his friend. "Has the city broken out? Has Antonius been murdered? Is the truce at an end? Are you alone?"

And Curio, who did not quite possess his leader's ability to "do all things at the same time," answered in a breath: "The city so far keeps tolerable order. Antonius is safe. The consuls and Senate still keep the peace; but so poorly that I thought it my duty to come to you and say things that cannot go in a letter."

"And who is this young man with you?"

"My friend," said Curio, turning to his companion, "is Quintus Livius Drusus, of whom I have had occasion to write no little."

The proconsul sprang forward and seized Drusus by both hands, and looked him fairly in the eye.

"*Papœ!* I see Sextus Drusus once more, the best tribune in his legion, and my dear friend. Your face should be cause for your welcome, if nothing else. Ah! how much we shall have to say! But you are travel-stained and weary. Words will keep while you bathe, and our dinner is prepared; for I myself have not dined, waiting, as I thought, for your despatches."

"Your excellency shows me too much courtesy," said Drusus, bowing in what was, to tell truth, some little embarrassment; "it is not fit that a young man like myself should dine at the same table with an imperator before whom nations have trembled."

And then it was that Drusus caught his first glimpse of that noble and sententious egotism which was a characteristic of the great proconsul.

"To be a friend of Cæsar is to be the peer of kings."

Drusus bowed again, and then, with Curio, followed the attendants who were leading them to comfortably, though not sumptuously, furnished apartments.

* * * * * * * * * *

Quintus Drusus in years to come sat at the boards of many great men, enjoyed their conversation, entered into their hopes and fears, but he never forgot the first dinner with the proconsul of the Gauls. Cæsar kept a double table. His hospitality was always ready for the people of note of the district where he happened to be staying, and for his own regular army officers. But he dined personally with such high-rank Romans

and very noble Provincials as chanced to be with him from
day to day. To this last select company Drusus found himself
that evening admitted ; and in fact he and Curio were the proconsul's only personal guests. The dinner itself was more
remarkable for the refinement of the whole service, the exquisite chasteness of the decorations of the dining room, the excellent cooking of the dishes, and the choiceness of the wines
than for any lavish display either of a great bill of fare, or of an
ostentatious amount of splendour. The company of officers and
gentlemen of the Ravenna district dined together in a spacious
hall, where Drusus imagined they had a rather more bounteous
repast than did the immediate guests of their entertainer. At
one end of this large hall was a broad alcove, raised a single
step, and here was laid the dinner for the proconsul. Cæsar
passed through the large company of his humbler guests, followed by Curio and Drusus, — now speaking a familiar word
to a favourite centurion; now congratulating a country visitor
on his election to his local Senate; now introducing the new-
comers to this or that friend. And so presently Drusus found
himself resting on his elbow on the same couch with Cæsar,
while Curio occupied the other end. For a time the latter
held by far the larger part of the conversation in his hands.
There were a myriad tales to tell of politics at the capital, a
myriad warnings to give. Cæsar listened to them all; and
only rarely interrupted, and then with words so terse and
penetrating that Drusus marvelled. The proconsul seemed to
know the innermost life history and life motives of everything
and everybody. He described a character with an epithet;
he fathomed a political problem with an expletive. Only now
and then did his words or motions betray any deep personal
concern or anxiety, and once only did Drusus see him flush
with passion.

"That affair of the magistrate of Coma, to whom you gave the franchise," said Curio, "was extremely unfortunate. You of course heard long ago how Marcellus, the consul, had him beaten with rods and sent home, to show[1] — as he said — to you, Cæsar, the print of his stripes."

The face of the proconsul reddened, then grew black with hardly reined fury.

"Yes, most unfortunate for Marcellus." It was all that Cæsar said, but Drusus would not have exchanged his life then, for that of Marcellus, for a thousand talents of gold.

"And our dear friend, Cato," went on Curio, who was perhaps not unwilling to stir the vials of his superior's wrath, "has just sworn with an oath in public, that as soon as your army is disbanded he will press an impeachment against you; and I've heard it reported that you will be compelled to plead, like Milo when he was tried for the Clodius affair, before judges overawed by armed men."

"I anticipate no such proceeding," said Cæsar, dryly, in an accent of infinite contempt. Then turning to Drusus, he entirely changed his intonation.

"So long," he said, with a shrug of his rather slight shoulders, "we have talked of comitias and senates! Praise to the gods, all life is not passed in the Forum or Curia! And now, my dear Quintus, let us put aside those tedious matters whereof we all three have talked and thought quite enough, and tell me of yourself; for, believe me, our friendship would be one-sided indeed, if all your trouble and exertion went for me, and you received no solicitude in return."

And Drusus, who had at first found his words coming awk-

---

[1] Cæsar had given the magistrates of towns of the north of Italy the Roman franchise: no Roman citizens could be lawfully flogged. By his action Marcellus denied Cæsar's right to confer the franchise.

wardly enough, presently grew fluent as he conversed with the proconsul. He told of his student days at Athens, of his stud- ies of rhetoric and philosophy, of his journey back to Præneste, and the incidents of the sea voyage, and land travel; of his welcome at Præneste by the old retainers and the familia of the Drusi, and then of his recent political work at Rome.

"These have been the chief events of my life, Cæsar," he concluded, "and since you have condescended to hear, I have ventured to tell; but why need I ask if such a commonplace tale of a young man who has yet his life to live, should inter- est you?"

Cæsar smiled, and laying down the beaker from which he was sipping very slowly, replied: —

"*Mehercle!* And do you wish to have all your exploits crowded into a few short years of youth, that mature age will have nothing to surpass? Listen, — I believe that when the historians, by whom our dear Cicero is so anxious to be remem- bered favourably, write their books, they will say something of my name, — good or bad, the Genius knows, — but fame at least will not be denied me. Twelve years ago when I was in Spain I was reading in some book of the exploits of Alexander the Great. Suddenly it seemed as though I could not control myself. I began to weep; and this was the explanation I gave to my friends, 'I have just cause to weep, when I consider that Alexander at my age had conquered so many nations, and I have all this time done nothing that is memorable.'"

"But even when your excellency went into Spain," remarked Drusus, "you had done that which should have given renown. Consider, you had won the prætorship, the office of Pontifex Maximus —"

"*St,*" interrupted the proconsul, "a list of titles is not a pledge from Fortune that she will grant fame. Besides, I was about to add — what folly it was for me to weep! Do I imagine now, that Alexander was happy and contented in the midst of his conquests? Rather, unless he were, indeed, of more than mortal stuff, for every morsel of fame, he paid a talent of care and anxiety. Rush not too quickly after fame; only with age comes the strength to pay the price thereof."

Drusus was half wondering at, half admiring, the unconscious comparison the proconsul was drawing between himself and Alexander. But Cæsar went on: —

"But you, O Drusus, have not dealt honestly with me, in that you have failed to tell that which lies nearest your heart, and which you consider the pivot of all your present life."

Drusus flushed. "Doubtless, your excellency will pardon a young man for speaking with diffidence on a subject, to recollect which is to cause pain."

Cæsar put off the half-careless air of the good-natured wit, which he had been affecting.

"Quintus Livius Drusus," and as he spoke, his auditor turned as if magnetized by his eye and voice, and hung on every word, "be not ashamed to own to me, of all men, that you claim a good woman's love, and for that love are ready to make sacrifice."

And as if to meet a flitting thought in the other's mind, Cæsar continued: —

"No, blush not before me, although the fashionable world of Rome will have its stories. I care not enough for such gossip to take pains to say it lies. But this would I have declared, when at your age, and let all the world hear, that I, Caius Cæsar, loved honourably, purely, and worthily; and for the sake of that love would and did defy death itself."

The proconsul's pale face flushed with something very akin to passion; his bright eyes were more lustrous than ever.

"*I was eighteen years old when I married Cornelia, the daughter of Cinna, the great leader of the 'Populares.' Sulla, then dictator, ordered me to put her away. Cornelia had not been the wife of my father's choice. He had wished to force upon me Cossutia, an heiress, but with little save riches to commend her. I gained neither riches, political influence, nor family good-will by the marriage. Sulla was in the fulness of his strength. I had seen nearly all my friends proscribed, exiled, or murdered. Sulla bade me put away my wife, and take such a one as he should appoint. He was graciously pleased to spare my life, in order that I might become his tool. Why did I refuse ? "

Cæsar was sitting upon the couch and speaking nervously, in a manner that betokened great and unusual excitement.

"I knew the dictator meant to favour me if I would only humour him in this matter. A word from him and all ambition of mine had probably been at an end. I take no praise to my-self for this. I refused him. I defied his threats. He seized my property, deprived me of my priesthood,[1] finally let loose his pack of assassins upon me. I almost became their victim. But my uncle, Aurelius Cotta, and some good friends of mine among the Vestal Virgins pleaded my cause. I escaped. Sulla said he was over-persuaded in sparing me; 'In me were many Mariuses.' But did I regret the loss, the danger, the check for the time being to my career? Quintus Drusus, I counted them as of little importance, not to be weighed beside the pure love that mastered me. And as the faithful husband of my Cornelia I remained, until cruel death closed her dear eyes for-ever. One can love once, and honourably, with his whole being, but not truly and honourably love a second time, at least not in a manner like unto the first. Therefore, my Quintus, blush

---

- Marius had made young Cæsar, Flamen Dialis : priest of Jupiter.

not to confess that which I know is yours, — a thing which too many of us Romans do not know in these declining days, — something that would almost convince me there were indeed celestial gods, who care for us and guide our darkened destinies. For when we reason of the gods, our reason tells us they are not. But when pure passion possesses our hearts, then we see tangible visions, then our dreams become no dreams but realities; we mount up on wings, we fly, we soar to Olympus, to Atlantis, to the Elysian fields; we no longer wish to know, we feel; we no longer wish to prove, we see; and what our reason bids us to reject, a surer monitor bids us to receive: the dangers and perils of this life of shades upon the earth are of no account, for we are transformed into immortals in whose veins courses the divine ichor, and whose food is ambrosial. Therefore while we love we do indeed dwell in the Islands of the Blessed: and when the vision fades away, its sweet memory remains to cheer us in our life below, and teach us that where the cold intellect may not go, there is indeed some way, on through the mists of the future, which leads we know not whither; but which leads to things purer and fairer than those which in our most ambitious moments we crave."

The voice of the conqueror of Gaul and German sank with a half tremor; his eye was moist, his lips continued moving after his words had ceased to flow. Drusus felt himself searched through and through by glance and speech. Was the proconsul a diviner to find all that was deepest in his soul and give it an utterance which Drusus had never expressed even to himself? The young man was thrilled, fascinated. And Cæsar, in quite another tone, recovered himself and spoke.

"Wherefore, O Drusus! be ashamed to tell how the Lady Cornelia loves you and you love her? What if the grim old consul-elect, like the jealous elder in the comedy, will stand in your way! *Phui!* What are the complaints, threats, and prohibitions of such as he? At present, the wind blows from his quarter, but it will not be ever so. Either Lentulus will be in no place to hinder you before long, or we all shall be beyond caring for his triumph or failure."

"Your excellency bids me hope!" cried Drusus.

"I bid you love," replied Cæsar, smiling. "I bid you go to Baiæ, for there I have heard your dear lady waits her long-absent Odysseus, and tell her that all will be well in time; for Cæsar will make it so."

"For Cæsar will make it so," repeated the young man, half-unconscious that he was speaking aloud.

"For Cæsar will make it so," reiterated the proconsul, as though Zeus on Olympus were nodding his head in awful and irrevocable promise.

And the proconsul took both of his guest's hands in his own, and said, with seriousness: —

"Quintus Drusus, why did you abandon your bride to support my cause?"

"Because," replied the other, with perfect frankness, "I should not be worthy to look Cornelia in the face, if I did not sacrifice all to aid the one Roman who can save the state."

"Young man," replied the proconsul, "many follow me for selfish gain, many follow me to pay off a grudge, but few follow me because they believe that because Cæsar is ambitious, he is ambitious as a god should be ambitious — to bestow the greatest benefits possible upon the men entrusted to his charge. I know not what thread for me the Fates have spun; but this I know, that Cæsar will never prove false to those who trust him to bring righteousness to Rome, and peace to the world."

*   *   *   *   *   *   *   *   *   *

That night, as Drusus was retiring, Curio spoke to him: —

"And what manner of man do you think is the proconsul?"

"I think," replied Drusus, "that I have discovered the one man in the world whom I craved to find."

"And who is that?"

"The man with an ideal."

CHAPTER XII

PRATINAS MEETS ILL-FORTUNE

I

PROBABLY of the various personages mentioned in the course of our story none was more thoroughly enjoying life about this time than Agias. Drusus had left him in the city when he started for Ravenna, with general instructions to keep an eye on Lucius Ahenobarbus and Pratinas, and also to gather all he could of the political drift among the lower classes. Agias was free now. He let his hair grow long in token of his newly gained liberty; paraded a many-folded toga; and used part of the donatives which Drusus and Fabia had lavished upon him, in buying one or two slave-boys of his own, whom, so far from treating gently on account of his own lately servile position, he cuffed and abused with grim satisfaction at being able to do what had so often been done to him.

Agias had been given lodgings by Drusus in a tenement house, owned by the latter, in the Subura.

The rooms were over a bakery, and at the sides were a doctor's and surgeon's office and a barber's shop — a rendezvous which gave the young Greek an admirable chance to pick up the current gossip. Every street-pedler, every forum-idler, had his political convictions and pet theories. The partisans who arrogated to themselves the modest epithet of "The Company of All Good Men," clamoured noisily that "Liberty and

Ancient Freedom " were in danger, if Cæsar set foot in Rome save as an impeached traitor. And the Populares — the supporters of the proconsul — raged equally fiercely against the greed of the Senate party that wished to perpetuate itself forever in office. Agias could only see that neither faction really understood the causes for and against which they fought; and observed in silence, trusting that his patron knew more of the issues than he.

But the newly manumitted freedman was thoroughly enjoying himself. The windy speeches in the Senate, the crowded and excited meetings in the Forum, the action and reaction of the tides of popular prejudice and fancy, the eloquence of Antonius, and the threatenings and ravings of Marcellus the consul — all these were interesting but not disturbing. Agias was catching glimpses of a little Olympus of his own — an Olympus in which he was at once Zeus, Poseidon, and Apollo; Sesostris — so he declared — the lame cup-bearer Hephæstus; and in place of Hera, Athena, and Aphrodite, were the smiles and laughter of Artemisia. Agias was head over ears in love with this pretty little cage-bird shut up in Pratinas's gloomy suite of rooms. Her "uncle" took her out now and then to the theatre or to the circus; but she had had little enough companionship save such as Sesostris could give; and to her, Agias was a wonderful hero, the master of every art, the victor over a hundred monsters. He had told her of his adventure with Phaon — not calling names, lest disagreeable consequences ensue — and Artemisia dreamed of him as the cleverest creature on the earth, able to outwit Hermes in subtlety. Agias had found out when Pratinas was likely to be away from home — and that worthy Hellene, be it said, never declined an invitation to dine with a friend — and Agias timed his visits accordingly. He taught Artemisia to play the cithera and to sing, and she made such rapid progress under his tutoring that the unconscious Pratinas commended her efforts to acquire the accomplishments he wished.   And Agias was never so happy as when those bright eyes were hanging on his lips or that merry tongue was chattering a thousand pointless remarks or jests.

Yes, Agias found himself in a condition when he could well ask to have no change.   The possibility that Pratinas would come home, and put an end to the romance once and for all, was just great enough to give the affair the zest of a dangerous ad‐venture.   Despite Sesostris's warnings that Artemisia might at any time be sold away by her pseudo-uncle, Agias could not dis‐cover that that danger was imminent enough to need frustration. He was content to live himself and to let Artemisia live, bask ing in the stolen sunshine of the hour, and to let the thought of the approaching shadows fade out of his mind.

Another person who saw the sunshine rather brighter than before was Pisander.   That excellent philosopher had received his share of the gratitude Drusus had bestowed on his deliver‐ ers.   But he was still in the service of Valeria, for Drusus saw that he had admirable opportunities for catching the stray bits of political gossip that inevitably intermixed themselves with the conversation of Valeria and her circle.   Pisander had con‐ tinued to read Plato to his mistress, and to groan silently at her frivolity; albeit, he did not groan so hopelessly as before, because he had good money in his pouch and knew where to procure more when he needed it.

So Agias enjoyed himself.   He was a youth; a Pagan youth; and in his short life he had seen many a scene of wickedness and shame.   Yet there was nothing unholy in the affection which he found was daily growing stronger and stronger for Artemisia.   She was a pure, innocent flower, that by the very whiteness of her simple sweet presence drove away anything that "defiled or made a lie." Agias did not worship her; she was too winning; too cunning and pretty to attract the least reverence; but in her company the young Greek was insensibly raised pinnacles above the murky moral atmosphere in which most men and youths of his station walked.

It was all like an Idyl of Theocritus; with the tenement of Pratinas for a shepherd's hut; and Sesostris for a black-backed sheep to whom the herdsmen and the nymph of his love could play on "oaten reed." At first, Agias had never dreamed of telling a word of his affection to Artemisia. In truth, it was very hard to tell, for she, with an absolute innocence, took all his advances for far more than they were worth; told him that next to her "uncle and dear Sesostris" he was quite the best friend she had; that she loved him, and was glad to hear him say that he loved her.

All this was delightful in the ears of her admirer, but very disconcerting. Agias thought of the hollow civilities of Valeria's life, as he had seen it; of the outward decorum of language, of the delicately veiled compliments, of the interchange of words that summed up, in a few polished commonplaces, a whole network of low intrigue and passion. Was this the same world! Could Valeria and Artemisia both be women! The one — a beauty, whose guilty heart was not ignorant of a single form of fashionable sin; the other — as it were, a blossom, that was pure sweetness, in whose opening petals the clear diamond of the morning dew still remained! Agias did not compare Artemisia with Cornelia; for Cornelia, in his eyes, was a goddess, and in beauty and passions was above the hope or regard of mortal men.

But what was one to do in an emergency like the following? Agias had been singing the "Love Song" from the "Cyclops," and trying to throw into the lines all the depth of tender affection which voice and look rendered possible.

> "One with eyes the fairest
>   Cometh from his dwelling,
> Some one loves thee, rarest,
>   Bright beyond my telling.
> In thy grace thou shinest
> Like some nymph divinest,
> In her caverns dewy ; —
> All delights pursue thee,
> Soon pied flowers, sweet-breathing,
> Shall thy head be wreathing." [1]

And at the conclusion of the song Artemisia threw her arms around Agias's neck and kissed him ; and then with astounding impartiality sprang into Sesostris's lap, and patted the old Ethiop's black cheeks, and bestowed on him all manner of endearing epithets. What was poor Agias to do in such a case ? He blankly concluded that it had proved easier to blast the plot of Pratinas and Ahenobarbus, than to win the love — as he meant "love" — of this provokingly affectionate girl. It was growing late. Pratinas might at any time return. And Agias constrained himself to depart.

"By Zeus !" was the exclamation he addressed to himself as he fought his way through the crowds toward his own quarters ; "where will this all end ? How much longer are you going to lie in the toils of that most innocent of Circes ? Will she never open her eyes ? If I could only make her cry, 'I hate you!' there would be some hope ; for when one hates, as I want her to, love is but a step away. Confound that Sesostris ! For me to have to sit there, and see that baboon kissed and fondled ! "

And so reflecting, he reached his rooms. One of the luck-

[1] Translated by Shelley.

less slave-boys who now addressed him as "Dominus," was waiting to tell him that a very gaunt, strange-looking man, with an enormous beard, had called to see him while he was out, and would return — so the visitor said — in the evening, for his business was important. "Pisander," remarked Agias; and he stayed in that evening to meet the philosopher, although he had arranged to share a dinner with one or two other freedmen, who were his friends.

The man of learning appeared at a very late hour. In fact, the water-clock showed that it wanted little of midnight before he came. His explanation was that Valeria had called him in to read verses to a company of friends who were supping with her, and he could not get away sooner. Besides, the dark streets were full of bandits, and he had therefore taken a circuitous route to avoid attack. Agias had to let him ramble through all the details, although he knew very well that Pisander would never have taken so much trouble to come if he had not had information of the first importance to impart.

"And now, my dear Pisander," ventured the young Greek, at length, "I will ask Dromo to set something to drink before us; and I hope you will tell me why you have come."

Pisander glanced timidly over his shoulder, pulled at his beard with suppressed excitement, then bent down, and in a very low voice burst out: —

"Pratinas and" — he hesitated — "Valeria!"

"Ai!" cried Agias, "I have suspected it for a very long time. You are sure the fox has snapped up his goose?"

"By Hercules, very sure! They are planning to go to Egypt. Pratinas has just had a wonderful stroke of luck. He received six hundred thousand sesterces[1] with which to

1 $24,000.

corrupt a jury for some poor wretch who expected to enlist
Pratinas's cunning to get him out of the toils of the law.
Pratinas calmly put the money in his strong-box, and let the
unhappy wight be cast.   He is not at all poor — he has
amassed a large fortune while he has been in Rome.   Shade
of Plato! how this knave has prospered!   And now he is
arranging with Valeria to strip poor Calatinus of nearly all
his valuables, before they fly the country."

"Ah, luckless Calatinus!" laughed Agias.   "That will be
the end of his marrying the handsomest woman in Rome.
And so this is what you came here to tell me?   It really was
a good secret to keep."

"*St!*" interrupted Pisander, "Pratinas has something else
to attend to.   Calatinus will get consolation for losing his
dear spouse.   I suppose Pratinas wishes to indemnify him,
but he himself will make a good bit at the same time."

In a twinkling a thought had flashed through Agias's mind,
that made a cold sweat break out all over him, and a hot surge
of blood mount to his head.

"Man, man!" he cried, grasping Pisander's wrists with all
his strength, "speak!   Don't look at me this way!   Don't
say that you mean Artemisia?"

"*Ai!*   You know the girl, then?" said the other, with the
most excruciating inquisitiveness.

"Know her?" raged Agias, "I love the sunbeam on which
her eyes rest.   Speak!   Tell me all, everything, all about it!
Quick!   I must know!"

Pisander drew himself together, and with a deliberation
that was nearly maddening to his auditor, began: —

"Well, you see, I had occasion this morning to be in Calatinus's library.   Yes, I remember, I was just putting the new
copy of Theognis back into the cupboard, when I noticed

that the Mimnermus was not neatly rolled, and so I happened to stay in the room, and — "

"By Zeus, speak faster and to the point!" cried Agias.

"Oh, there wasn't very much to it all! Why, how excited you are! Pratinas came into the atrium, and Calatinus was already there. I heard the latter say, 'So I am to give you forty thousand sesterces for the little girl you had with you at the circus yesterday?' And Pratinas replied, 'Yes, if she pleases you. I told you her name was Artemisia, and that I always taught her to believe that she was my niece.'"

"*Hei! Hei!*" groaned Agias, rushing up and down the room, half frantic. "Don't tell any more, I've heard enough! Fool, fool I have been, to sit in the sunshine, and never think of preparing to carry out my promise to Sesostris. No, you must tell me — you must tell me if you have learned any more. Did Calatinus fix on any time at which he was to take possession of the poor girl?"

"No," replied the still amazed Pisander. "I did not hear the whole conversation. There was something about 'a very few days,' and then Pratinas began to condole with Calatinus over being beaten for the tribunate after having spent so much money for the canvass. But why are you so stirred up? As Plato very admirably observes in his 'Philebus' — "

"The Furies seize upon your 'Philebus'!" thundered Agias. "Keep quiet, if you've nothing good to tell! Oh, Agias, Agias! where are your wits, where is your cunning? What in the world can I do?"

And so he poured out his distress and anger. But, after all, there was nothing to be done that night. Pisander, who at last began to realize the dilemma of his friend, ventured on a sort of sympathy which was worse than no sympathy at all, for philosophical platitudes are ever the worst of consolations.

Agias invited the good man to spend the night with him, and not risk a second time the robbers of the streets. The young Greek himself finally went to bed, with no definite purpose in his mind except to rescue Artemisia, at any and every hazard, from falling into the clutches of Calatinus, who was perhaps the one man in the world Agias detested the most heartily.

II

Early in the morning Agias was awake. He had slept very little. The face of Artemisia was ever before him, and he saw it bathed in tears, and clouded with anguish and terror. But, early as he arose, it was none too early. Dromo, one of his slaves, came to announce to his dread lord that an aged Ethiop was waiting to see him, and Agias did not need to be told that this was Sesostris.

That faithful servant of an unworthy master was indeed in a pitiable condition. His ordinarily neat and clean dress was crumpled and disarranged, as though he had not changed it during the night, but had rather been tossing and wakeful. His eyes were swollen, and tears were trickling down his cheeks. His voice had sunk to a husky choking, and when he stood before Agias he was unable to get out a word, but, after a few vain attempts which ended in prolonged sniffles, thrust into his young friend's hand a tablet.

It was in Greek, in the childish, awkward hand of Artemisia, and ran as follows : —

" Artemisia to her dear, dear Agias. I never wrote a letter before, and you must excuse the blunders in this. I don't know how to begin to tell you the dreadful thing that may happen to me. I will try and stop crying, and write it out just as it all happened. The day before yesterday Pratinas took me to the circus, where I enjoyed the racing very much.

Q

While we were sitting there, a very fine gentleman — at least he had purple stripes on his tunic and ever so many rings — came and sat down beside us. Pratinas told me that this gentleman was Lucius Calatinus, who was a great lord, but a friend of his. I tried to say something polite to Calatinus, but I didn't like him. He seemed coarse, and looked as though he might be cruel at times. He talked to me something the way you have talked — said I was pretty and my voice sounded very sweet. But I didn't enjoy these things from him, I can hardly tell why — though I'm delighted to hear you say them. Well, after quite a while he went away, and I didn't think anything more about him for a time, and yesterday you know how happy I was when you visited me. Only a little while after you left, Pratinas came back. I could see that he had something on his mind, although he said nothing. He seemed uneasy, and kept casting sidelong glances at me, which made me feel uncomfortable. I went up to him, and put my arms around his neck. 'Dear uncle,' I said, 'what is troubling you to-night?' 'Nothing,' he answered, and he half tried to take my arms away. Then he said, 'I was thinking how soon I was to go back to Alexandria.' 'To Alexandria!' I cried, and I was just going to clap my hands when I thought that, although Alexandria was a far nicer place than Rome, you could not go with us, and so I felt very sorry. Then Pratinas spoke again in a hard, cold voice he has never used to me before. 'Artemisia, I must tell you now the truth about yourself. I have let you call me uncle, and have tried to be kind to you. But you cannot come back to Alexandria with me. The day after to-morrow Calatinus, the gentleman you met at the circus yesterday, will come and take you away. He is a very rich man, and if you please him will give you everything you desire.' I couldn't understand at all what he meant, and

cried out, 'But, uncle, I don't like Calatinus, and you — you
don't really mean to leave me behind?' 'You little donkey,'
said Pratinas, laughing, oh! so heartlessly, 'I'm not your
uncle. You've been my slave, and I've sold you to Calatinus;
so don't quarrel with him, but learn to like him quickly.' I
don't remember what he said or I said next. I was so frightened and grieved that I don't know what I did. I know Pratinas finally whipped me, something he never did before. I
vent to bed feeling so sore, that I could not get really to sleep,
but dreadful visions of Calatinus kept frightening me. I don't
know which grieves me most, to know I am a slave, to know
that Pratinas is not my uncle and does not love me, or to be
about to be sold to Calatinus. Dear Sesostris has done all he
can to console me, but that's very little; and so, very early this
morning, I've written to you, Agias, just as soon as Pratinas
left the house, for I am sure that you, who are so clever and
wise, can see some way to get me out of my dreadful trouble."

It would be hardly necessary to say that, after reading this
appeal, Agias hurried away to do all that lay in his power to
console Artemisia, and deliver her from her danger. When
he reached Pratinas's tenement, Artemisia ran to meet him,
and kissed him again and again, and cuddled down in his
strong, young arms, quite content to believe that she had
found a protector on whom she could cast all her burdens.
And Agias? He laughed and bade her wipe away her tears,
and swore a great oath that, so long as he breathed, Calatinus
should not lay a finger upon her.

Artemisia had practically told all her story in her letter. It
was clear that Calatinus had caught sight of her several times,
— though she had remained in blissful ignorance, — and Pratinas had deliberately planned to waylay him as a customer
who would pay a good price for the girl, whom it would be

manifestly inconvenient for him to take with Valeria on his premeditated flight to Egypt. But this enlightenment did not make Agias's task any the easier. He knew perfectly well that he could never raise a tithe of the forty thousand sesterces that Pratinas was to receive from Calatinus, and so redeem Artemisia. He had no right to expect the gift of such a sum from Drusus. If Pratinas really owned the poor girl as a slave, he could do anything he listed with her, and no law could be invoked to say him nay. There was only one recourse left to Agias, and that was fairly desperate — to carry off Artemisia and keep her in hiding until Pratinas should give up the quest and depart for Egypt. That there was peril in such a step he was well aware. Not merely could Artemisia, if recaptured, receive any form whatsoever of brutal punishment, but he, as the abettor of her flight, would be liable to a heavy penalty. Slave property was necessarily very precarious property, and to aid a slave to escape was an extremely heinous crime. "So many slaves, so many enemies," ran the harsh maxim; and it was almost treason to society for a freedman to aid a servant to run away.

But Agias had no time to count the cost, no time to evolve a plan of escape that admitted no form of disaster. Artemisia besought him not to leave her for a moment, and accordingly he remained by her, laughing, poking fun, and making reckless gibes at her fears. Sesostris went about his simple household duties with a long face, and now and then a tear trickled down his cheek. Whatever came of the matter, Artemisia would have to be separated from him. He might never see her again, and the old Ethopian loved her more than he did life itself.

"You will not wrong the girl when she is with you?" he whispered dolefully to Agias.

"I swear by Zeus she shall be treated as if she were my own dear sister," was his reply.

"It is well. I can trust you; but *mu! mu!* it is hard, it is hard! I love her like my own eyes! Isis preserve her dear life!"

And so at last Artemisia, having cried out all her first burst of grief, was beginning to smile once more.

"And now, oh! makaira,"[1] said Agias, "I must go away for just a little while. I have ever so many things to attend to; and you must be a good, brave girl, and wait until I come back."

"*St!*" broke in Sesostris, "there's a step on the stairs. Pratinas is coming!"

"Hide me!" cried Agias, as the approaching feet grew nearer. There was no time to take refuge in one of the farther rooms.

"Here;" and Sesostris threw open the same iron clamped chest in which some time ago we saw Pratinas inspecting his treasure. "The money was taken out yesterday."

Agias bounded into the box, and Sesostris pushed down the cover. The luckless occupant had only a chance to push out a corner of his tunic through the slit to admit a little air, when Pratinas entered the room. Agias longed to spring forth and throttle him, but such an act would have been folly.

The young Greek's prison was sufficiently cramped and stuffy; but for a moment Agias tried to persuade himself that he had only to wait with patience until Pratinas should be gone, and no one would be the worse. An exclamation from the room without dispelled this comforting illusion.

"By Zeus!" cried Pratinas, "what is this? Whence came this new toga?

Agias writhed in his confinement. In the plentitude of the

[1] Blessed dear.

glory of his newly acquired freedom, he had come abroad in an elegant new toga; but he had laid it on a chair when he entered the room.

There was an awkward pause outside; then Pratinas burst out, "You worthless Ethiopian, you, where did this toga come from? It hasn't wings or feet! How came it here? Who's been here? Speak, speak, you fool, or I will teach you a lesson!"

Agias gathered himself for a spring; for he expected to hear Sesostris whimper out a confession, and see Pratinas's wickedly handsome face peering into the chest. "He shan't cut my throat without a struggle!" was his vow.

But, to his surprise, Sesostris answered with a tone of unlooked-for firmness, "Master, I cannot tell you where the toga came from."

The tone of Pratinas, in reply, indicated his passion. "Sheep! Dog! Have I had you all these years that you should need a thrashing for impertinence! What rascal has been here to ogle at this wretched girl?" He might have thundered his commands to Artemisia, who was sobbing in evident distress; but his anger was concentrated on Sesostris. "Will you not speak?"

"Master," came the same firm reply, "I will not tell you, though you take my life for refusing."

What followed was, as Agias heard it, a volley of curses, blows, groans, and scuffling; then a heavy fall; an extremely fierce execration from Pratinas, and a loud shrill scream from Artemisia, "O Sesostris; dear Sesostris! He doesn't speak! He doesn't move! You've killed him!"

"And I will kill you too if you won't tell the truth!" thundered Pratinas, in an ungovernable passion. Agias heard a blow as of a clinched fist, and a low moan. It was enough. One spring, and the ponderous cover flew back. The toga, the innocent cause of the catastrophe, lay on the chair close at hand. Agias grasped the whole picture in a twinkling: Sesostris lying beside a heavy wooden bench, with blood flowing from a great wound in his head which had struck in falling on a sharp corner; Artemisia crying in unspeakable dread on a divan; Pratinas, his face black as night, with uplifted hand prepared to strike a second time. Agias saw; and while he saw acted. Down over Pratinas's head dashed the broad linen folds of the toga, and two muscular arms drew it tight around the neck. Then began the struggle. Pratinas was of powerful physique, and resisted like a madman. The carpet was torn to shreds, the chairs shivered. But Agias, too, battled for grim life. He kept the hood over his opponent's eyes and never gave Pratinas a glimpse of the identity of his assailant. And at last a life of debauches and late dinners and unhealthy excitement began to tell against even so powerful a constitution as that of Pratinas. Tighter and tighter grew the pressure around his neck. And now Artemisia sprang up, and flew like a tiny tigress to her lover's assistance, and caught at her tormentor's hands, tearing them with her white little teeth, and pulling the enveloping mantle closer and closer. The contest could only have one end. Ere long, Pratinas was lying on the floor, bound hand and foot with strings of torn clothing, and his head still muffled in the toga. Agias, victorious, but with not a whole rag on his back, rose from his contest.

"Sesostris! help him!" cried Artemisia, trying in vain to get some response from the motionless form by the bench. Agias looked at the Ethiop. The hard wood had struck the top of his skull, and death must have been instantaneous.

"He does not feel any pain," explained the young Greek, who realized that this was no moment to indulge in emotions of any sort. "Now, Artemisia, you must hurry and put on a clean dress yourself; and give me at least a new tunic, for I cannot show this on the streets. Put into a basket all the bread you have, and some oil, and some olives, and some slices of salt fish."

Artemisia disappeared in the next room. Agias returned to his prisoner. Pratinas was coughing and twisting, and trying to ejaculate oaths.

"My good sir," said Agias, "I am not a bloodthirsty man, otherwise I would cut your throat, and so let you forget a predicament which doubtless embarrasses you not a little. But, since that is not to be, do not blame me if I arrange so that it will be unlikely that two such cold friends as you and myself will ever meet again. First of all, that purse which is at your side, and which, by its weight, shows that it contains a fair night's winnings, must go with me to speed me on my way. I have never stolen very much before. But I believe you, sir, are an Epicurean, who teach that pleasure is the highest good, and that all things are the result of chance. Now," and here he detached the purse, and counted over a very considerable sum, "you will observe that Fortune has thrown this money in my way, and it is my pleasure to take it. Therefore I am fulfilling the highest good. And you, as a philosopher, should be quite reconciled."

Artemisia came back into the room, having completed the few simple preparations.

"Now, my excellent sir," continued Agias, suiting his actions to his words, "I will stand you on your feet—so. I will push you, still bound, into this closet—so. I will pile furniture against the door, so that, when you have worked clear of your bonds, as I imagine you will in a few hours, even then you will not get out too quickly. And now, as your dear Roman friends say. *Vale!* We are off!"

Artemisia flung herself on the form of Sesostris, and covered the black, ugly face with kisses.

"He's growing cold," she lamented. "What is the matter? I can't leave him this way!"

But Agias did not dare to admit the least delaying.

"Dear Artemisia," he said, "we can't do anything for Sesostris. I will explain to you by and by about him. He is not feeling cold now at all. You must come at once with me. I will take you where Pratinas will never touch you."

III

If Agias had been a trifle more reckless he would have cut short Pratinas's thread of life then and there, and greatly diminished the chance of unpleasant consequences. But he had not sunk so low as that. Besides, he had already worked out in his versatile head a plan that seemed practicable, albeit utterly audacious. Cornelia was at Baiæ. Cornelia owed him a great debt of gratitude for saving Drusus. Cornelia might harbour Artemisia as a new maid, if he could contrive to get his charge over the hundred long miles that lay between Rome and Baiæ.

In the street he made Artemisia draw her mantle over her pretty face, and pressed through the crowds as fast as he could drag her onward. Quickly as he might he left the noisy Subura behind, and led on toward the Palatine. At length he turned in toward a large house, and by a narrow alley reached a garden gate, and gained admission to the rear By his confident movements he showed himself familiar with the spot. The dwelling, as a matter of fact, was that of Calatinus.

As Agias pushed open the gate, and led Artemisia into a little garden enclosed with a high stone wall, he surprised a dapper-appearing young slave-lad of about his age, who was lying idly on the tiny grass plot, and indulging in a solitary game of backgammon.[1]

"*Hem!* Iasus," was Agias's salutation, "can you do an old friend a favour?"

Iasus sprang to his feet, with eyes, nose, and mouth wide open. He turned red, turned white, turned red once more.

"*Phy!*" cried the other; "you aren't so silly as to take me for a shade from Hades? I've as much strength and muscle as you."

"Agias!" blurted out Iasus, "are you alive? Really alive? They didn't beat you to death! I am so glad! You know—"

"*St!*" interrupted Agias. "You did, indeed, serve me an awkward trick some time since; but who can blame you for wanting to save your own skin. Pisander and Arsinoë and Semiramis have kept the secret that I'm alive very well, for in some ways it shouldn't come to Valeria's ears. My story later. Where's her most noble ladyship?"

"The domina," replied Iasus, with a sniff, "has just gone out on a visit to a friend who has a country-house near Fidenæ, up the Tiber."

"Praise the gods! Far enough to be abroad for the day, and perhaps over night! This suits my purpose wonderfully. Is Pisander at home, and Arsinoë?"

"I will fetch them," replied Iasus; and in a minute the philosopher and the waiting-maid were in the garden.

A very few words explained to these two sympathetic souls the whole situation.

Artemisia shrank back at sight of Pisander.

"I am afraid of that man. He wears a great beard like Pratinas, and I don't love Pratinas any longer."

---

[1] *Duodecim scripta.*

"Oh, don't say that, my little swallow," said the worthy man of books, looking very sheepish. "I should be sorry to think that your bright eyes were vexed to see me."

"*Phui !* Pisander," laughed Arsinoë, "what have Zeno and Diogenes to do with 'bright eyes'?"

But for once Pisander's heart was wiser than his head, and he only tossed Artemisia an enormous Persian peach, at which, when she sampled the gift, she made peace at once, and forever after held Pisander in her toils as a devoted servant.

But Agias was soon gone; and Artemisia spent the rest of the morning and the whole of the afternoon in that very satisfactory Elysium of Syrian pears and honey-apples which Semiramis and Arsinoë supplied in full measure, with Pisander to sit by, and stare, boylike, at her clear, fair profile, and cast jealous glances at Iasus when that young man ventured to utilize his opportunity for a like advantage. Many of the servants had gone with Valeria, and the others readily agreed to preserve secrecy in a matter in which their former fellow-slave and favourite had so much at stake. So the day passed, and no one came to disturb her; and just as the shadows were falling Agias knocked at the garden gate.

"*St !*" were his words, "I have hired a gig which will carry us both. Pratinas is loose and has been raising heaven and earth to get at us. There is a crier going the rounds of the Forum offering a thousand sesterces for the return of Artemisia. Pratinas has gone before the *triumviri capitales* [1] and obtained from them an order on the *apparitores* [2] to track down the runaway and her abettor."

"*Eho !*" cried Pisander, "then you'd better leave your treasure here awhile, for us to take care of."

[1] One of their functions made these officers practically chiefs of police.
[2] A part of these public officers performed police duty.

"Not at all," replied Agias; "I could have taken her out of the city at once, but in the daytime we should have been certainly noticed and subsequently tracked. No one will imagine Artemisia is here — at least for a while. But this is a large familia; all may be my friends, but all may not have prudent tongues in their heads. The reward is large, and perhaps some will be tempted;" he glanced at Iasus, who, to do him justice, had never thought of a second deed of baseness. "I cannot risk that. No, Artemisia goes out of the city to-night, and she must get ready without the least delay."

Artemisia, who was charmed with her present surroundings and adulation, demurred at leaving her entertainers; but Agias was imperative, and the others realized well enough that there was not much time to be lost. Agias, however, waited until it had become tolerably dark before starting. Meantime, he proceeded to make certain changes of his own and Artemisia's costume that indicated the rather serious character of the risk he was preparing to run. For himself he put on a very full and flowing crimson evening dress, as if he were proceeding to a dinner-party; he piled a dozen odd rings upon his fingers, and laughingly asked Semiramis to arrange his hair for him in the most fashionable style, and anoint it heavily with Valeria's most pungent perfumes. At the same time, Arsinoë was quite transforming Artemisia. Valeria's cosmetic vials were for once put into play for a purpose, and when Artemisia reappeared from the dressing-room after her treatment, Agias saw before him no longer a fair-skinned little Greek, but a small, slender, but certainly very handsome Egyptian serving-lad, with bronzed skin, conspicuous carmine lips, and features that Arsinoë's paint and pencils had coarsened and exagger-

ated. Fortunately, the classic costume both for men and
women was so essentially alike, that Artemisia did not have
to undergo that mortification from a change of clothes which
might have befallen one at the present day in a like predicament. Her not very long black hair was loose, and shaken
over her shoulders. Agias had brought for her a short, varie-
gated *lacerna*,[1] which answered well enough as the habit of a
boy-valet who was on good terms with his master.

"*Eho!*" cried Agias, when he had witnessed the trans-
formation, "we must hasten or Valeria will be anxious to
keep you as her serving-boy! Ah, I forgot she is going with
her dear Pratinas to Egypt. Now, Arsinoë, and you, Semiramis, I shall not forget the good turn you have done me; don't
let Valeria miss her unguents and ask questions that might
prove disagreeable. Farewell, Iasus and Pisander; we shall
soon meet again, the gods willing."

The friends took leave of Artemisia; the slave-women
kissed her; Pisander, presuming on his age, kissed her, albeit
very sheepishly, as though he feared the ghosts of all the
Stoics would see him. Iasus cast an angry jealous glance at
the philosopher; he contented himself with a mere shake of
the hand.

Agias swung Artemisia into the gig and touched the lash to
the swift mules.

"Good-by, dear friends!" she cried, her merry Greek smile
shining out through her bronze disguise.

The gig rolled down the street, Agias glancing to right and
left to see that no inquisitive eye followed them.

"Oh! Agias," cried the girl, "am I at last going away with
you? Going away all alone, with only you to take care of me?
I feel — I feel queerly!"

---

[1] A sort of mantle held on the shoulders by a clasp.

Agias only touched the mules again, and laughed and squeezed Artemisia's hand, then more gravely said: —

"Now, makaira, you must do everything as I say, or we shall never get away from Pratinas. Remember, if I tell you to do anything you must do it instantly; and, above everything else, no matter what happens, speak not a word; don't scream or cry or utter a sound. If anybody questions us I shall say that I am a gentleman driving out to the suburbs to enjoy a late party at a friend's villa, and you are my valet, who is a mute, whom it is useless to question because he cannot answer. Do you understand?"

Artemisia nodded her little head, and bit her pretty lips very hard to keep from speaking. The fear of Pratinas made her all obedience.

It was after sundown, and driving was permitted in the city, though nearly all the teams that blocked Agias's way, as he drove down the crowded streets to turn on to the Via Appia, were heavy wagons loaded with timber and builders' stone.

So far, all was safe enough; but Agias knew perfectly well that Pratinas was an ʔwkward man to have for an enemy. The critical moment, however, was close at hand, and Agias called up all his wits to meet it. Under the damp arch of the ancient Porta Capena were pacing several men, whose lanterns and clinking sword-scabbards proclaimed them to be members of the city constabulary. There was no possibility of evading their scrutiny. No doubt any other gate was equally well watched. Agias drove straight ahead, as though he had seen nothing.

"Hold!" and one of the constables was at the heads of the mules, and another was waving a lantern up into the face of the occupants of the gig.

"Rascals," roared Agias, menacing with his whip, "are you highwaymen grown so impudent!"

"We have an order from the triumviri," began one officer.

"*Eho!*" replied Agias, settling back, as though relieved not to have to fight for his purse, "I can't see what for; I owe nothing. I have no suit pending."

"We are to search all carriages and pedestrians," recommenced the constable, "to find if we may a certain Artemisia, a runaway slave-girl of the most noble Greek gentleman, Pratinas."

"My good sirs," interrupted Agias, "I am already like to be very late at my dear friend Cimber's dinner party" —he mentioned the name of the owner of a very large villa not far down the road; "I have with me only Midas, my mute valet. If you detain me any longer I shall complain—"

And here a denarius slipped into the hands of the officer with the lantern.

"I think it's all right, Macer," was his report to his comrade. The latter left the heads of the mules.

"*Mehercle!* how handsome some of those Egyptians grow!" commented the first constable.

But the rest of his remarks were lost on Agias. He was whizzing down the "Queen of Roads," with a good team before him, Artemisia at his side, and a happy consciousness that two excellent officials had missed a chance to earn one thousand sesterces.

Hardly were they beyond earshot, when Artemisia burst out into an uncontrollable fit of giggling, which lasted a long time, only to be renewed and renewed, as often as a desperate effort seemed to have suppressed it. Then she drew the robes of the carriage round her, laid her head on Agias's shoulder, and with a confidence in her protector that would have inspired him to

go through fire and water for her sake, shook out her dark locks
and fell fast asleep, despite the fact that the mules were running their fastest. Agias grasped the reins with one hand, and
with the other pressed tight the sleeping girl. He would not
have exchanged his present position for all the wealth of
Sardanapalus.

*　*　*　*　*　*　*　*　*　*

Five days later Agias was back in Rome. He had succeeded
in reaching Baiæ, and introducing Artemisia into the familia
of the villa of the Lentuli, as a new waiting-maid from Rome
sent by Claudia to her daughter. For the present at least there
was practically no chance of Pratinas recovering his lost property. And indeed, when Agias reached Rome once more, all
fears in that direction were completely set at rest. The fashionable circle in which Claudia and Herennia were enmeshed
was in a flutter and a chatter over no ordinary scandal.
Valeria, wife of Calatinus, and Pratinas, the "charming"
Epicurean philosopher, had both fled Rome two days before,
and rumour had it that they had embarked together at Ostia on
a ship leaving direct for Egypt. Of course Calatinus was
receiving all the sympathy, and was a much abused man; and
so the tongues ran on.

To Agias this great event brought a considerable gain in
peace of mind, and some little loss. Valeria had taken with
her her two maids, Agias's good friends, and also Iasus.
Pisander ignominiously had been left behind. Calatinus had
no use for the man of learning, and Agias was fain to take him
before Drusus, who had returned from Ravenna, and induce
his patron to give Pisander sufficient capital to start afresh a
public school of philosophy, although the chances of acquiring
opulence in that profession were sufficiently meagre.

CHAPTER XIII

WHAT BEFELL AT BAIÆ

I

CORNELIA was at Baiæ, the famous watering-place, upon the classic Neapolitan bay, — which was the Brighton or Newport of the Roman. Here was the haunt of the sybarites, whose gay barks skimmed the shallow waters of the Lucrine lake; and not far off slumbered in its volcanic hollow that other lake, Avernus, renowned in legend and poetry, through whose caverns, fable had it, lay the entrance to the world of the dead. The whole country about was one city of stately villas, of cool groves, of bright gardens; a huge pleasure world, where freedom too often became license; where the dregs of the nectar cup too often meant physical ruin and moral death.

Cornelia had lost all desire to die now. She no longer thought of suicide. Lentulus's freedmen held her in close surveillance, but she was very happy. Drusus lived, was safe, would do great things, would win a name and a fame in the world of politics and arms. For herself she had but one ambition — to hear men say, "This woman is the wife of the great Quintus Drusus." That would have been Elysium indeed. Cornelia, in fact, was building around her a world of sweet fantasy, that grew so real, so tangible, that the stern realities of life, realities that had hitherto worn out her very

soul, became less galling. The reaction following the ̱ol
lapse of the plot against Drusus had thrown her into an
unnatural cheerfulness. For the time the one thought when
she arose in the morning, the one thought when she fell asleep
at night, was, "One day," or "One night more is gone, of the
time that severs me from Quintus." It was a strained, an
unhealthy cheerfulness; but while it lasted it made all the
world fair for Cornelia. Indeed, she had no right — from one
way of thinking — not to enjoy herself, unless it be that she
had no congenial companions. The villa of the Lentuli was
one of the newest and finest at Baiæ. It rested on a sort
of breakwater built out into the sea, so that the waves actually beat against the embankment at the foot of Cornelia's
chamber. The building rose in several stories, each smaller
than the one below it, an ornamental cupola highest of all.
On the successive terraces were formally plotted, but luxuriant, gardens. Cornelia, from her room in the second story,
could command a broad vista of the bay. Puteoli was only
two miles distant. Vesuvius was ten times as far; but the
eye swept clear down the verdant coast toward Surrentum
to the southward. At her feet was the sea, — the Italian,
Neapolitan sea, — dancing, sparkling, dimpling from the first
flush of morning to the last glint of the fading western
clouds at eve. The azure above glowed with living brightness, and by night the stars and planets burned and twinkled
down from a crystalline void, through which the unfettered
soul might soar and soar, swimming onward through the
sweet darkness of the infinite.

And there were pleasures enough for Cornelia if she would
join therein. Lentulus had ordered his freedmen not to deny
her amusements; anything, in fact, that would divert her
from her morbid infatuation for Drusus. The consul-desig-

nate had indeed reached the conclusion that his niece was suffering some serious mental derangement, or she would not thus continue to pursue a profitless passion, obviously impossible of fulfilment. So Cornelia had every chance to make herself a centre to those gay pleasure-seekers who were still at Baiæ; for the summer season was a little past, and all but confirmed or fashionable invalids and professional vacationers were drifting back to Rome. For a time all went merrily enough. Just sufficient of the Lucius Ahenobarbus affair had come to the Baiæans to make Cornelia the object of a great amount of curiosity. When she invited a select number of the pleasure-seekers to her dinner parties, she had the adulation and plaudits of every guest, and plenty of return favours. Lucius Ahenobarbus soon had a score of hot rivals; and Cornelia's pretty face was chipped on more than one admirer's seal ring. But presently it began to be said that the niece of the consul-designate was an extremely stoical and peculiar woman; she did not enjoy freedom which the very air of Baiæ seemed to render inevitable. She never lacked wit and vivacity, but there was around her an air of restraint and cold modesty that was admirable in every way — only it would never do in Baiæ. And so Cornelia, without ceasing to be admired, became less courted; and presently, quite tiring of the butterfly life, was thrown back more and more on herself and on her books. This did not disturb her A levee or a banquet had never given her perfect pleasure; and it was no delight to know that half the women of Baiæ hated her with a perfect jealousy. Cornelia read and studied, now Greek, now Latin; and sometimes caught herself half wishing to be a man and able to expound a cosmogony, or to decide the fate of empires by words flung down from the rostrum. Then finally Agias came bringing Artemisia, who as has been related, was introduced — by means of some little contriving — into the familia as a new serving-maid. Such Artemisia was in name; but Cornelia, whose gratitude to Agias had known no bounds, took the little thing into her heart, and determined to devote herself to instructing an innocence that must not continue too long, despite its charming naïveté.

Thus the days had passed for Cornelia. But only a little while after Agias left for Rome, — with a very large packet of letters for Drusus, — the pleasant, self-created world of fantasy, that had given Cornelia some portion of happiness, vanished. Like a clap of thunder from a cloudless sky Lucius Ahenobarbus suddenly arrived in Baiæ. He was tired of Rome, which was still very hot and uncomfortable. He loathed politics, they were stupid. He had lost a boon companion when Publius Gabinius was driven into outlawry. Marcus Læca was too deeply in debt to give any more dinners. Pratinas was fled to Egypt. And so he had come to Baiæ, to harass Cornelia by his presence; to gibe at her; and assure her that her uncle was more determined than ever that she should marry him — say and do what she might.

Ahenobarbus quartered himself in the Lentulan villa as the prospective nephew-in-law of its owner. He brought with him his customary train of underlings, and had travelled in appropriate state, in a litter with eight picked bearers, lolling on a cushion stuffed with rose-leaves, and covered with Maltese gauze, one garland on his head, another round his neck, and holding to his nose a smelling-bag of small-meshed linen filled with roses.

With all his effeminacy, he was beyond the least doubt desperately determined to possess himself of Cornelia. His passion was purely animal and unrefined, but none could doubt

As Cornelia feared to have him near her, and knew peace neither day nor night. He assumed all a master's rights over the slaves and freedmen, sending them hither and yon to do his bidding. He had recovered from the fear Cornelia had struck into him, in her first defiance, and met her threats and hauteur with open scorn.

"You are a most adorable actress!" was his constant sneer. And his every action told that he did not intend to let Cornelia play with him a second time. With all his profligacy and moral worthlessness, he had a tenacity of purpose and an energy in this matter that showed that either Cornelia must in the end bow to his will, or their contest would end in something very like a tragedy.

And if a tragedy, so be it, was the desperate resolve of Cornelia; whose eyes were too stern for tears when she saw that Lucius was still the former creature of appetite; full of intrigue, sweethearts, seashore revels, carouses, singing, and music parties and water excursions with creatures of his choice from morning until midnight. She could not altogether shun him, though she successfully resisted his half blandishments, half coercion, to make her join in his wild frivolities. One revenge she found she could take on him — a revenge that she enjoyed because it proclaimed her own intellectual superiority, and made Ahenobarbus writhe with impotent vexation — she had him at her mercy when they played at checkers;[1] and at last Lucius lost so much money and temper at this game of wit, not chance, that he would sulkily decline a challenge. But this was poor consolation to Cornelia. The time was drifting on. Before many days Lentulus Crus and Caius Clodius Marcellus would be consuls, and the anti-Cæsarians would be ready to work their great

[1] *Latrunculi.*

opponent's undoing, or be themselves forever undone. Where was Drusus? What was he doing? What part would he play in the struggle, perhaps of arms, about to begin? O for one sight of him, for one word! And the hunger in Cornelia's breast grew and grew.

Many are our wishes. Some flit through our hearts like birds darting under the foliage of trees, then out again, lost in the sunshine; others linger awhile and we nestle them in our bosoms until we forget that they are there, and the noble desire, the craving for something dear, for something that bears for us as it were a divine image, is gone — we are the poorer that we no longer wish to wish it. But some things there are --- some things too high or too deep for speech, too secret for really conscious thought, too holy to call from the innermost shrines of the heart; and there they linger and hover, demanding to be satisfied, and until they are satisfied there is void and dreariness within, be the sunshine never so bright without. And so Cornelia was a-hungered. She could fight against herself to save Drusus's life no longer; she could build around herself her dream castles no more; she must see him face to face, must hold his hand in hers, must feel his breath on her cheek.

Is it but a tale that is told, that soul can communicate to distant soul? That through two sundered hearts without visible communication can spring up, unforewarned, a single desire, a single purpose? Is there no magnetism subtle beyond all thought, that bounds from spirit to spirit, defying every bond, every space? We may not say; but if Cornelia longed, she longed not utterly in vain. One morning, as she was dressing, Cassandra, who was moving around the room aiding her mistress, let fall a very tiny slip of papyrus into Cornelia's lap, and with it a whisper, "Don't look; but keep it carefully." The injunction was needed, for several other serving-women were in the room, and Cornelia more than suspected that they were ready to spy on her to prevent unauthorized correspondence with Drusus. When she was dressed, and could walk alone on the terrace overlooking the sea, she unrolled the papyrus and read:—

"Delectissima, I have come from Rome to Puteoli. I cannot live longer without seeing you. Great things are stirring, and it may well be that ere long, if your uncle and his friends have their way, I may be a proscribed fugitive from Italy, or a dead man. But I must talk with your dear self first. Agias was known by the familia, and had no difficulty in seeing you quietly; but I have no such facility. I cannot remain long. Plan how we may meet and not be interrupted. I have taken Cassandra into my pay, and believe that she can be trusted. *Vale*."

There was no name of the sender; but Cornelia did not need to question. Cassandra, who evidently knew that her mistress would require her services, came carelessly strolling out on to the terrace.

"Cassandra," said Cornelia, "the last time I saw Quintus, you betrayed us to my uncle; will you be more faithful now?"

The woman hung down her head.

"*A!* domina, your uncle threatened me terribly. I did not intentionally betray you! Did I not receive my beating? And then Master Drusus is such a handsome and generous young gentleman."

"I can rely on you alone," replied Cornelia. "You must arrange everything. If you are untrue, be sure that it is not I who will in the end punish, but Master Drusus, whose memory is long. You have more schemes than I, now that

Agias is not here to devise for me. You must make up any stories that are necessary to save us from interruption, and see that no one discovers anything or grows suspicious. My hands are tied. I cannot see to plan. I will go to the library, and leave everything to you."

And with this stoical resolve to bear with equanimity whatever the Fates flung in her way for good or ill, Cornelia tried to bury herself in her Lucretius. Vain resolution! What care for the atomic theory when in a day, an hour, a moment, she might be straining to her heart another heart that was reaching out toward hers, as hers did toward it. It was useless to read; useless to try to admire the varying shades of blue on the sea, tones of green, and tones of deep cerulean, deepening and deepening, as her eye drifted off toward the horizon, like the blendings of a chromatic series. And so Cornelia passed the morning in a mood of joyful discontent. Lucius Ahenobarbus, who came to have his usual passage of arms with her, found her so extremely affable, yet half-preoccupied, that he was puzzled, yet on the whole delighted. "She must be yielding," he mentally commented; and when they played at draughts, Cornelia actually allowed herself to be beaten. Ahenobarbus started off for Puteoli in an excellent humour. His litter had barely swung down the road from the villa before Cassandra was knocking at her mistress's chamber door.

"*Io!* domina," was her joyful exclamation, "I think I have got every eavesdropper out of the way. Ahenobarbus is off for Puteoli. I have cooked up a story to keep the freedmen and other busybodies off. You have a desperate headache, and cannot leave the room, nor see any one. But remember the terrace over the water, where the colonnade shuts it in on all sides but toward the sea. This afternoon, if a boat with two strange-looking fishermen passes under the embankment, don't be surprised."

And having imparted this precious bit of information, the woman was off. Drusus's gold pieces had made her the most successful of schemers.

II

Cornelia feigned her headache, and succeeded in making herself so thoroughly petulant and exacting to all her maids, that when she ordered them out of the room, and told them on no account to disturb her in any respect for the rest of the day, they "rejoiced with trembling," and had no anxiety to thrust their attentions upon so unreasonable a mistress. And a little while later a visit of a strolling juggler — whose call had perhaps been prompted by Cassandra — made their respite from duty doubly welcome.

Cornelia was left to herself, and spent the next hour in a division of labour before her silver wall-mirror, dressing — something which was sufficiently troublesome for her, accustomed to the services of a bevy of maids — and at the window, gazing toward Puteoli for the fishing-boat that seemed never in sight. At last the toilet was completed to her satisfaction. Cornelia surveyed herself in her best silken purple flounced stola, thrust the last pin into her hair, and confined it all in a net of golden thread. Roman maidens were not as a rule taught to be modest about their charms, and Cornelia, with perfect frankness, said aloud to herself, "You are so beautiful that Drusus can't help loving you;" and with this candid confession, she was again on the terrace, straining her eyes toward Puteoli. Boats came, boats went, but there was none that approached the villa; and Cornelia began to harbour dark thoughts against Cassandra.

"If the wretched woman had played false to her mistress again — " but the threat was never formulated. There was a chink and click of a pair of oars moving on their thole-pins. For an instant a skiff was visible at the foot of the embankment; two occupants were in it. The boat disappeared under the friendly cover of the protecting sea-wall of the lower terrace. There was a little landing-place here, with a few steps leading upward, where now and then a yacht was moored. The embankment shut off this tiny wharf from view on either side. Cornelia dared not leave the upper terrace. Her heart beat faster and faster. Below she heard the slap, slap, of the waves on the sea-wall, and a rattle of rings and ropes as some skiff was being made fast. An instant more and Drusus was coming, with quick, athletic bounds, up the stairway to the second terrace. It was he! she saw him! In her eyes he was everything in physique and virile beauty that a maiden of the Republic could desire! The bitterness and waiting of months were worth the blessedness of the instant. Cornelia never knew what Drusus said to her, or what she said to him. She only knew that he was holding her in his strong arms and gazing into her eyes; while the hearts of both talked to one another so fast that they had neither time nor need for words. They were happy, happy! Long it was before their utterance passed beyond the merest words of endearment; longer still before they were composed enough for Cornelia to listen to Drusus while he gave his own account of Mamercus's heroic resistance to Dumnorix's gang at Præneste; and told of his own visit to Ravenna, of his intense admiration for the proconsul of the two Gauls; and of how he had come to Puteoli and opened communications with Cassandra, through Cappadox, the trusty body-servant who in the guise of a fisherman was waiting in the boat below.

"And as Homer puts it, so with us," cried Cornelia, at length: "'And so the pair had joy in happy love, and joyed in talking too, and each relating; she, the royal lady, what she had endured at home, watching the wasteful throng of suitors; and he, high-born Odysseus, what miseries he brought on other men, and bore himself in anguish;—all he told, and she was glad to hear.'"

So laughed Cornelia when all their stories were finished, likening their reunion to that of the son of Laërtes and the long-faithful Penelope.

"How long were Penelope and Odysseus asunder?" quoth Drusus.

"Twenty years."

"*Vah!* We have not been sundered twenty months or one-third as many. How shall we make the time fly more rapidly?"

"I know not," said Cornelia, for the first time looking down and sighing, "a lifetime seems very long; but lifetimes will pass. I shall be an old woman in a few years; and my hair will be all grey, and you won't love me."

"*Eho*," cried Drusus, "do you think I love you for your hair?"

"I don't know," replied Cornelia, shaking her head, "I am afraid so. What is there in me more than any other woman that you should love; except—" and here she raised her face half-seriously, half in play—"I am very beautiful? Ah! if I were a man, I would have something else to be loved for; I would have eloquence, or strength, or power of command, or wisdom in philosophy. But no, I can be loved for only two things; an ignoble or a poor man would take me if I were hideous as Atropos, for I am noble, and, if my uncle were an honest guardian, rich. But you need not regard these at all, so — " and she brushed her face across Drusus's cheek, touching it with her hair.

"O Cornelia," cried the young man, out of the fulness of his heart, "we must not waste this precious time asking why we love each other. Love each other we do as long as we view the sun. O carissima! we cannot trust ourselves to look too deeply into the whys and wherefores of things. We men and women are so ignorant! We know nothing. What is all our philosophy — words! What is all our state religion — empty form! What is all our life — a dream, mostly evil, that comes out of the eternal unconscious sleep and into that unconscious sleep will return! And yet not all a dream; for when I feel your hands in mine I know that I am not dreaming — for dreamers feel nothing so delicious as this! Not long ago I recalled what old Artabanus said to King Xerxes when the millions of Persia passed in review before their lord at Abydos, 'Short as our time is, death, through the wretchedness of our life, is the most sweet refuge of our race; and God, who gives us tastes that we enjoy of pleasant times, is seen, in His very gift, to be envious.' And I thought, 'How wise was the Persian!' And then I thought, 'No, though to live were to drag one's days in torture and in woe, if only love come once into life, an eternity of misery is endurable; yes, to be chained forever, as Prometheus, on drearest mountain crag, if only the fire which is stolen be that which kindles soul by soul.'"

"Ah!" cried Cornelia, "if only these were to be real souls! But what can we say? See my Lucretius here; read: 'I have shown the soul to be formed fine and to be of minute bodies and made up of much smaller first-beginnings than the liquid air, or mist, or smoke. As you see water, when the vessels are shattered, flow away on every side, and as mist and smoke vanish away into the air, believe that the soul, too, is shed abroad, and perishes much more quickly and dissolves sooner into its first bodies, when once it has been taken out of the limbs of a man and has withdrawn.' O Quintus, is the thing within me that loves you lighter, more fragile, than smoke? Shall I blow away, and vanish into nothingness? It is that which affrights me!"

And Drusus tried as best he might to comfort her, telling her there was no danger that she or he would be dissipated speedily, and that she must not fret her dear head with things that set the sagest greybeards a-wrangling. Then he told her about the political world, and how in a month at most either every cloud would have cleared away, and Lentulus be in no position to resist the legal claims which Drusus had on the hand of his niece; or, if war came, if fortune but favoured Cæsar, Cornelia's waiting for deliverance would not be for long. Drusus did not dwell on the alternative presented if civic strife came to arms; he only knew that, come what might, Cornelia could never be driven to become the bride of Lucius Ahenobarbus; and he had no need to exact a new pledge of her faithful devotion.

So at last, like everything terrestrial that is sweet and lovely, the slowly advancing afternoon warned Drusus that for this day, at least, they must separate.

"I will come again to-morrow, or the next day, if Cassandra can so arrange," said he, tearing himself away. "But part to-night we must, nor will it make amends to imitate Carbo, who, when he was being led to execution, was suddenly seized with a pain in the stomach, and begged not to be beheaded until he should feel a little better."

He kissed her, strained her to his breast, and stepped toward the landing-place. Cappadox had taken the boat out from the moorings to minimize a chance of discovery by some one in the house. Drusus was just turning for a last embrace, when many voices and the plash of oars sounded below. Cornelia staggered with dread.

"It's Ahenobarbus," she gasped, in a deathly whisper; "he sometimes comes back from Puteoli by boat. He will murder you when he finds you here!"

"Can't I escape through the house?"

The words, however, were no sooner out of Drusus's mouth, than Lucius Ahenobarbus, dressed in the most fashionably cut scarlet lacerna, perfumed and coiffured to a nicety, appeared on the terrace. Some evil genius had led him straight up without the least delay.

It was the first time that the two enemies had met face to face since Drusus had declined the invitation to Marcus Læca's supper. Be it said to Lucius's credit that he sensed the situation with only the minimum of confusion, and instantly realized all of Cornelia's worst fears. Drusus had drawn back from the steps to the lower terrace, and stood with stern brow and knotted fist, trapped by a blunder that could hardly have been guarded against, no submissive victim to what fate had in store. Cornelia, for once quite distraught with terror, cowered on a bench, unable to scream through sheer fright.

"*Salve!* amice," was the satirical salutation of Ahenobarbus. "How excellently well met. *Heus!* Phaon, bring your boatmen, quick! Not an instant to lose!"

"Pity! mercy!" gasped Cornelia, "I will do anything for you, but spare him;" and she made as if to fall on her knees before Ahenobarbus.

"Girl!" Drusus had never spoken in that way to her before; his tones were cold as ice. "Go into the house! Your place is not here. If Lucius Ahenobarbus intends to murder me —"

The boatmen and two or three other slaves that were always at Ahenobarbus's heels were crowding up on to the terrace ready to do their master's bidding.

"Throw me that fellow over the balcony," ordered Lucius, his sense of triumph and opportunity mastering every fear that Flaccus would execute his threat of prosecution. "See that he does not float!"

Cornelia found her voice. She screamed, screamed shrilly, and ran into the house. Already the familia was alarmed. Two or three freedmen of Lentulus were rushing toward the terrace. They were murdering Quintus! He was resisting, resisting with all the powers of a wild animal driven to its last lair. Outside, on the terrace, where but an instant before she and her lover were cooing in delicious ecstasy, there were oaths, blows, and the sharp pants and howls of mortal struggle. And she could do nothing — nothing! And it was through his love for her that Drusus was to go down to his untimely grave! The seconds of struggle and anguish moved on leaden feet. Every breath was agony, every sound maddening. And she could do nothing — nothing. Still they were fighting. Phaon — she knew his voice — was crying out as if in grievous pain. And now the voice of Lucius Ahenobarbus sounded again: "One thousand denarii if you fling him into the sea!" and she could do nothing — nothing! She tore down the purple tapestries around her bed, and dashed from its tripod a costly bowl of opal Alexandrian glass — all in the mere rage of impotence. And still they were fighting. What was that ornament hanging on the wall, half hid behind the torn tapestry? A scabbard — a sword, some relic of ancient wars! And all the combatants were unarmed! The antique weapon was held by stout thongs to the wall; she plucked it from its fastenings with the strength of a Titaness. The rusty blade

resisted an instant; she dragged it forth.   Then out on to the
terrace.   Really only a moment had elapsed since she left it.
One of the slaves was lying dead, or stunned, prone on the
turf.   Phaon was writhing and howling beside him, nursing a
broken jaw.   The other assailants had sunk back in temporary
repulse and were preparing for a second rush.   Drusus was
still standing.   He half leaned upon the stone pedestal of an
heroic-sized Athena, who seemed to be spreading her protecting ægis above him.   His garments were rent to the veriest
shreds.   His features were hidden behind streaming blood,
his arms and neck were bruised and bleeding; but clearly
his adversaries could not yet congratulate themselves that the
lion's strength was too sapped to be no longer dreaded.

"Come, you," was his hot challenge to Lucius Ahenobarbus,
who stood, half delighted, half afraid, shivering and laughing
spasmodically, as he surveyed the struggle from a safe distance.   "Come, you, and have your share in the villany!"

And again, for it was all the affair of the veriest moment,
the slaves rushed once more on their indocile victim.   "Freedom to the man wno pulls him down!" was the incentive of
Ahenobarbus.

But again Drusus, who, to tell the truth, had to contend with
only the flabby, soft-handed, unskilful underlings of Lucius,
struck out so furiously that another of his attackers fell backward with a groan and a gasp.   All this Cornelia saw while,
sword in hand, she flew toward the knot of writhing men.
She pushed aside the slaves by sheer force.   She asked no
civilities, received none.

"Pull her away!" shouted Lucius, and started himself to
accomplish his purpose.   A rude hand smote her in the face;
she staggered, fell; but as she fell a hand snatched the sword
out of her grasp.   She released her hold gladly, for did she

not know that hand? When she rose to her feet there were shrieks of fear and pain on every side. The slaves were cringing in dread before him. Drusus was standing under the Athena, with the keen steel in his hand — its blade dyed crimson; and at his feet lay Ahenobarbus's favourite valet — the wretch literally disembowelled by one deadly stroke.

"Fly, fly!" she implored; "they will bring arms! They will never let you escape."

"I'll pay you for letting him kill Crœsus," howled Lucius, facing himself resolutely toward his enemy. "How can he fly when the house is full of servants, and his boat is away from the landing? You give yourself trouble for no purpose, my lady! Lentulus's people will be here with swords in a moment!"

But as he spoke a blow of some unseen giant dashed him prostrate, and upon the terrace from below came Cappadox, foaming with anxious rage, his brow blacker than night, his brawny arms swinging a heavy paddle with which he clubbed the cowering slaves right and left.

"Have they killed him! Have the gods spared him!" These two demands came bounding in a breath from the honest servant's lips. And when he saw Drusus, bleeding, but still standing, he rushed forward to fling his arms about his master's neck.

"Fly! fly!" urged Cornelia, and out of the building, armed now with swords and staves, came flocking the freedmen of the house and as many slaves as they could muster.

"*Salve!* carissima," and Drusus, who never at the instant gave thought to the blood all over him, pressed her in one last kiss. He gained the terrace steps by a single bound ahead of his armed attackers. Cappadox smote down the foremost freedman with a buffet of the oar. Ahenobarbus staggered to his feet as Drusus sprang over him, and the latter tore a packet of tablets from his hand, never stopping in his own flight.

Then down on to the little landing-place pursuers and pursued tumbled. The large six-oared boat of Ahenobarbus was moored close beside Cappadox's skiff.

Drusus was into the skiff and casting loose before Lucius could descend from the upper terrace. The young Domitian was in a terrible distress.

"The letters! The letters! Freedom to you all if you save them! Cast off! Chase! Sink the skiff!"

But before any of the unskilful assailants could execute the order, Cappadox had driven the butt of his paddle clean through the bottom planking of the larger boat, and she was filling rapidly. The paddle shivered, but it was madness to embark on the stoven craft.

The skiff shot away from the landing as though an intelligent soul, rising equal to the needs of the crisis. The blue dancing water lapped between her gunwale and the shore. Drusus stood erect in the boat, brushed back the blood that was still streaming over his eyes, and looked landward. The slaves and freedmen were still on the landing, gazing blankly after their escaped prey. Ahenobarbus was pouring out upon their inefficiency a torrent of wrathful malediction, that promised employment for the "whipper" for some time to come. But Drusus gave heed to none of these things. Standing on the upper terrace, her hair now dishevelled and blowing in tresses upon the wind, was Cornelia, and on her all her lover's gaze was fixed.

"Safe?" and the melodious shout drifted out over the widening stretch of water.

"Safe! to live and to love!" And Drusus thought, with

his keen lover's eye, he could see the dimming face brighten, and the hands go up in a gesture of thanksgiving.

It was all that was said. Another boat might be procured at any time by Lucius Ahenobarbus; and with only one paddle Cappadox could make but slow headway. Stiff and bruised, the young man flung himself on the bottom of the skiff, and panted and nursed himself after his mortal struggle. Now that the combat was over he felt weak and sore enough, and was quite content to let Cappadox adjust such improvised bandages as were available, and scull him toward Puteoli. Fortunately none of the bruises was caused by any harder weapons than fists, and, though his body was black and blue, he had sustained no serious hurt. And so he rested his head on a wrap, and closed his eyes, and called up before his mind the vision of Cornelia. How beautiful she had been when he met her! How much more beautiful when she thrust her way through the fighting slaves and put the sword in his hand, at that moment of mortal combat, which he expected to be his last! Did he only love her because her face was sweet, her voice was sweet, and the touch of her hair was sweet? Happy was he, her lover; — he could say "no," and have never a fear that his sincerity would be tested. And Lucius Ahenobarbus? He hated him with a perfect hatred. A Roman who was no Roman! A womanish man whom every true woman must despise! A serpent who had not even the bright scales of a serpent! What would he do to Cornelia? Drusus's face grew hard. Had he, Drusus, yet done any injury worth mentioning to his enemy? Why had he not used the moment when Lucius lay prostrate, and run the sword through his body? Ill-timed, thoughtless mercy! But the letters, the packet he had wrenched from Ahenobarbus's hand? Why was it so precious? Drusus had flung it into the boat. He took up the packet.

Doubtless some *billet-doux.* Why should he degrade his mind by giving an instant's thought to any of his enemy's foul intrigues? He could only open his eyes with difficulty, but a curiosity that did not add to his self-esteem overmastered him. The seal! Could he believe his senses — the imprint of three trophies of victory? It was the seal of Pompeius! The instinct of the partisan and politician conquered every infirmity. He broke the wax, untied the thread, and opened. The letters were in cipher, and at first sight illegible. But this did not present any insuperable difficulty. Most classic ciphers were sufficiently simple to be solved without very much trouble. Drusus knew that in all Cæsar's correspondence a cipher had been used which consisted merely of substituting for each letter the fourth letter beyond it, as D for A; and a little examination showed that the present cryptogram was made on the same rude method. After a few guesses he struck the proper substitutions, and was able to read.

"Pompeius Magnus, Imperator, to the most excellent Lucius Domitius Ahenobarbus, Rome, tenth day before the Calends of January. If it is well with you, it is well; I am well.[1] I write to warn you that we are told that Quintus Drusus, your personal enemy and the friend of our own foes, is in Campania. We need not add more, for we trust to you to see to it that he stirs up no faction in favour of his master in those parts. Be assured that you will not be long troubled by this enemy. He is marked out as one of the earliest of those to pay with their lives for their conspiracy against the Republic. If possible see that Drusus is seized for some alleged offence, and lodged in prison until the new consuls come into office. After that time he can work little or no mischief. Use the

---

[1] *Si vales bene est ego valeo,* written commonly simply S. V. B. E. E. V.

uttermost endeavours in this matter; check him and his schemes at all hazards. I trust your energy and prudence, which your father and Lentulus Crus assure me will not fail. *Vale!*"

Drusus lay back in the bottom of the boat, and looked up into the blue dome. It was the same azure as ever, but a strange feeling of disenchantment seemed to have come over him. For the first time he realized the deadly stakes for which he and his party were playing their game. What fate had been treasured up for him in the impending chaos of civil war? If he perished in battle or by the executioner's axe, what awaited Cornelia? But he had chosen his road; he would follow it to the end. The battle spirit mounted in him.

The sky was darkening when the boat drew up to one of the busy quays of Puteoli. Stars had begun to twinkle. Cappadox aided his bruised and stiffened master to disembark.

"To-night rest," cried Drusus, forgetting all his wounds. "To-morrow away to Rome. And at Rome — the war of the Gods and the Giants!"

CHAPTER XIV

THE NEW CONSULS

I

IT had come — the great crisis that by crooked ways or straight was to set right all the follies and crimes of many a generation. On the Calends of January Lentulus Crus and Caius Clodius Marcellus were inaugurated consuls. In solemn procession with Senate, priesthoods, and people, they had gone up to the Capitol and sacrificed chosen white steers to Jupiter, "Best and Greatest,"[1] and invoked his blessing upon the Roman State. And so began the last consulship of the Free Republic.

Rome was in a ferment. All knew the intention of the consuls to move the recall of Cæsar from his government. All knew that Curio had brought a letter from Ravenna, the contents whereof he carefully guarded. That same afternoon the consuls convened the Senate in the Temple of Capitoline Jove, and every man knew to what purpose. All Rome swept in the direction of the Capitol. Drusus accompanied his friend, the tribune Antonius, as the latter's viator, for there was need of a trusty guard.

The excitement in the streets ran even higher than when Catilina's great plot was exposed. The streets were jammed

---

[1] *Optimus maximus.*

with crowds, — not of the idle and base born, but of equites and noble ladies, and young patricians not old enough to step into their fathers' places. They were howling and cheering for Pompeius and Lentulus, and cursing the absent proconsul. As Drusus passed along at the side of Antonius, he could not fail to hear the execrations and vile epithets flung from every side at him and his friend. He had always supposed the masses were on Cæsar's side, but now every man's hand seemed turned against the conqueror of the Gauls. Was there to be but a repetition of the same old tragedy of the Gracchi and of Marcus Drusus? A brave man standing out for the people, and the people deserting him in his hour of need?

They reached the Temple. The Senate was already nearly ready for business; every toothless consular who had been in public service for perquisites only, and who for years had been wasting his life enjoying the pickings of an unfortunate province — all such were in their seats on the front row of benches. Behind them were the *prætorii* and the *ædilicii*,[1] a full session of that great body which had matched its tireless wisdom and tenacity against Pyrrhus, Hannibal, and Antiochus the Great, and been victorious. Drusus ran his eye over the seats. There they sat, even in the midst of the general excitement, a body of calm, dignified elders, severe and immaculate in their long white togas and purple-edged tunics. The multitudes without were howling and jeering; within the temple, reigned silence — the silence that gathered about the most august and powerful assembly the world has ever seen.

The Temple was built of cool, grey stone; the assembly hall was quite apart from the shrine. The Senate had convened in a spacious semicircular vaulted chamber, cut off from the vulgar world by a row of close, low Doric columns. From

[1] Ex-prætors and ex-ædiles.

the shade of these pillars one could command a sweeping view of the Forum, packed with a turbulent multitude. Drusus stood on the Temple steps and looked out and in. Without, confusion; within, order; without, a leaderless mob; within, an assembly almost every member of which had been invested with some high command. For a moment the young man revived courage; after all, the Roman Senate was left as a bulwark against passion and popular wrath; and for the time being, as he looked on those motionless, venerable faces, his confidence in this court of final appeal was restored. Then he began to scan the features of the consulars, and his heart sank. There was Lucius Calpurnius Piso, with the visage of a philosopher, but within mere moral turpitude. There was Favonius; there were the two sanguinary Marcelli, consuls respectively for the two preceding years; there was Domitius; there was Cato, his hard face illumined doubtless by the near realization of unholy hopes; there was Faustus Sulla, another bitter oligarch. Drusus saw them all, and knew that the Cæsarian cause had been doomed without a hearing. Caius Marcellus, the new consul, sat in his separate seat, in all the splendid dignity of his embroidered toga. Around him stood his twelve lictors. But Lentulus, at whose behest the Senate had been convened, and who was to act as its president, had not come. Drusus followed Antonius over to the farther side of the house, where on a long, low bench [1] the other tribunes of the plebs were seated. Quintus Cassius was already there. The other tribunes darted angry glances at their newly arrived colleague. Drusus remained standing behind Antonius, ready to act as a body-guard, as much as to serve in mere official capacity. Even as they entered he had noticed a buzz and rustle pass along the tiers of seats, and whisper pass on

[1] *Subsellium.*

whisper, "There come the Cæsarians!" "What treason is in that letter!" "We must have an end of their impudence!" And Drusus ran his eye over the whole company, and sought for one friendly look; but he met with only stony glances or dark frowns. There was justice neither in the people nor in the Senate. Their hearts were drunk with a sense of revenge and self-willed passion; and Justice literally weighed out her bounty with blinded eyes.

There was another hum and rustle. And into the hall swept Lentulus Crus, in robes of office, with Scipio, the father-in-law of Pompeius, at his side. Before him strode his twelve lictors bearing their fasces erect. Not a word was spoken while Lentulus Crus seated himself in the ivory curule chair of office. No sign marked the extreme gravity of the occasion.

"Let the sacred chickens be brought," said Lentulus.

Never a lip twitched or curled in all that august multitude while several public attendants brought in a wooden cage containing three or four rather skinny specimens of poultry. Not even Drusus saw anything really ridiculous when Lentulus arose, took grain from an attendant, and scattered a quantity of it before the coop. Close at his elbow stood the augur, to interpret the omen, — a weazened, bald-headed old senator, who wore a purple-striped tunic,[1] and carried in his hand a long stick,[2] curved at its head into a spiral. Drusus knew perfectly well that the fowls had been kept without food all that day; but it would have seemed treason to all the traditions of his native land to cry out against this pompous farce. The hungry chickens pecked up the grain. The augur muttered formula after formula, and Lentulus took pains to repeat the meaningless jargon after him. Presently

---

[1] *Trabea.*   [2] *Lituus.*

the augur ceased his chatter and nodded to the consul. Lentulus turned toward the Senate.

"There is no evil sight or sound!"[1] was his announcement, meaning that business could be transacted.

Whereupon up from his seat sprang Marcus Antonius, flourishing in his hand a packet. Loudly Lentulus bade him hold his peace; loudly the tribunes who sided with the Senate party forbade him to read. But a rustle and stir of eager curiosity ran along all the benches, and first one voice, then many, cried out that the letter must be made public. With very ill grace the consul declared that Antonius should be allowed to read the communication from Cæsar.

Antonius read, and all were astonished at the moderation of the much-maligned proconsul. Cæsar made it clear that he would stand on his rights as to the second consulship; but to withdraw possibilities of seeming to issue a threat, he would disband his entire army if Pompeius would only do the same, or, if preferred, he would retain simply Cisalpine Gaul and Illyria with two legions, until the consular elections were over. In either event it would be out of his power to menace the constitution, and the public tranquillity would remain quite undisturbed.

But before the murmur of approbation at this unexpected docility wore away. Lentulus burst forth into a fiery invective. All knew why the Senate had been convened, nor would he allow a few smooth promises to bring the state into danger. The law provided that a proconsul should leave his province at a certain time; and if Cæsar thought that a special law exempted him from this requirement, it were well he were disabused of the notion. The Senate had been convened because the presiding consul felt that the continuance of

[1] *Silentium esse videtur.*

Cæsar in his governorship was a menace to the safety of the Republic. Let the Conscript Fathers express themselves boldly, and he, Lentulus, would not desert them; let them waver and try to court the favour of Cæsar as in former times, and the consul would have to look to his own safety —and he could make his own terms with Cæsar.

Lentulus had started out with studied moderation. His harangue ended with a stinging menace. A low mutter, difficult to interpret, ran through the Senate. Again Antonius leaped to his feet.

"Conscript Fathers, will you not consider the mild offers ol Cæsar? Do not reject them without debate."

"I ask the opinion of the Senate on my own proposition," broke in Lentulus. "Metellus Scipio, declare what is your judgment."

"I protest at this unseemly haste," cried Antonius; "let us consider the letter first!"

"And I protest against this boisterous and unlawful interruption," retorted the consul, fiercely. "Rise, Metellus Scipio!"

Antonius flushed with rage, but sank into his seat. Drusus leaned over his friend's shoulder and whispered "Veto." Antonius shook his head.

"They must speak. We should be foolish to shoot away our best arrow before the battle had really begun."

Scipio arose. He was not the "chief senator," [1] usually entitled to speak first; but everybody knew that his words were the mere expressions of his son-in-law, the mighty Pompeius. His oratory and physical presence were wretched, but all the Senate hung upon his words.

"Pompeius did not intend to abandon the Republic, if the Senate would support him; but let them act with energy, for

---

[1] *Princeps senatus.*

otherwise in the future they might need his aid never so much, and yet implore it in vain."

"You want to destroy the Republic!" cried Quintus Cassius, half leaping from his seat.

"We want to destroy *you!*" retorted Domitius, savagely.

But all men were not so blinded by fury, hate, and greed of power and revenge. To the dismay of his party Caius Marcellus, the second consul, counselled a certain kind of moderation. There was no love lost by the noble "Optimates" upon Pompeius, and Marcellus hinted this plainly when he said that all Italy must be put under arms, and with such an army at the disposal of the Senate, it could act as it saw fit, — to get rid of a troublesome protector, he implied, no less than an open enemy. And close after him followed Marcus Calidius and Marcus Rufus, two senators, who had at least the sagacity to perceive that it would not free the Commonwealth to crush Cæsar, by flinging themselves into the arms of Pompeius. "Let Pompeius go off to his Spanish province, to which he was accredited proconsul; it was but natural Cæsar should think himself ill treated, seeing that two legions had been taken from him for Eastern service, and Pompeius was keeping these very troops close to Rome."

For one moment it seemed to Drusus that wisdom and justice had not deserted the Senate of his native state. The consuls were divided; two influential men were counselling moderation. Surely the Senate would not push to extremities. But he had not reckoned on the spell which the malevolent spirit of Lentulus had cast over the assembly. In bitter words the presiding consul refused to put Calidius's proposal to a vote, and then, turning directly upon his colleague before the face of the whole multitude, he poured out reproof and vituperation. Marcellus turned red and then black in the face with rage. Drusus's heart was beating rapidly with hope. So long as the consuls were at enmity, little would be done! Suddenly Scipio started as if to leave the assembly. "He's going to call in Pompeius's cohorts!" belched Lentulus. Marcellus turned pale. Drusus saw Calidius's friends whispering with him, evidently warning and remonstrating. Senators cast uneasy glances toward the doorways, as if expecting to see a century of legionaries march in to enforce the decrees of Pompeius's spokesmen. Marcellus staggered to his feet. He was cowed, and evidently felt himself in personal danger.

"Conscript Fathers," he stammered, "I — I withdraw my motion to delay action for considering the recall of Cæsar."

"You have done well!" shouted Lentulus, triumphing savagely. Scipio ostentatiously settled back on his seat, while Cato called with warning, yet exultation: —

"Take care what you do. Cæsar is the only sober man among all those engaged in the plot to overturn the government. Remember with whom you must deal, and act!"

Then Scipio arose once more. Every one knew that his fiat was law. "Conscript Fathers," he began, "Marcus Cato speaks well. Consider the power of Cæsar. He has trained up bands of gladiators whom his friends, both senators and knights, are drilling for him. He is doubling his soldiers' pay, giving them extra corn, slaves, attendants, and land grants. A great part of the Senate, — yes, Cicero even, they say, — owes him money, at low and favourable rates of interest; he has actually made presents to freedmen and influential slaves. All young prodigals in debt are in his pay. He has made presents to win the favour of cities and princes, or been lending them troops without vote of the Senate. In Italy,

Gaul, and Spain, — yes, in Greece, too, and Asia, he is win-ning the good-will of communities by erecting splendid public buildings. So great is his present power! What he will do in a second consulship I dare not say. I dare not assign bounds to his ambition. Conscript Fathers, shall we vote ourselves freemen or slaves? What more can I add to the words of the consul? I vote to ratify the proposition of Lucius Lentulus, that Cæsar either disband his army on a fixed day, or be declared a public enemy!"

"And what is your opinion, Lucius Domitius?" demanded Lentulus, while never a voice was raised to oppose Scipio.

"Let the Senate remember," replied Domitius, "that Cæsar will justify the meaning of his name — the 'hard-hitter,' and let us strike the first and telling blow."

A ripple of applause swept down the Senate. The anti-Cæsarians had completely recovered from their first discom-fiture, and were carrying all sentiment before them. Already there were cries of "A vote! a vote! Divide the Senate! A vote!"

"Conscript Fathers," said Lentulus, "in days of great emer-gency like this, when your minds seem so happily united in favour of doing that which is for the manifest safety of the Republic, I will not ask for the opinions of each senator in turn. Let the Senate divide; let all who favour the recall of the proconsul of the Gauls pass to the right, those against to the left. And so may it be well and prosperous for the Commonwealth."

But Antonius was again on his feet; and at his side stood Quintus Cassius.

"Lucius Lentulus," he thundered, "I forbid the division. *Veto!*"

"*Veto!*" shouted Cassius.

Domitius, too, had risen. "Conscript Fathers, let the consuls remonstrate with the tribunes to withdraw their prohibition. And, if they do not succeed, let them lay before the Senate that order which is the safeguard of the Republic."

Everybody knew what Domitius meant. If Antonius would not give way, martial law was to be declared. Hot and furious raged the debate. More and more passionate the expressions of party hatred. More and more menacing the gestures directed upon the two Cæsarian tribunes. But even the impetuous fierceness of Lentulus, Cato, Scipio, and Domitius combined could not drive the browbeaten Senate to cast loose from its last mooring that night. Domitius's measure went over. It was late — the stars were shining outside. Lamps had been brought in, and threw their ruddy glare over the long tiers of seats and their august occupants. Finally the angry debate ended, because it was a physical impossibility to continue longer. Senators went away with dark frowns or care-knit foreheads. Out in the Forum bands of young "Optimates" were shouting for Pompeius, and cursing Cæsar and his followers. Drusus, following Antonius, felt that he was the adherent of a lost cause, the member of a routed army that was defending its last stronghold, which overwhelming numbers must take, be the defence never so valiant. And when very late he lay down on his bed that night, the howls of the fashionable mob were still ringing in his ears.

II

That night the most old-fashioned and sober Roman went to bed at an advanced hour. Men were gathered in little knots along the streets, in the forums, in the porticos and basilicas, arguing, gesticulating, wrangling. Military tribunes and centurions in armour of Pompeius's legions were parading on the *comitium*.[1] Veterans of that leader were jostling about in the crowd, clanking their newly furbished armour and shouting for their old general. If a man spoke for Cæsar, a crowd of bystanders was ready to hoot him down. Staid householders locked up their dwellings and stationed trusty slaves at the doors to see that the crowds did not take to riot and pillage. The sailors from the wharves had been drinking heavily in all the taverns, and now roved up and down the crowded streets, seeking opportunity for brawls. Thieves and cutpurses were plying their most successful work; but no officials had time to direct the efforts of the harassed and slender police corps. To Pompeius's palace, without the gates, every man whose voice or vote seemed worth the winning had been summoned. All the senators had streamed out thither; and there the Magnus had brought them under the spell of his martial authority and made them as wax in his hand. And all "that majesty that doth hedge about a king," or about a victorious general, exerted its full influence. The senators came into the palace of Pompeius as into the palace of their despot. He stood before them in his largest hall, wearing the embroidered robe of a triumphator, with the laurel crown of his victories upon his head. At his right hand, as first vizir of his state, stood Lentulus Crus; at his left Lucius Domitius. The senators came to him and bowed low, and said their "*Aves*" and "*Salves*" as though cringing before a Mithridates or Tigranes of the East; and Pompeius, by the cordiality or coolness of his response, indi-cated which of his vassals had or had not fallen under his disfavour.

Yes, despotism had come at last for Rome. The oligarchy had by its corrupt incapacity made a tyranny inevitable. They

---

[1] Assembly-place in the *Forum Romanum*.

could make choice of masters, but a master they must have. Many were the proud Fabii, Claudii, and Valerii present that night — men whose lines of curule ancestors were as long as the duration of the Republic — who ground their teeth with shame and inward rage the very moment they cried, " *Salve, Magne!* " Yet the recipient of all this adulation was in no enviable frame of mind. He looked harassed and weary, despite the splendour of his dress and crown. And many were the whispered conversations that passed between him and his ministers, or rather custodians, Lentulus and Domitius.

"Ah! poor Julia," sighed Pompeius, whose mind ever reverted to his dead wife, "what misery would have been yours if you had seen this day. Poor Julia; how I loved her; and Cæsar, her father, loved her too; and now — "

"Be yourself, Magnus," expostulated the consul at his side; "remember that for the good of the Republic every personal affection is to be put away. Recall Brutus, who put his own sons to death because they committed treason. Remember what Scipio Æmilianus said when he learned that Tiberius Gracchus, his dear brother-in-law, had been put to death for sedition. He quoted Homer's line: —

" 'So perish all who do the like again!' "

"And must I trample down every tie, every affection?" complained wretched Pompeius, who never ceased hoping against hope that something would avert the catastrophe.

"There is no tie, no affection, Magnus," said Domitius, sternly, "that binds you to Cæsar. Cast his friendship from your breast as you would a viper. Think only of being justly hailed with Romulus, Camillus, and Marius as the fourth founder of Rome. Strike, and win immortal glory."

And so to the last hour these confederates wrought upon

their supple instrument, and bent him to their will; and their tool in turn had all else at his mercy. Pompeius addressed the senators, and, well trained by his guardians, spoke with brutal frankness to those who had dared to advise moderation.

"You, Rufus," he said, pointing a menacing finger, before which that senator cowered in dread, "have been advising the Republic to tolerate the chief of its enemies. You bid me to disarm or withdraw from Italy, as though the lives and property of any good men would be safe the moment Cæsar was left unopposed to pour his cohorts of barbarous Gauls and Germans into the country. You, Calidius, have given the same untimely advice. Beware lest you repent the hour when you counselled that I should disarm or quit the neighbourhood of Rome." The two-edged suggestion contained in this last warning was too marked for the reproved men not to turn pale with dread, and slink away trembling behind their associates.

"But," continued Pompeius, "I have praise as well as blame; Marcus Cato has not deserted the Republic. He has advised, and advised well, that the proconsul of the Gauls be stripped of his legions." It was Cato's turn now to bite his lips with mortification, for in times past he had foretold that through Pompeius great miseries would come to the state, and in his prætorship had declared that Pompeius ought to go to his province, and not stay at home to stir up tumults and anarchy from which he could emerge as monarch. And such praise from the Magnus's lips, under the present circumstances, was gall and wormwood to his haughty soul.

"And," continued Pompeius, "I shall not forget to applaud the energetic counsels of Domitius and Lentulus Crus. Let those who wish to preserve life and property," he added, with a menacing significance, "see to it that they do as these gentlemen advise."

And thereupon there was a great shout of applause from all the more rabid senators, in which the rest thought it safer to join, with simulated heartiness. But Pompeius did not stop here. He brought before the senators tribunes from the two legions taken from Cæsar, and these tribunes loudly declaimed —having learned their lesson well—that their troops were ill-affected toward their former commander, and would follow Pompeius to the last. And the Magnus produced veteran officers of his old campaigns, whom hope of reward and promotion had induced to come and declare for their former commander. Late, very late, the informal session of the Senate broke up. The "Fathers of the Republic" went each man to his own dwelling; but there was no longer any doubt as to what was to come of the doings of the day.

Flaccus, the banker, had of course no access to the conference; but he had waited outside the gate of the palace, to learn the issue from an acquaintance in the Senate. His patience was at last rewarded.

"Tell me, friend," was his question, "what will be the outcome of this; shall I risk any loans to-morrow?"

The friendly senator seemed doubtful.

"Cæsar is a ruined man. Who imagines his legions will fight? We know Labienus is with Pompeius."

"You are wrong," said Flaccus.

"Wrong? I?" replied the senator. "I know whereof I speak."

"*Phy!*" cried the banker, "not Cæsar, but you are ruined. The legions will fight."

"Don't prophesy," sneered the acquaintance, "seeing that you brokers always keep out of politics."

"You politicians are blind," retorted Flaccus.

* * * * * * * * *

The debate raged on. But by law the Senate could **not** convene on the third and fourth of the month, and the question of setting aside the tribunician veto went over until the fifth. It was the last lull before the outbreak of the great tempest. The little group of Cæsarians put forth their final efforts. Drusus went in person to call on Cicero, the great orator, and plead with him to come out from his residence in the suburbs and argue for peace.   The destroyer of Catilina had declared that he would not forfeit his rights to a triumph for his Cilician victories by appearing prematurely in the Senate. Besides, he could never antagonize Pompeius.   Curio smiled grimly when his colleague reported his fruitless embassy.

"I think, my friends," said the politician, "we shall soon prove the old saying, 'Whom the gods would destroy, they first make mad.'"

CHAPTER XV

I

THE rapid march of events that week had taken Drusus out of himself, and made him forgetful of personal consequences; but it sobered him when he heard Curio and Cælius, his associates, telling Balbus where their wills would be found deposited if anything calamitous were to befall them. After all, life was very sweet to the young Livian. He could not at heart desire to drift off into nothingness — to stop breathing, thinking, feeling. And for the last time he reviewed his position; told himself that it was not an unworthy cause for which he was contending; that it was not treason, but patriotism, to wish to overthrow the great oligarchy of noble families, who by their federated influence had pulled the wires to every electoral assembly, so that hardly a man not of their own coterie had been elected to high office for many a long year; while the officials themselves had grown full and wanton on the revenues wrung from the score of unfortunate provinces.

The feeling against the Cæsarians was very bitter in the city. Cæsar had always been the friend and darling of the populace; but, now that his star seemed setting, hardly a voice was raised, save to cry up the patriotism and determination of the consuls and Pompeius Magnus. Soldiers of the latter's legions were everywhere. The Senate was to convene the afternoon of the

seventh, in the Curia of Pompeius, in the Campus Martius.
Lentulus Crus was dragging forth every obscure senator, every
retired politician, whose feet almost touched the grave, to swell
his majority. All knew that the tribunes' vetoes were to be set
aside, and arbitrary power decreed to the consuls. Drusus began
to realize that the personal peril was pressing.

"Won't his head look pretty for the crows to pick at?" commented Marcus Læca to a friend, as the two swept past Drusus
on the street. The Livian heard the loudly muttered words and
trembled. It was easy to laud the Decii who calmly sacrificed
their lives for the Republic, and many another martyr to patriotism; it was quite another thing to feel the mortal fear of death
coursing in one's veins, to reflect that soon perhaps the dogs
might be tearing this body which guarded that strange thing
one calls self; to reflect that all which soon will be left of one
is a bleaching skull, fixed high in some public place, at which
the heartless mob would point and gibber, saying, "That is the
head of Quintus Livius Drusus, the rebel!"

Drusus wandered on — on to the only place in Rome where
he could gain the moral courage to carry him undaunted through
that which was before him — to the Atrium of Vesta. He
entered the house of the Vestals and sent for his aunt. Fabia
came quickly enough, for her heart had been with her nephew
all these days that tried men's souls. The noble woman put
her arms around the youth — for he was still hardly more — and
pressed him to her breast.

"Aunt Fabia," said Drusus, growing very weak and pale,
now that he felt her warm, loving caress, "do you know that
in two or three days you will have as nephew a proscribed
insurgent, perhaps with a price on his head, who perhaps
is speedily to die by the executioner, like the most ignoble
felon?"

"Yes," said Fabia, also very pale, yet smiling with a sweet, grave smile — the smile of a goddess who grieves at the miseries of mortal men, yet with divine omniscience glances beyond, and sees the happiness evolved from pain. "Yes, I have heard of all that is passing in the Senate. And I know, too, that my Quintus will prove himself a Fabian and a Livian, to whom the right cause and the good of the Republic are all — and the fear of shame and death is nothing." And then she sat down with him upon a couch, and took his head in her lap, and stroked him as if she were his mother. "Ah! my Quintus," she said, "you are still very young, and it is easy for one like you to enlist with all your ardour in a cause that seems righteous; yes, and in the heat of the moment to make any sacrifice for it; but it is not so easy for you or any other man calmly to face shame and annihilation, when the actual shadow of danger can be seen creeping up hour by hour. I know that neither you nor many another man wise and good believes that there are any gods. And I — I am only a silly old woman, with little or no wisdom and wit — "

"Not silly and not old, carissima!" interrupted Drusus, smiling at her self-depreciation.

"We won't argue," said Fabia, in a bit lighter vein. "But — as I would say — I believe in gods, and that they order all things well."

"Why, then," protested the young man, "do we suffer wrong or grief? If gods there are, they are indifferent; or, far worse, malevolent, who love to work us woe."

Again Fabia shook her head.

"If we were gods," said she, "we would all be wise, and could see the good to come out of every seeming evil. There ! I am, as I said, silly and old, and little enough comfort can words of mine bring a bright young man whose head is crammed with all the learned lore of the schools of Athens. But know this, Quintus, so long as I live, you shall live in my heart — living or dead though you be. And believe me, the pleasure of life is but a very little thing; it is sweet, but how quickly it passes! And the curses or praises of men — these, too, only a few mouldy rolls of books keep for decay! What profits it to Miltiades this hour, that a few marks on a papyrus sheet ascribe to him renown; or how much is the joy of Sextus Tarquinius darkened because a group of other marks cast reproach upon his name? If so be death is a sleep, how much better to feel at the end, 'I die, but I die self-approved, and justified by self!' And if death is not all a sleep; if, as Socrates tells us, there are hopes that we but pass from a base life to another with less of dross, then how do pleasures and glories, griefs and dishonours, of this present life touch upon a man whose happiness or woe will be found all within?"

And so the good woman talked, giving to Drusus her own pure faith and hope and courage; and when the intellectual philosopher within him revolted at some of her simple premises and guileless sophistries, against his will he was persuaded by them, and was fain to own to himself that the heart of a good woman is past finding out; that its impulses are more genuine, its intuitions truer, its promptings surer, than all the fine-spun intellectuality of the most subtle metaphysician. When at last Drusus rose to leave his aunt, his face was glowing with a healthy colour, his step was elastic, his voice resonant with a noble courage. Fabia embraced him again and again. "Remember, whatever befalls," were her parting words, "I shall still love you." And when Drusus went out of the house he saw the dignified figure of the Vestal gazing after him. A few minutes later he passed no less a personage than the consular Lucius Domitius on his way to some political

conference. He did not know what that dignitary muttered
as he swept past in spotless toga, but the gloomy ferocity of
his brow needed no interpreter. Drusus, however, never for
a moment gave himself disquietude. He was fortified for the
best and the worst, not by any dumb resignation, not by any
cant of philosophy, but by an inward monitor which told him
that some power in some way would lead him forth out of all
dangers in a manner whereof man could neither ask nor think.

* * * * * * * * * *

On the sixth of January the debate, as already said, drew
toward its end. All measures of conciliation had been voted
down; the crisis was close at hand. On the seventh, after his
interview with Fabia, Drusus went back to his own lodgings,
made a few revisions in his will, and in the presence of two or
three friends declared Cappadox manumitted,[1] lest he, by some
chance, fall into the clutches of a brutal master. The young
man next wrote a long letter to Cornelia for Agias to forward
to Baiæ, and put in it such hope as he could glean from the
dark words of the philosophers; that even if destruction now
overtook him, death perhaps did not end all; that perhaps they
would meet beyond the grave. Then he took leave of his weep-
ing freedmen and slaves, and strolled out into the city, and
wandered about the Forum and the Sacred Way, to enjoy, perchance, a last view of the sites that were to the Roman so dear.
Then finally he turned toward the Campus Martius, and was
strolling down under the long marble-paved colonnade of
the Portico of Pompeius. Lost in a deep reverie, he was forgetful of all present events, until he was roused by a quick
twitch at the elbow; he looked around and found Agias before
him.

---

[1] *Manumissio inter amicos* was less formal than the regular ceremony
before the prætor.

"*A!* domine," cried the young Greek, "I have friends in the house of Lentulus. I have just been told by them that the consul has sworn that he will begin to play Sulla this very day. Neither you, nor Antonius, Cassius, Curio, nor the other supporters of Cæsar will be alive to-night. Do not go into the Curia. Get away, quickly! Warn your friends, and leave Rome, or to-night you will all be strangled in the Tullianum!"

The Tullianum! Drusus knew no other term to conjure up a like abode of horrors — the ancient prison of the city, a mere chamber sunk in the ground, and beneath that a dungeon, accessible only by an opening in the floor above — where the luckless Jugurtha had perished of cold and starvation, and where Lentulus Sura, Cethegus, and the other lieutenants of Catilina had been garroted, in defiance of all their legal rights, by the arbitrary decree of a rancorous Senate! So at last the danger had come! Drusus felt himself quiver at every fibre. He endured a sensation the like of which he had never felt before — one of utter moral faintness. But he steadied himself quickly. Shame at his own recurring cowardice overmastered him. "I am an unworthy Livian, indeed," he muttered, not perhaps realizing that it is far more heroic consciously to confront and receive the full terrors of a peril, and put them by, than to have them harmlessly roll off on some self-acting mental armour.

"Escape! There is yet time!" urged Agias, pulling his toga. Drusus shook his head.

"Not until the Senate has set aside the veto of the tribunes," he replied quietly.

"But the danger will then be imminent!"

"A good soldier does not leave his post, my excellent Agias," said the Roman, "until duty orders him away. Our duty is in the Senate until we can by our presence and voice do no more.

When that task is over, we go to Cæsar as fast as horse may bear us; but not until then."

"Then I have warned you all in vain!" cried Agias.

"Not at all. You may still be of the greatest service. Arrange so that we can leave Rome the instant we quit the Curia."

"But if the lictors seize you before you get out of the building?"

"We can only take our chance. I think we shall be permitted to go out. I had intended to ride out of the city this evening if nothing hindered and the final vote had been passed. But now I see that cannot be done. You have wit and cunning, Agias. Scheme, provide. We must escape from Rome at the earliest moment consistent with our duty and honour."

"I have it," said Agias, his face lighting up. "Come at once after leaving the Curia, to the rear of the Temple of Mars.[1] I know one or two of the temple servants, and they will give me the use of their rooms. There I will have ready some slave dresses for a disguise, and just across the Æmilian bridge I will have some fast horses waiting — that is, if you can give me an order on your stables."

Drusus took off his signet ring.

"Show that to Pausanias. He will honour every request you make, be it for a million sesterces."

Agias bowed and was off. For the last time Drusus was tempted to call him back and say that the flight would begin at once. But the nimble Greek was already out of sight, and heroism became a necessity. Drusus resolutely turned his steps toward the senate-house. Not having been able to forecast the immediate moves of the enemy, he had not arranged

[1] The Ædes Martis of the Campus Martius.

for hurried flight; it was to be regretted, although he had
known that on that day the end of the crisis would come.
He soon met Antonius, and imparted to him what he had
just learned from Agias, and the precautions taken.

Antonius shook his head, and remarked : —

"You ought not to go with me. Little enough can we who
are tribunes do; you have neither voice nor vote, and Lentulus is your personal foe. So back, before it is too late. Let
us shift for ourselves."

Drusus replied never a word, but simply took the tribune's
arm and walked the faster toward the Curia.

"I am a very young soldier," he said presently ; "do not be
angry if I wish to show that I am not afraid of the whizzing
arrows."

"Then, my friend, whatever befalls, so long as life is
in my body, remember you have a brother in Marcus
Antonius."

The two friends pressed one another's hands, and entered
the Curia Pompeii. There in one of the foremost seats sat the
Magnus,[1] the centre of a great flock of adulators, who were
basking in the sunshine of his favour. Yet Drusus, as he
glanced over at the Imperator, thought that the great man
looked harassed and worried — forced to be partner in a scheme
when he would cheerfully be absent. Fluttering in their broad
togas about the senate-house were Domitius, Cato, the Marcelli, and Scipio, busy whipping into line the few remaining
waverers. As Cato passed the tribune's bench, and saw the
handful of Cæsarians gathered there, he cast a glance of inde-

---

[1] Pompeius was not allowed by law to attend sessions of the Senate (so
long as he was proconsul of Spain) when held inside the old city limits ; but
the Curia which he himself built was outside the walls in the Campus Martius.
This meeting seems to have been convened there especially that he might
attend it.

scribable malignity upon them, a glance that made Drusus shudder, and think again of the horrors of the Tullianum.

"I know now how Cato looked," said he to Antonius, "when he denounced the Catilinarians and urged that they should be put to death without trial."

Antonius shrugged his shoulders, and replied: —

"Cato cannot forgive Cæsar. When Cæsar was consul, Cato interrupted his speech, and Cæsar had him haled off to prison. Marcus Cato never forgives or forgets."

Curio, Cælius, and Quintus Cassius had entered the senate-house — the only Cæsarians present besides Antonius and his viator. The first two went and took their seats in the body of the building, and Drusus noticed how their colleagues shrank away from them, refusing to sit near the supporters of the Gallic proconsul.

"*Eho!*" remarked Antonius, his spirits rising as the crisis drew on. "This is much like Catilina's days, to be sure! No one would sit with him when he went into the Senate. However, I imagine that these excellent gentlemen will hardly find Cæsar as easy to handle as Catilina."

Again Lentulus was in his curule chair, and again the solemn farce of taking the auspices, preparatory to commencing the session, was gone through.

Then for the last time in that memorable series of debates Lentulus arose and addressed the Senate, storming, browbeating, threatening, and finally ending with these words, that brought everything to a head: —

"Seeing then, Conscript Fathers, that Quintus Cassius and Marcus Antonius are using their tribunician office to aid Caius Cæsar to perpetuate his tyranny, the consuls ask you to clothe the magistrates with dictatorial power in order that the liberties of the Republic may not be subverted!"

The liberties of the Republic! Liberty to plunder provinces! To bribe! To rob the treasury! To defraud! To violate the law of man and God! To rule the whole world so that a corrupt oligarchy might be aggrandized! Far, far had the nation of the older Claudii, Fabii, and Cornelii fallen from that proud eminence when, a hundred years before, Polybius, contrasting the Romans with the degenerate Greeks, had exclaimed, "A statesman of Hellas, with ten checking clerks and ten seals, . . . cannot keep faith with a single talent; Romans, in their magistracies and embassies, handle great sums of money, and yet from pure respect of oath keep their faith intact."

But the words of selfish virulence and cant had been uttered, and up from the body of the house swelled a shout of approval, growing louder and louder every instant.

Then up rose Domitius, on his face the leer of a brutal triumph.

"Conscript Fathers," he said, "I call for a vote on the question of martial law. Have the Senate divide on the motion. ' Let the consuls, prætors, tribunes of the plebs, and men of consular rank see to it that the Republic suffers no harm.' "

Another shout of applause rolled along the seats, fiercer and fiercer, and through it all a shower of curses and abusive epithets upon the Cæsarians. All around Drusus seemed to be tossing and bellowing the breakers of some vast ocean, an ocean of human forms and faces, that was about to dash upon him and overwhelm him, in mad fury irresistible. The din was louder and louder. The bronze casings on the walls rattled, the pediments and pavements seemed to vibrate; outside, the vast mob swarming around the Curia reëchoed the shout. "Down with Cæsar!" "Down with the tribunes!" "*Io!* Pompeius!"

It was all as some wild distorted dream passing before Dru-

sus's eyes.   He could not bring himself to conceive the scene
as otherwise.   In a sort of stupor he saw the senators swarm·
ing to the right of the building, hastening to cast their votes
in favour of Domitius's motion.   Only two men — under a
storm of abuse and hootings, passed to the left and went on
record against the measure.   These were Curio and Cælius;
and they stood for some moments alone on the deserted side of
the house, defiantly glaring at the raging Senate.   Antonius
and Cassius contemptuously remained in their seats — for no
magistrate could vote in the Senate.

It was done; it could not be undone.   Not Cæsar, but the
Senate, had decreed the end of the glorious Republic.   Already,
with hasty ostentation, some senators were stepping outside the
Curia, and returning clad no longer in the toga of peace, but in
a military cloak [1] which a slave had been keeping close at hand
in readiness.   Already Cato was on his feet glaring at the
Cæsarian tribunes, and demanding that first of all they be sub·
jected to punishment for persisting in their veto.   The Senate
was getting more boisterous each minute.   A tumult was like
to break out, in which some deed of violence would be com·
mitted, which would give the key-note to the whole sanguinary
struggle impending.   Yet in the face of the raging tempest
Marcus Antonius arose and confronted the assembly.   It
raged, hooted, howled, cursed.   He still remained standing.
Cato tried to continue his invective.   The tempest that he had
done so much to raise drowned his own voice, and he relapsed
into his seat.   But still Antonius stood his ground, quietly,
with no attempt to shout down the raging Senate, as
steadfastly as though a thousand threats were not buzzing
around his ears.   Drusus's heart went with his friend that
instant.   He had never been in a battle, yet he realized

[1] *Sagum.*

that it was vastly more heroic to stand undaunted before this audience, than to walk into the bloodiest mêlée without a tremor.

Then of a sudden, like the interval between the recession of one wave and the advance of a second billow, came a moment of silence; and into that silence Antonius broke, with a voice so strong, so piercing, so resonant, that the most envenomed oligarch checked his clamour to give ear.

"Hearken, ye senators of the Republic, ye false *patres*, ye fathers of the people who are no fathers! So far have we waited; we wait no more! So much have we seen; we'll see no further! So much have we endured, — reproaches, repulses, deceits, insult, outrage, yes, for I see it in the consul's eye, next do we suffer violence itself; but that we will not tamely suffer. Ay! drive us from our seats, as Marcus Cato bids you! Ay! strike our names from the Senate list, as Domitius will propose! Ay! hound your lictors, sir consul, after us, to lay their rods across our backs! Ay! enforce your decree proclaiming martial law! So have you acted before to give legal fiction to your tyranny! But tell me this, senators, prætorii, consulars, and consuls, where will this mad violence of yours find end? Tiberius Gracchus you have murdered. Caius Gracchus you have murdered. Marcus Drusus you have murdered. Ten thousand good men has your creature Sulla murdered. Without trial, without defence, were the friends of Catilina murdered. And now will ye add one more deed of blood to those going before? Will ye strike down an inviolate tribune, in Rome, — in the shadow of the very Curia? Ah! days of the Decemvirs, when an evil Ten ruled over the state — would that those days might return! Not ten tyrants but a thousand oppress us now! Then despotism wore no cloak of patriotism or legal right, but walked unmasked in all its blackness!

"Hearken, ye senators, and in the evil days to come, remember all I say. Out of the seed which ye sow this hour come wars, civil wars; Roman against Roman, kinsman against kinsman, brother against brother! There comes impiety, violence, cruelty, bloodshed, anarchy! There comes the destruction of the old; there comes the birth, amid pain and anguish, of the new! Ye who grasp at money, at power, at high office; who trample on truth and right to serve your selfish ends; false, degenerate Romans, — one thing can wipe away your crimes — "

"What?" shouted Cato, across the senate-house; while Pompeius, who was shifting uncomfortably in his seat, had turned very red.

"Blood!" cried back Antonius, carried away by the frenzy of his own invective; then, shooting a lightning glance over the awe-struck Senate, he spoke as though gifted with some terrible prophetic omniscience. "Pompeius Magnus, the day of your prosperity is past — prepare ingloriously to die! Lentulus Crus, you, too, shall pay the forfeit of your crimes! Metellus Scipio, Marcus Cato, Lucius Domitius, within five years shall you all be dead — dead and with infamy upon your names! Your blood, your blood shall wipe away your folly and your lust for power. Ye stay, we go. Ye stay to pass once more unvetoed the decree declaring Cæsar and his friends enemies of the Republic; we go — go to endure our outlaw state. But we go to appeal from the unjust scales of your false Justice to the juster sword of an impartial Mars, and may the Furies that haunt the lives of tyrants and shedders of innocent blood attend you — attend your persons so long as ye are doomed to live, and your memory so long as men shall have power to heap on your names reproach!"

U

Drusus hardly knew that Antonius had so much as stopped, when he found his friend leading him out of the Curia.

Behind, all was still as they walked away toward the Temple of Mars. Then, as they proceeded a little distance, a great roar as of a distant storm-wind drifted out from the senate-house — so long had Antonius held his audience spellbound. "*Finitum est!*" said Curio, his eyes cast on the ground. "We have seen, my friends, the last day of the Republic."

II

Behind the Temple of Mars the faithful Agias was ready with the slaves' dresses which were to serve as a simple disguise. Antonius and his companions tossed off their cumbrous togas and put on the dark, coarse cloaks and slippers which were worn by slaves and people of the lower classes. These changes were quickly made, but valuable time was wasted while Antonius — who, as a bit of a dandy, wore his hair rather long [1] — underwent a few touches with the shears. It was now necessary to get across the Tiber without being recognized, and once fairly out of Rome the chances of a successful pursuit were not many. On leaving the friendly shelter of the Temple buildings, nothing untoward was to be seen. The crowds rushing to and fro, from the Curia and back, were too busy and excited to pay attention to a little group of slaves, who carefully kept from intruding themselves into notice. Occasionally the roar and echo of applause and shouting came from the now distant Curia, indicating that the Senate was still at its unholy work of voting wars and destructions. A short walk would bring them across the Pons Æmilius, and there, in the shelter of one of the groves of the new public gardens which Cæsar had just been laying out on Janiculum, were wait-

---

[1] Slaves were always close clipped.

ing several of the fastest mounts which the activity of Agias and the lavish expenditures of Pausanias had been able to procure.

The friends breathed more easily.

"I hardly think," said Quintus Cassius, "we shall be molested. The consuls cannot carry their mad hate so far."

They were close to the bridge. The way was lined with tall warehouses and grain storehouses,[1] the precursors of the modern "elevators." They could see the tawny Tiber water flashing between the stone arches of the bridge. The swarms of peasants and countrymen driving herds of lowing kine and bleating sheep toward the adjacent Forum Boarium seemed unsuspicious and inoffensive. A moment more and all Drusus's tremors and anxieties would have passed as harmless fantasy.

Their feet were on the bridge. They could notice the wind sweeping through the tall cypresses in the gardens where waited the steeds that were to take them to safety. The friends quickened their pace. A cloud had drifted across the sun; there was a moment's gloom. When the light danced back, Drusus caught Curio's arm with a start.

"Look!" The new sunbeams had glanced on the polished helmet of a soldier standing guard at the farther end of the bridge.

There was only an instant for hesitation.

"Lentulus has foreseen that we must try to escape by this way," said Curio, seriously, but without panic. "We must go back at once, and try to cross by the wooden bridge below or by some other means."

But a great herd of dirty silver-grey Etruscan cattle came over the causeway, and to get ahead of them would have been impracticable without attracting the most unusual attention. It was now evident enough that there was a considerable guard at

[1] *Horreæ.*

the head of the bridge, and to make a rush and overpower it was impossible. The heavy-uddered cows and snorting, bellowing bulls dragged by with a slow plodding that almost drove Drusus frantic. They were over at last, and the friends hastened after them, far more anxious to leave the bridge than they had been an instant before to set foot upon it. On they pressed, until as if by magic there stood across their path the twelve lictors of one of the consuls, with upraised fasces. Behind the lictors was a half-century of soldiers in full armour, led by their *optio*.[1]

"Sirs," announced the head lictor, "I am commanded by the consul, Lucius Lentulus Crus, to put you all under arrest for treason against the Republic. Spare yourselves the indignity of personal violence, by offering no resistance."

To resist would indeed have been suicide. The friends had worn their short swords under their cloaks, but counting Agias they were only six, and the lictors were twelve, to say nothing of the soldiers, of whom there were thirty or more.

The ground seemed swaying before Drusus's eyes; in his ears was a buzzing; his thoughts came to him, thick, confused, yet through them all ran the vision of Cornelia, and the conviction that he was never to see her again. He looked back. The soldiers at the head of the bridge had taken alarm and were marching down to complete the arrest. He looked before. The lictors, the troops, the stupid cattle and their stolid drivers, and the great black-sided warehouses, casting their gloomy shadow over the rippling river. Down stream; not a skiff seemed stirring. The water was plashing, dancing, glancing in the sunshine. Below the wooden bridge the spars of a huge merchantman were just covering with canvas, as she stood away from her quay. Up stream (the views were all compressed into the veriest moment) — with the current came working, or

---

[1] **Adjutant**, subordinate to a centurion.

rather drifting, a heavy barge loaded with timber. Only two men, handling rude paddles, stood upon her deck. The barge was about to pass under the very arch upon which stood the handful of entrapped Cæsarians. A word, a motion, and the last hope of escape would have been comprehended by the enemy, and all would have been lost. But in moments of extreme peril it is easy to make a glance full of pregnancy. [Antonius saw the face of his friend — saw and understood; and the other seemingly doomed men understood likewise. In an instant the barge would pass under the bridge!

"Fellow," replied Antonius (the whole inspection of the situation, formation of the plot, and visual dialogue had really been so rapid as to make no long break after the lictor ceased speaking), "do you dare thus to do what even the most profane and impious have never dared before? Will you lay hands on two inviolate tribunes of the plebs, and those under their personal protection; and by your very act become a *sacer* — an outlaw devoted to the gods, whom it is a pious thing for any man to slay?"

"I have my orders, sir," replied the head lictor, menacingly. "And I would have you know that neither you nor Quintus Cassius are reckoned tribunes longer by the Senate; so by no such plea can you escape arrest."

"Tribunes no longer!" cried Antonius; "has tyranny progressed so far that no magistrate can hold office after he ceases to humour the consuls?"

"We waste time, sir," said the lictor, sternly. "Forward, men; seize and bind them!"

But Antonius's brief parley had done its work. As the bow of the barge shot under the bridge, Curio, with a single bound over the parapet, sprang on to its deck; after him leaped Quintus Cassius, and after him Cælius. Before Drusus could follow, however, the stern of the barge had vanished under the arch-way. The lictors and soldiers had sprung forward, but a second had been lost by rushing to the eastern side of the bridge, where the barge had just disappeared from sight. Agias, Antonius, and Drusus were already standing on the western parapet. The lictors and soldiers were on them in an instant. The blow of one of the fasces smote down Antonius, but he fell directly into the vessel beneath — stunned but safe. A soldier caught Agias by the leg to drag him down. Drusus smote the man under the ear so that he fell without a groan; but Agias himself had been thrown from the parapet on to the bridge; the soldiers were thronging around. Drusus saw the naked steel of their swords flashing before his eyes; he knew that the barge was slipping away in the current. It was a time of seconds, but of seconds expanded for him into eternities. With one arm he dashed back a lictor, with the other cast Agias — he never knew whence came that strength which enabled him to do the feat — over the stonework, and into the arms of Curio in the receding boat. Then he himself leaped. A rude hand caught his cloak. It was torn from his back. A sword whisked past his head — he never learned how closely. He was in the air, saw that the barge was getting away, and next he was chilled by a sudden dash of water and Cælius was dragging him aboard; he had landed under the very stern of the barge. Struggling in the water, weighed down by their armour, were several soldiers who had leaped after him and had missed their distance completely.

The young man clambered on to the rude vessel. Its crew (two simple, harmless peasants) were cowering among the lumber. Curio had seized one of the paddles and was guiding the craft out into the middle of the current; for the soldiers were already running along the wharves and preparing to fling their darts. The other men, who had just been plucked out of the jaws of destruction, were all engaged in collecting their more or less scattered wits and trying to discover the next turn of calamity in store. Antonius — who, despite his fall, had come down upon a coil of rope and so escaped broken bones and serious bruises — was the first to sense the great peril of even their present situation.

"In a few moments," he remarked, casting a glance down the river, "we shall be under the Pons Sublicius, and we shall either be easily stopped and taken, or crushed with darts as we pass by. You see they are already signalling from the upper bridge to their guard at the lower. We shall drift down into their hands, and gain nothing by our first escape."

"Anchor," suggested Cassius, who was an impulsive and rather inconsiderate man. And he prepared to pitch overboard the heavy mooring-stone.

"*Phui!* You sheep," cried Curio, contemptuously, mincing no words at that dread moment. "How long will it be before there will be ten boatloads of soldiers alongside? Can we beat off all Pompeius's legions?"

Antonius caught up another paddle and passed it through a rower's thong.

"Friends," he said, with that ready command which his military life had given him, "these soldiers are in armour and can run none too swiftly. Once show them the back, and they must throw away their arms or give over the chase. It is madness to drift down upon the lower bridge. We must turn across the river, risk the darts, and try to land on the farther bank. Take oars!"

There was but one remaining paddle. Drusus seized it and pushed against the water with so much force that the tough wood bent and creaked, but did not snap. The unwieldy barge sluggishly answered this powerful pressure, and under the stroke of the three oars began to head diagonally across the current and move slowly toward the farther shore. The soldiers did not at once perceive the intent of this move. By their actions they showed that they had expected the barge to try to slip through the Pons Sublicius, and so escape down the river. They had run some little way along the south bank of the Tiber, to reënforce their comrades at the lower bridge, when they saw the new course taken by their expected prey. Much valuable time had thus been gained by the pursued, time which they needed sadly enough, for, despite their frantic rowing, their unwieldy craft would barely crawl across the current.

Long before the barge was within landing distance of the northern bank, the soldiers who had been on guard at the head of the Pons Æmilius had regained their former station, and were running along the shore to cut off any attempt there to escape. Soon a whizzing javelin dug into the plank at Drusus's feet, and a second rushed over Cælius's head, and plashed into the water beyond the barge. Other soldiers on the now receding southern bank were piling into a light skiff to second their comrades' efforts by a direct attack on the fugitives.

A third dart grazed Antonius's hair and buried its head in the pile of lumber. The tribune handed his oar to Cælius, and, deliberately wresting the weapon from the timber, flung it back with so deadly an aim that one pursuing legionary went down, pierced through the breastplate. The others recoiled for an instant, and no more javelins were thrown, which was some slight gain for the pursued.

It seemed, however, that the contest could have only a single ending. The soldiers were running parallel and apace with the barge, which was now as close to the northern bank as was safe in view of the missiles. The Pons Sublicius was getting minute by minute nearer, and upon it could be seen a considerable body of troops ready with darts and grapnels to cut off the last hope of escape.

But Antonius never withdrew his eye from the line of dark weatherbeaten warehouses that stretched down to the river's edge on the north bank just above the Pons Sublicius.

"Row," he exhorted his companions, "row! as life is dear! Row as never before!"

And under the combined impulse of the three desperate men, even the heavy barge leaped forward and a little eddy of foaming waves began to trail behind her stern. Drusus had no time to ask of himself or Antonius the special object of this last burst of speed. He only knew that he was flinging every pound of strength into the heavy handle of his oar, and that his life depended on making the broad blade push back the water as rapidly as possible. Antonius, however, had had good cause for his command. A searching scrutiny had revealed to him that a single very long warehouse ran clear down to the river's edge, and so made it impossible to continue running along the bank. A pursuer must double around the whole length of the building before continuing the chase of the barge. And for a small quay just beyond this warehouse Antonius headed his clumsy vessel. The soldiers continued their chase up to the very walls of the warehouse, where they, of a sudden, found themselves stopped by an impenetrable barrier. They lost an instant of valuable time in trying to wade along the bank, where the channel shelved off rapidly, and, finding the attempt useless, dashed a volley of their missiles after the barge. But the range was very long. Few reached the vessel; none did damage. The soldiers disappeared behind the warehouse, still running at a headlong pace. Before they reappeared on the other side, Antonius had brought his craft to the quay. There was no time for mooring, and the instant the barge lost way the hard-pressed Cæsarians were on shore. Another instant, and the clumsy vessel had been caught by the current, and swung out into the stream.

She had done her work. The pursued men broke into a dash for the nearest highway. The soldiers were close after them. But they had flung away their javelins, and what with their heavy armour and the fatigue of running were quite as exhausted as the Cæsarians, three of whom had been thoroughly winded by their desperate rowing. On the Pons Sublicius, where a great crowd had gathered to watch the exciting chase, there was shouting and tumult. No doubt voices few enough would have been raised for the Cæsarians if they had been captured; but, now that they bade fair to escape, the air was thick with gibes at the soldiers, and cries of encouragement to the pursued. On the two parties ran. Soon they were plunged in the tortuous, dirty lanes of the "Trans-Tiber" district, rushing at frantic speed past the shops of dirty Jews and the taverns of noisy fishermen and sailors. Already news of the chase had gone before them, and, as Drusus followed his friends under the half-arching shadows of the tall tenement houses, drunken pedlers and ribald women howled out their wishes of success, precisely as though they were in a race-course. Now the dirty streets were left behind and the fatigued runners panted up the slopes of the Janiculum, toward the gardens of Cæsar. They passed the little grove sacred to the Furies, and, even as for life he ran, Drusus recalled with shame how over this very road, to this very grove, had fled Caius Gracchus, the great tribune of the people, whom Drusus's own great grandfather, Marcus Livius Drusus, had hounded to his death; that day when all men encouraged him as he ran, but none would raise a hand to aid.

But now up from the bridge came the thunder of horses' hoofs, — cavalry, tearing at a furious gallop. Pompeius had evidently ordered out a *turma*[1] of mounted men to chase down the runaways. More and more frantic the race — Drusus's tongue hung from his mouth like a dog's. He flew past a running fountain, and was just desperate enough to wonder if it was safe to stop one instant and touch — he would not ask to drink — one drop of the cool water. Fortunately the Cæsarians were all active young men, of about equal physical powers, and they kept well together and encouraged one another, not by word — they had no breath for that — but by interchange of courage and sympathy from eye to eye. The heavy legionaries had given up the chase; it was the cavalry, now flying almost at their very heels, that urged them to their final burst of speed.

At last! Here were the gardens of Cæsar, and close by the roadway under a spreading oak, their grooms holding them in readiness for instant service, were six of the best specimens of horseflesh money could command.

None of the little party had breath left to speak a word. To fling themselves into the saddles, to snatch the reins from the attendants' hands, to plunge the heels of their sandals, in lieu of spurs, into the flanks of their already restless steeds, — these things were done in an instant, but none too soon. For, almost as the six riders turned out upon the road to give head to their horses, the cavalry were upon them. The foremost rider sent his lance over Curio's shoulder, grazing the skin and starting blood; a second struck with his short sword at Cælius's steed, but the horse shied, and before the blow could be repeated the

---

[1] Squadron of 30 horse.

frightened beast had taken a great bound ahead and out of danger. This exciting phase of the pursuit, however, was of only momentary duration. The horses of the Cæsarians were so incomparably superior to the common army hacks of the soldiers, that, as soon as the noble blooded animals began to stretch their long limbs on the hard Roman road, the troopers dropped back to a harmless distance in the rear. The cavalrymen's horses, furthermore, had been thoroughly winded by the fierce gallop over the bridge, and now it was out of the question for them to pursue. Before the flight had continued a mile, the Cæsarians had the satisfaction of seeing their enemies draw rein, then turn back to the city. The friends, however, did not check their pace until, safe beyond chance of overtaking, they reined in at an hospitable tavern in the old Etruscan town of Veii.

Here Drusus took leave of Agias.

"You are quite too unimportant an enemy," said he to the young Greek, "to be worth arrest by the consuls, if indeed they know what part you have had in our escape. I know not what perils are before me, and I have no right to ask you to share them. You have long ago paid off any debt of gratitude that you owed me and mine when Fabia saved your life. I am your patron no longer; go, and live honourably, and you will find deposited with Flaccus a sum that will provide for all your needs. If ever I return to Rome, my party victorious, myself in favour, then let us renew our friendship; but till then you and I meet no more."

Agias knelt and kissed Drusus's robe in a semi-Oriental obeisance.

"And is there nothing," he asked half wistfully at the parting, "that I can yet do for you?"

"Nothing," said Drusus, "except to see that no harm come

to my Aunt Fabia, and if it be possible deliver Cornelia from the clutches of her bloody uncle."

"Ah!" said Agias, smiling, "that is indeed *something!* But be not troubled, domine," — he spoke as if Drusus was still his master, — "I will find a way."

That evening, under the canopy of night, the five Cæsarians sped, swift as their horses could bear them, on their way to Ravenna.

CHAPTER XVI

THE RUBICON

I

IT was growing late, but the proconsul apparently was mani·
festing no impatience. All the afternoon he had been trans·
acting the routine business of a provincial governor—listening
to appeals to his judgment seat, signing requisitions for tax
imposts, making out commissions, and giving undivided attention to a multitude of seeming trifles. Only Decimus Mamercus,
the young centurion,—elder son of the veteran of Præneste,—
who stood guard at the doorway of the public office of the prætorium, thought he could observe a hidden nervousness and a
still more concealed petulance in his superior's manner that betokened anxiety and a desire to be done with the routine of the
day. Finally the last litigant departed, the governor descended
from the curule chair, the guard saluted as he passed out to his
own private rooms, and soon, as the autumn darkness began to
steal over the cantonment, nothing but the call of the sentries
broke the calm of the advancing night.

Cæsar was submitting to the attentions of his slaves, who
were exchanging his robes of state for the comfortable evening
synthesis. But the proconsul was in no mood for the publicity
of the evening banquet. When his chief freedman announced
that the invited guests had assembled, the master bade him go
to the company and inform them that their host was indisposed,
and wished them to make merry without him. The evening
advanced. Twice Cæsar touched to his lips a cup of spiced

wine, but partook of nothing else. Sending his servants from his chamber, he alternately read, and wrote nervously on his tablets, then erased all that he had inscribed, and paced up and down the room. Presently the anxious head-freedman thrust his head into the apartment.

"My lord, it is past midnight. The guests have long departed. There will be serious injury done your health, if you take no food and rest."

'My good Antiochus," replied the proconsul, "you are a faithful friend."

The freedman — an elderly, half-Hellenized Asiatic — knelt and kissed the Roman's robe.

"My lord knows that I would die for him."

"I believe you, Antiochus. The gods know I never needed a friend more than now! Do not leave the room."

The general's eyes were glittering, his cheeks flushed with an unhealthy colour. The freedman was startled.

"Domine, domine!" he began, "you are not well — let me send for Calchas, the physician; a mild sleeping powder — "

For the first time in his long service of Cæsar, Antiochus met with a burst of wrath from his master.

"Vagabond! Do you think a sleeping potion will give peace to *me?* Speak again of Calchas, and I'll have you crucified!"

"Domine, domine!" cried the trembling freedman; but Cæsar swept on: —

"Don't go from the room! I am desperate to-night. I may lay violent hands on myself. Why should I not ask you for a poisoned dagger?"

Antiochus cowered at his master's feet.

"Yes, why not? What have I to gain by living? I have won some little fame. I have conquered all Gaul. I have invaded Britain. I have made the Germans tremble. Life is an evil dream, a nightmare, a frightful delusion. Death is real. Sleep — sleep — forever sleep! No care, no ambition, no vexation, no anger, no sorrow. Cornelia, the wife of my love, is asleep. Julia is asleep. All that I loved sleep. Why not I also?"

"Domine, speak not so!" and Antiochus clasped the proconsul's knees.

Cæsar bent down and lifted him up by the hand. When he spoke again, the tone was entirely changed.

"Old friend, you have known me; have loved me. You were my *pedagogue*[1] when I went to school at Rome. You taught me to ride and fence and wrestle. You aided me to escape the myrmidons of Sulla. You were with me in Greece. You shared my joy in my political successes, my triumphs in the field. And now what am I to do? You know the last advices from Rome; you know the determination of the consuls to work my ruin. To-day no news has come at all, and for us no news is the worst of news."

"Domine," said Antiochus, wiping his eyes, "I cannot dream that the Senate and Pompeius will deny you your right to the second consulship."

"But if they do? You know what Curio reports. What then?"

Antiochus shook his head.

"It would mean war, bloody war, the upturning of the whole world!"

"War, or — " and Cæsar paused.

"What, my lord?" said the freedman.

"I cease either to be a care to myself or my enemies."

"I do not understand you, domine," ventured Antiochus, turning pale.

---

[1] Slave who looked after the welfare and conduct of a schoolboy

"I mean, good friend," said the proconsul, calmly, "that when I consider how little life often seems worth, and how much disaster the continuance of my act of living means to my fellow-men, I feel often that I have no right to live."

Antiochus staggered with dread. Cæsar was no longer talking wildly; and the freedman knew that when in a calm mood the proconsul was always perfectly serious.

"Domine, you have not rashly determined this?" he hinted.

"I have determined nothing. I never rashly determine anything. Hark! Some one is at the door."

There was a loud military knock, and the clang of armour.

"Enter," commanded Cæsar.

Decimus Mamercus hastened into the room. So great was his excitement that his Roman discipline had forsaken him. He neglected to salute.

"News! news! Imperator! from Rome! News which will set all Italy afire!"

Whereupon the man who had but just before been talking of suicide, with the greatest possible deliberation seated himself on a comfortable chair, arranged his dress, and remarked with perfect coldness: —

"No tidings can justify a soldier in neglecting to salute his general."

Decimus turned red with mortification, and saluted.

"Now," said Cæsar, icily, "what have you to report?"

"Imperator," replied Decimus, trying to speak with unimpassioned preciseness, "a messenger has just arrived from Rome. He reports that the Senate and consuls have declared the Republic in peril, that the veto of your tribunes has been overridden, and they themselves forced to flee for their lives."

Cæsar had carelessly dropped a writing tablet that he was holding, and now he stooped slowly and picked it up again.

x

"The messenger is here?" he inquired, after a pause.

"He is," replied the centurion.

"Has he been duly refreshed after a hard ride?" was the next question.

"He has just come."

"Then let him have the best food and drink my butler and cellarer can set before him."

"But his news is of extreme importance," gasped Decimus, only half believing his ears.

"I have spoken," said the general, sternly. "What is his name?"

"He is called Quintus Drusus, Imperator."

"Ah!" was his deliberate response, "send him to me when he will eat and drink no more."

Decimus saluted again, and withdrew, while his superior opened the roll in his hands, and with all apparent fixity and interest studied at the precepts and definitions of the grammar of Dionysius Thrax, the noted philologist.

At the end of some minutes Quintus Drusus stood before him.

The young Prænestian was covered with dust, was unkempt, ragged; his step was heavy, his arms hung wearily at his side, his head almost drooped on his breast with exhaustion. But when he came into the Imperator's presence, he straightened himself and tried to make a gesture of salutation. Cæsar had risen from his chair.

"Fools!" he cried, to the little group of slaves and soldiers, who were crowding into the room, "do you bring me this worn-out man, who needs rest? Who dared this? Has he been refreshed as I commanded?"

"He would take nothing but some wine —" began Decimus.

"I would have waited until morning, if necessary, before

seeing him. Here!" and while Cæsar spoke he half led, half thrust, the messenger into his own chair, and, anticipating the nimblest slave, unclasped the travel-soiled pænula from Drusus's shoulders. The young man tried to rise and shake off these ministrations, but the proconsul gently restrained him. A single look sufficed to send all the curious retinue from the room. Only Antiochus remained, sitting on a stool in a distant corner.

"And now, my friend," said Cæsar, smiling, and drawing a chair close up to that of Drusus, "tell me when it was that you left Rome."

"Two days ago," gasped the wearied messenger.

"*Mehercle!*" cried the general, "a hundred and sixty miles in two days! This is incredible! And you come alone?"

"I had Andræmon, the fastest horse in Rome. Antonius, Cælius, Cassius, Curio, and myself kept together as far as Clusium. There was no longer any danger of pursuit, no need for more than one to hasten." Drusus's sentences were coming in hot pants. "I rode ahead. Rode my horse dead. Took another at Arretium. And so I kept changing. And now — I am here." And with this last utterance he stopped, gasping.

Cæsar, instead of demanding the tidings from Rome, turned to Antiochus, and bade him bring a basin and perfumed water to wash Drusus's feet. Meantime the young man had recovered his breath.

"You have heard of the violence of the new consuls and how Antonius and Cassius withstood them. On the seventh the end came. The vetoes were set aside. Our protests were disregarded. The Senate has clothed the consuls and other magistrates with dictatorial power; they are about to make Lucius Domitius proconsul of Gaul."

"And I?" asked Cæsar, for the first time displaying any personal interest.

"You, Imperator, must disband your army and return to Rome speedily, or be declared an outlaw, as Sertorius or Catilina was."

"Ah!" and for a minute the proconsul sat motionless, while Drusus again kept silence.

"But you — my friends — the tribunes?" demanded the general, "you spoke of danger; why was it that you fled?"

"We fled in slaves' dresses, O Cæsar, because otherwise we should long ago have been strangled like bandits in the Tullianum. Lentulus Crus drove us with threats from the Senate. On the bridge, but for the favour of the gods, his lictors would have taken us. We were chased by Pompeius's foot soldiers as far as Janiculum. We ran away from his cavalry. If they hate us, your humble friends, so bitterly, how much the more must they hate you!"

"And the tribunes, and Curio, and Cælius are on their way hither?" asked Cæsar.

"They will be here very soon."

"That is well," replied the proconsul; then, with a totally unexpected turn, "Quintus Drusus, what do you advise me to do?"

"I — I advise, Imperator?" stammered the young man.

"And who should advise, if not he who has ridden so hard and fast in my service? Tell me, is there any hope of peace, of reconciliation with Pompeius?"

"None."

"Any chance that the senators will recover their senses, and propose a reasonable compromise?"

"None."

"Will not Cicero use his eloquence in the cause of peace and common justice?"

"I have seen him. He dare not open his mouth."

"Ah!" and again Cæsar was silent, this time with a smile, perhaps of scorn, playing around his mouth.

"Are the people, the equites, given body and soul over to the war party?"

Drusus nodded sadly. "So long as the consuls are in the ascendant, they need fear no revolution at home. The people are not at heart your enemies, Imperator; but they will wait to be led by the winning side."

"And you advise?" — pressed Cæsar, returning to the charge.

"War!" replied Drusus, with all the rash emphasis of youth.

"Young man," said Cæsar, gravely, half sadly, "what you have said is easy to utter. Do you know what war will mean?"

Drusus was silent.

"Let us grant that our cause is most just. Even then, if we fight, we destroy the Republic. If I conquer, it must be over the wreck of the Commonwealth. If Pompeius — on the same terms. I dare not harbour any illusions. The state cannot endure the farce of another Sullian restoration and reformation. A permanent government by one strong man will be the only one practicable to save the world from anarchy. Have you realized that?"

"I only know, Imperator," said Drusus, gloomily, "that no future state can be worse than ours to-day, when the magistrates of the Republic are the most grievous despots."

Cæsar shook his head.

"You magnify your own wrongs and mine If mere revenge prompts us, we are worse than Xerxes, or Sulla. The gods alone can tell us what is right."

"The gods!" cried Drusus, half sunken though he was in a weary lethargy, "do you believe there are any gods?"

Cæsar threw back his head. "Not always; but at moments

I do not *believe* in them, I *know!* And now I *know* that gods are guiding us!"

"Whither?" exclaimed the young man, starting from his weary drowsiness.

"I know not whither; neither do I care. Enough to be conscious that they guide us!"

And then, as though there was no pressing problem involving the peace of the civilized world weighing upon him, the proconsul stood by in kind attention while Antiochus and an attendant bathed the wearied messenger's feet before taking him away to rest.

After Drusus had been carried to his room, Cæsar collected the manuscripts and tablets scattered about the apartment, methodically placed them in the proper cases and presses, suffered himself to be undressed, and slept late into the following morning, as sweetly and soundly as a little child.

II

On the next day Cæsar called before him the thirteenth legion, — the only force he had at Ravenna, — and from a pulpit in front of the prætorium he told them the story of what had happened at Rome; of how the Senate had outraged the tribunes of the plebs, whom even the violent Sulla had respected; of how the mighty oligarchy had outraged every soldier in insulting their commander. Then Curio, just arrived, declaimed with indignant fervour of the violence and fury of the consuls and Pompeius; and when he concluded, the veterans could restrain their ardour and devotion no more, five thousand martial throats roared forth an oath of fealty, and as many swords were waved on high in mad defiance to the Senate and the Magnus. Then cohort after cohort cried out that on this campaign they would accept no pay; and the military tribunes and centurions pledged themselves, this officer for the support of two recruits, and that for three.

It was a great personal triumph for Cæsar. He stood receiving the pledges and plaudits, and repaying each protestation of loyalty with a few gracious words, or smiles, that were worth fifty talents to each acclaiming maniple. Drusus, who was standing back of the proconsul, beside Curio, realized that never before had he seen such outgoing of magnetism and personal energy from man to man, one mind holding in vassalage five thousand. Yet it was all very quickly over. Almost while the plaudits of the centuries were rending the air, Cæsar turned to the senior tribune of the legion.

"Are your men ready for the march, officer?"

The soldier instantly fell into rigid military pose. "Ready this instant, Imperator. We have expected the order."

"March to Ariminum, and take possession of the town. March rapidly."

The tribune saluted, and stepped back among his cohort. And as if some conjurer had flourished a wand of magic, in the twinkling of an eye the first century had formed in marching order; every legionary had flung over his shoulder his shield and pack, and at the harsh blare of the military trumpet the whole legion fell into line; the aquilifer with the bronze eagle, that had tossed on high in a score of hard-fought fights, swung off at the head of the van; and away went the legion, a thing not of thinking flesh and blood, but of brass and iron — a machine that marched as readily and carelessly against the consuls of the Roman Republic as against the wretched Gallic insurgents. The body of troops — cohort after cohort — was vanishing down the road in a cloud of dust, the pack train following after, almost before Drusus could realize that the order to advance had been given.

Cæsar was still standing on the little pulpit before the prætorium. Except for Curio and Drusus, almost all the vast company that had but just now been pressing about him with adulation and homage were disappearing from sight. For an instant the Imperator seemed alone, stripped of all the panoply of his high estate. He stood watching the legion until its dust-cloud settled behind some low-lying hills. Then he stepped down from the pulpit. Beyond a few menials and Drusus and that young man's late comrade in danger, no one else was visible. The transaction had been so sudden as to have something of the phantasmagoric about it.

Cæsar took his two friends, one by each hand, and led them back to his private study in the prætorium.

"The army is yours, Imperator," said Curio, breaking a rather oppressive silence. "The newest recruit is yours to the death."

"Yes, to the death," replied the general, abstractedly; and his keen eyes wandered down upon the mosaic, seemingly penetrating the stone and seeking something hidden beneath. "The thirteenth legion," he continued, "will do as a test of the loyalty of the others. They will not fail me. The eighth and the twelfth will soon be over the Alps. Fabius is at Narbo with three. They will check Pompeius's Spaniards. I must send to Trebonius for his four among the Belgæ; he is sending Fabius one." And then, as if wearied by this recapitulation, Cæsar's eyes wandered off again to the pavement.

Drusus had an uneasy sensation. What was this strange mingling of energy and listlessness? Why this soliloquy and internal debate, when the moment called for the most intense activity? The general being still silent, his friends did not venture to disturb him. But Antiochus passed in and out of the study, gathering up writing materials, tablets, and books;

and presently Drusus heard the freedman bidding an underling have ready and packed the marble slabs used for the tessel-
lated floor of the Imperator's tent — a bit of luxury that Cæsar
never denied himself while in the field. Presently the proconsul raised his eyes. He was smiling; there was not the
least cloud on his brow.

"There will be some public games here this afternoon," he
remarked, as though the sole end in view was to make their
stay pleasant to his guests: "I have promised the good people
of the town to act as *editor*,[1] and must not fail to honour them.
Perhaps the sport will amuse you, although the provincials
cannot of course get such good lanista-trained men as you see
at Rome. I have a new fencing school in which perhaps we
may find a few *threces*[2] and *retiarii*,[3] who will give some tolerable sword and net play."

"*Hei!*" groaned Curio, with a lugubrious whisper, "to
think of it, I have never a sesterce left that I can call my
own, to stake on the struggle!"

"At least," laughed Drusus, "I am a companion of your
grief; already Lentulus and Ahenobarbus have been sharing
my forfeited estate."

But the proconsul looked serious and sad.

"*Vah,* my friends! Would that I could say that your loyalty
to my cause would cost you nothing! It is easy to promise to
win back for you everything you have abandoned, but as the
poets say, 'All that lies in the lap of the gods.' But you shall
not be any longer the mere recipients of my bounty. Stern
work is before us. I need not ask you if you will play your
part. You, Curio, shall have a proper place on my staff of
legates as soon as I have enough troops concentrated; but **you,**

---

[1] President of the games.   [2] Buckler and cutlass men.
[3] Net and trident men.

my dear Drusus, what post would best reward you for your loyalty? Will you be a military tribune, and succeed your father?"

"Your kindness outruns your judgment, Imperator," replied Drusus. "Save repelling Dumnorix and Ahenobarbus, I never struck a blow in anger. Small service would I be to you, and little glory would I win as an officer, when the meanest legionary knows much that I may learn."

"Then, amice," said Cæsar, smiling, perhaps with the satisfaction of a man who knows when it is safe to make a gracious offer which he is aware will not be accepted, though none the less flattering, "if you will thus misappraise yourself, you shall act as centurion for the present, on my corps of *prætoriani*,[1] where you will be among friends and comrades of your father, and be near my person if I have any special need of you."

Drusus proffered the best thanks he could; it was a great honour — one almost as great as a tribuneship, though hardly as responsible; and he felt repaid for all the weariness of his desperate ride to Ravenna.

And then, with another of those strange alternations of behaviour, Cæsar led him and Curio off to inspect the fencing school; then showed them his favourite horse, pointed out its peculiar toelike hoofs, and related merrily how when it was a young colt, a soothsayer had predicted that its owner would be master of the world, and how he — Cæsar — had broken its fiery spirit, and made it perfectly docile, although no other man could ride the beast.

The afternoon wore on. Cæsar took his friends to the games, and watched with all apparent interest the rather sanguinary contests between the gladiators. Drusus noticed the effusive loyalty of the Ravenna citizens, who shouted a

---

[1] General's body-guard of picked veterans.

tumultuous welcome to the illustrious *editor*, but Cæsar acted precisely as though the presidency of the sports were his most important office. Only his young admirer observed that as often as a gladiator brought his opponent down and appealed to the *editor* for a decision on the life or death of the vanquished, Cæsar invariably waved his handkerchief, a sign of mercy, rather than brutally turned down his thumb, the sentence of death. After the games, the proconsul interchanged personal greetings with the more prominent townspeople. Drusus began to wonder whether the whole day and evening were to pass in this manner; and indeed so it seemed, for that night the Imperator dispensed his usual open-handed hospitality. His great banqueting hall contained indeed no army officers, but there were an abundance of the provincial gentry. Cæsar dined apart with his two friends. The courses went in and out. The proconsul continued an unceasing flow of light conversation: witty comments on Roman society and fashion, scraps of literary lore, now and then a bit of personal reminiscence of Gaul. Drusus forgot all else in the agreeable pleasure of the moment. Presently Cæsar arose and mingled with his less exalted guests; when he returned to the upper table the attendants were bringing on the beakers, and the Cisalpine provincials were pledging one another in draughts of many *cyathi*, "prosperity to the proconsul, and confusion to his enemies." Cæsar took a shallow glass of embossed blue and white bas-relief work, — a triumph of Alexandrian art, — poured into it a few drops of undiluted Cæcuban liquor, dashed down the potion, then dropped the priceless beaker on to the floor.

"An offering to Fortuna!" he cried, springing from his couch. "My friends, let us go!" And quietly leaving the table on the dais, the three found themselves outside the banqueting hall, while the provincials, unconscious that their host had departed, continued their noisy revelry.

Drusus at once saw that everything was ready for departure. Antiochus was at hand with travelling cloaks, and assured the young man that due care had been taken to send in advance for him a complete wardrobe and outfit. The proconsul evidently intended to waste no time in starting. Drusus realized by the tone of his voice that Cæsar the host had vanished, and Cæsar the imperator was present. His words were terse and to the point.

"Curio, you will find a fast horse awaiting you. Take it. Ride at full speed after the legion. Take command of the rear cohorts and of the others as you come up with them. Lead rapidly to Ariminum."

And Curio, who was a man of few words, when few were needed, saluted and disappeared in the darkness. Drusus followed the general out after him. But no saddle-horses were prepared for Cæsar. Antiochus and one or two slaves were ready with lanterns, and led the general and Drusus out of the gloomy cantonment, along a short stretch of road, to a mill building, where in the dim light of the last flickers of day could be seen a carriage with mules.

"I have hired this as you wished," said the freedman, briefly.

"It is well," responded his patron.

Antiochus clambered upon the front seat; a stout German serving-man was at the reins. Cæsar motioned to Drusus to sit beside him behind. There were a few necessaries in the carriage, but no other attendants, no luggage cart. The German shook the reins over the backs of the two mules, and admonished them in his barbarous native dialect. The dim shadow of the mill faded from sight; the lights of the prætorium grew dim

mer and dimmer: soon nothing was to be seen outside the
narrow circle of pale light shed on the ground ahead by the
lantern.

The autumn season was well advanced. The day however
had been warm. The night was sultry. There were no stars
above, no moon, no wind. A sickening miasmic odour rose
from the low flat country sloping off toward the Adriatic —
the smell of overripe fruit, of decaying vegetation, of the har-
vest grown old. There had been a drought, and now the dust
rose thick and heavy, making the mules and travellers cough,
and the latter cover their faces. Out of the darkness came
not the least sound: save the creaking of the dead boughs on
trees, whose dim tracery could just be distinguished against
the sombre background of the sky.

No one spoke, unless the incoherent shouts of the German
to the mules be termed speech. Antiochus and Cæsar were
sunk in stupor or reverie. Drusus settled back on the cushions, closed his eyes, and bade himself believe that it was all
a dream. Six months ago he had been a student at Athens,
wandering with his friends along the trickling Cephissus, or
climbing, in holiday sport, the marble cone of Hymettus.
And now — he was a proscribed rebel! Enemies thirsted for
his blood! He was riding beside a man who made no dis-
claimer of his intention to subvert the constitution! If Cæsar
failed, he, Drusus, would share in "that bad eminence"
awarded by fame to the execrated Catilinarians. Was it — was
it not all a dream? Connected thought became impossible.
Now he was in the dear old orchard at Praeneste playing
micare[1] with Cornelia and Æmilia; now back in Athens, now
in Rome. Poetry, prose, scraps of oratory, philosophy, and rules
of rhetoric, — Latin and Greek inextricably intermixed, — ideas

[1] A finger-guessing game.

without the least possible connection, raced through his head
How long he thus drifted on in his reverie he might not say.
Perhaps he fell asleep, for the fatigue of his extraordinary rid-
ing still wore on him. A cry from Antiochus, a curse from the
German, startled him out of his stupor. He stared about. It
was pitch dark. " The gods blast it ! " Antiochus was bawling
" The lantern has jolted out ! "

To relight it under existing circumstances, in an age when
friction matches were unknown, was practically impossible.

"Fellow," said the proconsul's steady voice, "do you know
the road to Ariminum ? "

The driver answered in his broken Latin that he was the
slave of the stable keeper who had let the carriage, and had
been often over the road, but to go safely in the dark was
more than he could vouch for. The only thing the German
saw to be done was to wait in the road until the morning, or
until the moon broke out through the clouds.

"Drusus," remarked the proconsul, "you are the youngest.
Can your eyes make out anything to tell us where we are ? "

The young man yawned, shook off his drowsiness, and stared
out into the gloomy void.

"I can just make out that to our left are tall trees, and I
imagine a thicket."

"Very good. If you can see as much as that here, it is safe
to proceed. Let us change places. I will take the reins. Do
you, Drusus, come and direct me."

"Oh! domine !" entreated Antiochus, "don't imperil your
self to-night! I'm sure some calamity impends before dawn.
I consulted a soothsayer before setting out, and the dove
which he examined had no heart — a certain sign of evil."

"Rascal !" retorted his patron, "the omens will be more
favourable when I please. A beast wants a heart — no very

great prodigy! men lose theirs very often, and think it slight disgrace. Change your seat, sirrah!"

Cæsar took the reins, smote the mules, and went off at so furious a pace that the worthy Antiochus was soon busy invoking first one, then another, member of the pantheon, to avert disaster. Drusus speedily found that the general's vision was far more keen than his own. Indeed, although the road, he knew, was rough and crooked, they met with no mishaps. Presently a light could be seen twinkling in the distance.

"We must get a guide," remarked the Imperator decisively, and he struck the mules again.

They at last approached what the owl-like discernment of Cæsar pronounced to be a small farmhouse with a few outbuildings. But it was no easy matter to arouse the drowsy countrymen, and a still more difficult task to convince the good man of the house that his nocturnal visitors were not brigands. At last it was explained that two gentlemen from Ravenna were bound for Ariminum, on urgent business, and he must furnish a guide for which he would be amply paid. As a result, the German driver at last resumed the reins, and sped away with a fresh lantern, and at his side a stupid peasant boy, who was almost too shy to make himself useful.

But more misfortune was in store. Barely a mile had they traversed, before an ominous crack proclaimed the splitting of an axletree. The cheap hired vehicle could go no farther.

"'Tis a sure sign the gods are against our proceeding this night," expostulated Antiochus; "let us walk back to the farmhouse, my lord."

Cæsar did not deign to give him an answer. He deliberately descended, clasped his pænula over his shoulders, and bade the German make the best of his way back to Ravenna. The peasant boy, he declared, could lead them on foot until dawn.

The freedman groaned, but he was helpless. The guide, bearing the lantern, convoyed them out of the highroad, to strike what he assured them was a less circuitous route; and soon had his travellers, now plunged in quagmires that in daylight would have seemed impassable, now clambering over stocks and stones, now leaping broad ditches. At last, after thoroughly exhausting the patience of his companions, the wretched fellow confessed that he had missed the by-path, and indeed did not know the way back.

Antiochus was now too frightened to declare his warnings confirmed. Drusus liked the prospect of a halt on these swampy, miasmic fields little enough. But again the proconsul was all resources. With almost omniscience he led his companions through blind mazes of fallow land and stubble fields: came upon a brook at the only point where there appeared to be any stepping-stones; and at length, just as the murky clouds seemed about to lift, and the first beams of the moon struggled out into the black chaos, the wanderers saw a multitude of fires twinkling before them, and knew that they had come upon the rear cohort of the thirteenth legion, on its way to Ariminum.

The challenge of the sentry was met by a quick return of the watchword, but the effusively loyal soldier was bidden to hold his peace and not disturb his comrades.

"What time is it?" inquired his general. The fellow replied it lacked one hour of morn. Cæsar skirted the sleeping camp, and soon came out again on the highroad. There was a faint paleness in the east; a single lark sang from out the mist of grey ether overhead; an ox of the baggage train rattled his tethering chain and bellowed. A soft, damp river fog touched on Drusus's face. Suddenly an early horseman, coming at a moderate gallop, was heard down the road. In the stillness, the pounding of his steed crept slowly nearer and nearer: then, as he was almost on them, came the hollow clatter of the hoofs upon the planks of a bridge. *Cæsar stopped.* Drusus felt himself clutched by the arm so tightly that the grasp almost meant pain.

"Do you hear? Do you see?" muttered the Imperator's voice in his ear. "The bridge, the river — we have reached it!"

"Your excellency — " began Drusus, sorely at a loss.

"No compliments, this is the Rubicon; the boundaries of Cisalpine Gaul and Italy. On this side I am still the Proconsul — not as yet rightly deposed. On the other — Cæsar, the Outlaw, the Insurgent, the Enemy of his Country, whose hand is against every man, every man's hand against him. What say you? Speak! speak quickly! Shall I cross? Shall I turn back?"

"Imperator," said the young man, struggling to collect his wits and realize the gravity of his own words, "if you did not intend to cross, why send the legion over to commence the invasion? Why harangue them, if you had no test to place upon their loyalty?"

"Because," was his answer, "I would not through my own indecision throw away my chance to strike. But the troops can be recalled. It is not too late. No blood has been shed. I am merely in a position to strike if so I decide. No, — nothing is settled."

Drusus had never felt greater embarrassment. Before he could make reply, Cæsar had bidden Antiochus and the peasant boy remain in the roadway, and had led the young man down the embankment that ran sloping toward the river. The light was growing stronger every moment, though the mist still hung heavy and dank. Below their feet the slender stream — it was the end of the season — ran with a monotonous gurgle.

now and then casting up a little fleck of foam, as it rolled by a small boulder in its bed.

"Imperator," said Drusus, while Cæsar pressed his hand tighter and tighter, "why advise with an inexperienced young man like myself? Why did you send Curio away? I have no wisdom to offer; nor dare proffer it, if such I had."

"Quintus Drusus," replied Cæsar, sinking rather wearily down upon the dry, dying grass, "if I had needed the counsel of a soldier, I should have waited until Marcus Antonius arrived; if I had needed that of a politician, I was a fool to send away Curio; if I desire the counsel of one who is, as yet, neither a man of the camp, nor a man of the Forum, but who can see things with clear eyes, can tell what may be neither glorious nor expedient, but what will be the will," — and here the Imperator hesitated, — "the will of the gods, tell me to whom I shall go."

Drusus was silent; the other continued : —

"Listen, Quintus Drusus. I do not believe in blind fate. We were not given wills only to have them broken. The function of a limb is not to be maimed, nor severed from the body. A limb is to serve a man; just so a man and his actions are to serve the ends of a power higher and nobler than he. If he refuse to serve that power, he is like the mortifying limb, — a thing of evil to be cut off. And this is true of all of us; we all have some end to serve, we are not created for no purpose." Cæsar paused. When he began again it was in a different tone of voice. "I have brought you with me, because I know you are intelligent, are humane, love your country, and can make sacrifices for her; because you are my friend and to a certain extent share my destiny; because you are too young to have become overprejudiced, and cal- loused to pet foibles and transgressions. Therefore I took

you with me, having put off the final decision to the last possi
ble instant. And now I desire your counsel."

"How can I counsel peace!" replied Drusus, warming to a
sense of the situation. "Is not Italy in the hand of tyrants?
Is not Pompeius the tool of coarse schemers? Do they not
pray for proscriptions and confiscations and abolition of debt?
Will there be any peace, any happiness in life, so long as we
call ourselves freemen, yet endure the chains of a despotism
worse than that of the Parthians?"

"Ah! amice!" said Cæsar, twisting the long limp grass,
"every enemy is a tyrant, if he has the upper hand. Consider,
what will the war be? Blood, the blood of the noblest Romans!
The overturning of time-honoured institutions! A shock that
will make the world to tremble, kings be laid low, cities anni-
hilated! East, west, north, south—all involved—so great has
our Roman world become!"

"And are there not wrongs, abuses, Imperator, which cry for
vengeance and for righting?" replied Drusus, vehemently.
"Since the fall of Carthage, have not the fears of Scipio
Æmilianus almost come true: Troy has fallen, Carthage has
fallen; has not Rome almost fallen, fallen not by the might of
her enemies, but by the decay of her morals, the degeneracy of
her statesmen? What is the name of liberty, without the
semblance! Is it liberty for a few mighty families to enrich
themselves, while the Republic groans? Is it liberty for the
law courts to have their price, for the provinces to be the farms
of a handful of nobles?"

Cæsar shook his head.

"You do not know what you say. This is no moment for
declamation. Every man has his own life to live, his own
death to die. Our intellects cannot assure us of any consciousness the instant that breath has left our bodies. It is then at

if we had never hoped, had never feared; it is rest, peace, Quintus Drusus, I have dared many things in my life. I defied Sulla; it was boyish impetuosity. I took the unpopular and perilous side when Catilina's confederates were sent to their deaths; it was the ardour of a young politician. I defied the rage of the Senate, while I was prætor; still more hot madness. I faced death a thousand times in Gaul, against the Nervii, in the campaign with Vercingetorix; all this was the mere courage of the common soldier. But it is not of death I am afraid; be it death on the field of battle, or death at the hands of the executioner, should I fall into the power of my enemies. I fear myself.

"You ask me to explain?" went on the general, without pausing for a question. "Hearken! I am a man, you are a man, our enemies are men. I have slain a hundred thousand men in Gaul. Cruel? No, for had they lived the great designs which the deity wills to accomplish in that country could not be executed! But then my mind was at rest. I said, 'Let these men die,' and no Nemesis has required their blood at my hands. What profit these considerations? The Republic is nothing but a name, without substance or reality. It is doomed to fall. Sulla was a fool to abdicate the dictatorship. Why did he not establish a despotism, and save us all this turmoil of politics? But Lentulus Crus, Pompeius, Cato, Scipio — they are men with as much ambition, as much love of life, as myself. The Republic will fall into their hands. Why will it be worse off than in mine? Why shed rivers of blood? After death one knows no regrets. If I were dead, what would it matter to me if obloquy was imputed to my name, if my enemies triumphed, if the world went to chaos over my grave. It would not mean so much as a single evil dream in my perpetual slumber"

Cæsar was no longer resting on the bank. He was pacing to and fro, with rapid, nervous steps, crushing the dry twigs under his shoes, pressing his hands together behind his back, knitting and unknitting his fingers.

Drusus knew enough to be aware that he was present as a spectator of that most terrible of all conflicts — a strong man's wrestle with his own misgivings. To say something, to say anything, that would ease the shock of the contest — that was the young man's compelling desire; but he felt as helpless as though he, single handed, confronted ten legions.

"But your friends, Imperator," he faltered, "think of them! They have made sacrifices for you. They trust in you. Do not abandon them to their enemies!"

Cæsar stopped in his impetuous pacings.

"Look here," he exclaimed, almost fiercely, "you wish to be happy. You are still very young; life is sweet. You have just forsaken wealth, friends, love, because you have a fantastic attachment for my cause. You will live to repent of your boyish decision. You will wish to win back all you have lost. Well, I will give you the chance; do what I tell you, and you shall ride into Rome the hero of Senate and people! The consuls will be to you all smiles. Pompeius will canvass for you if you desire to become a candidate for curule office before you reach the legal age limit. Cicero will extol your name in an immortal oration, in which he will laud your deed above the slaying of the dangerous demagogue Mælius by Servilius Ahala. Will you do as I shall bid you?"

Drusus's eyes had been riveted on those of the general. He saw that at Cæsar's side was girded a long slender dagger in an embossed silver sheath. He saw the Imperator draw out the blade halfway, then point off into the river where the water ran sluggishly through a single deep mist-shaded pool.

"Do you understand?" went on Cæsar, as calmly as though he had been expounding a problem of metaphysics. "You can take this ring of mine, and by its aid go through the whole legion, and obtain the best horses for flight, before anything is discovered. Your conscience need not trouble you. You will only have done as I earnestly requested."

The cold sweat started to Drusus's forehead, his head swam; he knew that it was more than the mist of the river-fog that drifted before his eyes. Then, filled with a sudden impulse, he sprang on the general and wrenched the dagger from its sheath.

"Here!" cried Cæsar, tearing back the mantle from his breast.

"There!" cried Drusus, and the bright blade glinted once in the air, and splashed down into the dark ripple. He caught the Imperator about the arms, and flung his head on the other's neck.

"Oh! Imperator," he cried, "do not desert us. Do not desert the Commonwealth! Do not hand us back to new ruin, new tyrants, new wars! Strike, strike, and so be merciful! Surely the gods have not led you thus far, and no farther! But yesterday you said they were leading us. To-day they still must guide! To you it has been given to pull down and to build up. Fail not! If there be gods, trust in them! If there be none slay me first, then do whatever you will!"

Cæsar shook himself. His voice was harsh with command.

"Unhand me! I must accomplish my own fate!" and then, in a totally different tone, "Quintus Drusus, I have been a coward for the first time in my life. Are you ashamed of your general?"

"I never admired you more, Imperator."

"Thank you. And will you go aside a little, please? I will need a few moments for meditation."

Drusus hesitated. His eyes wandered off to the river. In one spot it was quite deep.

"*Phui!*" said the proconsul, carelessly, "I am too brave for such a venture now. Leave me on my embankment, like Diogenes and his tub."

Drusus clambered part way up the slope, and seated himself under a stunted oak tree. The light was growing stronger. The east was overshot with ripples of crimson and orange, here blending into lines each more gorgeous than a moment before. The wind was chasing in from the bosom of Adria, and driving the fleeting mists up the little valley. The hills were springing out of the gloom, the thrushes were swinging in the boughs overhead, and pouring out their morning song. Out from the camp the bugles were calling the soldiers for the march; the baggage trains were rumbling over the bridge. But still below on the marge lingered the solitary figure; now walking, now motionless, now silent, now speaking in indistinct monologue. Drusus overheard only an occasional word, "Pompeius, poor tool of knaves! I pity him! I must show mercy to Cato if I can! Sulla is not to be imitated! The Republic is fallen; what I put in its place must not fall." Then, after a long pause, "So this was to be my end in life — to destroy the Commonwealth; what is destined, is destined!" And a moment later Drusus saw the general coming up the embankment.

"We shall find horses, I think, a little way over the bridge," said Cæsar; "the sun is nearly risen. It is nine miles to Ariminum; there we can find refreshment."

The Imperator's brow was clear, his step elastic, the fatigues of the night seemed to have only added to his vigorous good humour. Antiochus met them. The good man evidently was relieved of a load of anxiety. The three approached the bridge; as they did so, a little knot of officers of the rear cohort, Asinius Pollio and others, rode up and saluted. The golden rim of the sun was just glittering above the eastern lowlands. Cæsar put foot upon the bridge. Drusus saw the blood recede from his face, his muscles contract, his frame quiver. The general turned to his officers.

"Gentlemen," he said quietly, "we may still retreat; but if we once pass this little bridge, nothing is left for us but to fight it out in arms."

The group was silent, each waiting for the other to speak. At this instant a mountebank piper sitting by the roadway struck up his ditty, and a few idle soldiers and wayfaring shepherds ran up to him to catch the music. The man flung down his pipe, snatched a trumpet from a bugler, and, springing up, blew a shrill blast. It was the "advance." Cæsar turned again to his officers.

"Gentlemen," he said, "let us go where the omens of the gods and the iniquity of our enemies call us! *The die is now cast!*"

And he strode over the bridge, looking neither to the right hand nor to the left. As his feet touched the dust of the road beyond, the full sun touched the horizon, the landscape was bathed with living, quivering gold, and the brightness shed itself over the steadfast countenance, not of Cæsar the Proconsul, but of Cæsar the Insurgent.

The Rubicon was crossed!

CHAPTER XVII

THE PROFITABLE CAREER OF GABINIUS

VERY wretched had been the remnants of Dumnorix's band of gladiators, when nightfall had covered them from pursuit by the enraged Prænestians. And for some days the defeated assassins led a desperate struggle for existence on the uplands above the Latin plain. Then, when the hue and cry aroused by their mad exploit had died away, Dumnorix was able to reorganize his men into a regular horde of banditti. In the sheltered valleys of the upper Apennines they found moderately safe and comfortable fastnesses, and soon around them gathered a number of unattached highwaymen, who sought protection and profit in allying themselves with the band led by the redoubtable lanista. But if Dumnorix was the right arm of this noble company, Publius Gabinius was its head. The Roman had sorely missed the loss of the thousand and one luxuries that made his former life worth living. But, as has been said, he had become sated with almost every current amusement and vice; and when the freshness of the physical hardships of his new career was over, he discovered that he had just begun to taste joys of which he would not soon grow weary.

And so for a while the bandits ranged over the mountains, infested the roads, stopped travellers to ease them of their purses, or even dashed down on outlying country houses, which they plundered, and left burning as beacons of their handiwork. Even this occupation after a time, however, grew monotonous to Gabinius. To be sure, a goodly pile of money was accumulating in the hut where he and Dumnorix, his fellow-leader, made their headquarters; and the bandits carried away with them to their stronghold a number of slave and peasant girls, who aided to make the camp the scene of enough riot and orgy to satisfy the most graceless; but Gabinius had higher ambitions than these. He could not spend the gold on dinner parties, or bronze statuettes; and the maidens picked up in the country made a poor contrast to his city sweethearts. Gabinius was planning a great piece of *finesse*. He had not forgotten Fabia; least of all had he forgotten how he had had her as it were in his very arms, and let her vanish from him as though she had been a " shade " of thin air. If he must be a bandit, he would be an original one. A Vestal taken captive by robbers! A Vestal imprisoned in the hold of banditti, forced to become the consort, lawful or unlawful, of the brigands' chief! The very thought grew and grew in Gabinius's imagination, until he could think of little else. Dumnorix and his comrades trusted him almost implicitly; he had been successful as their schemer and leader in several dark enterprises, that proved his craft if not his valour. He would not fail in this.

An overmastering influence was drawing him to Rome. He took one or two fellow-spirits in his company, and ventured over hill and valley to the suburbs of the city on a reconnoissance, while by night he ventured inside the walls.

The capital he found in the ferment that preceded the expulsion of the tribunes, on the fateful seventh of January. Along with many another evil-doer, he and his followers filched more than one wallet during the commotions and tumults. He dared not show himself very openly. His crime had been too notorious to be passed over, even if committed against a doomed Cæsarian like Drusus; besides, he was utterly without any political influence that would stand him in good stead. But around the Atrium Vestæ he lurked in the dark, spying out the land and waiting for a glimpse of Fabia. Once only his eye caught a white-robed stately figure appearing in the doorway toward evening, a figure which instinct told him was the object of his passion. He had to restrain himself, or he would have thrown off all concealment then and there, and snatched her away in his arms. He saved himself that folly, but his quest seemed hopeless. However weak the patrol in other parts of the city, there was always an ample watch around the Atrium Vestæ.

Gabinius saw that his stay around Rome was only likely to bring him into the clutches of the law, and reluctantly he started back, by a night journey in a stolen wagon, for the safer hill country beyond the Anio. But he was not utterly cast down. He had overheard the street talk of two equites, whom in more happy days he had known as rising politicians.

"I hope the consuls are right," the first had said, "that Cæsar's army will desert him."

"*Perpol,*" responded the other, "your wish is mine! If the proconsul really *does* advance, nothing will stand between him and the city!"

Gabinius kept his own counsel. "In times of war and confusion, the extremity of the many is the opportunity of the few," was the maxim he repeated to himself.

When he was well out of the city and moving up the Via Salaria, the trot and rattle of an approaching carriage drifted up upon him.

"Shall we stop and strip them?" asked Dromo, one of the accompanying brigands, in a matter-of-fact tone.

"Ay," responded Gabinius, reining in his own plodding draught-horse, and pulling out a short sword. "Let us take what the Fates send!"

A moment later and Servius Flaccus was being tumbled out of his comfortable travelling carriage, while one brigand stood guard over him with drawn sabre, a second held at bay his trembling driver and whimpering valet, and a third rifled his own person and his conveyance. There was a bright moon, and the luckless traveller's gaze fastened itself on the third bandit.

"By all the gods, Gabinius!" cried Servius, forgetting to lisp his Greekisms, "don't you know me? Let me go, for old friendship's sake!"

Gabinius turned from his task, and held to his nose a glass scent-bottle he had found in the vehicle.

"Ah! amice," he responded deliberately, "I really did not anticipate the pleasure of meeting you thus! You are returning very late to Rome from your Fidenæ villa. But this is very excellent oil of rose!"

"Enough of this, man!" expostulated the other. "The jest has gone quite far enough. Make this horrible fellow lower that sword."

"Not until I have finished making up my package of little articles," replied Gabinius, "and," suiting the action to the word, "relieved your fingers of the weight of those very heavy rings."

"Gabinius," roared Servius, in impotent fury, "what are you doing? Are you a common bandit?"

"A bandit, my excellent friend," was his answer, "but not a common one; no ordinary footpad could strip the noble Servius Flaccus without a harder struggle."

Servius burst into lamentations.

"My box of unguents! My precious rings! My money-bag! You are not leaving me one valuable! Have you sunk as low as this?"

"Really," returned the robber, "I have no time to convince you that the brigand's life is the only one worth living. You do not care to join our illustrious brotherhood? No? Well, I must put these trinkets and fat little wallet in my own wagon. I leave you your cloak out of old friendship's sake. Really you must not blame me. Remember Euripides's line:—

"'Money can warp the judgment of a God.'

Thus I err in good company. And with this, *vale!*"

Flaccus was left with his menials to clamber back into his plundered carriage. Gabinius drove his horse at topmost speed, and before morning was saluted by the remainder of the banditti, near their mountain stronghold. Dumnorix met him with news.

"It is rumoured in the country towns that Cæsar is driving all before him in the north, and will be down on Rome in less days than I have fingers."

Gabinius clapped his hands.

"And we will be down on Rome, and away from it, before a legionary shows himself at the gates!"

CHAPTER XVIII

HOW POMPEIUS STAMPED WITH HIS FEET

I

A MESSENGER to the consuls! He had ridden fast and furious, his horse was flecked with foam and straining on his last burst of speed. On over the Mulvian Bridge he thundered; on across the Campus Martius; on to the Porta Ratumena — with all the hucksters and street rabble howling and chasing at his heels.

"News! News for the consuls!"

"What news?" howled old Læca, who was never backward in a street press.

"Terrible!" shouted the messenger, drawing rein, "Cæsar is sweeping all before him! All Thermus's troops have deserted him at Iguvium. Attius Varus has evacuated Auximum, and his troops too have dispersed, or joined Cæsar. All the towns are declaring for the enemy. *Vah!* He will be here in a few days at most! I am the last of the relay with the news. I have hardly breathed from Eretum!"

And the courier plunged the spur into his hard-driven mount, and forced his way into the city, through the mob. "Cæsar advancing on Rome!" The Jewish pedlers took up the tale, and carried it to the remotest tenement houses of Janiculum. The lazy street-idlers shouted it shrilly. Læca, catching sight of Lucius Ahenobarbus, just back from Baiæ, and a little knot

of kindred spirits about him, was in an instant pouring it all
in their ears. The news spread, flew, grew. The bankers on
the Via Sacra closed their credit books, raised their shutters,
and sent trusted clerks off to suburban villas, with due orders
how to bury and hide weighty money-bags. The news came
to that very noble lady Claudia, sister-in-law of the consul,
just at the moment when she was discussing the latest style
of hairdressing with the most excellent Herennia; and the
cheeks of those patrician ladies grew pale, and they forgot
whether or not it was proper to wear ivory pins or a jewel-set
head-band, at the dinner-party of Lucius Piso that evening.
The news came to Lentulus Crus while he was wrangling with
Domitius as to who should be Cæsar's successor as Pontifex
Maximus — and those distinguished statesmen found other
things to think of.

The news flew and grew. The noble senators overheard
their slaves whispering, — how it was rumoured on the street
or in the Forum that Cæsar was in full advance on the city,
that his cavalry were close to the gates. Cæsar at the gates!
Why had they not remembered how rapidly he could advance? Why had they trusted the assurance of the traitor
Labienus that the legions would desert their Imperator? Resist? By what means? The walls were walls only in name;
the city had long outgrown them, spreading through a thousand breaches. There was not a trained soldier this side of
Capua, whither Pompeius had departed only the day before to
take command of the Apulian legions. Cæsar was coming!
Cæsar — whose tribunes the oligarchs had chased from the
Senate! Cæsar — whom they had proclaimed a rebel and public enemy! He was coming like a second Marius, who thirty-
eight years before had swept down on Rome, and taken a
terrible vengeance on enemies less bitter to him than they to

the great Julian. "*Moriendum est*,"[1] had been the only reply to every plea for mercy. And would Cæsar now be more lenient to those who had aimed to blast his honour and shed his blood?

Evening drew on, but the calamity was only delayed. There was not a soldier to confront the invader. Few men that night could sleep. Rich and poor alike, all trembled. To their imaginations their foe was an ogre, implacable, unsparing. "Remember how it was in Sulla's day," croaked Læca to Ahenobarbus. "Remember how he proscribed forty senators and sixteen hundred equites with one stroke. A fine example for Cæsar! And Drusus, who is with the rebels, is little likely to say a good word in your behalf, eh?"

"The gods blast your tongue!" cried the young man, wringing his hands in terror; for that Drusus would ruin him, if he gained the chance, Lucius had not the least doubt in the world.

So passed the night, in fear and panic. When morning came everything save flight seemed suicide. There was a great government treasure in the Temple of Saturn. The Senate had voted that the money be delivered to Pompeius. But the consuls were too demoralized to take away a denarius. They left the great hoard under mere lock and key — a present to their bitterest enemy. Then began the great exodus. Hardly a man had done more than gather a few valuables together: property, children, wives — all these were left to the avenger. Down the Via Appia, toward Campania, where was their only safety, poured the panic-stricken company. Every carriage, every horse, was in service. The hard-driven chariots of the consuls were the tokens merely of the swiftest flight. Lentulus Crus fled; Caius Mar

[1] He has got to die.

cellus, his colleague, was close behind; Domitius fled, with
his sons; Cato fled, ironically exclaiming that they would
have to leave everything to Pompeius now, "for those who
can raise up great evils can best allay them." Favonius fled,
whose first words, when he met the Magnus, were to command
him to "stamp on the ground for the legions so sorely needed."
Piso, Scipio, and many another fled—their guilty hearts adding
wings to their goings. Cicero fled — gazing in cynical disgust
at the panic and incompetence, yet with a sword of Damocles,
as he believed, hanging over his head also. "I fear that
Cæsar will be a very Phalaris, and that we may expect the
very worst," he wrote to his intimate friend Atticus, who,
safe from harm and turmoil, was dwelling under the calm
Athenian sky. A great fraction of the Senate departed; only
those stayed who felt that their loyalty to the advancing
Imperator was beyond dispute, or who deemed themselves too
insignificant to fall beneath his displeasure. In the hour of
crisis the old ties of religion and superstition reasserted themselves. Senators and magistrates, who had deemed it a polite
avocation to mock at the gods and deny the existence of any
absolute ethical standards, now, before they climbed into
their carriages for flight, went, with due ritual, into the
temples of the gods of their fathers, and swore hecatombs of
milk-white Umbrian steers to Capitoline Jove, if the awful
deity would restore them to the native land they then were
quitting. And as they went down from the temples and
hastened toward the gates, friends and clients who could not
join their flight crowded after them, sighing, lamenting, and
moaning. Out over the Campagna they streamed, this company of senators, prætors, consuls — men who had voted thrones
to kings, and decreed the deposition of monarchs; whose
personal wealth was princely, whose lineage the noblest in the

world, whose ancestors had beaten down Etruscan, Gaul, Samnite, and Carthaginian, that their posterity might enjoy the glory of unequalled empire. And these descendants fled, fled not before any foe, but before their own guilty consciences; abandoning the city of their fathers when not a sword had flashed against her gates! The war had been of their making; to send Cæsar into outlawry the aristocracy had laboured ten long years. And now the noble lords were exiles, wanderers among the nations. To Capua they went, to find small comfort there, and thence to join Pompeius in further flight beyond the seas to Greece. But we anticipate. Enough that neither Lentulus Crus, nor Domitius, nor Cato, nor the great Magnus himself, ever saw Rome again.

II

Agias stood in a shop by the Sacred Way watching the stream of fugitives pouring down toward the Porta Capena. At his side was a person whom a glance proclaimed to be a fellow-Greek. The stranger was perhaps fifty, his frame presented a faultless picture of symmetry and manly vigour, great of stature, the limbs large but not ungainly. His features were regular, but possessed just enough prominence to make them free from the least tinge of weakness. The Greek's long, thick, dark but grey-streaked beard streamed down upon his breast; his hair, of similar hue, was long, and tossed back over his shoulders in loose curls. His dress was rich, yet rude, his chiton and cloak short, but of choice Milesian wool and dyed scarlet and purple; around his neck dangled a very heavy gold chain set with conspicuously blazing jewels. The ankles, however, were bare, and the sandals of the slightest and meanest description. The stranger must once have been of a light, not to say fair, complexion; but cheeks, throat, arms, and feet were all deeply bronzed, evidently by prolonged exposure to wind and weather. Agias and his companion watched the throng of panic-struck exiles. The younger Greek was pointing out, with the complacency of familiar knowledge, the names and dignities of the illustrious fugitives.

"Yonder goes Cato," he was saying; "mark his bitter scowl! There goes Marcus Marcellus, the consular. There drives the chariot of Lucius Domitius, Cæsar's great enemy." And Agias stopped, for his friend had seized his arm with a sudden grasp, crushing as iron. "Why, by all the gods, Demetrius, why are you staring at him that way?"

"By Zeus!" muttered the other, "if I had only my sword! It would be easy to stab him, and then escape in this crowd!"

"Stab him!" cried Agias. "Demetrius, good cousin, control yourself. You are not on the deck of your trireme, with all your men about you. Why should you be thus sanguinary, when you see Lucius Domitius? Why hate him more than any other Roman?"

The consular, unaware of the threat against him, but with a compelling fear of Cæsar's Gallic cavalry lending strength to the arm with which he plied the whip — for the law against driving inside the city no man respected that day — whirled out of sight.

Demetrius still strained at his cousin's arm.

"Listen, Agias," he said, still hoarsely. "Only yesterday I ran upon you by chance in the crowd. We have many things to tell one another, chiefly I to tell you. Why do I hate Lucius Domitius? Why should you hate him? Who made you a slave and me an outlaw? Your father died bankrupt; you know it was said that Philias, his partner, ruined him. That was truth, but not the whole truth. Philias was under deep obligations to a certain Roman then in the East, who knew of several crimes Philias *had* committed, crimes that would bring him to the cross if discovered. Do you understand?"

"Hardly," said Agias, still bewildered. "I was very young then."

"I will go on. It was shortly before Pompeius returned to Rome from the East. Your father had charge of the banking firm in Alexandria, Philias of the branch at Antioch. I was a clerk in the Antioch banking-house. I knew that Philias was misusing his partner's name and credit. The Roman whom I have mentioned knew it too, and had a supple Greek confidant who shared his spoils and gave the touches to his schemes. He had good cause to know: he was levying blackmail on Philias. At last a crisis came; the defalcation could be concealed no longer. Philias was duly punished; he was less guilty than he seemed. But the Roman — who had forced from him the money — he was high on the staff of the proconsul — let his confederate and tool suffer for his own fault. He kept his peace. I would not have kept mine; I would not have let the real ruiner of my uncle escape. But the Roman had me seized, with the aid of his Greek ally; he charged me with treasonable correspondence with the Parthians. He, through his influence with the proconsul, had me bound to the oar as a galley slave for life. I would have been executed but for another Roman, of the governor's suite, who was my friend. He pleaded for my life; he believed me innocent. He saved my life — on what terms! But that is not all he did. He bribed my guards; I escaped and turned outlaw. I joined the last remnants of the Cilician pirates, the few free mariners who have survived Pompeius's raid. And here I am in Rome with one of my ships, disguised as a trader, riding at the river wharf."

"And the name of the Roman who ruined you and my father?" said Agias.

"Was Lucius Domitius. The friend who saved me was Sextus Drusus, son of Marcus Drusus, the reformer. And if I do not recompense them both as they deserve, I am not Demetrius the pirate, captain of seven ships!"

"You will never recompense Sextus Drusus," remarked Agias, quietly. "He has been dead, slain in Gaul, these five years."

"Such is the will of the gods," said Demetrius, looking down.

"But he has left a son."

"Ah! What sort of a man?"

"The noblest of all noble Romans. He is the Quintus Drusus who saved my life, as last night I told you."

"Mithras be praised! The name is so common among these Latins that I did not imagine any connection when you mentioned it. What can I do to serve him?"

"Immediately, nothing. He is with Cæsar, and, as you see, the enemies of the Imperator are not likely, at present, to work his friends much mischief. Yet it is singular that his chief enemy and yours are so near akin. Lucius Ahenobarbus, son of Domitius, is thirsting for Drusus's blood."

"If I had my sword!" muttered Demetrius, clapping his hand to his thigh. "It is not too late to run after the fugitives!"

"Come, come," remonstrated Agias, feeling that his newly found cousin was indeed a fearful and wonderful man after twelve years of lawless and godless freebooter's life. "At my lodgings we will talk it all over; and there will be time enough to scheme the undoing of Domitius and all his family."

And with these words he led the sanguinary sea-king away.

* * * * * * * * * *

Agias indeed found in Demetrius a perfect mine of bloody romance and adventure. It had been the banking clerk's misfortune, not his fault, that every man's hand had been against him and his against every man. Demetrius had been declared an outlaw to Roman authority; and Roman authority at that time stretched over very nearly every quarter of the civilized world. Demetrius had been to India, to intercept the Red Sea traders. He had been beyond the Pillars of Hercules and set foot on those then half-mythical islands of the Canaries. He had plundered a hundred merchantmen; he had fought a score of Roman government galleys; he had been principal or accessory to the taking of ten thousand lives. All this had been forced upon him, because there was no tolerable spot on the planet where he might settle down and be free from the grasp of punishment for a crime he had never committed.

Demetrius had boldly come up to Rome on a light undecked yacht.[1] The harbor masters had been given to understand that the captain of the craft was an Asiatic princeling, who was visiting the capital of the world out of a quite legitimate curiosity. If they had had any doubts, they accepted extremely large fees and said nothing. The real object of the venture was to dispose of a large collection of rare gems and other valuables that Demetrius had collected in the course of his wanderings. Despite the perturbed state of the city, the worthy pirate had had little difficulty in arranging with certain wealthy jewellers, who asked no questions, when they bought, at a very large discount, bargains of a most satisfactory character. And so it came to pass, by the merest luck, that the two cousins were thrown together in a crowd, and partly

[1] A *celox* of one bank of oars, a small ship much used by the pirates.

Agias, through his dim childish recollections of his unfortunate relative, and partly Demetrius, through memories of his uncle's boy and the close resemblance of the lad to his father, had been prompted first to conversation, then to mutual inquiries, then to recognition.

Demetrius had no intention of leaving Rome for a few days. Under existing circumstances the chances of his arrest were not worth considering. His cousin was eager to show him all the sights; and the freebooter was glad of a little relaxation from his roving life, glad to forget for an instant that his country was his squadron, his rights at law were his cutlass. Moreover, he had taken a vast liking to Agias; deeply dipped in blood himself, he dared not desire his cousin to join him in his career of violence — yet he could not part with the bright, genial lad so hastily. Agias needed no entreaties, therefore, to induce his cousin to enjoy his hospitality.

III

Fabia the Vestal was in direful perplexity. Her heart had gone with Drusus in his flight to Ravenna; she had wished herself beside him, to be a man, able to fight a man's battles and win a man's glory. For the first time in her life the quiet routine of the Temple service brought her no contentment; for the first time she felt herself bound to a career that could not satisfy. She was restless and moody. The younger Vestals, whose attendance on the sacred fire and care of the Temple she oversaw, wondered at her exacting petulance. Little Livia brought her aunt to her senses, by asking why she, Fabia, did not love her any more. The lady summoned all her strength of character, and resumed her outward placidity. She knew that Drusus was safe with Cæsar, and exposed only to the ordinary chances of war. She became more at ease as each successive messenger came into the city, bearing the tidings of the Gallic proconsul's advance. Too innocent herself of the political turmoils of the day to decide upon the merits of the parties, her hopes and wishes had gone with those of her nephew; so pure and unquestioning was her belief that he would espouse only the right. And when the great panic came; when trembling consulars and pallid magistrates rushed to the Temple of Vesta to proffer their last hurried vows, before speeding away to Capua, their refuge; Fabia stood all day beside the altar, stately, gracious, yet awe-inspiring, the fitting personification of the benignant Hearth Goddess, who was above the petty passions of mortals and granted to each an impartial favour.

Yet Fabia was sorely distressed, and that too on the very day of the great exodus of the Senate. She had heard for some time past rumours of the depredations of a certain band of robbers upon the Sabine and Æquian country. It was said that a gang of bandits, headed by a gigantic Gaul, had plundered some farms near Carsioli and infested the mountain regions round about. Fabia had connected this gang and its chieftain with Dumnorix and the remnant of his gladiators, who escaped after their disastrous affray at Præneste. As for Publius Gabinius, who had on one occasion given her such distress, nothing had been heard or seen of him since the Præneste affair. It was generally believed, however, that he was still with Dumnorix. And a few days before the panic in the city, Fabia had received a letter. A strange slave had left it at the Atrium Vestæ, and had gone away without explanations. It ran thus:—

"To the very noble Vestal, the Lady Fabia, greeting:—

Though I am now so unfortunate as to be barred from the doors of all law-abiding men, do not imagine this will forever continue. In the confusion and readjustments of war, and the calamities of many, the affairs of some, one time enemies of Fortune, come to a happy issue. Do not say that Mars may not lead Amor and Hymen in his train. All things come to them who wait. I wait. Remember the life you spend in the Temple is no longer obligatory. Be no cage bird who will not fly out into the sunlight when the door is opened freely. Be surprised and angry at nothing. *Vale.*"

There was no date, no signature. The hand was distorted, evidently for disguise. Fabia was in a dilemma. She did not need to be told that in all probability — though she had no proof — the writer was Gabinius. She was extremely reluctant to tell any one of her escape from his clutches in the villa by the Appian Way. However, some confidant seemed necessary. She knew that Fonteia, the senior Vestal, the Maxima, would never treat her other than as a sister, and to her she read the letter and imparted her story and fears. Fonteia did not regard the matter in a very serious light. She was herself an old woman, grown grey in the service of Vesta. She said that Fabia had been most fortunate to remain in the Temple service so long as she had and not be harassed by more than one impious and overbold suitor. The only thing to do was to be careful and avoid anything that would give false appearances. As for Fabia's fears that Gabinius would attempt to carry her away perforce, as he had perhaps treated earlier sweethearts, Fonteia scoffed at the suggestion. The Atrium Vestæ was in the heart of the city; there was a constant patrol on duty. For a man to enter the building at night meant the death penalty. Whosoever did violence to a Vestal fell under a religious curse; he was a *homo sacer*, a " sacred man," a victim devoted to the gods, whom it was a pious deed to slay. And thus comforted, with the assurance that the whole power of the Republic would rise for her personal defence, Fabia was fain to put the disquieting letter from her heart.

Then followed the night of panic, and the succeeding day. There were no longer any magistrates in Rome. The great palaces of the patricians stood deserted, exposed to the unfaithful guardianship of freedmen and slaves. The bankers' booths were closed, the shops did not raise their shutters. On the streets swarmed the irresponsible and the vicious. Men of property who had not fled barred their doors and stood guard with their servants to beat back would-be plunderers. There were no watchmen at the gates, no courts sitting in the basilicas. After the great flight of the early morning, Rome was a city without warders, police, or government.

Fabia did not realize this fact until late in the afternoon, when she started forth, on foot and unattended, to visit a friend on the Cælian. The half-deserted streets and barricaded houses filled her with uneasy tremors. The low, brutish creatures that she met gave her little heed; but the sight of them, alone and not offset by any more respectable fellow-strollers, made her turn back to the Atrium Vestæ. As she hastened on her way homeward an uneasy sensation haunted her that she was being followed. She halted, faced about. The street was narrow, the light was beginning to fade. The figure of a man was vanishing in the booth of some bold vintner, who had ventured to risk plunder for the sake of sales. She proceeded. A moment later a half glance over the shoulder and a straining of the eyes told her that the stranger was continuing his pursuit. He kept very close to the side of the buildings. His face and form were quite lost in shadow. Fabia quickened her pace; the stranger increased his also, yet made no effort to cut down the distance between them. The Vestal began to feel the blood mantling to her cheeks and leaving them again.

She was so near to the Forum and the Atrium Vestæ now that she could not be overtaken. But why did the stranger follow?

There was a gap in the houses ahead. Through a narrow alley the dying light was streaming. Fabia passed it, timed herself, glanced back. For an instant, and only an instant (for the stranger walked rapidly), the light glared full upon his face. But Fabia needed to see no more. It was the face of Publius Gabinius. By a mighty effort she prevented herself from breaking into a run. She passed into the doorway of the Atrium Vestæ, and sank upon a divan, shivering with fright. Recollecting herself, she went to Fonteia and told her the discovery. The Maxima, however, by that singular fatuity which sometimes takes possession of the wisest of people, — especially when the possible danger is one which never in all their long experience has come to a head, — received her warnings with blank incredulity.

"You should not go out of the house and Temple," she said, "until there is some proper policing of the city. No doubt Gabinius has come back for the sake of riot and plunder, and having met with you by chance could not resist the temptation to try to have an interview; but you are in no possible danger here."

"But, Fonteia," urged the younger Vestal, "I know him to be a bold, desperate man, who fears not the gods, and who from the law can expect no mercy. And we in this house are but weak women folk. Our only defence is our purity and the reverence of the people. But only the evil wander the streets to-night; and our virtuous lives make us only the more attractive prey to such men as Gabinius."

"Fabia," said the other Vestal, severely, "I am older than you. I have beheld sights you have never seen. I saw the riots when Saturninus and Glaucia came to their ends; when

Marius was chased from Rome and Sulpicius put to death; when Marius returned with Cinna; and all the massacres and strife attending the taking of the city by Sulla. But never has the name of Vesta been insufficient to protect us from the violence of the basest or the most godless. Nor will it now. I will trust in the goddess, and the fear of her, which protects her maidens against all men. We will sleep to-night as usual. I will not send anywhere to have guards stationed around the house and Temple."

Fabia bowed her head. The word of the aged Maxima was law in the little community. Fabia told herself that Fonteia was right — not even Gabinius would dare to set unhallowed foot inside the Atrium Vestæ. But the vision of the coarse, sensual face of her unloved lover was ever before her. In ordinary times she would have been tempted to go to one of the consuls and demand that Fonteia be overruled; but in ordinary times there would not have been the least need of adding to the already sufficient city watch. It lacked four hours of midnight before she brought herself to take her tablets and write the following brief note: —

"Fabia the Vestal to Agias her good friend, greeting. I am in some anxiety to-night. Gabinius, Lucius Ahenobarbus's friend, is in the city. He means, I fear, to work me some mischief, though the cause whereby I have good reason to dread him is too long here to write. The Atrium Vestæ has nothing to protect it to-night — as you well may understand — from impious, violent men. Can you not guard me overnight? I do not know how. Gabinius may have all Dumnorix's band with him. But you alone are equal to an host. I trust you, as Drusus and Cornelia have trusted you. *Vale.*"

Fabia called one of the young slave-girls who waited on the Vestals. The relation between servant and mistress in the Temple company, was almost ideal in its gentle loyalty. The slaves were happy in their bondage.

"Erigone," she said, putting the tablets in the girl's hand, "I am about to ask of you a very brave thing. Do you dare to take this letter through the city?" and she told her how to find Agias's lodgings. "Come back in the morning if you dread a double journey. But do not tell Fonteia; she would be angry if she knew I sent you, though there is nothing but what is right in the letter."

"I will carry the tablets to Scythia for you, domina," replied the girl, kissing the hem of her mistress's robe. "I know all the streets. If I live, the letter shall be delivered."

"Go by the alleys," enjoined Fabia; "they are safer, for you will not be seen. Speak to no one. Let none stop you."

Erigone was gone in the night, and Fabia went to her chamber. She was reproaching herself for having sent the letter. Rome by darkness was an evil place for a young maid to traverse, and never worse than that night. Fabia repeated to herself that she had committed an act of selfish folly, possibly sacrificing an implicitly loyal servant to the mere gratification of a perfectly ungrounded panic. She was undressed by her other women, and lay down with Livia fast asleep in her arms; and she kissed the little one again and again before slumber stole over her.

IV

Demetrius had been astonishing his cousin that evening by the quantity of strong wine he could imbibe without becoming in the least tipsy. Agias marvelled at the worthy pirate's capacity and hardness of head, and, fortunately for his own wits, did not attempt to emulate the other's potations. Consequently, as the evening advanced, Demetrius simply became more and more good-natured and talkative, and Agias more entranced with his cousin's narration of the Indian voyage.

The younger Greek was about to order his yawning servants to fill up another *krater*,[1] when the conversation and drinking were interrupted by the arrival of Erigone. She, poor girl, had set out bravely enough; but once outside of the Atrium Vestæ every shadow had been a refuge of cutthroats, every noise the oncoming of goblins. Fortunately for her, she did not know the contents of the tablets she carried pressed to her breast, or she would have been all the more timorous. Once a few half-sober topers screamed ribald words after her, as she stole past a low tavern. She had lost her way, in the darkness and fright, among the alleys; she had dodged into a doorway more than once to hide from approaching night rovers. But at last she had reached her destination, and, pale and weary, placed the letter in Agias's hands. The young Greek read and grew grave. Even better than Fabia he understood how reckless a profligate Publius Gabinius might be, and how opportune was the night for carrying out any deed of darkness.

"Brave girl!" he said, commending Erigone for persevering on her errand. "But how long ago did you leave your mistress?"

"It was the second hour of the night[2] when I started," she replied.

Agias glanced at the water-clock.

"By Zeus!" he cried, "it is now the fourth hour! You

[1] Wine-mixing bowl.

[2] The Romans divided the night into 12 hours (from sunrise to sunset); thus the length of the hour varied with the seasons: but at the time here mentioned the "second hour" was about 8 P.M. The water-clocks could show only regular, not solar, time.

have been two hours on the way! Immortal gods! What's to be done? Look here, Demetrius!"

And he thrust the letter before his cousin, and explained its meaning as rapidly as he could.

Demetrius puffed hard through his nostrils.

"*Mū! mū!* This is bad business. If there were time I could have twenty as stout men as ever swung sword up from the yacht and on guard to die for any relative or friend of Sextus Drusus. But there's not a moment to lose. Have you any arms?"

Agias dragged two short swords out of a chest. Demetrius was already throwing on his cloak.

"Those are poor, light weapons," commented the pirate. "I want my heavy cutlass. But take what the gods send;" and he girded one about him. "At least, they will cut a throat. Do you know how to wield them?"

"After a fashion," replied Agias, modestly, making haste to clasp his pænula.

Leaving Erigone to be cared for by the slaves and sent home the next morning, the two Greeks hastened from the house. Agias could hardly keep pace with his cousin's tremendous stride. Demetrius was like a war-horse, which snuffs the battle from afar and tugs at the rein to join in the fray. They plunged through the dark streets. Once a man sprang out from a doorway before them with a cudgel. He may have been a footpad; but Demetrius, without pausing in his haste, smote the fellow between the eyes with a terrible fist, and the wretched creature dropped without a groan. Demetrius seemed guided to the Forum and Via Sacra as if by an inborn instinct. Agias almost ran at his heels.

"How many may this Dumnorix have with him?" shouted the pirate over his shoulder.

"Perhaps ten, perhaps twenty!" gasped Agias.

"A very pretty number! Some little credit to throttle them," was his answer; and Demetrius plunged on.

The night was cloudy, there was no moonlight. The cold chill wind swept down the Tiber valley, and howled mournfully among the tall, silent basilicas and temples of the Forum. The feet of the two Greeks echoed and reëchoed as they crossed the pavement of the enclosure. None addressed them, none met them. It was as if they walked in a city of the dead. In the darkness, like weird phantoms, rose the tall columns and pediments of the deserted buildings. From nowhere twinkled the ray of lamp. Dim against the sky-line the outlines of the Capitoline and its shrines were now and then visible, when the night seemed for an instant to grow less dark.

They were close to the Atrium Vestæ. All was quiet. No light within, no sound but that of the wind and their own breathing without.

"We are not too late," whispered Agias.

The two groped their way in among the pillars of the portico of the *Regia*,[1] and crouched down under cover of the masonry, half sheltered from the chilly blasts. They could from their post command a tolerably good view of one side of the Atrium Vestæ. Still the darkness was very great, and they dared not divide their force by one of them standing watch on the other side. The moments passed. It was extremely cold. Agias shivered and wound himself in his mantle. The wine was making him drowsy, and he felt himself sinking into semiconsciousness, when a touch on his arm aroused him.

"*St!*" whispered Demetrius. "I saw a light moving."

Agias stared into the darkness.

"There," continued the pirate, "see, it is a lantern carefully

[1] The official residence of the Pontifex Maximus.

covered! Only a little glint on the ground now and then. Some one is creeping along the wall to enter the house of the vestals!"

"I see nothing," confessed Agias, rubbing his eyes.

"You are no sailor; look harder. I can count four men in the gloom. They are stealing up to the gate of the building. Is your sword ready? Now—"

But at this instant Demetrius was cut short by a scream— a scream of mortal terror—from within the Atrium Vestæ. There were shouts, howls, commands, moans, entreaties, shrieks. Light after light blazed up in the building; women rushed panic-struck to the doorway to burst forth into the night; and at the open portal Agias saw a gigantic figure with upraised long sword, a Titan, malevolent, destroying, terrible,—at the sight whereof the women shrank back, screaming yet the more.

"Dumnorix!" shouted Agias; but before he spoke Demetrius had leaped forward.

Right past the sword-wielding monster sprang the pirate, and Agias, all reckless, was at his heels. The twain were in the atrium of the house. A torch was spluttering and blazing on the pavement, shedding all around a bright, flickering, red glare. Young Vestals and maid-servants were cowering on their knees, or prone on cushions, writhing and screaming with fear unspeakable. A swart Spanish brigand, with his sabre gripped in his teeth, was tearing a gold-thread and silk covering from a pillow; a second plunderer was wrenching from its chain a silver lamp. Demetrius rushed past these also, before any could inquire whether he was not a comrade in infamy. But there were other shouts from the peristylium, other cries and moanings. As the pirate sprang to the head of the passage leading to the inner house, a swarm of desperadoes poured through it, Gauls, Germans, Africans, **Italian** renegadoes, — perhaps ten in all, — and in their midst — **half** borne, half dragged — something white!

"*Io triumphe!*" called a voice from the throng, "my bird will leave her cage!"

"The lady! Gabinius!" cried Agias, and, without waiting for his cousin, the young Greek flung himself forward. One stroke of his short sword sent a leering negro prone upon the pavement; one snatch of his hand seized the white mantle, and held it — held it though half a dozen blades were flashing in his face in an eye's twinkling. But the prowess of twenty men was in the arm of Demetrius; his sword was at once attacker and shield; with a single sweeping blow he smote down the guard and cleft the skull of a towering Teuton; with a lightning dart he caught up the ponderous long sword of the falling brigand, passed his own shorter weapon to his left hand, and so fought, — doubly armed, — parrying with his left and striking with his right. And how he struck! The whole agile, supple nature of the Greek entered into every fence. He struck and foiled with his entire body. Now a bound to one side; now a dart at an opponent's head; fighting with feet, head, frame, and not with hands only. And Agias — he fought too, and knew not how he fought! When a blow was aimed at him, Demetrius always parried it before he could raise his sword; if he struck, Demetrius had felled the man first; but he never let go of the white dress, nor quitted the side of the lady. And presently, he did not know after how long — for hours make minutes, and minutes hours, in such a mêlée — there was a moment's silence, and he saw Publius Gabinius sinking down upon the pavement, the blood streaming over his cloak; and the brigands, such as were left of them, scurrying out of the atrium cowed and panic-struck at the fall of their leader. Then, as he threw his arms about Fabia, and tried to raise her to her feet, he saw the giant Dumnorix, with his flail-like sword, rushing back to the rescue.

Four brigands lay dead in the atrium and none of the others dared look the redoubtable Greek swordsman in the eyes; but Dumnorix came on — the incarnation of brute fury. Then again Demetrius fought, — fought as the angler fights the fish that he doubts not to land, yet only after due play; and the Gaul, like some awkward Polyphemus, rushed upon him, flinging at him barbarous curses in his own tongue, and snorting and raging like a bull. Thrice the Greek sprang back before the monster; thrice the giant swung his mighty sword to cleave his foeman down, and cut the empty air; but at the fourth onset the Hellene smote the ex-lanista once across the neck, and the great eyes rolled, and the panting stopped, and the mighty Gaul lay silent in a spreading pool of blood.

Already there were shouts and cries in the Forum. Torches were dancing hither and thither. The slave-maids of the Vestals ran down the Via Sacra shrieking and calling for aid. Out from the dark tenements rushed the people. The thieves ran from their lairs; the late drinkers sprang from their wine. And when the wretched remnants of Dumnorix's band of ex-gladiators and brigands strove to flee from the holy house they had polluted, a hundred hands were put forth against each one, and they were torn to pieces by the frenzied mob. Into the Atrium Vestæ swarmed the people, howling, shouting, praising the goddess, fighting one another — every man imagining his neighbour a cutthroat and abductor.

Agias stood bearing up Fabia in his arms; she was pale as the driven snow. Her lips moved, but no sound passed from them. Fonteia, the old Maxima, with her white hair tumbling over her shoulders, was still huddled in one corner, groaning and moaning in a paroxysm of unreasoning terror, without dignity or self-control. A frightened maid had touched the torch to the tall candelabra, and the room blazed with a score of lights; while in at the doorway pressed the multitude — the mob of low tapsters, brutal butchers, coarse pedlers, and drunkards just staggering from their cups. The scene was one of pandemonium. Dumnorix lay prone on a costly rug, whose graceful patterns were being dyed to a hideous crimson; over one divan lay a brigand — struggling in the last agony of a mortal wound. Three comrades lay stretched stiff and motionless on the floor. Gory swords and daggers were strewn all over the atrium; the presses of costly wood had been torn open, their contents scattered across the room. There was blood on the frescoes, blood on the marble feet of the magnificent Diomedes, which stood rigid in cold majesty on its pedestal, dominating the wreck below.

Agias with Fabia stood at the end of the atrium near the exit to the peristylium. Demetrius, seemingly hardly breathed by his exertions, leaned on his captured long sword at his cousin's side. The multitude, for an instant, as they saw the ruin and slaughter, drew back with a hush. Men turned away their faces as from a sight of evil omen. Who were they to set foot in the mansion of the servants of the awful Vesta? But others from behind, who saw and heard nothing, pressed their fellows forward. The mob swept on. As with one consent all eyes were riveted on Fabia. What had happened? Who was guilty? Why had these men of violence done this wrong to the home of the hearth goddess? And then out of a farther corner, while yet the people hesitated from reverence, staggered a figure, its face streaming with blood, its hands pressing its side.

"*Quirites*," cried a voice, the voice of one speaking with but one remaining breath, "ye have rewarded me as the law demands; see that *she*," and a bloody forefinger pointed at Fabia, "who led me to this deed, is not unpunished. *She* is the more guilty!"

And with a groan the figure fell like a statue of wood to the pavement; fell heavily, and lay stirring not, neither giving any sound. In his last moment Publius Gabinius had sought a terrible revenge.

And then madness seized on the people.

"She is his sweetheart! She is his paramour!" cried a score of filthy voices. "She has brought down this insult to the goddess! There is no pontifex here to try her! Tear her in pieces! Strike! Slay!"

But Demetrius had turned to his cousin.

"Agias," he said, making himself heard despite the clamour, "do you believe the charge of that man?"

"No villain ever would avenge himself more basely."

"Then at all costs we must save the lady."

It was time. A fat butcher, flourishing a heavy cleaver, had leaped forward; Fabia saw him with glassy, frightened eyes, but neither shrieked nor drew back. But Demetrius smote the man with his long sword through the body, and the brute dropped the cleaver as he fell.

"Now," and Demetrius seized the Vestal around the waist, as lightly as a girl would raise a kitten, and flung her across his shoulders. One stride and he was in the passage leading to the peristylium; and before the mob could follow Agias had dashed the door in their faces, and shot the bolt.

"It will hold them back a moment," muttered Demetrius, "but we must hasten."

They ran across the peristylium, the pirate chief with his

burden no less swift than Agias. The door to the rear street was flung open, and they were out in a narrow alleyway. Just as they did so, a howl of many voices proclaimed that the peristylium door had yielded.

"Guide me by the straightest way," commanded the sea rover.

"Where?" was Agias's question.

"To the wharves. The yacht is the only safe place for the lady. There I will teach her how I can honour a friend of Sextus Drusus."

Agias felt that it was no time for expostulation. A Vestal Virgin take refuge on a pirate ship! But it was a matter of life and death now, and there was no time for forming another plan. Once let the mob overtake them, and the lives of all three were not worth a sesterce. Agias found it necessary to keep himself collected while he ran, or he would lose the way in the maze of streets. The yacht was moored far below the Pons Sublicius, and the whole way was full of peril. It was no use to turn off into alleys and by-paths; to do so at night meant to be involved in a labyrinth as deadly for them as that of the Cretan Minos. The mob was on their heels, howling, raging. The people were beginning to wake in their houses along the streets. Men bawled "Stop thief!" from the windows, imagining there had been a robbery. Once two or three figures actually swung out into the way before them, but at a stray glint of lantern light falling on Demetrius's naked long sword, they vanished in the gloom. But still the mob pressed on, ever gaining accessions, ever howling the more fiercely. Agias realized that the weight of his burden was beginning to tell on even the iron frame of his cousin. The pursuers and pursued were drawing closer together. The mob was ever reënforced by relays; the handicap on Demetrius was too

great. They had passed down the Vicus Tuscus, flown past the dark shadow of the lower end of the Circus Maximus. At the Porta Trigemina the unguarded portal had stood open; there was none to stop them. They passed by the Pons Sublicius, and skirted the Aventine. Stones and billets of wood began to whistle past their ears, — the missiles of the on-rushing multitude. At last the wharves! Out in the darkness stood the huge bulk of a Spanish lumberman; but there was no refuge there. The grain wharves and the oil wharves were passed; the sniff of the mackerel fisher, the faint odour from the great Alexandrian merchantman loaded with the spices of India, were come and gone. A stone struck Agias in the shoulder, he felt numb in one arm, to drag his feet was a burden; the flight with the Cæsarians to the Janiculum had not been like to this, — death at the naked sword had been at least in store then, and now to be plucked in pieces by a mob! Another stone brushed forward his hair and dashed, not against Demetrius ahead, but against his burden. There was — Agias could hear — a low moan; but at the same instant the fleeing pirate uttered a whistle so loud, so piercing, that the foremost pursuers came to a momentary stand, in half-defined fright. In an instant there came an answering whistle from the wharf just ahead. In a twinkling half a dozen torches had flashed out all over a small vessel, now barely visible in the night, at one of the mooring rings. There was a strange jargon of voices calling in some Oriental tongue; and Demetrius, as he ran, answered them in a like language. Then over Agias's head and into the thick press of the mob behind, something — arrows no doubt — flew whistling; and there were groans and cries of pain. And Agias found uncouth, bearded men helping or rather casting him over the side of the vessel. The yacht was alive with men: some were bounding ashore to loose the hawsers, others were lifting ponderous oars, still more were shooting fast and cruelly in the direction of the mob, while its luckless leaders struggled to turn in flight, and the multitude behind, ignorant of the slaughter, was forcing them on to death. Above the clamour, the howls of the mob, the shouts of the sailors, the grating of oars, and the creaking of cables, rang the voice of Demetrius; and at his word a dozen ready hands put each command into action. The narrow, easy-moving yacht caught the current; a long tier of white oars glinted in the torchlight, smote the water, and the yacht bounded away, while a parting flight of arrows left misery and death upon the quay.

Agias, sorely bewildered, clambered on to the little poop. His cousin stood grasping one of the steering paddles; the ruddy lantern light gleamed on the pirate's frame and face, and made him the perfect personification of a sea-king; he was some grandly stern Poseidon, the "Storm-gatherer" and the "Earth-shaker." When he spoke to Agias, it was in the tone of a despot to a subject.

"The lady is below. Go to her. You are to care for her until I rejoin my fleet. Tell her my sister shall not be more honoured than she, nor otherwise treated. When I am aboard my flag-ship, she shall have proper maids and attendance. Go!"

Agias obeyed, saying nothing. He found Fabia lying on a rude pallet, with a small bale of purple silk thrust under her head for a pillow. She stared at him with wild, frightened eyes, then round the little cabin, which, while bereft of all but the most necessary comforts, was decorated with bejeweled armour, golden lamps, costly Indian tapestries and ivory — the trophies of half a score of voyages.

"Agias," she faintly whispered, "tell me what has happened since I awoke from my sleep and found Gabinius's ruffians about me. By whatsoever god you reverence most, speak truly!"

Agias fell on his knees, kissed the hem of her robe, kissed her hands. Then he told her all, — as well as his own sorely confused wits would admit. Fabia heard him through to the end, then laid her face between her hands.

"Would that — would that they had murdered me as they wished! It would be all over now," she agonized. "I have no wish again to see the light. Whether they believe me innocent or guilty of the charge is little; I can never be happy again."

"And why not, dear lady?" cried Agias.

"Don't ask me! I do not know. I do not know anything! Leave me! It is not fit that you should see me crying like a child. Leave me! Leave me!"

And thus conjured, Agias went up to the poop once more.

The yacht was flying down the current under her powerful oarage. Demetrius was still standing with his hands fixed on the steering paddle; his gaze was drifting along in the plashing water. The shadowy outlines of the great city had vanished; the yacht was well on her way down the river to Ostia. Save for the need to avoid a belated merchantman anchored in midstream for the night, there was little requiring the master's skill. Agias told his cousin how Fabia had sent him away.

"*A!* Poor lady!" replied the pirate, "perhaps she was the Vestal I saw a few days since, and envied her, to see the consuls' lictors lowering their rods to her, and all the people making way before her; she, protected by the whole might of this terrible Roman people, and honoured by them all; and I, a poor outlaw, massing gold whereof I have no need, slaying men when I would be their friend, with only an open sea and a few planks for native land. And now, see how the Fates

bring her down so low, that at my hands she receives nospi-
tality, nay, life!"

"You did not seem so very loath to shed blood to-night,"
commented Agias, dryly.

"No, by Zeus!" was his frank answer. "It is easy to send
men over the Styx after having been Charon's substitute for so
many years. But the trade was not pleasant to learn, and,
bless the gods, you may not have to be apprenticed to it."

"Then you will not take me with you in your rover's life?"
asked Agias, half-disappointedly.

"Apollo forbid! I will take you and the lady to some place
where she can be safe until she may return vindicated, and
where you can earn an honest livelihood, marry a wife of
station, in accordance with the means which I shall give you,
dwell peaceably, and be happy."

"But I cannot accept your present," protested the younger
Greek.

"*Phui!* What use have I of money? To paraphrase
Æschylus: 'For more of money than I would is mine.' I
can't eat it, or beat swords out of gold, or repair my ships
therewith."

"Then why amass it at all?"

"Why drink when you know it is better to keep sober? I
can no more stop plundering than a toper leave a wine-jar.
Besides, perhaps some day I may see a road to amnesty open,
— and, then, what will not money do for a man or woman?"

"Quintus Drusus, my patron, the Lady Cornelia, and the
Lady Fabia all are rich. But I would not take up their
sorrows for all their wealth."

"True," and Demetrius stared down into the inky water.
"It will not give back those who are gone forever. Achilles
could ask Hephæstus for his armour, but he could not put

breath into the body of Patroclus. *Plutus* and *Cratus*[1] are, after all, but weaklings. *A!* This is an unequal world!"

When Agias fell asleep that night, or rather that morning, on a hard seaman's pallet, two names were stirring in his heart, names inextricably connected: Cornelia, whom he had promised Quintus Drusus to save from Ahenobarbus's clutches, and Artemisia. In the morning the yacht, having run her sixteen miles to Ostia, stood out to sea, naught hindering.

*   *   *   *   *   *   *   *   *   *

It was two months later when Quintus Drusus reëntered Rome, no more a fugitive, but a trusted staff officer of the lawfully appointed dictator Julius Cæsar. He had taken part in a desperate struggle around Corfinium, where his general had cut off and captured the army with which Domitius had aimed to check his advance. Drusus had been severely wounded, and had not recovered in time to participate in the futile siege of Brundusium, when Cæsar vainly strove to prevent Pompeius's flight across the sea to Greece. Soon as he was convalescent, the young officer had hurried away to Rome; and there he was met by a story concerning his aunt, whereof no rational explanation seemed possible. And when, upon this mystery, was added a tale he received from Baiæ, he marvelled, yet dreaded, the more.

[1] Riches and strength.

CHAPTER XIX

THE HOSPITALITY OF DEMETRIUS

I

W**HILE** grave senators were contending, tribunes haranguing, imperators girding on the sword, legions marching, cohorts clashing, — while all this history was being made in the outside world, Cornelia, very desolate, very lonely, was enduring her imprisonment at Baiæ.

If she had had manacles on her wrists and fetters on her feet, she would not have been the more a prisoner. Lentulus Crus had determined, with the same grim tenacity of purpose which led him to plunge a world into war, that his niece should comply with his will and marry Lucius Ahenobarbus. He sent down to Baiæ, Phaon, — the evil-eyed freedman of Ahenobarbus, — and gave to that worthy full power to do anything he wished to break the will of his prospective patroness. Cassandra had been taken away from Cornelia — she could not learn so much as whether the woman had been scourged to death for arranging the interview with Drusus, or no. Two ill-favoured slatternly Gallic maids, the scourings of the Puteoli slave-market, had been forced upon Cornelia as her attendants — creatures who stood in abject fear of the whip of Phaon, and who obeyed his mandates to the letter. Cornelia was never out of sight of some person who she knew was devoted to Lentulus, or rather to Phaon and his patron. She received no letters save those from her mother, uncle, or Ahenobarbus; she saw no visitors; she was not allowed to go outside of the walls of the villa, nor indeed upon any of its terraces where she would be exposed to sight from without, whether by land or sea. At every step, at every motion, she was confronted with the barriers built around her, and by the consciousness that, so long as she persisted in her present attitude, her durance was likely to continue unrelaxed.

Cornelia was thirsty for the news from the world without. Her keepers were dumb to the most harmless inquiry. Her mother wrote more of the latest fashions than of the progress of events in the Senate and in the field; besides, Claudia — as Cornelia knew very well — never took her political notions from any one except her brother-in-law, and Cornelia noted her mother's rambling observations accordingly. Lentulus studiously refrained from adverting to politics in letters to his niece. Ahenobarbus wrote of wars and rumours of wars, but in a tone of such partisan venom and overreaching sarcasm touching all things Cæsarian, that Cornelia did not need her prejudices to tell her that Lucius was simply abusing her credulity.

Then at last all the letters stopped. Phaon had no explanation to give. He would not suffer his evil, smiling lips to tell the story of the flight of the oligarchs from Rome, and confess that Lentulus and Claudia were no farther off than Capua. The consul had ordered that his niece should not know of their proximity and its cause, — lest she pluck up hope, and all his coercion be wasted. So there was silence, and that was all. Even her mother did not write to her. Cornelia grew very, very lonely and desolate — more than words may tell. She had one consolation — Drusus was not dead, or she would have been informed of it! Proof that her lover was dead would have been a most delightful weapon in Lentulus's hands.

too delightful to fail to use instantly. And so Cornelia hoped on.

She tried again to build a world of fantasy, of unreal delight, around her; to close her eyes, and wander abroad with her imagination. She roamed in reverie over land and sea, from Atlantis to Serica; and dwelt in the dull country of the Hyperboreans and saw the gold-sanded plains of the Ethiops. She took her Homer and fared with Odysseus into Polyphemus's cave, and out to the land of Circe; and heard the Sirens sing, and abode on Calypso's fairy isle; and saw the maiden Nausicaä and her maids at the ball-play on the marge of the stream. But it was sorry work; for ever and again the dream-woven mist would break, and the present — stern, unchanging, joyless — she would see, and that only.

Cornelia was thrown more and more back on her books. In fact, had she been deprived of that diversion, she must have succumbed in sheer wretchedness; but Phaon, for all his crafty guile, did not realize that a roll of Æschylus did almost as much to undo his jailer's work as a traitor among his underlings.

The library was a capacious, well-lighted room, prettily frescoed, and provided with comfortably upholstered couches. In the niches were a few choice busts: a Sophocles, a Xenophon, an Ennius, and one or two others. Around the room in wooden presses were the rolled volumes on Egyptian papyrus, each labelled with author and title in bright red marked on the tablet attached to the cylinder of the roll. Here were the poets and historians of Hellas; the works of Plato, Aristotle, Callimachus, Apollonius Rhodius and the later Greek philosophers. Here, too, were books which the Greek-hating young lady loved best of all — the rough metres of Livius Andronicus and Cnæus Nævius, whose uncouth lines of the old Saturnian verse breathed of the hale, hearty, uncultured, uncorrupted life of the period of the First Punic War. Beside them were the other great Latinists: Ennius, Plautus, Terence, and furthermore, Pacuvius and Cato Major, Lucilius, the memoirs of Sulla, the orations of Antonius "the orator" and Gracchus, and the histories of Claudius Quadrigarius and Valerius Antias.

The library became virtually Cornelia's prison. She read tragedy, comedy, history, philosophy, — anything to drive from her breast her arch enemy, thought. But if, for example, she turned to Apollonius Rhodius and read —

> "Amidst them all, the son of Æson chief
> Shone forth divinely in his comeliness,
> And graces of his form. On him the maid
> Looked still askance, and gazed him o'er;"[1]

straightway she herself became Medea, Jason took on the form of Drusus, and she would read no more; "while," as the next line of the learned poet had it, "grief consumed her heart."

Only one other recreation was left her. Artemisia had not been taken away by Phaon, who decided that the girl was quite impotent to thwart his ends. Cornelia devoted much of her time to teaching the bright little Greek. The latter picked up the scraps of knowledge with a surprising readiness, and would set Cornelia a-laughing by her *naïveté*, when she soberly intermixed her speech with bits of grave poetical and philosophical lore, uttered more for sake of sound than sense.

As a matter of fact, however, Cornelia was fast approaching a point where her position would have been intolerable. She did not even have the stimulus that comes from an active aggressive persecution. Drusus was in the world of action, not forgetful of his sweetheart, yet not pent up to solitary broodings on his ill-fated passion. Cornelia was thrust back

[1] Elton, translator.

upon herself, and found herself a very discontented, wretched, love-lorn, and withal — despite her polite learning — ignorant young woman, who took pleasure neither in sunlight nor star light; who saw a mocking defiance in every dimple of the sapphire bay; who saw in each new day merely a new period for impotent discontent. Something had to determine her situation, or perhaps she would not indeed have bowed her head to her uncle's will; but she certainly would have been driven to resolutions of the most desperate nature.

Cornelia had practically lost reckoning of time and seasons. She had ceased hoping for a letter from her mother; even a taunting missive from Ahenobarbus would have been a diversion. She was so closely guarded that she found herself praying that Drusus would not try to steal a second interview, for the attempt might end in his murder. Only one stray crumb of comfort at last did she obtain, and it was Artemisia who brought it to her. The girl had been allowed by Phaon to walk outside the grounds of the villa for a little way, and her pretty face had won the good graces of one or two slave-boys in an adjoining seaside house. Artemisia came back full of news which they had imparted: the consuls had fled from Rome; Pompeius was retreating before Cæsar; the latest rumour had it that Domitius was shut up in Corfinium and likely to come off hardly.

The words were precious as rubies to Cornelia. She went all that day and the next with her head in the air. Perhaps with a lover's subtle omniscience she imagined that it was Drusus who had some part in bringing Domitius to bay. She pictured the hour when he — with a legion no doubt at his back — would come to Baiæ, not a stealthy, forbidden lover, but a conqueror, splendid in the triumph of his arms; would enter the villa with a strong hand, and lead her forth in the eyes of all the world — his wife! and then back to Praeneste, to Rome — happy as the Immortals on Olympus; and what came after, Cornelia neither thought nor cared.

On those days the sea was lovely, the sunlight fair, and all the circling sea-gulls as they hovered over the waves cried shrilly one to the other; "How good is all the world!" And then, just as Cornelia was beginning to count the hours, — to wonder whether it would be one day or ten before Drusus would be sufficiently at liberty to ride over hill and dale to Baiae, — Phaon thrust himself upon her.

"Your ladyship," was his curt statement, "will have all things prepared in readiness to take ship for Greece, to-morrow morning."

"For Greece!" was the agonized exclamation.

"Certainly; it is useless to conceal matters from your ladyship now. Caesar has swept all Italy. Corfinium may fall at any time. His excellency the consul Lentulus is now at Brundusium. He orders me to put you on board a vessel that has just finished her lading for the Piraeus."

This then was the end of all those glittering day-dreams! Caesar's victories only would transfer Cornelia to a more secure bondage. She had enough pride left not to moan aloud and plead with an animal like Phaon not to crush her utterly. In fact she was benumbed, and did not fully sense the changed situation. She went through a mechanical process of collecting her wardrobe, of putting her jewellery in cases and boxes, of laying aside for carriage a few necessaries for Artemisia. Phaon, who had expected a terrible scene when he made his announcement, observed to himself that, "The domina is more sensible than I supposed. I think her uncle will have his way now soon enough, if Master Lucius does not get his throat cut at Corfinium." And having thus concluded to himself, —

2 B

satisfactorily, if erroneously, — he, too, made arrangements for the voyage impending.

II

Cornelia's sleeping room was large and airy. It had windows overlooking the sea — windows closed by the then extravagant luxury of panes of glass. When these were swung back the full sweep of the southwest wind poured its mild freshness into the room. The apartment was decorated and furnished with every taste and luxury. In one corner was the occupant's couch, — the frame inlaid with ivory and tortoise-shell, the mattress soft with the very choicest feathers of white German geese. Heaped on the cushion were gorgeous coverlets, of purple wool or even silk, and embroidered with elaborate figures, or covered with rare feather tapestry. Around the room were silver mirrors, chairs, divans, cabinets, dressers, and elegant tripods.

On one of the divans slept Artemisia, and just outside of the door one of the Gallic maids, whom Cornelia detested so heartily.

When Artemisia's curly head touched her pillow, its owner was fast asleep in an instant. When her patroness sank back on the cushions worth a king's ransom, Somnus, Hypnus, or whatever name the drowsy god may be called by, was far from present. Cornelia tossed on the pillows, tossed and cried softly to herself. The battle was too hard! She had tried: tried to be true to Drusus and her own higher aspirations. But there was some limit to her strength, and Cornelia felt that limit very near at hand. Earlier in the conflict with her uncle she had exulted in the idea that suicide was always in her power; now she trembled at the thought of death, at the thought of everything contained in the unlovely future. She did not want to die, to flicker out in nothingness, never to smile and never to laugh again. Why should she not be happy — rightly happy? Was she not a Cornelian, a Claudian, born to a position that a princess might enjoy? Was not wealth hers, and a fair degree of wit and a handsome face? Why then should she, the patrician maiden, eat her heart out, while close at hand Artemisia, poor little foundling Greek, was sleeping as sweetly as though people never grieved nor sorrows tore the soul?

Cornelia was almost angry with Artemisia for being thus oblivious to and shielded from calamity. So hot in fact did her indignation become against the innocent girl, that Cornelia herself began to smile at her own passion. And there was one thought very comforting to her pride.

" Artemisia is only an uneducated slave, or little better than a slave; if she were in my station she would be just as unhappy. I am wretched just in proportion to the greatness of my rank;" then she added to herself, " *Hei!* but how wretched then the gods must be!" And then again she smiled at admitting for an instant that there were any gods at all; had not her philosophy taught her much better?

So at last Cornelia turned over the pillows for the last time, and finally slept, in heavy, dreamless slumber.

*   *   *   *   *   *   *   *   *   *

Cornelia did not know at what watch of the night she awoke; awoke, not suddenly, but slowly, as consciousness stole over her that *something* was happening. It was a dark, cloudy night, yet a strange red light was glinting faintly through the windows and making very dim panels on the rugs of the floor. There was a bare gleam of fire from the charcoal in the portable metal stove that stood in a remote corner of the room to dispel the chill of night. Artemisia was stirring in her sleep,

and saying something — probably in a one-sided dream-dia
logue. Cornelia opened her eyes, shut them again; peeped
forth a second time, and sat up in bed. There was a confused
din without, many voices speaking at once, all quite unintelli-
gible, though now and then she caught a few syllables of
Greek. The din grew louder and louder. At the same time,
as if directly connected with the babel, the strange light flamed
up more brightly — as if from many advancing torches. Cornelia shook the sleep from her eyes, and flung back the coverlets. What was it? She had not yet reached the stage of
feeling any terror.

Suddenly, drowning all lesser noise, came the blows of a heavy
timber beating on the main door of the villa.

Crash! and with the stroke, a torrent of wild shouts, oaths,
and imprecations burst forth from many score throats.

Crash! The slaves sleeping near the front door began to
howl and shout. The great Molossian hound that stood watch
was barking and snapping. The Gallic maid sprang from her
pallet by Cornelia's door, and gave a shrill, piercing scream.
Artemisia was sitting up on her bed, rubbing her eyes, blink-
ing at the strange light, and about to begin to cry. Cornelia
ran over the floor to her.

"*A! A!* what is going to happen!" whimpered the girl.

"I do not know, *philotata*,"[1] said Cornelia in Greek, putting
her hand on Artemisia's cheek; "but don't cry, and I'll soon
find out."

Crash! and at this the door could be heard to fall inward.
Then, with yells of triumph and passion, there was a great
sweep of feet over the threshold, and the clang of weapons and
armour. Cornelia found herself beginning to tremble. As she
stepped across the room, she passed before her largest mirror

---

[1] Dearest one.

whereon the outside light was shining directly. She saw herself
for an instant; her hair streaming down her back, her only dress
her loose white tunic, her arms bare, and nothing on her throat
except a string of yellow amber beads. "And my feet are
bare," she added to herself, diverted from her panic by her
womanly embarrassment. She advanced toward the door, but
had not long to wait. Down below the invaders had burst loose
in wild pillage, then up into the sleeping room came flying
a man—Phaon, his teeth chattering, his face ghastly with
fright.

"Domina! domina!" and he knelt and seized Cornelia's
robe. "Save, *A!* save! We are undone! Pirates! They
will kill us all! *Mu! mu!* don't let them murder me!"

A moment longer and Cornelia, in her rising contempt,
would have spurned him with her foot. There were more
feet on the stairway. Glaring torches were tossing over gold
inlaid armour. A man of unusual height and physique strode
at the head of the oncomers, clutching and dragging by the
wrist a quivering slave-boy.

"Your mistress, boy! where is she? Point quickly, if you
would not die!" cried the invader, whom we shall at once
recognize as Demetrius.

Cornelia advanced to the doorway, and stood in her maid-
enly dignity, confronting the pirates, who fell back a step, as
though before an apparition.

"I am the Lady Cornelia, mistress of the villa," she said
slowly, speaking in tones of high command. "On what
errand do you come thus unseasonably, and with violence?"

Whereat, out from the little group of armed men sprang
one clad in costly, jewel-set armour, like the rest, but shorter
than the others, and with fair hair flowing down from his
helmet on to his shoulders.

"Domina, do you not know me? Do not be afraid."

"Agias!" cried Cornelia, in turn giving back a step.

"Assuredly," quoth the young Hellene, nothing dismayed; "and with your leave, this great man is Demetrius, my cousin, whose trade, perchance, is a little irregular, but who has come hither not so much to plunder as to save you from the clutches of his arch-enemy's son, Lucius Ahenobarbus."

Cornelia staggered, and caught the curtain in the doorway to keep from falling.

"Has Master Drusus sent him to me?" she asked, very pale around the lips.

"Master Drusus is at Corfinium. No one knows what will be the issue of the war, for Pompeius is making off. It is I who counselled my cousin to come to Baiæ."

"Then what will you do with me? How may I dare to trust you? Deliver myself into the hands of pirates! Ah! Agias, I did not think that *you* would turn to such a trade!"

The youth flushed visibly, even under the ruddy torchlight.

"Oh, lady," he cried, "have I not always been true to you? I am no pirate, and you will not blame my cousin, when you have heard his story. But do not fear us. Come down to the ship — Fabia is there, waiting for you."

"Fabia!" and again Cornelia was startled. Then, fixing her deep gaze full on Agias, "I believe you speak the truth If not you — who? Take — take me!"

And she fell forward in a swoon, and Demetrius caught her in his powerful arms.

"This is the affianced wife of Quintus Drusus?" he cried to Agias.

"None other."

"She is worthy of Sextus's son. A right brave lady!" cried the pirate. "But this is no place for her. poor thing

Here, Eurybiades," and he addressed a lieutenant, — an athletic, handsome Hellene like himself, — "carry the lady down to the landing, put her on the trireme, and give her to Madam Fabia. Mind you lift her gently."

"Never fear," replied the other, picking up his burden carefully. "Who would not delight to bear Aphrodite to the arms of Artemis!"

And so for a while sight, sound, and feeling were at an end for Cornelia, but for Agias the adventures of the evening were but just begun. The pirates had broken loose in the villa, and Demetrius made not the slightest effort to restrain them. On into the deserted bedroom, ahead of the others, for reasons of his own, rushed Agias. As he came in, some one cried out his name, and a second vision in white confronted him.

"*Ai! ai!* Agias, I knew you would come!" and then and there, with the sword-blades glinting, and the armed men all around, Artemisia tossed her plump arms around his neck.

"The nymph, attendant on Aphrodite!" cried Demetrius, laughing. And then, when Artemisia saw the strange throng and the torches, and heard the din over the villa, she hung down her head in mingled fear and mortification. But Agias whispered something in her ear, that made her lift her face, laughing, and then he in turn caught her up in his arms to hasten down to the landing — for the scene was becoming one of little profit for a maid. Groans and entreaties checked him. Two powerful Phœnician seamen were dragging forward Phaon, half clothed, trembling at every joint. "Mercy! Mercy! Oh! Master Agias, oh! Your excellency, *clarissime*,[1] *despotes!*[2]" whined the wretched man, now in Latin, now in Greek, "ask them to spare me; don't let them murder me in cold blood!"

---

[1] **Very distinguished sir.**   [2] **Master.**

"*Ai!*" cried Demetrius. "What fool have we here? Do you know him, Agias?"

"He is the freedman of Lucius Ahenobarbus. I can vouch for his character, after its way."

"*Ō-op!*"[1] thundered the chief, "drag him down to the boats! I'll speak with him later!"

And Agias carried his precious burden down to the landing-place, while the seamen followed with their captive.

Once Artemisia safe on her way to the trireme, which was a little off shore, Agias ran back to the villa; the pirates were ransacking it thoroughly. Everything that could be of the slightest value was ruthlessly seized upon, everything else recklessly destroyed. The pirates had not confined their attack to the Lentulan residence alone. Rushing down upon the no less elaborate neighbouring villas, they forced in the gates, overcame what slight opposition the trembling slaves might make, and gave full sway to their passion for plunder and rapine. The noble ladies and fine gentlemen who had dared the political situation and lingered late in the season to enjoy the pleasures of Baiæ, now found themselves roughly dragged away into captivity to enrich the freebooters by their ransoms. From pillage the pirates turned to arson, Demetrius in fact making no effort to control his men. First a fragile wooden summer-house caught the blaze of a torch and flared up; then a villa itself, and another and another. The flames shot higher and higher, great glowing, wavering pyramids of heat, roaring and crackling, flinging a red circle of glowing light in toward the mainland by Cumæ, and shimmering out over the bay toward Prochyta. Overhead was the inky dome of the heavens, and below fire; fire, and men with passions unreined.

[1] *Ō-op* — avast there.

Demetrius stood on the terrace of the burning villa of the Lentuli, barely himself out of range of the raging heat. As Agias came near to him, the gilded Medusa head emblazoned on his breastplate glared out; the loose scarlet mantle he wore under his armour was red as if dipped in hot blood; he seemed the personification of Ares, the destroyer, the waster of cities. The pirate was gazing fixedly on the blazing wreck and ruin. His firm lips were set with an expression grave and hard. He took no part in the annihilating frenzy of his men.

"This is terrible destruction!" cried Agias in his ear, for the roar of the flames was deafening, he himself beginning to turn sick at the sight of the ruin.

"It is frightful," replied Demetrius, gloomily; "why did the gods ever drive me to this? My men are but children to exult as they do; as boys love to tear the thatch from the roof of a useless hovel, in sheer wantonness. I cannot restrain them."

At this instant a seaman rushed up in breathless haste.

"*Eleleu!* Captain, the soldiers are on us. There must have been a cohort in Cumæ."

Whereat the voice of Demetrius rang above the shouts of the plunderers and the crash and roar of the conflagration, like a trumpet: —

"Arms, men! Gather the spoil and back to the ships! Back for your lives!"

Already the cohort of Pompeian troops, that had not yet evacuated Cumæ, was coming up on the double-quick, easily guided by the burning buildings which made the vicinity bright as day. The pirates ran like cats out of the blazing villas, bounded over terraces and walls, and gathered near the landing-place by the Lentulan villa. The soldiers were already on them. For a moment it seemed as though the cohort was about to drive the whole swarm of the marauders over the sea-wall, and make them pay dear for their night's diversion. But the masterly energy of Demetrius turned the scale. With barely a score of men behind him, he charged the nearest century so impetuously that it broke like water before him; and when sheer numbers had swept his little group back, the other pirates had rallied on the very brink of the sea-wall, and returned to the charge.

Never was battle waged more desperately. The pirates knew that to be driven back meant to fall over a high embankment into water so shallow as to give little safety in a dive; capture implied crucifixion. Their only hope was to hold their own while their boats took them off to the ships in small detachments. The conflagration made the narrow battle-field as bright as day. The soldiers were brave, and for new recruits moderately disciplined. The pirates could hardly bear up under the crushing discharge of darts, and the steady onset of the maniples. Up and down the contest raged, swaying to and fro like the waves of the sea. Again and again the pirates were driven so near to the brink of the sea-wall that one or two would fall, dashed to instant death on the submerged rocks below. Demetrius was everywhere at once, as it were, precisely when he was most needed, always exposing himself, always aggressive. Even while he himself fought for dear life, Agias admired as never before the intelligently ordered puissance of his cousin.

The boats to and from the landing were pulled with frantic energy. The ships had run in as close as possible, but they could not use their *balistæ*,[1] for fear of striking down friend as well as foe. As relays of pirates were carried away, the position of the remainder became the more desperate with their

---

[1] Missile-throwing engines.

lessening numbers. The boats came back for the last relay. Demetrius drew the remnant of his men together, and charged so furiously that the whole cohort gave way, leaving the ground strewn with its own slain. The pirates rushed madly aboard the boats, they sunk them to the gunwales; other fugitives clung to the oars. At perilous risk of upsetting they thrust off, just as the rallied soldiers ran down to the landing-place. Demetrius and Agias were the only ones standing on the embankment. They had been the last to retire, and therefore the boats had filled without them.

A great cry went up from the pirates.

"Save the captain!" and some boats began to back water, loaded as they were; but Demetrius motioned them back with his hand.

"Can you swim, boy!" he shouted to Agias, while both tore off their body-armour. Their shields had already dropped. Agias shook his head doubtfully.

"My arm is hurt," he muttered.

"No matter!" and Demetrius seized his cousin under one armpit, and stepped down from the little landing-platform into the water just below. A single powerful stroke sent the two out of reach of the swing of the sword of the nearest soldier. The front files of the cohort had pressed down on to the landing in a dense mass, loath to let go its prey.

"Let fly, men!" cried Demetrius, as he swam, and javelins spat into the water about him.

It was a cruel thing to do. The three pirate vessels, two large triremes and the yacht, discharged all their enginery. Heavy stones crashed down upon the soldiers, crushing several men together. Huge arrows tore through shield and armour, impaling more than one body. It was impossible to miss working havoc in so close a throng. The troops, impotent to make effective reply, turned in panic and fled toward the upper terraces to get beyond the decimating artillery. The pirates raised a great shout of triumph that shook the smoke-veiled skies. A fresh boat, pulling out from one of the vessels, rescued the captain and Agias; and soon the two cousins were safe on board the trireme Demetrius used as his flagship.

The pirates swarmed on the decks and rigging and cheered the escape of their commander. On shore the burning buildings were still sending up their pillars of flame. The water and sky far out to sea were red, and beyond, blackness. Again the pirates shouted, then at the order of their commander the cables creaked, the anchors rose, hundreds of long oars flashed in the lurid glare, and the three vessels slipped over the dark waves.

Demetrius remained on the poop of his ship; Agias was below in the cabin, bending over Artemisia, who was already smiling in her sleep.

III

When Cornelia awoke, it was with Fabia bending over her at the bedside. The portholes of the cabin were open; the warm, fresh southern wind was pouring in its balmy sweetness. Cornelia pressed her hands to her eyes, then looked forth. The cabin ceiling was low, but studded with rare ornamental bronze work; the furniture glittered with gilding and the smooth sheen of polished ivory; the tapestry of the curtains and on the walls was of the choicest scarlet wool, and Coan silk, semi-transparent and striped with gold. Gold plating shone on the section of the mast enclosed within the cabin. An odour of the rarest Arabian frankincense was wafted from the pastils burning on a curiously wrought tripod of Corinthian brass. The upholsteries and rugs were more splendid than any that Cornelia had seen gracing the palace of Roman patrician.

Thus it came to pass that Fabia repeated over and over again to Cornelia the tale of recent happenings, until the latter's sorely perturbed brain might comprehend. And then, when Cornelia understood it all: how that she was not to go to Greece with Phaon; how that she was under the protection of a man who owed his life to Sextus Drusus, and hated the Ahenobarbi with a perfect hatred; how that Demetrius had sworn to carry her to Alexandria, where, safe out of the way of war and commotion, she might await the hour when Drusus should be free to come for her — when, we repeat, she understood all this, and how it came to pass that the Vestal herself was on the vessel, — then Cornelia strained Fabia to her breast, and laid her head on the elder woman's shoulder, and cried and cried for very relief of soul. Then she arose and let the maids Demetrius had sent to serve her — dark-skinned Hindoos, whose words were few, but whose fingers quick and dexterous — dress her from the very complete wardrobe that the sea prince had placed at her disposal.

Never before had the sunlight shone so fair; never before had the sniff of the sea-breeze been so sweet. The galleys were still in the bay, close by Prochyta, scarce a mile and a half from the nearest mainland. The pirates were landing to procure water from the desolate, unsettled isle. The bay was dancing and sparkling with ten million golden ripples; the sun had risen high enough above the green hills of the coastland to spread a broad pathway of shimmering fire across the waters. Not a cloud flecked the light-bathed azure. Up from the forward part of the ships sounded the notes of tinkling cithera and the low-breathing double flutes[1] in softest Lydian mood. In and out of the cabin passed bronzed-faced Ethiopian mutes with silver cups of the precious Mareotic white wine of Egypt for the lady, and plates of African pomegranates, Armenian apricots, and strange sweetmeats flavoured with a marvellous powder, an Oriental product worth its weight in gold as a medicine, which later generations were to designate under the name of sugar.

And so Cornelia was refreshed and dressed; and when the maids held the mirror before her and she saw that the gold trinkets were shining in her hair, and the jewels which Demetrius had sent her were sparkling brightly at her throat, and realized that she was very fair to see, — then she laughed, the first real, unforced laugh for many a weary day, whereupon she laughed again and again, and grew the more pleased with her own face when she beheld a smile upon it. Then Fabia kissed her, and told her that no woman was ever more beautiful; and the dark Indian maids drew back, saying nothing, but admiring with their eyes. So Cornelia went up upon the deck, where Demetrius came to meet her. If she had been a Semiramis rewarding a deserving general, she could not have been more queenly. For she thanked him and his lieutenants with a warm gratitude which made every rough seaman feel himself more than repaid, and yet throughout it all bore herself as though the mere privilege on their part of rescuing her ought to be sufficient reward and honour. Then Demetrius knelt down before all his men, and kissed the hem of her robe, and swore that he would devote himself and all that was his to her service, until she and Quintus Drusus should meet, with no foe to come between; so swore all the pirates after their captain, and thus it was Cornelia entered into her life on the ship of the freebooters.

[1] *Tibiæ.*

Other work, however, was before Demetrius that day, than casting glances of dutiful admiration at the stately lady that had deigned to accept his hospitality. Out from the various other cabins, less luxurious assuredly than the one in which Cornelia had awakened, the pirates led their several captives to stand before the chief. Demetrius, indeed, had accomplished what he euphemistically described as "a fair night's work." Half a dozen once very fashionable and now very disordered and dejected noble ladies and about as many more sadly bedraggled fine gentlemen were haled before his tribunal for judgment. The pirate prince stood on the raised roof of a cabin, a step higher than the rest of the poop. He was again in his splendid armour, his naked sword was in his hand, at his side was stationed Eurybiades and half a score more stalwart seamen, all swinging their bare cutlasses. Demetrius nevertheless conducted his interrogations with perhaps superfluous demonstrations of courtesy, and a general distribution of polite "domini" "dominæ," "clarissimi," and "illustres." He spoke in perfectly good Latin, with only the slightest foreign accent; and Cornelia, who — unregenerate pagan that she was — was taking thorough delight in the dilemma of persons who she knew had made her the butt of their scandalous gibes, could only admire the skilful manner in which he brought home to the several captives the necessity of finding a very large sum of money at their bankers' in a very short time, or enduring an indefinite captivity. After more or less of surly threats and resistance on the part of the men, and screaming on the part of the women, the prisoners one and all capitulated, and put their names to the papyri they were commanded to sign; and away went a boat dancing over the waves to Puteoli to cash the money orders, after which the captives would be set ashore at Baiæ.

Last of the wretches brought before Demetrius came **Phaon.**
The freedman had been roughly handled; across his brow a
great welt had risen where a pirate had struck him with a rope's
end. His arms were pinioned behind his back. He was per
fectly pale, and his eyes wandered from one person to another
as if vainly seeking some intercessor.

"*Euge! Kyrios!*[1]" cried the pirate chief, "you indeed seem
to enjoy our hospitality but ill."

Phaon fell on his knees.

"I am a poor man," he began to whimper. "I have no
means of paying a ransom. My patron is not here to protect or rescue me. I have nothing to plunder. *Mu! mu!*
set me free, most noble pirate! Oh! most excellent prince,
what have I done, that you should bear a grudge against
me?"

"Get up, fellow," snapped Demetrius; "I'm not one of those
crocodile-headed Egyptian gods that they grovel before in the
Nile country. My cousin Agias here says he knows you. Now
answer — are you a Greek?"

"I am an Athenian born."

"Don't you think I can smell your Doric accent by that
broad alpha? You are a Sicilian, I'll be bound!"

Phaon made a motion of sorrowful assent.

"*Phui!*" continued Demetrius, "tell me, Agias, is this the
creature that tried to murder Quintus Drusus?"

Agias nodded.

"A fit minister for such a man as I imagine the son of Lucius
Domitius to be. Eurybiades, take off that fellow's bands; he
is not worth one stroke of the sword."

"The captain will not spare the knave!" remonstrated the
sanguinary lieutenant.

[1] **Your Highness.**

"What I have said, I have said," retorted the other; then, when Phaon's arms hung free, "See, on the strength of our fellowship in our both being Greeks, I have set you at large!"

Phaon again sank to his knees to proffer thanks.

"Hold!" cried Demetrius, with a menacing gesture. "Don't waste your gratitude. Greek you pretend to be, more the shame! Such as you it is that have brought Hellas under the heel of the oppressor; such as you have made the word of a Hellene almost valueless in the Roman courts, so that juries have to be warned to consider us all liars; such as you have dragged down into the pit many an honest man; ay, myself too!"

Phaon left off his thanks and began again to supplicate.

"Stop whining, hound!" roared Demetrius; "haven't I said you are free? Free, but on one condition!"

"Anything, anything, my lord," professed the freedman, "money, service —"

"On this condition," and a broad, wicked smile overspread the face of the pirate, "that you quit this ship instantly!"

"Gladly, gladly, merciful sir!" commenced Phaon again; "where is the boat?"

"Wretch!" shouted the other, "what did I say about a boat? Depart — depart into the sea! Swim ashore, if the load on your legs be not too heavy. Seize him and see that he sinks," — this last to Eurybiades and the seamen.

Phaon's terror choked his utterance; he turned livid with mortal fright. He pleaded for life; life on the terms most degrading, most painful, most joyless — life, life and that only. He cried out to Cornelia to save him, he confessed his villanies, and vowed repentance a score of times all in one breath. But Cornelia lived in an age when the wisest and best — whatever

2 c

the philosophers might theorize — thought it no shame to reward evil for evil, not less than good for good. When Deme-trius asked her, "Shall I spare this man, lady?" she replied: "As he has made my life bitter for many days, why should I spare him a brief moment's pain? Death ends all woe!"

There was a dull splash over the side, a circle spreading out in the water, wider and wider, until it could be seen no more among the waves.

"There were heavy stones to his feet, Captain," reported Eurybiades, "and the cords will hold."

"It is well," answered Demetrius, very grave. . . .

Later in the day the boat returned from Puteoli, and with it sundry small round-bellied bags, which the pirate prince duly stowed away in his strong chest. The ransomed captives were put on board a small unarmed yacht that had come out to receive them. Demetrius himself handed the ladies over the side, and salaamed to them as the craft shot off from the flag-ship. Then the pirates again weighed anchor, the great purple [1] square sail of each of the ships was cast to the piping breeze, the triple tiers of silver-plated oars [1] began to rise and fall in unison to the soft notes of the piper. The land grew fainter and more faint, and the three ships sprang away, speeding over the broad breast of the sea.

That night Cornelia and Fabia held each other in their arms for a long time. They were leaving Rome, leaving Italy, their closest friend at hand was only the quondam slave-boy Agias, yet Cornelia, at least, was happy — almost as happy as the girl Artemisia; and when she lay down to sleep, it was to enjoy the first sound slumber, unhaunted by dread of trouble, for nigh unto half a year.

---

[1] These were real affectations of the Cilician pirates.

CHAPTER XX

CLEOPATRA

I

A "CLEAR singing zephyr" out of the west sped the ships on their way. Down they fared along the coast, past the isle of Capreæ, then, leaving the Campanian main behind, cut the blue billows of the Tyrrhenian Sea; all that day and night, and more sail and oar swept them on. They flew past the beaches of Magna Græcia, then, betwixt Scylla and Charybdis, and Sicilia and its smoke-beclouded cone of Ætna faded out of view, and the long, dark swells of the Ionian Sea caught them. No feeble merchantman, hugging coasts and headlands, was Demetrius. He pushed his three barques boldly forward toward the watery sky-line; the rising and setting sun by day and the slowly circling stars by night were all-sufficient pilots; and so the ships flew onward, and, late though the season was, no tempest racked them, no swollen billow tossed them.

Cornelia sat for hours on the poop, beneath a crimson awning, watching the foam scudding out from under the swift-moving keel, and feeling the soft, balmy Notos, the kind wind of the south, now and then puff against her face, when the west wind veered away, and so brought up a whiff of the spices and tropic bloom of the great southern continent, over the parching deserts and the treacherous quicksands of the Syrtes and the broad "unharvested sea."

Cornelia had seen the cone of Ætna sinking away in the west, and then she looked westward no more. For eastward and ever eastward fared the ships, and on beyond them on pinions of mind flew Cornelia. To Africa, to the Orient! And she dreamed of the half-fabulous kingdoms of Assyria and Babylonia; of the splendours of Memphis and Nineveh and Susa and Ecbatana; of Eastern kings and Eastern gold, and Eastern pomp and circumstance of war; of Ninus, and Cyrus the Great, and Alexander; of Cheops and Sesostris and Amasis; of the hanging gardens; of the treasures of Sardanapalus; of the labyrinth of Lake Mœris; of a thousand and one things rare and wonderful. Half was she persuaded that in the East the heart might not ache nor the soul grow cold with pain. And all life was fair to Cornelia. She was sure of meeting Drusus soon or late now, if so be the gods — she could not help using the expression despite her atheism — spared him in war. She could wait; she could be very patient. She was still very young. And when she counted her remaining years to threescore, they seemed an eternity. The pall which had rested on her life since her uncle and her lover parted after their stormy interview was lifted; she could smile, could laugh, could breathe in the fresh air, and cry, "How good it all is!"

Demetrius held his men under control with an iron hand. If ever the pirate ship was filled with sights and sounds unseemly for a lady's eyes and ears, there were none of them now. Cornelia was a princess, abjectly waited on by her subjects. Demetrius's attention outran all her least desires. He wearied her with presents of jewellery and costly dresses, though, as he quietly remarked to Agias, the gifts meant no more of sacrifice to him than an obol to a rich spendthrift. He filled her ears with music all day long; he entertained her with inimitable narrations of his own adventurous voyages and battles. And only dimly could Cornelia realize that the gems she wore in her hair, her silken dress, nay, almost everything she touched, had come from earlier owners with scant process of law.

Demetrius was no common rover. He had been a young man of rare culture before misfortune struck him. He knew his Homer and his Plato as well as how to swing a sword. "Yet," as he remarked with half jest, half sigh, "all his philosophy did not make him one whit more an honest man."

And in his crew of Greeks, Orientals, and Spaniards were many more whom calamity, not innate wickedness, so Cornelia discovered, had driven to a life of violence and rapine.

Demetrius, too, gave no little heed to Artemisia. That pretty creature had been basking in the sunshine of Agias's presence ever since coming on shipboard. It was tacitly understood that Cornelia would care for the welfare and education of Pratinas's runaway, until she reached a maturity at which Agias could assert his claims. The young Hellene himself had been not a little anxious lest his cousin cast obstacles in the way of an alliance with a masterless slave-girl; for of late Demetrius had been boasting to his kinsman that their family, before business misfortunes, had been wealthy and honourable among the merchant princes of Alexandria. But the worthy pirate had not an objection to make; on the contrary, he would sit for hours staring at Artemisia, and when Agias demanded if he was about to turn rival, shook his head and replied, rather brusquely:—

"I was only thinking that Daphne might be about her age, and look perhaps like her."

"Then you do not think your little daughter is dead?" asked Agias, sympathetic, yet personally relieved.

"I know nothing, nothing," replied his cousin, a look of ineffable pain passing over his fine features; "she was a mere infant when I was arrested. When I broke loose, I had to flee for my life. When I could set searchers after her, she had vanished. Poor motherless thing; I imagine she is the slave of some gay lady at Antioch or Ephesus or Rome now."

"And you do not know who stole her?" asked Agias.

"Don't tear open old wounds," was the retort. "I know nothing. I think — but it matters little what I think. There was that sly-eyed, smooth-tongued Greek, like that Phaon who met his deserts, who was no stranger to Domitius's blackmailings. I *feel* that he did it. Never mind his name. If ever I get the snake into my power — " and Demetrius's fingers tightened around the thick, hard cable he was clutching, and crushed the solid hemp into soft, loose strands; then he broke out again, "Never mention this another time, Agias, or I shall go mad, and plunge down, down into the waves, to go to sleep and forget it all!"

Agias was faithful to the injunction; but he observed that Demetrius showed Artemisia the same attention as Cornelia, albeit mingled with a little gracious and unoffending familiarity.

II

After a voyage in which one pleasant day succeeded another, Cornelia awoke one morning to hear the creak of blocks and tackle as the sailors were lowering sail. The full banks of oars were plashing in the waves, and on deck many feet were rushing to and fro, while officers shouted their orders. Coming out of her cabin, the young lady saw that the end of her seafaring was close at hand. Even to one fresh from the

azure atmosphere of the Campanian Bay, the sky was marvellously clear. The water was of a soft green tint, that shaded
off here and there into dark cerulean. The wind was blowing
in cool puffs out of the north. A long, slow swell made the
stately triremes rock gracefully. Before them, in clear view,
rose the tall tower of the Pharos, — the lighthouse of Alexandria, — and beyond it, on the low-lying mainland, rose in
splendid relief against the cloudless sky the glittering piles
and fanes of the city of the Ptolemies. It was a magnificent
picture, — a "picture" because the colours everywhere were as
bright as though laid on freshly by a painter's brush. The
stonework of the buildings, painted to gaudy hues, brought out
all the details of column, cornice, and pediment. Here Demetrius pointed out the Royal Palace, here the Theatre; here,
farther inland, the Museum, where was the great University;
in the distance the whole looked like a painting in miniature.
Only there was more movement in this picture: a splendid
yacht, with the gold and ivory glittering on its prow and poop,
was shooting out from the royal dockyards in front of the
palace; a ponderous corn-ship was spreading her dirty sails to
try to beat out against the adverse breeze, and venture on a
voyage to Rome, at a season when the Italian traffic was usually suspended. The harbour and quays were one forest of
masts. Boats and small craft were gliding everywhere.
Behind the pirate's triremes several large merchantmen were
bearing into the harbour under a full press of sail.

"And this, your ladyship," said Demetrius, smiling, "is
Egypt. Does the first sight please you?"

"Does it not!" exclaimed Cornelia, drinking in the matchless spectacle. "But you, kind sir, do you not run personal
peril by putting into this haven for my sake?"

Demetrius laughed.

"It speaks ill for the law-abiding qualities of my country. men, lady," said he, "that I have nothing now to fear. I have too many great friends both in the court and in the city to fear arrest or annoyance. Here I may not stay long, for if it were to be noised in Rome that a pirate were harboured habitually at Alexandria, a demand for my arrest would come to the king quickly enough, and he must needs comply. But for a few days, especially while all Rome is in chaos, I am safe; and, come what may, I would be first warned if any one intended to lay hands on me."

Indeed, Demetrius's boast as to his own importance in Alexandria was soon verified. The customs officials were all obsequiousness when they went through the form of levying on the cargo of the ship. The master of the port was soon in Demetrius's own cabin over a crater of excellent wine, and no sooner had the vessels touched the quay than their crews were fraternizing with the hosts of stevedores and flower-girls who swarmed to meet the new arrivals.

* * * * * * * * * *

A few days later Cornelia and Fabia found themselves received as members of the household of no less a person than Cleomenes, a distant kinsman of Demetrius and Agias, and himself one of the great merchant princes of the Egyptian capital. The Roman ladies found a certain amount of shyness to overcome on their own part and on that of their hosts. Cleomenes himself was a widower, and his ample house was presided over by two dark-skinned, dark-eyed daughters, Berenice and Monime — girls who blended with the handsome Greek features of their father the soft, sensuous charm of his dead Egyptian wife. Bashful indeed had been these maidens in contact with the strangers who came bearing with them the haughty pride of all-conquering Rome. But after a day or two, when

Cornelia had cast off the hauteur begotten of diffidence, and Fabia had opened the depths of her pure womanly character, the barriers were thrown down rapidly enough; and Cornelia and Fabia gained, not merely an access to a new world of life and ideas, but two friends that they could regard almost as sisters.

It was a new thing for these Roman ladies to meet a foreigner on terms approaching equality. A non-Roman had been for them a servant, an intelligent underling, nothing more; even Agias and Demetrius they had regarded as friends, very close and agreeable, but whom it was a distinct condescension not to treat with ostentatious superiority. But to sustain this feeling long with Berenice and Monime was impossible. The young Egyptians were every whit as cultured, as intelligent, as themselves, every whit as accustomed to deference from others, and implicitly assumed the right to demand it. The result was that Cornelia found herself thinking less and less about being a Roman, and more and more regarded her gracious hosts as persons in every way equal to herself.

And less and less of a Roman, Cornelia, the Hellene-hater, became. Greek was the only tongue now that sounded in her ear, unless she talked privately with Fabia or was beguiled into trying to learn a little Egyptian — a language Berenice and Monime spoke fluently. The clothes she wore were no longer stola and palla, but chiton and himation. The whole atmosphere about her was foreign, down to the cries on the streets. And Italy was very far away, and the last memories thereof none the most pleasant.

It chanced that one morning Cleomenes, Monime, and Cornelia were driving down the great central street, under the shadow of seemingly endless colonnades.

"*A!* dearest one," cried Monime, "why must you think

of leaving our lovely Alexandria, of going back to cold, cheerless Rome? What good thing does Rome send out but stern men and sharp iron?"

Cornelia shook her head and made answer —

"You Alexandrians are not one nation, but all the world; therefore you think all who are less cosmopolitan poor. See, I count in the crowds not only the dark Egyptians and fair Greeks, but a Persian in his splendid long kaftan, and a very venerable Jew, and a wiry little Arab, and Syrians, and negroes, and, I think, a Hindoo."

"And yourself, my lady, a Roman," concluded Cleomenes. "Truly all the earth has met in our city."

They whirled down the splendid highway that ran straight as an arrow the whole length of the city, lined on either side by a forest of the infinite number of columns of the great stretches of porticos. Handsomely dressed cavalrymen of the palace guard were dashing to and fro over the clean, hard pavement; elegant carriages containing the noble and wealthy were whirling in every direction. At each glance, the eye lit on some pleasing bit of sculpture, some delicate curve of architecture. Statues were everywhere, everywhere colour, everywhere crowds of gayly dressed citizens and foreigners. Cornelia contrasted the symmetrical streets, all broad, swept, and at right angles — the triumph of the wise architectural planning of Dinocrates — with the dirty, unsightly, and crooked lanes of the City of the Seven Hills, and told herself, as she had told herself often in recent days, that Romans had much yet to learn.

They drove on past the Amphitheatre toward the Egyptian quarter of the Rhacotis; and here, at the intersection of the Great Street with the other broad way leading from the "Gate of the Moon" on the harbour to the "Gate of the Sun" on Lake Mareotis, a moving hedge of outriders, cavalrymen, and footguards met them.

"The queen coming from the Serapeum," said Cleomenes, drawing rein.

Cornelia saw half-naked Numidian footmen thrusting back the crowd that bustled in the Omphalos — the great square where the two highroads met. Behind them pushed a squadron of light cavalry in silvered armour and splendid purple and scarlet uniforms. Then, in the midst of all, moved a chariot drawn by four horses white as snow, the harness resplendent with gold and jewels; at either side ran fan-bearers, waving great masses of bright ostrich plumes; a gaudy parasol swept over the carriage itself. There were three occupants, whereof two stood: an Egyptian, gaunt and of great height, clad in plain white linen, who was driving, and a handsome, gaudily dressed Greek youth, who was holding the parasol. Cornelia could just catch the profile of a young woman seated between them. The face was not quite regular, but marvellously intelligent and sensitive; the skin not pale, yet far from dark, and perfectly healthy and clear; the eyes restive and piercing. The queen was dressed plainly in Greek fashion; her himation was white, her only ornament a great diamond that was blazing like a star on her breast. Upon the coils of her heavy, dark hair sat a golden circlet faced in front with the likeness of the head of the venomous uræus snake — the emblem of Egyptian royalty. This was all Cornelia could observe in the brief time the queen was in view. Some of the people — Egyptians mostly — cried out to her in their own tongue: —

"Hail to the ever glorious Daughter of Ra!"

But the queen paid them little heed. Once her restless eyes lit on the carriage of Cleomenes, and she made a slight inclination of the head in return to that gentleman's salute, for Cleomenes had standing at court as one of the "friends of the king."[1]

---

[1] A high order of Egyptian nobility.

The cortège rolled away toward the palace.

"This Cleopatra is a rather remarkable woman," observed Cornelia, for the sake of saying something.

"Indeed, that is true," replied Cleomenes, as he turned to drive homeward. "She is worthy to have lived in the days of the first Ptolemies, of Ptolemæus Soter and Philadelphus and Euergetes. She is still very young, only twenty, and yet five years ago she was so fascinating that when Antonius, of whom I have heard you speak, came here with Gabinius's expedition, he quite lost his heart to her. She has a marvellous talent for statecraft and intrigue and diplomacy. You know that, nominally at least, she has to share her crown with young Ptolemæus, her younger brother. He is a worthless rascal, but his tutor, the eunuch Pothinus, really wields him. Pothinus, as the custom is, was brought up with him as his playmate, and now Pothinus wants to drive out the queen, and rule Egypt through his power over the king. His ambition is notorious, but the queen has not been able to lay hands on him for treason."

Cleopatra and her fortunes and perils played a slight part in Cornelia's mind, however, that day. To know Alexandria in its sunlight and shadows was indeed to know a miniature world. First of all to notice, besides the heterogeneous nature of the crowds on the streets, was the fact that every person, high as well as low, was engaged in some trade. Very far was the typical Alexandrian from the quiet "leisure" which the average Greek or Latin believed requisite for a refined life — 'a life in which slaves did all the necessary work, and amassed an income for the master to expend in polite recreations. In Rome, for a free citizen to have been a handicraftsman would have been a disgrace; he could be farmer, banker, soldier, — nothing more. In Alexandria the glass-workers, paper-makers, and linen weavers were those who were proudest and most jealous of their title of "Men of Macedonia." [1] Money, Cornelia soon discovered, was even a greater god here than in Rome. Cleomenes himself was not ashamed to spend a large part of the day inspecting his factories, and did not hesitate to declare that during a period when he and his family had been in great distress, following the failure of the banking house of Agias's father, he had toiled with his own hands to win bread for his daughters.

The conception that any honest labour, except a certain genteel agriculture, might not make a man the less of a gentleman, or a woman the less of a lady, was as new to Cornelia as the idea that some non-Romans could claim equality with herself. Neither proposition did she accept consciously. The prejudice wore quietly away. But other things about the city she gathered quickly enough from the caustic explanations of Cleomenes.

"Here in Alexandria," he asserted on one occasion, "we are always ripe for a riot. Never a chariot race without stone-throwing and throat-cutting after it. An unpopular official is torn in pieces by a mob. If you chance to kill a cat, the Egyptians are after you for your life. The Greeks hate the Jews, and are always ready to plunder their quarter; the Egyptians are on bad terms with both. We talk about being free citizens of the capital of the Ptolemies, and pretend to go to the Gymnasium for discussion, and claim a right to consult with the king; but our precious Senate, and all our tribes and wards, are only fictions. We are as much slaves as the poor creatures down in the royal quarries; only we demand the right to riot and give nicknames. We called the last Ptolemæus, Auletes "the Piper," because in that way we have punished him in all history for the way he oppressed us. *Euge!* **Have** we not a wonderful city!"

It was on the very next day that Cleopatra was recalled to Cornelia's mind in a quite marked fashion. It was rather early, and she was upon the roof-garden, on the third story of the house, where there was a commanding view of the city. Berenice was busy reading from a papyrus the Egyptian legend of the "Adventures of Sinuhit," translating into Greek as she read.

Cleomenes broke in upon the reading. His face wore a mysterious smile.

"I have a rather strange piece of news for you, my lady," he said. "A chamberlain of the court has just been here, and brings a royal command."

"I am not accustomed to being commanded," interrupted Cornelia, all her Roman haughtiness rising.

"I do not think you will be found disobedient. The queen, it seems, noticed you in my carriage yesterday, and at once divined, with that wonderfully quick wit of hers, that you must be a Roman lady of rank. She immediately made inquiries, and now sends her chamberlain to ask you and the Lady Fabia, as well as myself, to dine with her at the palace to-night. You may be sure nothing will be lacking to do you honour."

Cornelia meekly acquiesced in this royal mandate. Fabia, however, could not stir from the house. The shock to her finely strung nature when she was taken from Rome had, indeed, produced a physical reaction. She was not seriously ill, but could endure no excitement. So it was with only Cleomenes for an escort that Cornelia mounted into one of the splendid royal chariots sent from the palace about dusk, and drove away surrounded by a cloud of guardsmen sent to do honour to the guests of the queen.

Cornelia herself felt highly strung and slightly nervous. She wished, for the first time since she reached Alexandria, that she could go dressed in the native costume of a Roman lady. She was going to enjoy the hospitality of a princess who was the successor of thirty odd dynasties of Pharaohs; who was worshipped herself as a goddess by millions of Egyptians; who was hailed as "Daughter of the Sun," and with fifty other fulsome titles; a princess, furthermore, who was supposed to dispose of the lives of her subjects as seemed right in her own eyes, without law of man or god to hinder. Cornelia was not afraid, nay rather, anticipatory; only she had never before been so thoroughly conscious that she was Roman down to her finger-tips — Roman, and hence could look upon the faces of princes unabashed.

The people saw the royal chariot, and some shouted salutations to the guests whom the queen delighted to honour. The company swept up under the magnificent archway leading to the palace; above them rose tall Ionic columns of red granite of Syene, building rising above building, labyrinths of pillars, myriads of statues. Torches were blazing from every direction. The palace grounds were as bright as day. The light breeze was sweeping through rare Indian ferns and tropical palms. The air was heavy with the breath of innumerable roses. Huge fountains were tossing up showers of spray, which fell tinkling into broad basins wherein the cups of the blue and white lotus were floating. It was indeed as if one had been led on to enchanted ground.

Cornelia and her friend dismounted from their chariot, and were led through an endless colonnade, past a second, lower gateway, and then into a hall, not very high or large, but admirable in its proportions, with a whole gallery of choice mythological paintings on its walls. Small heed did Cornelia give to them. For at the end of the hall rose a low dais, whereon sat, in a gilded chair, the same person who had been pointed out to Cornelia the day before as the mistress of Upper and Lower Egypt.

The light was too dim to discover in the distance anything new in the face of the queen. She wore a loose, long gown of some light blue silken stuff; and her belt, shoes, neck, breast, and ears were all glittering with gems. At the foot of the dais was a group of half a dozen showily dressed chamberlains and courtiers, who made a slight motion of greeting when the two guests darkened the doorway. One of these functionaries advanced to Cornelia.

"Your ladyship," he began, in a smooth, colourless voice, "I have the honour to be the Royal Introducing Chamberlain.[1] In approaching the queen, do as I shall direct. First, before advancing to the dais bow slightly; then at the foot of the dais it is proper — "

"Sir," interrupted Cornelia, drawing herself up to her full height, "I am not accustomed to your prostrations and genuflections, and of them my countrymen make sorry work; pray excuse me." And without waiting for reply or expostulation she advanced straight toward the dais. The hall was small, the steps from the door to the queen's chair few; but never did Cornelia fare on more tedious journey. She knew that a half-horrified titter was passing through the group of courtiers. She knew that Cleopatra herself had stirred in her seat, as if to rise. But one word sounded in Cornelia's ears, and that word was "Rome." Were not Roman citizens nobles among nobles, and Roman senators peers of kings! And she, daughter of the Cornelii and Claudii, whose ancestors had broken the might of Antiochus the Great and Mithridates — should she

<hr>

[1] εἰσαγγελεύς.

not look in the face the heiress of the Lagidæ? Had not one hundred years before Popilius, the Roman commissioner, come unarmed into the presence of Antiochus Epiphanes, while he was advancing to the gates of defenceless Alexandria, drawn a circle in the dust about the king, and bidden him answer, before he stepped over, whether he would court destruction or obey the mandate of the Republic and leave Egypt in peace? And had not the great king obeyed — humbly? Why, then, should not a Roman patrician maiden look down on a mere monarch, who was a pawn in the hands of her kinsfolk and countrymen?

To repeat these things is long. The mind moves faster than the sunlight. Cornelia came to the dais, and there gave the slightest inclination of her head — the greeting of a mistress to slaves — to the group of courtiers. She advanced straight toward the royal chair and stretched forth her hand.

"I am your debtor, O queen, for a kindness that I may not soon, I fear, repay — unless you come to Rome."

She spoke as a superior addressing an inferior who had rendered some slight service. The queen rose from her seat and took the proffered hand without the least hesitation.

"And I will ask for none other reward than that you do honour to my entertainment."

The voice was wonderfully soft, modulated, and ringing; like an instrument of many strings. Every syllable blended into the next in perfect harmony; to hear a few words was like listening unto music.

Cornelia knew later, when she was older and had thought more, that the queen had instantly caught the defiant mood of her guest, and thereupon left nothing unspared to conciliate it. At that moment, however, she attempted no such analysis of motive. She was conscious of only one thing: the luminous

2 D

personality of Cleopatra. The queen was all that Cornelia had noticed her to be when they met at the Great Square; but she was more than a beautiful woman. In fact, in mere bodily perfection Monime or Berenice might well have stood beside her. The glance of the queen went through and through her guests like arrows of softly burning light. It was impossible to withdraw one's eyes from her; impossible to shake off the spell of an enjoyable magnetism. If she moved her long, shapely fingers, it was speech; if she raised her hand, eloquence. As shade after shade of varying emotion seemed to pass across Cleopatra's face, it was as if one saw the workings of a masterful spirit as in a mirror; and now could cry, "This is one of the Graces," and now "This is one of the Fates," as half-girlish candour and sweetness was followed by a lightning flash from the eyes, disclosing the deep, far-recessed subtleties of the soul within. Cornelia had entered the hall haughty, defiant; a word and a look — she was the most obedient vassal.

Cornelia had seen many a splendid banquet and dinner party in Rome. Even Oriental kings had not a great deal to teach the "masters of the toga" in ostentatious luxury. Perhaps the queen had realized this. The present occasion called, indeed, for very little formality, for, besides Cornelia, Cleomenes was the only guest; and when that gentleman inquired politely if his Majesty, the King Ptolemæus, was to honour them with his presence, Cleopatra replied, with an eloquent raising of the eyebrows: —

"The king will be to-night, as he always is, with his tutor — Pothinus."

There was indescribable scorn in the last word.

The doors of the reception hall had been flung back on noiseless pivots by unseen hands. The banqueting room disclosed within was not so much a room as a garden. Flowers, flowers were everywhere, roses, violets, narcissuses, and a score of others breathing forth a heavy fragrance. Overhead, the gold-studded ceiling was converted into a vast arbour of blending flowery tints. The room was large, very large for only three banqueters; on the walls, from out between the potted tropical plants, shone marvellous marble reliefs, one hundred in all; and in betwixt them were matchless paintings. Framing, after a fashion, the pictures, were equally perfect embroideries, portraying in silk and fine linen the stories of Thebes, the kingly house of Argos, and many another myth of fame. The pillars of the room represented palm trees and Bacchic thyrsi; skins of wild beasts were fastened high up to the walls; and everywhere was the sheen of silver and gold, the splendour of scarlet and purple tapestries.

"The decorations of this room," said the queen, as her two guests entered, "are nearly all preserved from the great banqueting pavilion of Ptolemæus Philadelphus, which he erected for the grand festival that ushered in his reign."

Cornelia drew back as her foot crossed the threshold. Her sandals trod on the fair white cup of a blooming lily. The queen laughed as merrily as a little girl at her confusion.

"In Rome, I doubt not," she said, smiling, "there are not flowers enough at this time of year to have them for a carpet. But this is Alexandria. Flowers are never out of bloom."

So Cornelia advanced, but perhaps it grieved her more to tread on the innocent flowers, than any small thing had since she left Baiæ.

And then the banquet, if such it may be termed when there are but three to enjoy it, began. Cleopatra knew well that she could not overwhelm her Roman guest with show of plate and gems, nor did she try. But Cornelia forgot about such things long before they rose. For the queen displayed to her a myriad dainty perfections and refinements that never had endeared themselves to the grosser Italian gourmands. Cleomenes had whispered to his companion, before they reached the palace, "Plato tells of four sorts of flattery; but I can promise you a thousand sorts from Cleopatra if she but cares to win your friendship." And surely the queen did thus desire. For Cornelia was surfeited with strange dishes, and rare sherbets, flowers, and music; surfeited with everything save the words that fell from the lips of Cleopatra.

The more the queen spoke, the more complete became the vassalage of her guest. Cornelia discovered that this woman, who was but little older than she, could speak fluently seven languages, and carried about with her an exceedingly accurate knowledge, not merely of the administration of Egypt, but of the politics of Rome, and the details of the great contest racking the Republic. When Cleopatra asked questions concerning Roman affairs, Cornelia was fain to confess ignorance and be put to shame. And as the evening advanced, Cornelia found herself talking with more and more confidence to this woman that she had never addressed until an hour before. Cleopatra of course knew, as all Alexandria knew, that Cornelia and Fabia were Roman ladies of the highest rank, who had been forced to take refuge abroad until the political crisis was over. But now Cornelia told the queen the true reasons that had led her to be willing to submit to Demetrius's friendly kidnapping; and when, in a burst of frankness, — which in a saner moment Cornelia would have deemed unwise, — she told of her betrothal to Drusus and willingness to wait long for him, if they might only come together in the end, the queen seemed unable to speak with her usual bright vivacity. Presently she said: —

" So you love this young man as none other? You are willing to be all your life his handmaid, his slave?"

"I love him, assuredly," said Cornelia, with a little heat. " And so far as being all my life his slave, I've given that never so much as a thought. Where love is, there slavery cannot be."

" And where love is not, there slavery must be, doubtless you wish to add?" broke in the queen.

"I should be very miserable if I had nothing to love, which I might love purely, and feel myself the nobler and happier thereby."

"Then pity us poor mortals who cannot climb up to your Olympus! Eh, my very noble Cleomenes," went on the queen, addressing the Greek, "do I not deserve compassion, that I have not been able to find some Tigranes of Armenia, or Parthian prince, who will be all in all to me, and make me forget everything in worshipping him?"

These were the first words that evening that had grated on Cornelia. A little ruffled, she replied: —

"I fear, O queen, that if you are awaiting a Tigranes or an Artavasdes to sue for your hand, you will indeed never find a lord to worship. Quintus Drusus is indeed wealthy at Rome, his family noble, he may rise to great things; but I would not lay down my life for him because of his wealth, his lineage, or his fair prospects. It is not these things which make a common woman love a man."

"But I am not a common woman," responded Cleopatra, with emphasis. "I am ambitious, not to be led, but to lead. I must rule or I must die. I cannot love a master, only fear him. Why, because I was born a woman, must I give up all my royal aspirations to rise to a great place among princes, to build up a great empire in the East, to make Alexandria a capital with the power of Rome, the culture of Athens, the splendour of Babylon, all in one? It is because I have these hopes stirring in me that I may love no man, can love no man! Nothing shall stand in my way; nothing shall oppose me. Whoever thwarts my ambitions, the worse for him; let him die — all things must die, but not I, until I have won my power and glory!"

For once, at least, the queen's emotions had run away with her; she spoke hotly, passionately, as though tearing her words from the recesses of her throbbing heart. Her wonderful voice was keyed in half-bitter defiance. For the moment Cornelia was mistress, and not the queen.

"O queen," broke in the young Roman, "would you know how I feel toward you?"

Cleopatra looked at her with dilated eyes.

"I feel for you a very great sorrow. I know not whether you will or will not do as you wish — set your empire over the far East, a rival, friendly, I hope, to our Rome; but this I know, that with your glory, and with your renown among men for all time, you will go down to your grave with an empty heart. And I know not what may compensate for that."

Cleomenes was clearly a little disturbed at this turn to the conversation; but Cleopatra bowed her head on her hands. It was only for an instant. When she looked up once more there were tears in her eyes, which she made no effort to conceal. The look of high defiance had faded from her face.

"Think kindly of me, Lady Cornelia," she said; "I am but a wilful girl with many things to learn. Perhaps you yourself know that purple robes do not make a light heart."

"That I know well and sadly."

"Therefore," went on the queen, "if I forget myself, and half envy a cup of happiness that seems dashed from my lips, do not be over blameful."

"Never," responded the young Roman.

"Time advances," said the queen; "let us forget that any barriers shut us out from perfect bliss. Let us call in the Egyptian musicians; and cry out upon me if my looks grow sad!"

Whereat a whole section in the side of the room turned on a pivot, and there entered three native harpers and eight pretty Egyptian girls, in gauzy dresses, who danced in intricate figures, and juggled with balls; now with two, now with three, catching them with their hands crossed. Boys ran in and out and sprinkled *kyphi*[1] on the heads of the three feasters, and flung huge wreaths of flowers round their necks, and thrust lotus flowers in their hair. And all the time the girls sang sweetly.

The queen kept her guests very late.

"We of Alexandria," said she, "make little difference between night and day. Our city is a new Sybaris."

And all through the evening Cleopatra kept close to Cornelia, often with her hand upon her, as though extremely loath to let her go. At last the moon crept up into the heavens, and as the queen and her guests roved out of the heated banqueting hall into the cool gardens, the pale yellow light gently bathed the sweep of the city, which lay in full view of the palace terrace.

"All sleep," said Cleopatra, "all but ourselves. Let there be one more song, and then farewell! — but soon to meet again."

The chorus of maidens, which followed them, sang, in Greek, the hymn of Onomacritus :[2] —

"Heavenly Selene ! goddess queen ! that shed'st abroad the light !
Bull-horned moon ! air-habiting ! thou wanderer through the night !

[1] A mixture of myrrh, frankincense, and other aromatic materials.
[2] Elton, translator.

> Moon bearer of mighty torch ! thou star-encircled maid!
> Woman thou, yet male the same, still fresh and undecayed !
> Thou that in thy steeds delightest, as they travel through the sky,
> Clothed in brightness ! mighty mother of the rapid years that fly ;
> Fruit dispenser ! amber-visaged ! melancholy, yet serene !
> All beholding ! sleep-enamour'd ! still with trooping planets seen !
> Quiet loving ; who in pleasance and in plenty tak'st delight ;
> Joy diffusing ! Fruit maturing ! Sparkling ornament of night !
> Swiftly pacing ! ample-vested ! star-bright ! all divining maid !
> Come benignant ! come spontaneous ! with starry sheen arrayed !
> Sweetly shining ! save us virgin, give thy holy suppliants aid !"

"Yes," said Cleopatra, passing her hand over her brow, "give us aid, either thou, O moon, or some other power, for we are full weak ourselves."

When the queen parted with her guests she put her arms around Cornelia's waist and kissed her on the forehead.

"I sent for you," said Cleopatra, "half intending to amuse myself with the boorishness and clumsy insolence which I conceived a noble Roman lady to possess. I have been punished. Promise to come to see me often, very often, or I shall call my body-guards and keep you prisoner. For I have very few friends."

While the chariot was bearing the two guests away, Cleomenes asked Cornelia what she thought of the queen.

"She is the most wonderful woman I have ever met," was her answer, enthusiastic and characteristically feminine. "I admire her. I am almost her slave."

The frequency of Cornelia's visits to the palace on following days seemed to prove that the admiration was not unreciprocated. Indeed, Monime and Berenice grew jealous of the queen for stealing their new friend from them.

CHAPTER XXI

HOW ULAMHALA'S WORDS CAME TRUE

I

THE sentries were going their rounds; the camp-fires were burning low. Over on the western hills bounding the Thessalian plain-land lingered the last bars of light. It was oppressively warm, and man and beast were utterly fatigued. Quintus Drusus stripped off his armour, and flung himself on the turf inside his tattered leather tent. Vast had been the changes eighteen months of campaigning had made in him He had fought in Italy, in Spain, in the long blockade of the Pompeians at Dyrrachium. He had learned the art of war in no gentle school. He had ceased even so much as to grumble inwardly at the hardships endured by the hard-pressed Cæsarian army. The campaign was not going well. Pompeius had broken through the blockade; and now the two armies had been executing tedious manœuvres, fencing for a vantage-ground before joining pitched battle.

Drusus was exceedingly weary. The events of the past two years, — loves, hates, pleasures, perils, battles, — all coursed through his mind; the fairest and most hideous of things were blended into buzzing confusion; and out of that confusion came a dull consciousness that he, Quintus Drusus, was thoroughly weary of everything and anything — was heavy of heart, was consumed with hatred, was chafing against a hundred barriers of time, space, and circumstance, and was utterly impotent to contend against them.

The Imperator — how he loved and adored him! Through all the campaigning nothing could seem to break the strength of that nervous, agile, finely strung physique. Sleeping in carriages or litters; ever moving; dictating continually books and letters to a secretary if for an hour there was a halt; dictating even while on horseback, in fact, and composing two letters at the same time; riding the most ungovernable horses fearlessly and without a fall; galloping at full speed with his hands clasped behind his back, — these were the mere external traits that made him wonderful among men. Worthy of all praise was the discipline by which the Imperator had held his troops to him by bonds firmer than iron; neither noticing all petty transgressions, nor punishing according to a rigid rule; swift and sure to apprehend mutineers and deserters; certain to relax the tight bands of discipline after a hard-fought battle with the genial remark that "his soldiers fought none the worse for being well oiled"; ever treating the troops as comrades, and addressing them as "fellow-soldiers," as if they were but sharers with him in the honour of struggling for a single great end. Drusus had known him to ride one hundred miles a day in a light chariot without baggage, march continually at the head of his legions on foot, sharing their fatigues in the most malignant weather, swim a swollen river on a float of inflated skins, always travelling faster than the news of his coming might fly before him. Tireless, unsleeping, all providing, all accomplishing, omniscient, — this was what made Drusus look upon his general as a being raised up by the Fates, to go up and down the world, destroying here and building there. The immediate future might be sombre enough, with all the military advantages falling, one after another, into Pompeius's lap; but doubt the ultimate triumph of Cæsar? The young Livian would have as readily questioned his own existence.

Some one thrust back the flaps of the tent, and called inside into the darkness : —

"Are you here, Drusus?"

"I am," was the wearied answer. "Is that Antonius?"

"Yes. Come out. We may as well dispose of our cold *puls* before the moon rises, and while we can imagine it peacocks, Lucrine oysters, or what not."

' If sight were the only sense!" grumbled Drusus, as he pulled himself together by a considerable effort, and staggered to his feet.

Outside the tent Antonius was waiting with a helmet half full of the delectable viand, which the two friends proceeded to share together as equally as they might in the increasing darkness.

"You are over sober to-night," said Antonius, when this scarcely elaborate meal was nearly finished.

"*Perpol!*" replied Drusus, "have I been as a rule drunken of late? My throat hardly knows the feeling of good Falernian, it is so long since I have tasted any."

"I doubt if there is so much as a draught of *posca*[1] in the army," said Antonius, yawning. "I imagine that among our friends, the Pompeians, there is plenty, and more to spare. *Mehercle*, I feel that we must storm their camp just to get something worth drinking. But I would stake my best villa that you have not been so gloomy for mere lack of victuals, unless you have just joined the Pythagoreans, and have taken a vow not to eat fish or beans."

"I do not know that I am especially gloomy to-night,"

[1] A drink of vinegar and water very common among the soldiers.

replied Drusus, a bit testily. "I know little whereon to make merry."

"The arrows of Amor," hinted Antonius, "sink deep in the soul, and the god is unfair; he shoots venomed darts; the poison ever makes the pain greater."

"I would you could endure your own troubles," retorted the other, "and let me care for mine!"

"*Perpol*, friend," replied Antonius, "don't be vexed! I see it is a case of your wanting little said on a sore point. Well, keep silent, I won't tease you. Doesn't Theognis declare : —

> "'Caress me not with words, while far away
> Thy heart is absent and thy feelings stray'?[1]

And doubtless you would reverse the saying and put 'my heart' for 'thy heart.' Forgive me."

But Drusus, now that the ice was broken, was glad to talk.

"Now, amice, I won't harbour any ill feeling. I know that you don't look at women the way I do. If you had ever fallen in love with one like Cornelia, it would have been different. As it is, you can only stare at me, and say to yourself, 'How strange a sensible fellow like Drusus should care for a girl from whom he has been parted for nearly two years!' That's why I doubt if your sympathy can be of any great solace to me."

"Well," said Antonius, washing down his *puls* with a draught of water from a second helmet at hand, "I can't say that I would be full of grief two years from the day my beloved Fulvia was taken from me. But there are women of many a sort. Some are vipers to sting your breast, some are playthings, some are — what shall I call them — goddesses? no, one may not

[1] Elton, translator.

kiss Juno; flowers? they fade too early; silver and gold? that is rubbish. I have no name for them. But believe me, Quintus, I have met this Cornelia of yours once or twice, and I believe that she is one of those women for whom my words grow weak."

"Then you can sympathize, can feel, for me," said Drusus, as he lay back with his head on the dark green sward.

"Yes, as a poor man who has always possessed nothing can feel for a rich merchant whose whole fortune is about to founder at sea. Do not spurn my feeble sort of pity. But do you know nothing of her, not a word, a sign? Is she alive or dead? Much less, does she still care for you?"

"Nothing!" answered Drusus, and the sense of vexation and helplessness choked his utterance. "She vanished out of sight at Baiæ, as a flash of lightning passes away in the sky. I cannot imagine the cause of her disappearance. The pirates, indeed, might have wished to take her for ransom; but no, they bore her off with never a demand for money from any friend or relative. I have tried to trace them — the Pompeian ships on every sea make it impossible. I have questioned many prisoners and spies; she is not at the Pompeian camp with her uncle. Neither can I discover that her kinsmen among the enemy themselves know where she is. And to this is added that other mystery: whither has my Aunt Fabia vanished? How much of the account of those who followed her to the river dock is to be believed — that pirates saved her from Gabinius, and then abducted her? Upon all, my clever freedman Agias is gone — gone without ever a word, though I counted him faithful as my own soul!"

"And what then do you expect?" asked Antonius, not without friendly interest.

"What can a man, who dares to look the situation in the

face, expect, except something too horrible to utter?" and Drusus groaned in his agony.

"You mean —" began his friend.

"That the pirates have kept Cornelia and perhaps Fabia in their vile clutches until this hour; unless, indeed, the Fates have been merciful and they are dead! Do you wonder at my pain?"

"*Phui!* we will not imagine any such disagreeable thing!" said Antonius, in a sickly effort to make banter at the other's fears.

"Don't speak again unless you want me your enemy," threatened Drusus, springing up in fury. Antonius knew his own interests enough to keep quiet; besides, his friend's pain cut him to the heart, and he knew himself that Drusus's dread was justified under the circumstances.

"Do you think there will be a battle to-morrow?" demanded Drusus, after some interval of gloomy silence.

"I would to the gods it might be so," was his answer; "are you thirsting for blood?"

Drusus half drew his short sword, which even in camp never left the side of officer or private during that campaign.

"Thirst for blood?" he growled. "Yes, for the lives of Lucius Lentulus, and Domitius and his accursed younger son. I am hot as an old gladiator for a chance to spill their blood! If Cornelia suffers woe unutterable, it will be they — they who brought the evil upon her! It may not be a philosophic mood, but all the animal has risen within me, and rises more and more the longer I think upon them and on *her*."

"Come," said Antonius, lifting his friend by the arm, "and let us lie down in the tent. There will be toil enough to morrow; and we must take what rest we may."

II

On that same night, in a very sumptuous tent, fresh from an ample dinner and a season over choice wines, the high and the mighty of Cæsar's enemies were taking counsel together. No longer were they despairing, panic-stricken fugitives, driven from their native land which they had abandoned a prey to the invader. The strength of the East had gathered about them. Jews, Armenians, and Arabians were among their auxiliary forces; Asia Minor, Greece, the Archipelago, had poured out for them levies and subsidies. In the encampment were the vassal kings, Deiotarus of Galatia and Ariarathes of Cappadocia, allies who would share the triumph of the victorious Pompeius.

For none could doubt that the Magnus had proved his right to be called the favoured child of Fortune. Had not Cæsar been utterly defeated at Dyrrachium? Was he not now almost a fugitive in the interior of Greece, — liable at any moment to have his forces cut to pieces, and he himself to be slain in battle like a second Catilina, or to die by the executioner's axe like another Carbo? Had not several delighted Pompeians just hastened away to Lesbos, to convey to Cornelia, the wife of the Magnus, the joyful tidings that Cæsar's power was broken and the war was over?

Throughout the Pompeian camps there was feasting and revelry, soldiers trolled low songs deriding their opponents, and drunk themselves stupid, celebrating in advance the return of the victorious army to Italy. Their officers were looking forward even more eagerly to their reinstatement in their old haunts and pleasures at Rome. Lucius Ahenobarbus, who was outside the tent of the Magnus, while his father was taking part in the conference, was busy recounting to a crony the arrangements he was making.

"I have sent a freedman back to Rome to see that my rooms are furnished and put in order. But I have told him that I need a suite near the Forum, if possible, so as to be convenient for the canvass when I sue for quæstor at the next election, for it is time I began on my 'round of offices.'" (A "round of offices" being, according to this worthy young gentleman, an inalienable right to every male scion of his family.)

Within the debate was waxing hot. Not that any one had the least doubts that the Cæsarians were at their last gasp; rather it was so extremely difficult to decide how the spoils of victory were to be equitably shared, and what was almost equally important, how the hostile and the neutral were to be punished. The noble lords were busy settling amongst themselves who should be consuls for several years to come, and how the confiscated villas of the proscribed Cæsarians should be divided. As to the military situation, they were all complaisance.

"There is no need for a real battle," Pompeius was saying. "Our superior cavalry will rout their whole army before the infantry join the attack."

And Labienus, the only officer who had deserted Cæsar, protested that the opposing legions had long since been thinned of their Gallic veterans, that only raw recruits composed them now.

Loudly the councillors wrangled over the successor to Cæsar's pontificate; Scipio, Domitius, and another great noble, Lentulus Spinther, all had their claims. Domitius was clamouring against delay in disposing of Cæsar, and in returning to Italy, to begin a general distribution of spoils, and sanguinary requital of enemies and neutrals. The contest over the pontificate grew more and more acrimonious each minute.

"Gentlemen," broke in Pompeius, "I would that you could agree amongst yourselves. It is a grievous thing that we must thus quarrel with bitterness, when victory is within our grasp."

But the war of words went on hotter and hotter. Lentulus Crus noticed that Pompeius looked pale and worried.

"You look careworn, Magnus," he whispered; "it will be a relief for the burdens of war to be off your shoulders!"

"I know not how this all will come out," said the general. "All the chances are in our favour. We have numbers, the best position, cavalry, the prestige of victory. Labienus cannot be mistaken in his estimate of Cæsar's men; yet I am afraid, I am almost timorous."

"It is but the natural fear lest some slight event dim your excellency's great glory. Our position is too secure for reverse," remarked Lentulus, soothingly.

"Great glory —" repeated Pompeius, "yes, that makes me afraid. Remember Ulamhala's words, — they haunt me: —

> "'He that is highest shall rise yet higher,
> He that is second shall utterly fall.'

Lentulus, I *know* Cæsar is greater than I!"

Before he could continue, Labienus had risen to his feet in the council.

"An oath! an oath, gentlemen!" cried the renegade legate. "Swear all after me! 'By Jupiter Capitolinus, Optimus, Maximus, I swear not to return from the battle until victorious over Cæsar!'"

All the council rose.

"We swear!" cried a score of tongues, as though their oath was the lightest thing imaginable.

"Bravely done!" shouted Labienus, while the two Lentuli and Domitius and Scipio and many another scion of the great noble houses joined in the oath. "*Hem!* Most excellent

2 B

Magnus, you do not have confidence enough in your own cause to join us. Do you doubt our loyalty or soldierly qualities!"

"*Perpol!*" replied Pompeius, with a rather ill-concealed effort to speak gayly, "do you think, good Labienus, that I am as distrustful of you as Cæsar ought to be of his men?"

And the Magnus also took the oath.

Outside the tent the sentries were exchanging their challenges. It was the end of the second watch of the night.[1]

"It is late, gentlemen," said Pompeius. "I believe that I have given my orders. Remember our watch-word for tomorrow."

"*Hercules Invictus!*" shouted one and all.

"'Unconquerable' we shall be, I trust," continued the commander-in-chief. "Good-night, gentlemen; we meet to-morrow."

The council broke up, and filed out of the tent. Lentulus Spinther paused to cast a look of savage anger at Scipio, who lingered behind. The contest over the pontificate still rankled in his breast. That four and twenty hours hence both of these aristocratic gentlemen might have more pressing things to think of seemingly entered the head of neither. Lentulus Crus, Domitius, and Scipio waited after the others were gone.

"I have been wondering all day," said the genial Domitius, when the tent had emptied, "how Cæsar will comport himself if he is taken prisoner and not slain in battle. I give him credit for not being likely to flee away."

"I trust he will die a soldier's death," replied Pompeius, gloomily. "It would be a grievous thing to have him fall into my hands. He has been my friend, my father-in-law. I could not treat him harshly."

"Doubtless," said the ever suave Lentulus Crus, "it would

[1] Midnight.

be most disagreeable for you, Magnus, to have to reward such an enemy of the Republic as he deserves. But your excellency will, of course, bow to the decrees of the Senate, and—I fear it will be very hard to persuade the conscript fathers that Cæsar has earned any mercy."

"*Vah!* gentlemen," retorted Pompeius, pressing his hands together, and walking up and down: "I have been your tool a long while! I never at heart desired this war! A hundred times I would draw back, but you in some way prevented. I have been made to say things that I would fain have left unsaid. I am perhaps less educated and more superstitious than you. I believe that there are gods, and they punish the shedders of innocent blood. And much good Roman blood has been shed since you had your way, and drove Cæsar into open enmity!"

"Of course," interposed Domitius, his face a little flushed with suppressed anger, "it is a painful thing to take the lives of fellow-countrymen; but consider the price that patriots must pay for liberty."

"Price paid for liberty," snorted Pompeius, in rising disgust, "*phui!* Let us at least be honest, gentlemen! It is very easy to cry out on tyrants when our ambition has been disappointed. But I am wasting words. Only this let me say. When, to-morrow, we have slain or captured our enemy, it will be *I* that determine the future policy of the state, and not *you!* I will prove myself indeed the Magnus! I will be a tool no longer."

The three consulars stared at each other, at loss for words.

"Time wastes, gentlemen," said Pompeius. "To your several commands! You have your orders."

The Magnus spoke in a tone that admonished the three oligarchs to bow in silence and go out without a word.

" His excellency is a bit tempted to play the high tragedian to-night," sneered Domitius, recovering from his first consternation. " He will think differently to-morrow. But of all things, my good Lentulus (if it comes your way), see that Cæsar is quietly killed — no matter what fashion; it will save us endless trouble."

" *Mehercle!* " quoth the other, " do I need that advice ? And again remind me to-morrow of this. We must arrange the dividing of the estate of that young reprobate, Quintus Drusus, who gave us some anxiety two years ago. But I imagine that must be deferred until after the battle."

And so they separated, and the two armies — scarce five miles apart — slept; and the stars watched over them.

III

The sun was climbing out of the dark bank of clouds that pressed down upon the eastern horizon. The green plain of Pharsalus lay spread out far and wide under the strengthening light; the distant hills were peering dimly out from the mist; the acropolis of Pharsalus itself, — perhaps the Homeric Phthia, dwelling of Achilles, — with its two peaked crags, five hundred feet in height, frowned down upon the Cæsarian camp. The Enipeus and one or two minor streams were threading their way in silver ribbons down toward the distant Peneus. The fertile plain was green and verdant with the bursting summer. The scent of clover hung in the air, and with it the fragrance of thyme. Wild flowers were scattered under the feet. The early honeybee was hovering over the dew-laden petals. Wakeful thrushes were carolling out of the thickets. A thin grey fog was drifting off of the valley, soon to vanish in the blue of a perfect day. Clear and sweet the notes of the trumpets called the soldiers from their camp. The weary men shook the sleep from their eyes. There was a hurried pounding of grain in the stone mortars, breakfasts even more hurried. Then again the trumpets called out their signal. Busy hands tore up the tent pegs, other hands were folding the coverings, gathering up the poles and impedimenta, and loading them on the baggage animals.

The soldiers were grumbling as soldiers will. Drusus, who emerged from his own tent just as it was about to be pulled down about his ears, heard one private growl to another: "Look at the sun rising! What a hot day we shall have! *Ædepol!* will there never be an end to this marching and countermarching, skirmishing and intrenching, — water to drink, *puls* to eat, — I didn't take the oath[1] for that. No plunder here, and the sack of Gomphi, the last town stormed, amounted to nothing."

Drusus would have rebuked the man for breeding discontent in the army, but at that moment he and every other around him for once relaxed that stringent discipline that held them in bands of iron. A third trumpet call cut the air, quick, shrill, penetrating.

"To arms!" Every centurion was shouting it to his men. The baggage animals were left unladen. A cohort that was about to leave the camp in marching order halted, and began to throw away its impedimenta, when Cæsar himself rode up to them.

"Fellow-soldiers," said the Imperator, smiling as though he had to reveal a great piece of good fortune, "we can postpone the march. Let us put our hearts into the battle for which we have longed, and meet the foe with resolute souls, for now or never is our opportunity!"

"*Io! Io!*" cried a thousand hoarse throats.

[1] The military oath of obedience.

Out of confusion came the most perfect order. Drusus ran to the horse that he had yielded for a pack animal on the march, saddled, mounted, flew away to Cæsar's side, his heart pounding in his breast.

"Pompeius is leading out his men!" soldier was shouting to soldier. Legion after legion filed forth from the camp. Cæsar, sitting with easy grace on his own favourite charger which he himself had bred, gave in calm, deliberate voice the last orders to his legates. Drusus drew rein at the general's side, ready to go anywhere or do anything that was needed, his position being one of general aide-de-camp.

Cæsar was facing east; Pompeius, west. Five miles of mainly level country had extended between the camps, but Pompeius had pitched on a hill site, with a river and hills to flank him. There he might safely have defied attack. But he had come down from the eminence. He had led his army out into the plain, and the camp was a full mile behind. The long ranks of the Pompeians were splendid with all the bravery of war. On the right wing by the river lay his Cilician and Spanish cohorts, led by Lentulus Crus, — the flower of the Pompeian infantry. Scipio held the centre with two Syrian legions. On the left, Domitius was in command and Pompeius accompanied him. Seven cohorts were behind in the fortified camp. A great mass of auxiliaries and volunteers, as well as two thousand reënlisted veterans, gave strength to the lines of fully recruited cohorts. Out on the left wing, reaching up on to the foothills, lay the pride of the oligarchs, seven thousand splendid cavalry, the pick and flower of the exiled youth and nobility of Rome, reënforced by the best squadrons of the East. Here Labienus led. The Pompeian ranks were in three lines, drawn up ten deep. Forty-five thousand heavy infantry were they; and the horse and light troops were half as many —

Spaniards, Africans, Italian exiles, Greeks, Asiatics — the glory
of every warlike, classic race.

Slowly, slowly, the Cæsarian legionaries advanced over the
plain.   Drusus knew that one of the most crucial hours of his
life was before him, yet he was very calm.   He saw some wild
roses growing on a bush by the way, and thought how pretty
they would look in a wreath on Cornelia's hair.   He exchanged
jokes with his fellow-officers; scolded a soldier who had come
away without his sword in his sheath; asked Antonius, when
he came across him, if he did not envy Achilles for his country-
seat.   It was as if he were going on the same tedious march of
days and days gone by.   Yet, with it all, he felt himself far
more intensely excited than ever before.   He knew that his
calm was so unnatural that he wished to cry aloud, to run,
weep, to do anything to break it.   This was to be the end of
the great drama that had begun the day Lentulus and Marcellus
first sat down as consuls !

Slowly, slowly, that long snake, the marching army,
dragged out of the camp.   The sun was high in the sky;
the last cloud had vanished; the blue above was as clear
and translucent as it is conceivable anything may be and
yet retain its colour — not become clear light.   The head of
the column was six hundred paces from the silent Pompeian lines which awaited them.   Then cohort after cohort
filed off to the right and left, and the line of battle was ready.
On the right was the tenth legion, on the left the weak ninth,
reënforced by the eighth.   There were eighty cohorts in all,
to oppose one hundred and ten.   But the ranks of Cæsar's
cohorts were thin.   The numbers were scarce half as many as
in those of the foe.   And to confront Labienus and his cavalry Cæsar had but one thousand horse.   His army stood in
three lines, facing the enemy's infantry; but, though it weak-

ened his own legions dangerously, there was but one thing to
do, unless Labienus was to force around the flank, and sweep
all before him. Six cohorts Cæsar stationed at the rear of his
right wing, a defence against the hostile cavalry. The third
line of the legions the Imperator commanded to hold back
until he ordered them otherwise, for on them lay the turning
of the battle.

Antonius commanded the left, Publius Sulla the right, Cal-
vinus the centre. Cæsar himself took post on his own right
wing opposite Pompeius. Then, when the lines were formed, he
rode down before his men, and addressed them; not in gaudy
eloquence, as if to stir a flagging courage, but a manly request
that they quit themselves as became his soldiers. Ever had
he sought reconciliation, he said, ever peace; unwillingly had
he exposed his own soldiers, and unwillingly attacked his enemies. And to the six chosen cohorts in the fourth line he
gave a special word, for he bade them remember that doubtless on their firmness would depend the fate of the battle.

"Yes," he said in closing, while every scarred and tattered
veteran laughed at the jest, "only thrust your pila in the
faces of those brave cavaliers. They will turn and flee if
their handsome faces are likely to be bruised." And a grim
chuckle went down the line, relieving the tension that was
making the oldest warriors nervous.

Cæsar galloped back to his position on his own right wing.
The legions were growing restive, and there was no longer
cause for delay. The officers were shouting the battle-cry
down the lines. The Imperator nodded to his trumpeter, and
a single sharp, long peal cut the air. The note was drowned
in the rush of twenty thousand feet, the howl of myriads of
voices.

"*Venus victrix!*" The battle-cry was tossed from mouth to

mouth, louder and louder, as the mighty mass of men in iron
swept on.

"*Venus victrix!*" And the shout itself was dimmed in the
crash of mortal battle, when the foremost Cæsarians sent their
pila dashing in upon the enemy, and closed with the short
sword, while their comrades piled in upon them. Crash after
crash, as cohort struck cohort; and so the battle joined.

* * * * * * * * * *

Why was the battle of Pharsalus more to the world than
fifty other stricken fields where armies of strength equal to
those engaged there joined in conflict? Why can these other
battles be passed over as dates and names to the historian,
while he assigns to this a position beside Marathon and
Arbela and Tours and the Defeat of the Armada and Waterloo
and Gettysburg? What was at stake — that Cæsar or Pompeius and his satellites should rule the world? Infinitely
more — the struggle was for the very existence of civilization,
to determine whether or not the fabric of ordered society was
to be flung back into chaos. The Roman Republic had conquered the civilized world; it had thrown down kings; it had
destroyed the political existence of nations. What but feeble-
ness, corruption, decay, anarchy, disintegration, disruption,
recurring barbarism, had the oligarchs, for whom Pompeius
was fighting his battle, to put in the place of what the Republic had destroyed? Could a Senate where almost every man
had his price, where almost every member looked on the provinces as a mere feeding ground for personal enrichment —
could such a body govern the world? Were not German and
Gaul ready to pluck this unsound organism called the Republic limb from limb, and where was the reviving, regenerating
force that was to hold them back with an iron hand until a
force greater than that of the sword was ready to carry its

evangel unto all nations, Jew, Greek, Roman, barbarian, — bond and free? These were the questions asked and answered on that ninth day of August, forty-nine years before the birth of a mightier than Pompeius Magnus or Julius Cæsar. And because men fought and agonized and died on those plains by Pharsalus, the edict could go from Rome that all the world should be taxed, and a naturalized Roman citizen could scorn the howls of the provincial mobs, could mock at Sanhedrins seeking his blood, and cry: *"Civis Romanus sum. Cæsarem appello!"*

How long did the battle last? Drusus did not know. No one knew. He flew at the heels of his general's charger, for where Cæsar went there the fight was thickest. He saw the Pompeian heavy infantry standing stolidly in their ranks to receive the charge — a fatal blunder, that lost them all the enthusiasm aggression engenders. The Cæsarian veterans would halt before closing in battle, draw breath, and dash over the remaining interval with redoubled vigour. The Pompeians received them manfully, sending back javelin for javelin; then the short swords flashed from their scabbards, and man pressed against man — staring into one another's face — seeking one another's blood; striking, striking with one thought, hope, instinct — to stride across his enemy's dead body.

The Pompeian reserves ran up to aid their comrades in the line. The odds against the Cæsarian cohorts were tremendous. The pressure of shield against shield never abated. Woe to the man who lost footing and fell; his life was trampled out in a twinkling! The battle-cries grew fewer and fewer; shouting requires breath; breath, energy; and every scruple of energy was needed in pushing on those shields. There were few pila left now. The short swords dashed upon the armour, but in the press even to swing a blade was difficult. More and more intense grew the strain; Cæsarians gave ground here and then regained it. Pompeians did the like yonder. The long reach of the line swayed to and fro, rippling like a dark ribbon in the wind. Now and then a combatant would receive a mortal wound, and go down out of sight in the throng, which closed over him almost ere he could utter one sharp cry.

Cæsar was everywhere. His voice rang like a clarion down the lines; he knew, as it were, each soldier by name — and when a stout blow was to be struck, or a stand was needed to bear up against the weight of hostile numbers, Cæsar's praise or admonition to stand firm was as a fresh cohort flung into the scale. Drusus rode with him, both mounted, hence unable to mingle in the press, but exposed to the showers of arrows and sling-stones which the Pompeian auxiliaries rained upon them. Cæsar's red paludamentum marked him out a conspicuous figure for the aim of the missiles, but he bore a charmed life.

Drusus himself did what he could to steady the men. The contest in the line of battle could not continue long, flesh and blood might not endure the strain.

"Imperator," cried Drusus, riding up to his chief, "you see that this can last no longer. Our men are overmatched. Shall I order up the third line? The centurion Crastinus, who swore that he would win your gratitude living or dead, is slain after performing deeds worthy of his boast. Many others have gone down. What shall I do?"

Cæsar drew rein, and cast his eyes down the swaying lines.

"I dare not order up the third line so early," he began; then, with a glance to the extreme right, "Ah, *Mehercle!* we are at the crisis now! Our cavalry have given way before the enemy's horse. They are outflanking us!"

"The six cohorts!" cried Drusus.

"The six cohorts — ride!　Make them stop those horse, or all is lost!　On your life, go!"

And away went Drusus.　The supreme moment of his life had come.　The whole act of being, he felt, he knew, had been only that he might live at that instant.　What the next hour had in store — life, death — he cared not at all.　The Cæsarian horse, outnumbered seven to one, had fought valiantly, but been borne back by sheer weight of numbers.　With not a man in sight to oppose them, the whole mass of the splendid Pompeian cavalry was sweeping around to crush the unprotected flank of the tenth legion.　The sight of the on-rushing squadrons was beyond words magnificent.　The tossing mass of their panoplies was a sea of scarlet, purple, brass, and flashing steel; the roar of the hoof-beats of seven thousand blooded coursers swept on like the approaching of the wind leading the clouds in whose breast are thunder and lightning unfettered.　Behind them rose the dun vapour of the dust, drifting up toward heaven, — the whirling vortex of the storm.　It was indeed the crisis.

The six cohorts were standing, resting on their shields, in the rear of the extreme right flank of the third line.　They were in an oblique formation.　The most distant cohort extended far back, and far beyond the Cæsarian line of battle.　The hearts of the soldiers were in the deathly press ahead, but they were veterans; discipline held them quiet, albeit restive in soul.

On swept the roar of the advancing Pompeians.　What must be done must be done quickly.　Drusus drove the spurs into his horse, and approached the cohorts on a headlong gallop.

"Forward!　I will lead you against the enemy!"

No need of second command.　The maniples rushed onward

as though the men were runners in a race, not soldiers clothed in armour. Drusus flew down the ranks and swung the farthest cohorts into alignment with the others. There was not a moment to lose.

"Now, men, if ye be indeed soldiers of Cæsar, at them!"

Drusus was astounded at the resonance of his own voice; a thousand others caught up the shout.

"*Venus victrix!*" And straight into the teeth of the galloping hosts charged the thin line of infantry.

The line was weak, its members strong. They were rural Italians, uncorrupted by city life, hardy, god-fearing peasants and sons of peasants, worthy descendants of the men who died in the legions at Cannæ, or triumphed at the Metaurus. Steady as on a review the six cohorts bore down into action. And when they struck the great mass of horsemen they thrust their pila into the riders' eyes and prodded the steeds. The foremost cavalrymen drew rein; the horses reared. The squadrons were colliding and plunging. In an eye's twinkling their momentum had been checked.

"Charge! Charge!" Drusus sent the word tossing down along the cohorts, and the legionaries pressed forward. It was done. The whole splendid array of horsemen broke in rout; they went streaming back in disordered squadrons over the plain, each trooper striving to outride his fellow in the flight. Pompeius had launched his most deadly bolt, and it had failed.

Now was Drusus's chance. No further order had been given him; to pursue cavalry with infantry were folly; he needed no new commands. The six cohorts followed his lead like machinery. The crash of battle dimmed his voice; the sight of his example led the legionaries on. They fell on the Pompeian archers and slingers and dispersed them like smoke.

They wheeled about as on a pivot and struck the enemy's left wing; struck the Pompeian fighting line from the rear, and crushed it betwixt the upper and nether millstone of themselves and the tenth legion. Drusus drove into the very foremost of the fight; it was no longer a press, it was flight, pursuit, slaughter, and he forced his horse over one enemy after another — transformed, transfigured as he was into a demon of destruction, while the delirium of battle gained upon him.

Drusus saw the figure of a horseman clothed, like Cæsar, in a red general's cloak spurring away to the enemy's camp. He called to his men that Pompeius had taken panic and fled away; that the battle was won. He saw the third line of the Cæsarians drive through the Pompeian centre and right as a plough cuts through the sandy field, and then spread terror, panic, rout — the battle became a massacre.

So the Cæsarians hunted their foes over the plain to the camp. And, though the sun on high rained down a pitiless heat, none faltered when the Imperator bade them use their favour with Fortune, and lose not a moment in storming the encampment. They assailed the ramparts. The Pompeian reserve cohorts stood against them like men; the Thracian and other auxiliary light troops sent down clouds of missiles — of what avail? There are times when mortal might can pass seas of fire and mountains of steel; and this was one of those moments. The Pompeians were swept from the ramparts by a pitiless shower of javelins. The panic still was upon them; standards of cohorts, eagles of legions, they threw them all away. They fled — fled casting behind shields, helmets, swords, anything that hindered their running. The hills, the mountain tops, were their only safety. Their centurions and tribunes were foremost among the fugitives. And from these mountain crests they were to come down the next morning and surrender themselves prisoners to the conquerors — petitioners for their lives.

Not all were thus fated. For in the flight from the camp Domitius fell down from fatigue, and Marcus Antonius, whose hand knew no weariness, neither his heart remorse or mercy, slew him as a man would slay a snake. And so perished one of the evil spirits that hounded Pompeius to his death, the Roman oligarchy to its downfall.

Drusus sought far and wide for Lentulus and Lucius Ahenobarbus. The consular had fought on the most distant wing, and in the flight he and his mortal enemy did not meet. Neither did Drusus come upon the younger son of the slain Domitius. Fortune kept the two asunder. But slaying enough for one day the young Livian had wrought. He rode with Cæsar through the splendid camp just captured. The flowers had been twined over the arbours under which the victory was to be celebrated; the plate was on the tables; choice viands and wines were ready; the floors of the tents were covered with fresh sods; over the pavilion of Lentulus Crus was a great shade of ivy. The victors rode out from the arbours toward the newly taken ramparts. There lay the dead, heaps upon heaps, the patrician dress proclaiming the proud lineage of the fallen; Claudii, Fabii, Æmilii, Furii, Cornelii, Sempronii, and a dozen more great *gentes* were represented — scions of the most magnificent oligarchy the world has ever seen. And this was their end! Cæsar passed his hand over his forehead and pressed his fingers upon his eyes.

"They would have it so," he said, in quiet sadness, to the little knot of officers around him. "After all that I had done for my country, I, Caius Cæsar, would have been condemned by them like a criminal, if I had not appealed to my army."

And so ended that day and that battle. On the field and in

the camp lay dead two hundred Cæsarians and fifteen thousand Pompeians.   Twenty-four thousand prisoners had been taken, one hundred and eighty standards, nine eagles.   As for the Magnus, he had stripped off his general's cloak and was riding with might and main for the seacoast, accompanied by thirty horsemen.

CHAPTER XXII

THE END OF THE MAGNUS

1

THE months had come and gone for Cornelia as well as for Quintus Drusus, albeit in a very different manner. The war was raging upon land and sea. The Pompeian fleet controlled all the water avenues; the Italian peninsula was held by the Cæsarians. Cornelia wrote several times to old Mamercus at Præneste, enclosing a letter which she begged him to forward to her lover wherever he might be. But no answer came. Once she learned definitely that the ship had been captured. For the other times she could imagine the same catastrophe. Still she had her comfort. Rumours of battles, of sieges, and arduous campaigning drifted over the Mediterranean. Now it was that a few days more would see Cæsar an outlaw without a man around him, and then Cornelia would believe none of it. Now it was that Pompeius was in sore straits, and then she was all credulity. Yet beside these tidings there were other stray bits of news very dear to her heart. Cæsar, so it was said, possessed a young aide-de-camp of great valour and ability, one Quintus Drusus, and the Imperator was already entrusting him with posts of danger and of responsibility. He had behaved gallantly at Ilerda; he had won more laurels at the siege of Massilia. At Dyrrachium he had gained yet more credit. And on account of these tidings, it may easily be imagined that Cornelia was prepared to be very patient and to be willing to take the trying vicissitudes of her own life more lightly.

As a matter of fact, her own position at Alexandria had begun to grow complicated. First of all, Agias had made one day a discovery in the city which it was exceeding well for Artemisia was not postponed for a later occasion. Pratinas was in Alexandria. The young Greek had not been recognized when, as chance meetings will occur, he came across his one-time antagonist face to face on the street. He had no fears for himself. But Artemisia was no longer safe in the city. Cleomenes arranged that the girl should be sent to a villa, owned by the relatives of his late wife, some distance up the Nile. Artemisia would thus be parted from Agias, but she would be quite safe; and to secure that, any sacrifice of stolen looks and pretty coquetry was cheerfully accepted.

Soon after this unpleasant little discovery, a far more serious event occurred. Pothinus the eunuch, Achillas, the Egyptian commander of the army, and Theodotus, a "rhetoric teacher," whose real business was to spin, not words, but court intrigues, had plotted together to place the young King Ptolemæus in sole power. The conspiracy ran its course. There was a rising of the "Macedonian"[1] guard at the palace, a gathering of citizens in the squares of the capital, culminating in bloody riots and proclamations declaring the king vested with the only supreme power. Hot on the heels of this announcement it was bruited around the city that Cleopatra had escaped safely to Palestine, where, in due time, she would doubtless be collecting an army at the courts of Hyrcanus, the

---

[1] Macedonian it is needless to say was a mere name. The Græco-Egyptian soldiery and citizen body of Alexandria probably had hardly a drop of Macedonian blood in their veins.

Jewish prince, and other Syrian potentates, to return and retake the crown.

Alexandria was accustomed to such dynastic disruptions. The rioting over, the people were ready to go back to the paper and linen factories, and willing to call Ptolemæus the "Son of Ra," or "King," until his sister should defeat him in battle. Cornelia grieved that Cleopatra should thus be forced into exile. She had grown more and more intimate with the queen. The first glamour of Cleopatra's presence had worn away. Cornelia saw her as a woman very beautiful, very wilful, gifted with every talent, yet utterly lacking that moral stability which would have been the crown of a perfect human organism. The two women had grown more and more in friendship and intimacy; and when Cornelia studied in detail the dark, and often hideous, coils and twistings of the history of the Hellenistic royal families, the more vividly she realized that Cleopatra was the heiress of generations of legalized license,[1] of cultured sensuality, of veneered cruelty, and sheer blood-thirstiness. Therefore Cornelia had pitied, not blamed, the queen, and, now that misfortune had fallen upon her, was distressed for the plight of Cleopatra.

That Cornelia had been an intimate of the queen was perfectly well known in Alexandria. In fact, Cleomenes himself was of sufficiently high rank to make any guest he might long entertain more or less of a public personage. Cornelia was a familiar sight to the crowds, as she drove daily on the streets and attended the theatre. Cleomenes began to entertain suspicions that the new government was not quite pleased to leave such a friend of Cleopatra's at liberty; and Agias took pains to discover that Pratinas was deep in the counsels of the virtual

[1] As, for instance, the repeated wedlock of brothers and sisters among the Ptolemies.

regent — Pothinus. But Cornelia scoffed at any suggestions that it might be safer to leave the city and join Artemisia in the retreat up the Nile. She had taken no part whatsoever in Egyptian politics, and she was incapable of assisting to restore Cleopatra. As for the possible influence of Pratinas in court, it seemed to her incredible that a man of his caliber could work her any injury, save by the dagger and poison cup. That an ignoble intriguer of his type could influence the policy of state she refused to believe.

Thus it came to pass that Cornelia had only herself to thank, when the blow, such as it was, fell. The eunuch prime minister knew how to cover his actions with a velvet glove. One evening a splendidly uniformed division of Macedonian guard, led by one of the royal *somatophylakes*,[1] came with an empty chariot to the house of Cleomenes. The request they bore was signed with the royal seal, and was politeness itself. It overflowed with semi-Oriental compliment and laudation; but the purport was clear. On account of the great danger in the city to foreigners from riots — ran the gist of the letter — and the extremely disturbed condition of the times, the king was constrained to request Cornelia and Fabia to take up their residence in the palace, where they could receive proper protection and be provided for in a princely manner, as became their rank.

Cornelia had enough wisdom to see that only by taking the letter for the intentions written on its face could she submit to the implied command without loss of dignity. She had much difficulty in persuading Fabia to yield; for the Vestal was for standing on her Roman prerogatives and giving way to nothing except sheer force. But Cleomenes added his word, that only harm would come from resistance; and the two

[1] Commanders of the body-guard.

Roman ladies accompanied the escort back to the palace. It was not pleasant to pass into the power of a creature like Pothinus, even though the smooth-faced eunuch received his unwilling guests with Oriental salaams and profuse requests to be allowed to humour their least desires. But the restraint, if such it can be called, could hardly take a less objectionable form. Monime and Berenice, as ladies whose father was known as a merchant prince of colourless politics, were allowed free access to their friends at the palace. Young Ptolemæus, who was a dark-eyed and, at bottom, dark-hearted youth, completely under the thumb of Pothinus, exerted himself, after a fashion, to be agreeable to his visitors; but he was too unfavourable a contrast to his gifted sister to win much grace in Cornelia's eyes. Agias, who was living with Cleomenes, nominally for the purpose of learning the latter's business, preparatory to becoming a partner on capital to come from his predatory cousin, as a matter of fact spent a great part of his time at the palace also, dancing attendance upon his Roman friends. Pratinas, indeed, was on hand, not really to distress them, but to vex by the mere knowledge of his presence. Cornelia met the Greek with a stony haughtiness that chilled all his professions of desire to serve her and to renew the acquaintance formed at Rome. Agias had discovered that Pratinas had advised Pothinus to keep his hands on the ladies, especially on Cornelia, because whichever side of the Roman factions won, there were those who would reward suitably any who could deliver her over to them. From this Cornelia had to infer that the defeat of the Cæsarians meant her own enthralment to her uncle and Lucius Ahenobarbus. Such a contingency she would not admit as possible. She was simply rendered far more anxious. Pratinas had given up seeking Drusus's life, it was clear; his interest in the matter had ended the very instant the chance to levy blackmail on Aheno barbus had disappeared. Pratinas, in fact, Agias learned for her, was never weary ridiculing the Roman oligarchs, and professing his disgust with them; so Cornelia no longer had immediate cause to fear him, though she hated him none the less.

After all, Pratinas thrust himself little upon her. He had his own life to live, and it ran far apart from hers. Perhaps it was as well for Cornelia that she was forced to spend the winter and ensuing months in the ample purlieus of the palace If living were but the gratification of sensuous indolence, if existence were but luxurious dozing and half-waking, then the palace of the Ptolemies were indeed an Elysium, with its soft-footed, silent, swift, intelligent Oriental servants; rooms where the eye grew weary of rare sculpture or fresco; books drawn from the greatest library in the world — the Museum close at hand; a broad view of the blue Mediterranean, ever changing and ever the same, and of the swarming harbour and the bustling city; and gardens upon gardens shut off from the outside by lofty walls — some great enclosures containing besides forests of rare trees a vast menagerie of wild beasts, whose roarings from their cages made one think the groves a tropical jungle; some gardens, dainty, secluded spots laid out in Egyptian fashion, under the shade of a few fine old sycamores, with a vineyard and a stone trellis-work in the midst, with arbours and little parks of exotic plants, a palm or two, and a tank where the half-tame water-fowl would plash among the lotus and papyrus plants. In such a nook as this Cornelia would sit and read all the day long, and put lotus flowers in her hair, look down into the water, and, Narcissus-like, fall in love with her own face, and tell herself that Drusus would be delighted that she had not grown ugly since he parted with her.

So passed the winter and the spring and early summer months; and, however hot and parched might be the city under the burning sun, there was coolness and refreshment in the gardens of the palace.

With it all, however, Cornelia began to wax restive. It is no light thing to command one's self to remain quiet in Sybaritic ease. More and more she began to wish that this butterfly existence, this passive basking in the sun of indolent luxury, would come to an end. She commenced again to wish that she were a man, with the tongue of an orator, the sword of a soldier, able to sway senates and to lead legions. Pothinus finally discovered that he was having some difficulty in keeping his cage-bird contented. The eunuch had entertained great expectations of being able to win credit and favour with the conquerors among the Romans by delivering over Cornelia safe and sound either to Lentulus Crus or Quintus Drusus. Now he began to fear that Pratinas had advised him ill; that Cornelia and Fabia were incapable of intriguing in Cleopatra's favour, and by his "protection at the palace" he was only earning the enmity of his noble guests. But it was too late to retrace his steps, and he accordingly plied Cornelia with so many additional attentions, presents, and obsequious flatteries, that she grew heartily disgusted and repined even more over her present situation.

Bad news came, which added to her discomfort. Cæsar had been driven from his lines at Dyrrachium. He had lost a great many men. If the Pompeian sources of information were to be believed, he was now really a negligible military factor, and the war was practically over. The tidings fell on Cornelia's soul like lead. She knew perfectly well that the defeat of the Cæsarians would mean the death of Quintus Drusus. Her uncle and the Domitii, father and son, would be all powerful, and they never forgave an enmity. As for herself — but she did not think much thereon; if Drusus was slain or executed, she really had very little to live for, and there were many ways of getting out of the world. For the first time since the memorable night of the raid on Baiæ, she went about with an aching heart. Fabia, too, suffered, but, older and wiser, comforted Cornelia not so much by what she might say, by way of extending hopes, as by the warm, silent contact of her pure, noble nature. Monime and Berenice were grieved that their friends were so sad, and used a thousand gentle arts to comfort them. Cornelia bore up more bravely because of the sympathy — she did not have to endure her burden alone, as at Rome and Baiæ; but, nevertheless, for her the days crept slowly.

And then out of the gloom came the dazzling brightness. A Rhodian merchantman came speeding into the haven with news. "Is Cæsar taken?" cried the inquisitive crowd on the quay, as the vessel swung up to her mooring. "Is Pompeius not already here?" came back from the deck. And in a twinkling it was all over the city: in the Serapeium, in the Museum, under the colonnades, in the factories, in the palace. "Pompeius's army has been destroyed. The Magnus barely escaped with his life. Lucius Domitius is slain. Cæsar is master of the world!"

Never did the notes of the great water-organ of the palace sound so sweet in any ears as these words in those of the Roman ladies. They bore with complacency a piece of petty tyranny on the part of Pothinus, which at another time they would have found galling indeed. Report had it that Cleopatra had gathered an army in Syria, and the eunuch, with his royal puppet, was going forth to the frontier town of Pelusium, to head the forces that should resist the invasion. Cornelia and

Fabia were informed that they would accompany the royal party on its progress to the frontier. Pothinus clearly was beginning to fear the results of his "honourable entertainment," and did not care to have his guests out of his sight. It was vexatious to be thus at his mercy; but Cornelia was too joyous in soul, at that time, to bear the indignity heavily. They had to part with Monime and Berenice, but Agias went with them; and Cornelia sent off another letter to Italy, in renewed hope that the seas would be clear and it would find its way safely to Drusus.

Very luxurious was the progress of the royal party to Pelusium. The king, his escort, and his unwilling guests travelled slowly by water, in magnificent river barges that were fitted with every requisite or ornament that mind of man might ask or think. They crossed the Lake Mareotis, glided along one of the minor outlets of the delta until they reached the Bolbitinic branch of the Nile, then, by canals and natural watercourses, worked their way across to Bubastis, and thence straight down the Pelusiac Nile to Pelusium. And thus it was Cornelia caught glimpses of that strange, un-Hellenized country that stretched away to the southward, tens and hundreds of miles, to Memphis and its pyramids, and Thebes and its temples — ancient, weird, wonderful; a civilization whereof everything was older than human thought might trace; a civilization that was almost like the stars, the same yesterday, to-day, and forever. Almost would Cornelia have been glad if the prows of the barges had been turned up the river, and she been enabled to behold with her own eyes the mighty piles of Cheops, Chephren, Mycerinus, Sesostris, Rhampsinitus, and a score of other Pharaohs whose deeds are recorded in stone imperishable. But the barges glided again northward, and Cornelia only occasionally caught some glimpse of a massive temple, under whose huge propylons the priests had chanted their litanies to Pakht or Ptah for two thousand years, or passed some boat gliding with its mourners to the necropolis, there to leave the mummy that was to await the judgment of Osiris. And down the long valley swept the hot winds from the realm of the Pygmies, and from those strange lakes and mountains whence issued the boundless river, which was the life-giver and mother of all the fertile country of Egypt.

Thus with a glimpse, all too short, of the "Black Land,"[1] as its native denizens called it, the royal party reached the half-Hellenized town of Pelusium, where the army was in waiting and a most splendid camp was ready for Ptolemæus and his train. Cleopatra had not yet advanced. The journey was over, and the novelty of the luxurious quarters provided in the frontier fortress soon died away. Cornelia could only possess her soul in patience, and wonder how long it would be before a letter could reach Italy, and the answer return. Where was Drusus? Had aught befallen him in the great battle? Did he think of her? And so, hour by hour, she repeated her questions — and waited.

II

Cleopatra's forces had not reached proportions sufficient for her to risk an engagement, when a little squadron appeared before Pelusium bearing no less a person than Pompeius himself, who sent ashore to demand, on the strength of former services to the late King Ptolemæus Auletes, a safe asylum, and assistance to make fresh head against the Cæsarians. There was a hurried convening of the council of Pothinus — a select company of eunuchs, amateur generals, intriguing rhetoricians. The conference was long; access to its debates

[1] "Black" because of the black fertile mud deposited by the inundation.

closely guarded. The issue could not be evaded; on the decision depended the reëstablishment of the Pompeians in a new and firm stronghold, or their abandonment to further wanderings over the ocean. All Pelusium realized what was at stake, and the excitement ran high.

Cornelia beyond others was agitated by the report of the arrival of the Magnus. Rumour had it that Lucius Lentulus was close behind him. If the council of Pothinus voted to receive the fugitives, her own position would be unhappy indeed. For a time at least she would fall into the power of her uncle and of Lucius Ahenobarbus. She was fully determined, if it was decided to harbour the Pompeians, to try to escape from the luxurious semi-captivity in which she was restrained. She could escape across the frontier to the camp of Cleopatra, where she knew a friendly welcome was in waiting. Agias, ever resourceful, ever anxious to anticipate the slightest wish on the part of the Roman ladies, actually began to bethink himself of the ways and means for a flight. When finally it was announced in the camp and city that Pompeius was to be received as a guest of the king, Cornelia was on the point of demanding of Agias immediate action toward escape.

"In a few days," were her words, "my uncle will be here; and I am undone, if not you also. There is not an hour to lose."

But Agias reasoned otherwise. If Pothinus and Achillas had really consented to receive the Magnus, flight was indeed necessary. Agias, however, had grounds, he thought, for hesitancy. He knew that Achillas, the head of the army, bitterly opposed the idea of letting Pompeius land; he knew, what was almost as much to the point, that Pratinas did not care to enew certain acquaintanceships contracted at Rome. There fore the young Hellene calmed Cornelia's fears, and waited as best he might.

The council had convened early in the day; the herald went through the squares of Pelusium announcing that Ptolemæus, " Son of Ra," would receive as his guest the Roman suppliant. The shore fronting the anchorage was covered with the files of the royal army in full array. Several Egyptian men-of-war had been drawn down into the water and their crews were hastening on board. Out in the haven rode the little fleet of the Pompeians. Agias had heard the proclamation, and hurried down to the mole to bear the earliest definite information to his mistress. Presently, out of the throng of officers and court magnates on the quay, stepped Achillas in a splendid panoply of gilded armour, with a purple chiton flowing down from beneath. Beside him, with the firm swinging step of the Roman legionary, strode two other officers in magnificent armour, whom Agias at once recognized as Lucius Septimius, a Roman tribune now in Egyptian service, and a certain Salvius, who had once been a centurion of the Republic. The three advanced on to the quay and stood for a moment at a loss. Agias, who was quite near, could hear their conversation.

" The yacht is not ready for us."

" We cannot delay a moment."

There was a large open boat moored to the quay, a fisher man's craft. In a moment a few subalterns had taken possession of it and there was a call for rowers. Agias, who, like all his race, never declined a chance " to see or hear some new thing," took his seat on one of the benches, and soon the craft shot away from the mole with the three officers in its stern.

It was a short pull to the Pompeian ships; Agias, as he glanced over his shoulder thought he could see a motion on board the vessels as if to sheer away from the boat; but in a moment the little craft was alongside, under the lee of the flagship.

"Where is Pompeius Magnus?" cried Achillas, rising from his seat; "we are sent to carry him to the king."

A martial, commanding figure was seen peering over the side, — a figure that every inhabitant of Rome knew right well.

"I am he; but why do you come thus meanly with only a fisher's boat? Is this honourable, is this worthy of a great king's guest?"

"Assuredly, kyrios," began Achillas, "we are forced to come in this small craft, because the water is too shallow for larger ships to approach the shore."

Agias knew that this was a lie; he was very certain that he was about to be witness to a deed of the darkest treachery. A vague feeling of shrinking and horror froze his limbs, and made his tongue swell in his mouth. Yet he was perfectly powerless to warn; a sign or a word would have meant his instant death.

"*Salve*, Imperator!" shouted Septimius in Latin, rising in turn. "Don't you remember the campaign I had with you against the pirates?"

The fugitive general's care-worn face lighted up at the recognition of an old officer.

"*Eu!*" he answered, "I shall not want for good friends, I see! How glad I shall be to grasp your hands! But is not this a very small boat? I see men going on board the galleys by the shore."

"You shall be satisfied in a moment, kyrios," repeated Achillas, with suave assurance, "that the quicksands by the mole are very dangerous to large vessels. Will you do us the honour to come aboard?"

Agias felt as though he must howl, scream, spring into the

sea — do anything to break the horrible suspense that oppressed him.

A woman was taking leave of Pompeius on the deck, a tall, stately, patrician lady, with a sweet, trouble-worn face; Agias knew that she was Cornelia Scipionis. She was adjuring her husband not to go ashore, and he was replying that it was impossible to refuse; that if the Egyptians meant evil, they could easily master all the fugitives with their armament. Several of the Magnus's servants came down into the boat — a couple of trusted centurions, a valued freedman called Philip, a slave named Scythes. Finally Pompeius tore himself from his wife's arms.

" Do not grieve, all will be well ! " were his words, while the boat's crew put out their hands to receive him ; and he added, " We must make the best choice of evils. I am no longer my own master. Remember Sophocles's iambics,

> " ' He that once enters at a tyrant's door
> Becomes a slave, though he were free before.' "

The general seated himself on the stern seat between the Egyptian officers. Agias bent to his oar in sheer relief at finding some way in which to vent his feelings; and tugged at the heavy paddle until its tough blade bent almost to cracking. The silence on the part of the officers was ominous. Not a word, not a hint of recognition, came from Achillas or his Italian associates, from the instant that Pompeius set foot in the boat. The stillness became awkward. The Magnus, flushed and embarrassed, turned to Septimius. " I was not mistaken in understanding that you were my fellow-soldier in years past ? " His answer was a surly nod. Pompeius, however, reined his rising feelings, and took up and began to re read some tablets on which he had written an address in Greek to be delivered before the king. Agias rowed on with the energy of helpless desperation. They were very close to the quay. A company of the royal body-guard in gala armour stood as if awaiting the distinguished visitor. For a moment the young Hellene believed that Achillas was sincere in his errand.

The boat drew up to the landing; one or two of the rowers sprang to the dock and made her fast. Agias was unshipping his oar. His thought was that he must now contrive the escape of Cornelia. Pompeius half rose from his seat; the boat was pitching in the choppy harbour swell; the general steadied himself by grasping the hands of Philip the freedman. Suddenly, like the swoop of a hawk on its prey, Agias saw the right hand of Septimius tear his short sword from its sheath. A scream broke from the Hellene's lips; before the Magnus could turn his head, the blow was struck. Pompeius received the blade full in the back, and staggered, while Salvius and Achillas likewise drew and thrust at him. Agias gazed on, paralyzed with horror. The general seized his red paludamentum, threw it over his face, groaned once, and fell. Even as he did so Septimius struck him across the neck, decapitating the corpse. The brutal boatmen tore the blood-soaked clothes off of the body, and flung it overboard, to drift ashore with the current. And so it ended with Pompeius Magnus, Imperator, the Fortunate, the favourite general of Sulla, the chieftain of "godlike and incredible virtue," the conquerer of the kingdoms of the East, thrice consul, thrice triumphator, joint ruler with Cæsar of the civilized world!

Agias hastened back to Cornelia to tell her that the danger was past, that there was no need of a flight to Cleopatra; but he was sick at heart when he thought of the treachery in which he had shared, albeit so unwillingly.

CHAPTER XXIII

BITTERNESS AND JOY

I

CORNELIA knew not whether to be merry or to weep when the report of the fate of Pompeius reached her. That she would be delivered up to her uncle was no longer to be dreaded; but into the hands of what manner of men had she herself fallen? Her own life and that of Fabia, she realized, would be snuffed out in a twinkling, by Pothinus and his confederates, the instant they saw in such a deed the least advantage. The splendid life of the court at the garrison city went on; there was an unending round of fêtes, contests in the gymnasium and stadium; chariot races; contests of poets and actors for prizes in dramatic art. To the outward eye nothing could be more decorous and magnificent than the pleasures of the Egyptian king. And so some days passed while Cornelia crushed her fears, and waited for the news that she was sure would come — that Cæsar was pressing on the tracks of his rival.

Late one afternoon, as the king and his suite were just returned from a visit by boat up the river to inspect a temple under restoration at Sethroë, Agias sought the private apartment of his patroness. His face was extremely grave, and Cornelia at once realized that he brought serious news.

"Domina," he said, speaking in Latin to evade the curiosity

of the maids present, " when you are at leisure, I have a curious story to tell you."

Cornelia presently found pretexts to get rid of all her women. Agias reconnoitred, made certain that there was no eavesdropper, and began afresh.

"What I have to say is so different from that which we feared a few days since, that I scarce know how you will receive it. I have just learned that your uncle Lucius Lentulus and Lucius Ahenobarbus made a landing on the coast the day after Pompeius was murdered; they have been quietly arrested and the matter hushed up. I believe that Pothinus intends to execute them without your knowledge. Only by a friendship with some of the officers of the guard did I get at this."

Cornelia's lips twitched; her hands pressed on her cheeks till the pale skin flushed red. In her heart a hundred conflicting emotions held sway. She said nothing for a long time, and then it was only to ask where the prisoners were confined.

"They are in the dungeon of the fortress," said Agias. "That is all that I can discover."

"I must see them at once," declared the lady.

"I do not know how Pothinus will take this," replied the young freedman; "the discovery of his secret will be rightly attributed to me, and your ladyship would not care to imperil my life unless something very great is to be gained thereby."

"I shall miss you very much," said Cornelia, soberly. "But though Lucius Lentulus has done me grievous ill, he is my uncle. You must leave Pelusium this very night, and keep out of danger until Pothinus's vexation can abate. In the morning I shall demand to see the prisoners and to learn the eunuch's intentions touching them."

Agias accordingly fared away, much to Cornelia's regret,

2 G

but not quite so much to his own, because his enforced journeying would take him to the Nile villa, where was the pretty Artemisia. Early on the following day Cornelia boldly went to Pothinus, and, without any explanations, demanded to see her uncle. The regent, who had tried to keep the matter profoundly secret, first was irate, then equivocated, and tried to deny that he had any Roman prisoners; then, driven to bay by Cornelia's persistency and quiet inflexibility before his denials and protests, gave her permission to be taken to the prison and see the captives.

To pass from the palace of Pelusium to the fortress-prison was to pass, by a few steps, from the Oriental life, in all its sensuous splendour, to Orientalism in its most degraded savagery. The prison was a half-underground kennel of stone and brick, on which the parching sun beat pitilessly, and made the galleries and cells like so many furnaces in heat. The fetid odour of human beings confined in the most limited space in which life can be maintained; the rattle of fetters; the grating of ponderous doors on slow-turning pivots; the coarse oaths and brutish aspect of both jailers and prisoners; the indescribable squalor, filth, misery, — these may not be enlarged upon. The attendants led Cornelia to the cell, hardly better than the rest, wherein Lentulus and Ahenobarbus were confined.

But another had been before Cornelia to visit the unfortunates. As the lady drew toward the open door she saw the graceful, easy form of Pratinas on the threshold, one hand carelessly thrust in the folds of his himation, the other gesturing animatedly, while he leaned against the stone casing.

Lucius Lentulus, his purple-lined tunic dirty and torn, his hair disordered, his face knitted into a bitter frown, crouched on a stool in the little low-ceiled room, confronting the Hellene. Cowering on a mass of filthy straw, his head bowed, his body quaking in a paroxysm of fear, was another whose name Cornelia knew full well.

Pratinas was evidently just concluding a series of remarks.

"And so, my friends, amici, as we say at Rome," he was jauntily vapouring, "I regret indeed that the atomic theory, — which my good Ahenobarbus, I am sure, holds in common with myself, — can leave us no hope of meeting in a future world, where I can expect to win any more of his good sesterces with loaded dice. But let him console himself! He will shortly cease from any pangs of consciousness that our good friend Quintus Drusus will, in all probability, enjoy the fortune that he has inherited from his father, and marry the lady for whose hand the very noble Ahenobarbus for some time disputed. Therefore let me wish you both a safe voyage to the kingdom of Hades; and if you need money for the ferryman, accept now, as always, the use of my poor credit."

"May all the infernal gods requite you!" broke forth Lentulus, half rising, and uplifting his fettered hands to call down a solemn curse.

"It has been often observed by philosophers," said Pratinas, with a smile, "that even among the most sceptical, in times of great extremity, there exists a certain belief in the existence of gods. Your excellency sees how the observation is confirmed."

"The gods blast you!" howled Lentulus, in impotent fury. Before further words could pass, Cornelia put Pratinas aside, and entered the cell.

"Your presence, sir," she said haughtily, to the Hellene, "is needed no longer." And she pointed down the gallery.

Pratinas flushed, hesitated as if for once at a loss, and nimbly vanished. Lentulus sat in speechless astonishment

"Uncle," continued Cornelia, "what may I do for you? I did not know till last evening that you were here."

But ere the other could reply the figure in the corner had sprung up, and flung itself at the lady's feet.

"Save me! save me! By all that you hold dear, save my life! I have loved you. I thought once that you loved me. Plead for me! Pray for me! Anything that I may but live!"

"*Vah*, wretch!" cried the consular; and he spurned Ahenobarbus with his foot. "It is indeed well that you have not married into family of mine! If you can do naught else, you can at least die with dignity as becomes a Roman patrician — and not beg intercession from this woman who has cut herself off from all her kin by disobedience."

"Uncle," cried Cornelia in distress, "must we be foes to the end? Must our last words be of bitterness?"

"Girl," thundered the unbending Lentulus, "when a Roman maiden disobeys, there is no expiation. You are no niece of mine. I care not how you came here. I accept nothing at your hands. I will not hear your story. If I must die, it is to die cursing your name. Go! I have no more words for you!"

But Ahenobarbus caught the skirt of Cornelia's robe, and pleaded and moaned. "Let them imprison him in the lowest dungeons, load him with the heaviest fetters; place upon him the most toilsome labour — only let him still see the light and breathe the air!"

"Uncle," said Cornelia, "I will plead for you despite your wrath — though little may my effort avail. You are my father's brother, and neither act of yours nor of mine can make you otherwise. But as for you, Lucius Ahenobarbus," — and her words came hot and thick, as she hissed out her contempt, — "though I beg for your life, know this, that if I despised you less I would not so do. I despise you too much to hate; and if I ask to have you live, it is because I know the pains of a base and ignoble life are a myriad fold more than those of a swift and honourable death. Were I your judge — I would doom you; doom you *to live* and know the sting of your ignominy!"

She left them; and hatred and pity, triumph and anguish, mingled within her. She went to the young King Ptolemæus and besought him to spare the prisoners; the lad professed his inability to take a step without the initiative of Pothinus. She went to Pothinus; the eunuch listened to her courteously, then as courteously told her that grave reasons of state made it impossible to comply with the request — much, as he blandly added, it would delight him personally to gratify her. Cornelia could do no more. Pratinas she would not appeal to, though he had great influence with Pothinus. She went back to her rooms to spend the day with Fabia, very heavy of heart. The world, as a whole, she beheld as a thing very evil; treachery, guile, wrath, hatred, were everywhere. The sight of Ahenobarbus had filled her with loathsome memories of past days. The sunlight fell in bright warm panels over the rich rugs on the floor of her room. The sea-breeze sweeping in from the north blew fresh and sweet; out against the azure light, into which she could gaze, a swarm of swallows was in silhouette — black dots crawling along across the dome of light. Out in one of the public squares of the city great crowds of people were gathering. Cornelia knew the reason of the concourse — the heads of two noble Romans, just decapitated, were being exposed to the gibes and howls of the coarse Greek and Egyptian mob. And Cornelia wished that she were herself a swallow, and might fly up into the face of the sun, until the earth beneath her had vanished.

But while she leaned from the parapet by the window of the room, footsteps sounded on the mosaic pavement without; the drapery in the doorway was flung aside; Agias entered, and after him — another.

II

Drusus ran to Cornelia and caught her in his arms; and she — neither fainted nor turned pale, but gave a little laugh, and cried softly: —

"I always knew you were coming!"

What more followed Agias did not know; his little affair with Artemisia had taught him that his Hellenic inquisitiveness sometimes would do more harm than good.

Very different from the good-humoured, careless, half-boyish student youth who had driven down the Præneste road two years before, was the soldierly figure that Cornelia pressed to her heart. The campaigning life had left its mark upon Drusus. Half of a little finger the stroke of a Spanish sword had cleft away at Ilerda; across his forehead was the broad scar left by the fight at Pharsalus, from a blow that he had never felt in the heat of the battle. During the forced marchings and voyages no razor had touched his cheeks, and he was thickly bearded. But what cared Cornelia? Had not her ideal, her idol, gone forth into the great world and stood its storm and stress, and fought in its battles, and won due glory? Was he not alive, and safe, and in health of mind and body after ten thousand had fallen around him? Were not the clouds sped away, the lightnings ceased? And she? She was happy.

So Drusus told her of all that had befallen him since the day he escaped out of Lucius Ahenobarbus's hands at Baiæ. And Cornelia told of her imprisonment at the villa, and how

Demetrius had saved her, and how it came to pass that she was here at the Egyptian court. In turn Drusus related how Cæsar had pursued Pompeius into Asia, and then, hearing that the Magnus had fled to Egypt, placed two legions on shipboard and sailed straight for Alexandria.

"And when he landed," continued the young officer, "the magistrates of the city came to Cæsar, and gave him first Pompeius's seal-ring of a lion holding a sword in his paw, and then another black-faced and black-hearted Egyptian, without noticing the distress the Imperator was in, came up and uncovered something he had wrapped in a mantle. I was beside the general when the bundle was unwrapped. I am sickened when I speak of it. It was the head of Pompeius Magnus. The fools thought to give Cæsar a great delight."

"And what did the Imperator do or say?" asked Cornelia.

"He shrank back from the horror as though the Egyptian had been a murderer, as indeed all of his race are. Cæsar said nothing. Yet all saw how great was his grief and anger. Soon or late he will requite the men who slew thus foully the husband of his daughter Julia."

"You must take me away from them," said Cornelia, shuddering; "I am afraid every hour."

"And I, till you are safe among our troops at Alexandria," replied Drusus. "I doubt if they would have let me see you, but for Agias. He met us on the road from Alexandria and told me about you. I had received a special despatch from Cæsar to bear with all haste to the king. So across the Delta I started, hardly waiting for the troops to disembark, for there was need for speed. Agias I took back with me, and my first demand when I came here was to see the king and deliver my letter, which was easily done an hour ago; and my next to see you. Whereat that nasty sheep Pothinus declared that you had been sent some days before up the river on a trip to the Memphis palace to see the pyramids. But Agias was close at hand, and I gave the eunuch the lie without difficulty. The rascal blandly said, 'that he had not seen you of late; had only spoken by hearsay about you, and he might have been misinformed;' and so — What do I look like?"

"You look like Quintus Livius Drusus, the Roman soldier," said Cornelia, "and I would not have you otherwise than what you are."

"*Eho!*" replied Drusus, passing his hand over her hair. "Do you want me to tell you something?"

"What is it?" said Cornelia, pressing closer.

"I can never write a cosmology. I shall never be able to evolve a new system of ethics. I cannot improve on Plato's ideal state. I know I am a very ignorant man, with only a few ideas worth uttering, with a hand that is very heavy, with a mind that works to little purpose save when it deals with politics and war. In short" — and Drusus's voice grew really pathetic — "all my learning carries me no farther than did the wisdom of Socrates, 'I know that I know nothing;' and I have no time to spend in advancing beyond that stage."

"But Socrates," said Cornelia, laughing, "was the wisest man in Greece, and for that very reason."

"Well," said Drusus, ignoring the compliment, as a certain type of men will when the mood is on them, "what do you wish me to make of myself?"

"I wish you to make nothing different," was her reply, "for you are precisely what I have always wanted you to be. When you have read as much as I have," this with an air of utter weariness, "you will realize the futility of philosophic study."

"*Eho!*" remarked Drusus again. "So you would have me

feel that I am turning my back on nothing very great, after all ? "

" And so I mean."

" Seriously ? "

" I am serious, Quintus." And indeed Cornelia was. " I can read Aristotle and Plato, and Zeno and Cleanthes, and Pyrrho, and a score of others. I can spin out of my own brain a hundred theories of the universe as good as theirs, but my heart will not be the happier, if things outside make me sad. I am sick of the learning that is no learning, that answers our questions by other questions that are more riddling."

" Ah, scoffer at the wise," laughed Drusus, " what do you wish, then ? " He spoke in Greek.

" Speak in Latin, in Latin, Quintus," was her retort. " I am weary of this fine, sweet language that tinkles so delicately, every word of which hides a hundred meanings, every sentence attuned like the notes for a harp. Let us have our own language, blunt and to the point; the language, not of men who wonder what they ought to do, but who *do*. We are Romans, not Greeks. We have to rule the world, not growl as to how Jupiter made it. When you came back from Athens I said, 'I love Quintus Drusus, but I would love him more if he were less a Hellene.' And, now I see you wholly Roman, I love you wholly. And for myself, I wish neither to be a Sappho, nor an Aspasia, nor a Semiramis, but Cornelia the Roman matron, who obeys her husband, Quintus Drusus, who cares for his house, and whom, in turn, her household fears and obeys."

"*O tempora ! O mores !*" cried the young soldier, in delight. " When had ever a woman such ambition in these degenerate days ? *Eu !* Then I will burn my books, if you can get no profit out of them."

"I do not think books are bad," said Cornelia, still soberly, 'but I know that they can never make me happy."

"What can?" demanded her tormenter.

"*You!*"

* * * * * * * * * *

So the hours of the afternoon ran on, and the lovers gave them little heed. But they were not too selfish to refuse to Fabia's sharing in their joy; and Drusus knew that he was dear no less, though differently, in the eyes of his aunt than of his betrothed. And there were duties to perform that not even the long-deferred delights of the afternoon could postpone. Chief of these were the arrangements for the immediate departure of the Roman ladies for Alexandria. Agias, who was called into the council, was invaluable in information and suggestion. He said that Pothinus had acted at Pratinas's advice, when he took Fabia and Cornelia to the palace. The eunuch had expected to use them half as hostages, half as captives to be put to ransom. If Cæsar had delayed a few days, Pothinus would not have lied when he made excuse that the ladies had been sent up the river. But now Agias believed that the regent was afraid, having overreached himself, and it was best to make a prompt demand for conveyance to Alexandria. This, indeed, proved advantageous policy. The eunuch made difficulties and suggested obstacles, but Drusus made his native Italian haughtiness stand him in good stead. It would largely depend, he said insinuatingly, on the way in which his demand was complied with, what sort of a report he made to Cæsar touching the execution of Lucius Lentulus and Ahenobarbus. During his interview with Pothinus, the Roman came face to face with Pratinas. No words were exchanged, but Drusus noticed that the elegant Hellene flushed, and then turned pale, when he fastened upon him a gaze steady and half menacing. Pothinus ended by yielding everything — the use of the royal chariots and horses, the use of the Nile boats needed for swift transit across the Delta, and orders on the local garrisons and governors to provide entertainment and assistance.

As a result Cornelia speedily found herself again journeying, not this time in a slow barge following the main branches of the Nile, but by more rapid, if less luxurious, conveyance, now by land, now by water, hurrying westward. They passed through Sethroë and Tanis, Mendes and Sebennytus, Xaïs and Saïs, where were the tomb of Osiris and the great Egyptian university in this the capital of the mighty Pharaohs who had wrested the nation from the clutches of Assyria. Then they fared up the Nile to the old Milesian trading factory of Naucratis, — now dropping into decline beside the thriving Alexandria, — and then by boat they pressed on to the capital itself. Never more delightful journey for Cornelia or for Drusus; they saw the strange land through one another's eyes; they expressed their own thoughts through one another's lips; they were happy together, as if children at play; and Fabia was their never exacting, ever beneficent, guardian goddess.

Drusus and Cornelia were neither of them the same young persons who had met in the gardens of the villa of the Lentuli two short years before. They saw life with a soberer gaze; they had both the wisdom that experience teaches. Yet for the time not a cloud was drifting across their sky. Their passions and hates had been too fierce, too pagan, to feel the death of even Cornelia's uncle very keenly. Lucius Ahenobarbus was dead — they had no more thought for him than for a dead viper. Lucius Domitius was dead. Gabinius and Dumnorix were dead. Pompeius, the tool of guiltier men than himself, was dead. Pratinas alone of all those who had crossed their path remained; but the wily Greek was a mere creature of self-interest — what had he to gain by pressing his animosity, if he had any, against them? Cæsar was triumphant. His enemies were barely lifting their heads in Africa. Doubtless there was stern work awaiting the Imperator there, but what of it? Was he not invincible? Was he not about to commence a new order of things in the world, to tear down the old and decaying, to raise up a steadfast fabric? Therefore the little party took its pleasure, and enjoyed every ancient temple of the Amenhoteps, Thothmeses, and Ramesides that they hurriedly visited; won the favour of the wrinkled old priests by their plentiful votives of bright philippi; heard a hundred time-honoured tales that they knew not whether to believe or laugh at; speculated among themselves as to the sources of the Nile, the cause of the vocal Memnon, and fifty more darkened wonders, and resolved to solve every mystery during a second and more prolonged visit.

So they came to Alexandria, but on the way called at the Nile villa where was Artemisia, and, to the great satisfaction of that young lady and of Agias, carried her along with them to the house of Cleomenes, where that affable host and Berenice and Monime received them with open arms.

Their pleasure at this reunion, however, began to abate when they realized the disturbed state of the city.

"I can't say I like the situation," admitted Cleomenes, as soon as he had been introduced to Drusus, and the first greetings were over; "you know when Cæsar landed he took his consular insignia with him, and the mob made this mean that he was intending to overthrow the government and make Egypt a Roman province. If you had not left for Pelusium so hastily, you would have been present at a very serious riot, that was with great difficulty put down. The soldiers of the royal garrison are in an ugly mood, and so are the people. I suspect the king, or rather Pothinus, is doing nothing to quiet them. There have been slight riots for several days past, and a good many Roman soldiers who have straggled away from the palace into the lower quarters of the city have been murdered."

"I am glad," replied Drusus, "that I can leave Cornelia and my aunt under your protection, for my duty may keep me continuously with the Imperator."

The young officer at once hastened to the palace and reported for service. Cæsar questioned him as to the situation at Pelusium, and Drusus described the unpromising attitude of Pothinus, and also mentioned how he had found Cornelia and his aunt.

The general, engrossed as he was with his business of state and threatening war, put all his duties aside and at once went to the house of Cleomenes. It was the first time Cornelia had ever met the man whose career had exerted such an influence upon her own life. She had at first known of him only through the filthy, slanderous verses of such oligarchs as Catullus and Calvus; then through her lover she had come to look upon Cæsar as an incarnation as it were of omniscience, omnipotence, and benevolence — the man for whom everything was worth sacrificing, from whom every noble thing was to be expected.

She met the conquerer of Ariovistus, Vercingetorix, and Pompeius like the frank-hearted, patrician maiden that she was, without shyness, without servility.

"My father died in your army," she said on meeting; "my affianced husband has taught me to admire you, as he himself does. Let us be friends!"

And Cæsar bowed as became the polished gentleman, who had been the centre of the most brilliant salons of Rome, and took the hand she offered, and replied: —

"Ah! Lady Cornelia, we have been friends long, though never we met before! But I am doubly the friend of whosoever is the friend of Quintus Livius Drusus."

Whereupon Cornelia was more completely the vassal of the Imperator than ever, and words flew fast between them. In short, just as in the case with Cleopatra, she opened her heart before she knew that she had said anything, and told of all her life, with its shadows and brightness; and Cæsar listened and sympathized as might a father; and Drusus perfectly realized, if Cornelia could not — how many-sided was the man who could thus turn from weighing the fate of empires to entering unfeignedly into a sharing of the hopes and fears of a very young, and still quite unsophisticated, woman.

When the Imperator departed Drusus accompanied him to the palace. Neither of the two, general nor subaltern, spoke for a long while; at last Cæsar remarked : —

"Do you know what is uppermost in my mind, after meeting women like Fabia or Cornelia ? "

Drusus shook his head.

"I believe that there are gods, who bring such creatures into the world. They are not chance accretions of atoms." And then Cæsar added, half dreamily : "You ought to be a very happy man. I was once — it was many years ago. Her name was Cornelia also."

* * * * * * * * * *

Serious and more serious grew the situation at Alexandria. King Ptolemæus and Pothinus came to the city from Pelusium. Cæsar had announced that he intended to examine the title of the young monarch to the undivided crown, and make him show cause why he had expelled Cleopatra. This the will of Ptolemæus Auletes had enjoined the Roman government to do; for in it he had commissioned his allies to see that his oldest children shared the inheritance equally.

But Pothinus came to Alexandria, and trouble came with him. He threw every possible obstacle in Cæsar's way when the latter tried to collect a heavy loan due the Romans by the late king. The etesian winds made it impossible to bring up reënforcements, and Cæsar's force was very small. Pothinus grew more insolent each day. For the first time, Drusus observed that his general was nervous, and suspicious lest he be assassinated. Finally the Imperator determined to force a crisis. To leave Egypt without humbling Pothinus meant a great lowering of prestige. He sent off a private message to Palestine that Cleopatra should come to Alexandria.

Cleopatra came, not in royal procession, for she knew too well the finesse of the regent's underlings; but entered the harbour in disguise in a small boat; and Apollodorus, her Sicilian confidant, carried her into Cæsar's presence wrapped in a bale of bedding which he had slung across his back.

The queen's suit was won. Cleopatra and the Imperator met, and the two strong personalities recognized each other's affinity instantly. Her coming was as a thunder-clap to Pothinus and his puppet Ptolemæus. They could only cringe and acquiesce when Cæsar ordered them to be reconciled with the queen, and seal her restoration by a splendid court banquet.

The palace servants made ready for the feast. The rich and noble of Alexandria were invited. The stores of gold and silver vessels treasured in the vaults of the Lagidæ were brought forth. The arches and columns of the palace were festooned with flowers. The best pipers and harpers of the great city were summoned to delight with their music. Precious wine of Tanis was ready to flow like water.

Drusus saw the preparations with a glad heart. Cornelia would be present in all her radiancy; and who there would be more radiant than she?

CHAPTER XXIV

BATTLING FOR LIFE

I

AND then it was, — with the chariots bearing the guests almost driving in at the gates of the palace, — that Cerrinius, Cæsar's barber, came before his master with an alarming tale. The worthy man declared that he had lighted on nothing less than a plot to murder the Romans, one and all, by admitting Achillas's soldiery to the palace enclosure, while all the banqueters were helpless with drugged wine. Pratinas, who had been supposed to be at Pelusium, Cerrinius had caught in retired conference with Pothinus, planning the arrangement of the feast. Achillas's mercenary army was advancing by stealthy marches to enter the city in the course of the even-ing. The mob had been aroused by agitators, until it was in a mood to rise *en masse* against the Romans, and join in destroying them. Such, in short, was the barber's story.

There was no time to delay. Cæsar was a stranger in a strange and probably hostile land, and to fail to take warn-ing were suicide. He sent for Pothinus, and demanded the whereabouts of Achillas's army. The regent stammered that it was at Pelusium. Cæsar followed up the charge by inquir-ing about Pratinas. Pothinus swore that he was at Pelusium also. But Cæsar cut his network of lies short, by command-ing that a malefactor should be forced to swallow a beaker of the wine prepared for the banquet. In a few moments the man was in a helpless stupor.

The case was proved and Cæsar became all action. A squad of legionaries haled Pothinus away to an execution not long delayed. Other legionaries disarmed and replaced the detachment of the royal guard that controlled the palace gates and walls. And barely had these steps been taken, when a courier thundered into the palace, hardly escaped through the raging mob that was gaining control of the city. Achillas, he reported, had wantonly murdered Dioscorides and Serapion, whom Cæsar had sent as envoys to Pelusium, and was marching on the city with his whole army of Italian renegades, Syrian banditti, convicts, and runaway slaves, twenty thousand strong.

There was nothing to do but to prepare to weather the storm in the palace enclosure, which, with its high walls, was practically a fortress in itself. There were only four thousand Romans, and yet there was a long circuit of defences to man. But Drusus never saw his general putting forth greater energy. That night, instead of feasting, the soldiers laboured, piling up the ramparts by the light of torches. The city was surging and thundering without the palace gates. Cæsar had placed the king under guard, but Arsinoë — his younger sister — had slipped out of the palace to join herself to the advancing host of Achillas, and speedily that general would be at hand. Cæsar as usual was everywhere, with new schemes for the defences, new enthusiasm for his officers, new inspiration for his men. No one slept nor cared to sleep inside the palace walls. They toiled for dear life, for with morning, at most, Achillas would be upon them; and by morning, if Pothinus's plans had not failed, they would have been drugged and helpless to a man, none able to draw sword from scabbard. It was a new experience to one and all, for these Romans to stand on the defensive

2 н

For once Cæsar had made a false step—he ought to have taken on his voyage more men. He stood with his handful, with the sea on one side of him and a great city and a nation in arms against him on the other. The struggle was not to be for empire, but for life. But the Romans were too busy that night to realize anything save the need of untiring exertion. If they had counted the odds against them, four thousand against a nation, they might well have despaired, though their chieftain were Cæsar.

Two years earlier Drusus, as he hurried to and fro transmitting orders for his general, might have been fain to draw aside and muse on the strangeness of the night scene. The sky was clear, as almost always in a land where a thunder-storm is often as rare as an eclipse; the stars twinkled out of heavens of soft blackness; the crescent of a new moon hung like a silvered bow out over the harbour, and made a thin pathway of lustre across the moving, shimmering waters. Dimly the sky-line was visible; by the Pharos and its mole loomed the vague tracery of masts. On the west and the south lay the white and dark masses of the city, now and then brought into clearer relief as the moonbeams swept across some stately pile, and touched on its Corinthian columns and nobly wrought pediments. But Drusus was a soldier; and the best of poets doubtless work poorly when their lives are hanging in the balance. Over the flower-strewn walks, under the festooned colonnades, ran the busy legionaries, bestirring themselves as never before; while Diomedes, and Hector, and Patroclus, and fifty other heroic worthies waged perpetual battle on their marble heights above the soldiers' heads. On occasion Drusus was called to one of the upper terraces and pinnacles of the palace buildings, and then he could catch a glimpse of the whole sweep of the mighty city. Over to the southeast, where was the Jewish quarter, the sky was beginning to redden. The mob had begun to vent its passions on the innocent Israelites, and the incendiary was at his work. A deep, low, growling hum, as of ten thousand angry voices, drifted upon the night air. The beast called the Alexandrian rabble was loose, and it was a terrible animal.

It was midnight. Drusus had toiled since noon. He had hardly tasted food or drink since morning, but there were three feet more of brick, stone, and rubbish to be added still to this and that rampart before it would be secure, and a whole wing of the overgrown palace must be pulled down to furnish the material. He had climbed out upon the roof to aid in tearing up the tiles and to encourage the men by his example, when some one plucked him from behind on the cloak — it was Cæsar.

"You are not needed here," said the general, in a voice that seemed a bit strained to keep calm. "Read this — take all the men you want."

And the Imperator himself held up the torch, while Drusus took the tablet thrust into his hands and read the hastily scribbled lines: —

"Cleomenes to Drusus. The ladies are in danger. I will resist the mob as long as I can. Send help."

Drusus threw down the tablet; forgot to so much as salute his commander. He had laid off his armour during the work on the ramparts; he ran for it, put it on with feverish haste. A moment more and he was running among the soldiers, calling this and that legionary by name. The troops all knew him, and would have followed him to the death. When he asked for thirty volunteers for dangerous service, none demanded of him the occasion; he simply selected his men as fast as he might. He secured four chariots and placed in them the fastest horses in the royal stables and trusted men for drivers.

He mounted the rest of his thirty on other steeds, and the preparations were over. The gate was thrown open; Decimus Mamercus, who was his subaltern, led out the little company. Drusus rode out last, in one of the chariots. The troops on the walls cheered them as they departed.

In the immediate neighbourhood of the palace there prevailed an ominous silence. Earlier in the night a few cohorts had charged out and scattered the street rabble; and the mob had kept at a distance. There was no light save that of the moon and the distant glow of the burning buildings. Drusus felt his breath coming thick and fast, the drops of sweat were hanging on his forehead, something within was driving his heart into his throat. "If — " he never went further; unless he brought Cornelia and Fabia back to the palace unscathed, he knew the Alexandrian rabble would howl over his unconscious body.

"Ride!" he commanded, as if the rush of the chariots and horses would drown the fears that nearly drove him frantic. "Ride!"

The drivers lashed the teams, the horsemen pricked with the spur. Drusus caught the reins from his chariot companion, and swung the lash himself over the four steeds. Faster and faster they flew down the splendidly paved and built highways. Temples and majestic public buildings rose in sombre grandeur above their heads; above them winged "Victories" seemed springing up into dark void, their sculptured symmetries just visible in the moonlight. On and on, swift and more swift — persons began shouting from the buildings which they passed, now a few voices, now many, now a hundred. A volley of stones was dashed down from the safe recesses of the pillars at the head of the long flight of steps leading up to a temple. Presently an arrow whirred over Drusus's head and smote on the masonry across the street. There were lights ahead — scores of torches waving — a small building was on fire; the glare grew redder and brighter every instant; and a din, a din lifted by ten thousand men when their brute instincts are enkindled, grew and grew. Drusus dashed the cold sweat from his brow, his hand was trembling. He had a quiver and bow in the chariot, — a powerful Parthian bow, and the arrows were abundant. Mamercus had taught him to be a good archer, as a boy. Could he turn his old skill to account? Not unless his hand became more steady.

Women screamed out at him and his band from the house roofs; a tile struck one of the chariot horses and made it plunge wildly; Drusus flung his strength into the reins, and curbed in the raging beast; he tossed the lines back to his driver and tore the bow from its casings. His car had rushed on ahead of Decimus Mamercus and the rest; two furlongs more would bring him to the house of Cleomenes on one of the squares of the city. The chariot swung around a street corner for the final stretch, the way was broad, the buildings on either side (the residences of the Alexandrian gentry) high; but the whole street from wall to wall was a seething mass of human forms. The fire was spreading; the brightening flames shone down on the tossing, howling multitude — excited Egyptians from the quarter of Rhacotis, frenzied Asiatics in their turbans, mad sailors from the Eunostian port and the Pharos island. At the head of the street the flames were pressing in upon a stately mansion around which the raging mob was packed thickly. On the roof of the threatened house figures could be seen in the lurid light, running to and fro, flinging down bricks and stones, and trying to beat back the fire. It was the house of Cleomenes. Insensibly the veteran who had been driving reined in the horses, who themselves drew back, loath to plunge into the living barriers ahead. But Drusus was past fear or prudence; with his own hands he sent the lash stinging over all the four, and the team, that had won more than a single trophy in the games, shot forward. The chariot struck the multitude and went, not through it, but over it. The on-rush was too rapid, too unexpected, for resistance. To right and left, as the water gives way before the bows of an on-rushing ship, the crowd surged back, the instinct of panic reigning in every breast. Thick and fast, as quickly as he might set shaft to string, flew Drusus's arrows — not a shaft that failed a mark, as it cut into the living masses. The chariot reeled again and again, as this wheel or that passed over something animate and struggling. The horses caught the fire of conflict; they raced, they ran — and the others sped after them. The mob left off howling: it screamed with a single voice of mortal dread. And before Drusus or any one else realized, the deed was done, the long lane was cleared, and the drivers were drawing rein before the house of Cleomenes.

The heavily barred carriage-way was thrown open, the valiant merchant and his faithful employees and slaves greeted their rescuers as the little cavalcade drove in. There was not a moment to lose. Cleomenes and his household might indeed have long made good the house against the mere attacks of the mob; but the rioters had set the torch to some adjacent buildings, and all efforts to beat back the flames were proving futile. There was no time to condole with the merchant over the loss of his house. The mob had surged again into the streets and was pressing back, this time more or less prepared to resist the Romans. The colonnades and the house roofs were swarming, the din was indescribable, and the crackling and roar of the advancing flames grew ever louder.

The only alternative was a return to the palace. Cleomenes's employees and slaves were to scatter into the crowd, where they would easily escape notice; he himself, with his daughters, Artemisia, and the Roman ladies, must go in the chariots to the palace. Cornelia came down from her chamber, her face more flushed with excitement than alarm. Troubles enough she had had, but never before personal danger; and she could not easily grasp the peril.

"Are you afraid, carissima," said Drusus, lifting her into his chariot, "to ride back with me to the palace, through that wolf pack?"

"With you?" she said, admiring the ease with which he sprang about in full armour; "I would laugh at Medusa or the Hydra of Lerna with you beside me."

Cleomenes had been again upon the housetop to watch the progress of the fire. He came down, and Drusus instantly saw that there was dismay written on his face. The merchant, who was himself armed with sword and target, drew the officer aside and whispered: —

"Pray, Roman, to all your native gods! I can see a *lochos*[1] of regular troops filing into the square before the house. Achillas is entering the city with his men. We shall have to fight our way through his thousands."

Drusus uttered a deep and silent curse on himself for the mad bravado that led him to leave the palace with but thirty men; why had he not waited to assemble more? He could ride over the mob; to master Achillas's disciplined forces was otherwise.

A freedman came running down from the roof, crying out that it was already on fire. It was a time for action, not thought, yet even at the moment Drusus's schoolboy Polyb·

[1] A company of about one hundred men.

ius was running through his mind — the description of th
great riot when Agathocles, the wicked regent of Ptolemæus
Philopator, and his sister Agathocleia, and his mother Oenan-
the, had been seized by the multitude and torn in pieces, bit
by bit, while yet they lived. Cornelia seemed to have caught
some new cause for fear; she was trembling and shivering
when Drusus took her in his arms and swung her into the
chariot. He lifted in Fabia likewise, but the Vestal only
bowed her head in calm silence. She had overheard Cleomenes's tidings, but, by stress of all the force of her strong
nature, remained composed. Decimus Mamercus took Artemisia, frightened and crying, into his own chariot. Monime,
Berenice, and their father were to go in the other cars. The
fire was gaining on the roof, smoke was pouring down into the
court-yard, and now and then a gleam came from a firebrand.
The horses were growing restive and frightened.

"Throw open the gate!" commanded Drusus; his anxieties
and despair were driving him almost to frenzy, but the gods,
if gods there were, knew that it was not for himself that he
was fearful. His voice sounded hollow in his throat; he
would have given a talent of gold for a draught of water.
One of his men flung back the gateway, and in at the entrance
came the glare of great bonfires lighted in the streets, of
hundreds of tossing torches. The yelling of the multitude
was louder than ever. There it was, packed thick on all
sides: in its midst Drusus could see bright lines of tossing
steel — the armour of Achillas's soldiery! As the portal
opened, a mighty howl of triumph burst from the people;
the fire had driven forth to the mob its prey. Cornelia
heard the howl — the voice of a wild and raging beast — and
trembled more.

"Cornelia," said Drusus, lowering his head so as to mak

himself heard, "do not look above the framework of the chariot. Cling to it tightly, for we may have to pass over obstacles. Above all, do not spring out, however much we may be swayed and shaken."

"I will not, Quintus," and that was all she could be heard to say in the din.

And so the little cavalcade drove forth. Cornelia cowered in the chariot and saw nothing and heard everything, which was the same as nothing. Was she frightened? She did not know. The peril was awful. Of course she realized that; but how could calamity come to pass, when it was Drusus whose powerful form towered above her, when it was Drusus whose voice rang like a trumpet out into the press swaying around?

It was very dark crouching in the body of the chariot. She could just see the face of Fabia opposite, very white, but, she knew, very calm. She reached out and caught the Vestal's hand, and discovered that her own was trembling, while the other's was perfectly steady. But the contest, the fighting all about! Now the horses were dashing forward, making the chariot spring as though it were a thing of life; now reined in sharply, and the heavily loaded car swayed this way and that, almost to overturning. The uproar above her head passed the telling by words; but there was one shout, now in Greek, now in Egyptian, that drowned all others: "Death to the Romans! tear them in pieces!" Missiles smote against the chariot; an arrow went cutting into the wood, driving its keen point home, and Cornelia experienced a thrill of pain in her shoulder. She felt for the smart, found the mere tip of the point only had penetrated the wood; but her fingers were wet when she took them away. Drusus was shooting; his bow-string snapped and snapped. Once a soldier in armour sprang behind the chariot when it came to a stop, and his javelin was poised to discharge; but an arrow tore through his throat, and he went down to the pavement with a crash. The car rocked more and more; once the wheels slipped without revolving, as though sliding over some smooth liquid — not water. Cornelia felt powers of discriminating sensation becoming fainter and fainter; a great force seemed pressing out from within her; the clamour and shocks were maddening. She felt driven to raise her head, to look out into the raging chaos, though the first glance were death. Peering back out of the body of the chariot now and then, she saw a little. The Romans were charging this way and that, forcing their passage down the street, barred no longer by a mere mob, but by Achillas's infantrymen, who were hastening into action. The chariot horses were wounded, some seriously; she was sure of that. They could not be driven through the spearmen, and the little handful of cavalry was trying to break through the enemy and make space for a rush. It was thirty against thousands; yet even in the mortal peril, which Cornelia realized now if she had never before, she had a strange sort of pride. Her countrymen were showing these Orientals how one Roman could slay his tens, could put in terror his hundreds. Drusus was giving orders with the same mechanical exactitude of the drill, albeit his voice was high-pitched and strained — not entirely, perhaps, because of the need of calling above the din.

"Form in line by fours!"

Cornelia raised her head above the chariot frame. The Romans had worked their way down into a square formed by the intersection of streets. Behind them and on every building were swarming the people; right across the eastern avenue, where their escape lay, stood the bristling files of one of Achillas's companies. Stones and roof-tiles were being tossed

in a perfect hail from the houses, and now and then an arrow
or a dart. The four chariots — one had only three horses left
— were standing in the little plaza, and the troopers were
forming before them. The arrows of the chariot warriors
made the mob behind keep a respectful distance. It was the
triumph of discipline over man's animal sense of fear. Even
the mob felt this, when it saw the little squadron fall into line
with as much precision as on the parade ground. A tile smote
one soldier upon the head, and he tumbled from his horse like
a stone. His comrades never paused in their evolution. Then,
for the first time, Cornelia screamed with horror and fright.
Drusus, who was setting a new arrow to his bow, looked down
upon her; he had never seemed so handsome before, with the
fierce light of the battle in his eyes, with his whole form
swelling with the exertions of conflict.

"Down, Cornelia!" commanded the officer; and Cornelia
did so implicitly — to disobey him at that moment was
inconceivable.

"At them, men!"

And then came a new bound from the horses, and then a
mighty crash and clash of bodies, blades, and shields, the snort
of dying beasts, the splintering of spear-shafts, the groans
and cries of men in battle for their lives. The car rose on one
wheel higher and higher; Cornelia was thrown against Fabia,
and the two women clung to each other, too terrified and
crushed to scream; then on a sudden it righted, and as it did
so the soldier who had acted as charioteer reeled, his face
bathed in blood, the death-rattle in his throat. Back he fell,
pierced in face and breast, and tumbled from the car; and, as
if answering to this lightening of their burden, the hoofs of the
hard-pressed horses bit on the pavement, and the team bounded
onward.

"*Io triumphe!*" It was Drusus who called; and in answer to his shout came the deep Cæsarian battle-cry from hundreds of throats, "*Venus Victrix!*"

The chariot was advancing, but less rapidly. Cornelia rose and looked forth again, not this time to be rebuked. Down the moon-lighted street were moving several infantry cohorts from the palace; the avenue was clear, the mob and hostile soldiery had melted away like a mist; a mounted officer came flying down the street ahead of the legionaries.

"The ladies are safe, Imperator!" Drusus was reporting with military exactitude. "I have lost twelve men."

Cæsar galloped along beside the chariot. He had his horse under absolute control, and he extended his hand, first to Fabia, then to Cornelia.

"Fortune has been kind to us," said he, smiling.

"Vesta has protected us," said Fabia, bowing her head.

Cæsar cast a single inquiring, keen glance at the Vestal.

"Your excellency doubts the omnipotence of the goddess," continued she, looking him steadily in the face.

"That a power has protected you," was his answer, "I am the last to deny."

But the Imperator and Drusus were exchanging glances; that a woman of the intelligence of Fabia could believe in the regular, personal intervention of the Deity in human affairs was to them, not an absurdity, but a mystery unfathomable.

And so, safe-guarded by the troops, they rode back to the palace, where the preparations for defence were ready, and all were awaiting the onset of Achillas. The weary men on the walls cheered as the carriages with their precious burdens rolled in at the gate; and cheered again for Drusus and his eighteen who had taught the Alexandrian rabble how Roman steel could bite. But Drusus himself was sad when he thought of the twelve good men that he had left behind — who need not have been sacrificed but for his headlong rashness.

And how had the mob come to attack the house of Cleomenes? It was a long story, but in a few words probably this. Pratinas had come and demanded of Cleomenes that he surrender the ladies (doubtless because they would be useful hostages) to go with him to Achillas. Cleomenes had refused, the more especially as Cornelia adjured him not to deliver them over to the clutches of such a creature; and Pratinas went away full of anger and threatenings. How he came to be in Alexandria, and had returned so soon from Achillas's forces, if he had indeed gone to Achillas, was neither clear nor important. But that he had excited the mob to assail Cleomenes's mansion needed no great proof. Cleomenes himself had seen his artful fellow-countryman surveying the riot from a house-top, though doubtless he had kept at a prudent distance during the fighting.

So ended that exciting day, or rather that night. It was Cleopatra who with her own hands laid the bandages on Cornelia's wounded shoulder, but the hurt was not serious; only, as Drusus laughingly assured her, it was an honourable scar, as became the descendant of so many fighting Claudii and Cornelii.

"Ah! delectissime," replied she, "it isn't the hurt that gives me pain; it is that I was frightened — frightened when you were acting like one of the Heroes!"

"Mehercle!" laughed Drusus, before he left her to snatch a few hours of well-earned rest and see to the dressing of his own bruises, "I would not blame a veteran for being panic-struck in that mêlée, if he didn't have a chance to swing a weapon and so keep his heart from standing still."

II

On the next day Achillas moved up his thousands and attacked the palace fortifications. There was a desperate struggle in the streets outside the royal residence; the assailants were five to the defenders' one, and the mob was arming to aid in the assault; but the Egyptians soon realized that it was no light thing to carry barricades held by men who had fought in Gaul, Britain, Germany, Spain, Italy, and Greece, and never tasted overthrow. Fiercest of all was the fight at the harbour, where the navy of the king lay, and which, if seized, would have put Cæsar at his enemies' mercy. But here, also, Roman valour prevailed over Oriental temerity. All the ships that Cæsar could not use were burned. With the rest he sailed over to the Pharos island, and landed men to make good the tower on that point of vantage. So ended the first round of battle; and the initial danger of being overwhelmed by sheer force was over.

But day after day of conflict followed. Princess Arsinoë and Achillas quarrelled in the camp of the besiegers, and this occasioned some respite to the Romans. Still there was no end to the fighting. Cæsar sent off to Asia Minor, Syria, and Crete for reënforcements; but these, all knew, could not come at once. A sharp struggle cleared the houses nearest to the palace, and the general caused them to be razed and the positions thoroughly fortified. He seized the low-lying ground which ran as an insignificant valley down between the halves of the city and tried to cut his enemies' position in twain. So the struggle dragged on. Achillas had been murdered by Arsinoë, and she had placed in command her governor, the eunuch Ganymed, who was more dangerous by his sly craft than fifty common generals. One day a frightened centurion reported to Cæsar that all the cisterns used by the troops were becoming flooded with sea-water. It was a contrivance of Ganymed. The soldiers were in a panic, and it was all that their leader could do to pacify them. And then one of those strokes of fortune which will always come to a favoured few was vouchsafed; as the terrified Romans delved in the earth where rain had seldom fallen, lo! on the very first night of their toil fresh water bubbled up, and all the danger was at an end.

But it is needless to tell how the contest was waged; how the thirty-seventh legion arrived as help, how the wind kept them off port exposed to the enemy, and how Cæsar sailed out and succoured them, and worsted the Alexandrian ships. Then, again, Ganymed stirred the disheartened citizens to build another fleet, and, by tremendous exertions, a new flotilla arose to threaten to cut Cæsar off; and there was a second battle for dear life — this time on sea close by the city; while Roman and Alexandrian stood staring on the housetops, with their hearts beating quickly, for defeat meant ruin to the Romans. And, again, the gods of the waters fought for Cæsar, and the beaten Alexandrian fleet drifted back to the shelter of its mole in the harbour of Eunostus.

Next came a great struggle for the possession of the Pharos. The fighting was severe, the footing on the island hard to win, up steep crags and rocks swept by volleys of missiles; but Italian courage seemed inexhaustible. The legionaries, without ladders or fascines, stormed towers and battlements. The town on the island was taken and the fort by it; then came the contest along the mole, driving the Alexandrians to the fort at the lower end. On the next day the second fort, too, was taken. There was a bridge at the lower end of the mole, and the Alexandrians had tried to sail under to attack the Cæsarians in the western harbour. The legionaries toiled to fill up the passage. All seemed going well, but of a sudden befell calamity.

* * * * * * * * * *

Panic will seize the most hardened veterans, and so it was that day. A flank attack from the Alexandrian ships, and of other foes by land, a sudden giving way on the part of some sailors who were defending the working party, and then terror spread among the three veteran cohorts at the lower fort. Cæsar had been among his men directing the work, with him had gone Drusus, as aide-de-camp, and Agias, who had long been chafing under the restraints of the beleaguered palace and imagined the position safe and unassailable. The panic came more quickly than words may tell: a few hostile shouts from behind, cries of fear and alarm, a volley of darts, and the men who had hunted the Magnus to his death fled like raw recruits at their first arrow.

The Cæsarian ships beside the mole began to thrust back, lest the enemy seize them. The terrified legionaries rushed from their ranks, cast away shield and cuirass, sword and dart. Every man cared but to save himself, the spirit of mere fear uppermost. Cæsar and Drusus rushed into the press, and commanded and exhorted; they might have better striven to turn the flight of a herd of frightened cattle; their words fell on deaf ears; the panic-struck soldiers swept them aside in a mad dash to get on board the receding shipping. The danger was terrible. On either side the enemy were rushing down the mole, and over the defences just forsaken by the Romans. Cæsar had been caught in the swirl of his men and carried along despite his resistance. He fell, and Drusus, who struggled to be near him, ran to his side.

" We must escape, Imperator! " cried he, in his commander's ear. He saw that there was blood on the general's face, and for an instant that thought overpowered all others.

"Save yourselves," gasped Cæsar, striving to struggle to his feet. " You cannot aid me."

A burly Egyptian soldier was running toward them, far ahead of the other enemies, flourishing a battle-axe. Did he realize the prize that lay almost in his power? Drusus had not been fighting, but his sword was now out. One blow of the terrible weapon of the legionary sent the oncomer sprawling in his own gore. A trifling respite had been gained. Cæsar steadied himself and looked about him. They were alone with Agias facing the foe; the legionaries were struggling one over another at the edge of the causeway, battling for dear life to force their way into the only galley that had not thrust off.

"Come," said Cæsar, turning; and the three joined in the flight. To linger were madness.

It was only a trifling distance across the mole, but a frightful tragedy was enacted before their eyes as they ran. The galley by the mole was none too large; as the frightened men piled into her, the shifting and increasing weight threw her on an uneven keel; and then came the horror. A cry of mortal agony burst from hundreds of throats as the ship capsized. Drusus, as he ran, saw, but for a twinkling, her deck black with writhing men, then her curving sides and keel, ere all vanished behind the embankment of the mole. The three fugitives ran to the edge of the causeway: below them, the water full of men battling for life; behind, the foe, now fully aware of their advantage and pressing on with exultant shouts. Never had the Imperator been in greater peril. Drusus glanced at his chief and saw that he was very pale, evidently

2 ɪ

hurt in the scuffle. There was not a ship within hail, not a ship within two arrow-flights; and all seemed pulling back as if to escape from the danger.

"Leap, swim!" cried Cæsar, casting off his breastplate.[1]

"There is no ship within reach, Imperator," replied the young man, gravely.

"You are young and strong," was his answer, "and will come away safe." Cæsar was preparing to spring over the edge.

"And you?" cried Drusus, catching him by the wrist. He knew that Cæsar could never swim the distance to the nearest ship.

"In the hands of the Fates."

But Agias, whose eyes had been straining out into the western harbour, cried, "Help! A galley is coming!"

"Imperator," said Drusus, "you must wait for this galley." The foe were almost on them.

"Are you mad?" was the exclamation of the general.

"I can hold them off until it is safe to swim," and Drusus had covered himself behind a coping in the masonry.

Cæsar measured the distance with his eye.

"We play at dice with Fortuna, whatever we do," was his comment. "Come, then." And the three steadied themselves on the narrow footing behind the parapet, one thrust being enough to send them headlong. Fortunately weapons were ready — thrown away by the luckless fugitives. When the Alexandrians rushed up, three pila crashed in upon them, and, caught unawares by the little volley, they held back an instant. The three desperate men were counting their hearts' beats, while the distance from the friendly galley lessened. Then the rush came, but it was met, and, narrow as was the ledge,

[1] *Lorica.*

the attempt to carry it failed. The victors were stripping the dead, and, thus engaged, few joined in the attack. Cæsar had laid down his paludamentum, and the attackers thought they had to deal simply with three ordinary Romans, who meant to sell their lives dearly. Another rush; the Imperator was forced hard, so that another push would have sent him plunging into the sea; but his companions sent the attackers reeling back, and there was more breathing time. The Alexandrians had received a taste of these Roman blades, and they did not enjoy it. Stripping the dead and picking up lost arms was more profitable than bearding the three lions. The galley was drawing nearer. Drusus began to think of something else besides thrusting at men before him.

"They will give us time to escape, Imperator."

"I think so;" but as Cæsar spoke all three started in dismay. There was a new face among the little band immediately opposed to them — Pratinas.

The Greek had never looked so handsome as in armour. His beautifully polished mail sat on him with perfect grace; he was a model for an artist's Ares, the beautiful genius of battle. *He*, at least, knew whose were those three stern, set faces defiantly peering over the low parapet that ran waist-high along the edge of the mole.

"At them!" cried the Hellene. "A thousand drachmas to the man who brings the middle Roman down!"

The "middle Roman" was Cæsar. The enemy came on again, this time some springing over the parapet to run along the narrow outer platform and attack from either side. But the galley was still nearer.

"Throw off your armour and leap!" It was Drusus who commanded now, and Cæsar who obeyed. The Imperator tore off his greaves and helmet, caught his general's cloak in his

teeth, that it might not fall as a trophy to the foe, and sprang
down into the waves; it was all done in a twinkling. But,
quick as the leap had been, it was but just in time. A rush
of irresistible numbers carried Drusus off of his feet, and he
fell also — but fell in all his armour. It was an instant too
crowded for sensations. He just realized that his helmet
tumbled from his head as he fell backward. The weight of
his greaves righted him while he was in the air. He struck
the water with his feet. There was a chilling shock; and then,
as he went down, the shield on his left arm caught the water
in its hollow and bore him upward. Nature reasserted itself;
by a mighty tug at the straps he wrenched away his breastplate, and could make shift to float. The short harbour
waves lifted him, and he saw Cæsar striking out boldly toward
the now rapidly approaching galley. Even as the general
swam, Drusus observed that he held up a package of papyri in
his left hand to keep it out of the wet; in uttermost perils
Cæsar could not forget his books. But while the young man
gazed seaward, shook the water from his eyes, and struck out
to reach the friendly galley, groans and shouts arose from the
waters near beside him. A voice — Agias's voice — was calling out for help. The sound of his freedman's cries drove the
Roman to action. Twice the waves lifted him, and he saw
nothing; but at the third time he lit on two forms clinging to
a bit of wreckage, and yet struggling together. A few powerful strokes sent him beside them, and, to his unutterable
astonishment, he beheld in the person who was battling with
Agias for possession of the float none other than Pratinas.
There are times when nothing has opportunity to appear wonderful. This moment was one of these. Actions, not words,
were wanted. The elder Greek had made shift to draw a
dagger, and was making a vicious effort to stab the other, who

had gripped him round the neck with a tenacity that would end only with life. One stroke of Drusus's fist as he surged alongside the wreckage sent the dagger flying; and in a twinkling he had borne Pratinas down and had him pinioned fast on the planking of the rude raft. There was a great shout rising from the enemy on the mole. A few darts spat in the water beside the fugitives; but at the sight of the approaching galley the Alexandrians gave way, for on her decks were swarming archers and slingers, and her powerful ballistæ were already working havoc. The pulsations of her banks of oars grew slower as she swept up to the fugitives, the great column of white spray curling around her prow sank, and while she drifted past them a boat shot forth. In a minute Drusus was standing on her deck, and the sailors were passing up Pratinas, still feebly resisting, and Agias, who was weak and helpless with his wounds. On the poop Cæsar was conversing with a seaman of magnificent presence, who was in the act of assuring the Imperator that his vessel and crew were at the general's service.

III

The boats of the rescuer were pulling about, taking up such few Romans as had been able to keep afloat; but Drusus was too exhausted to give them further heed. He realized that the vessel he was aboard was no member of the Roman squadron, that its crew were neither Cæsarians nor Alexandrians. Deft hands aided him off with his water-soaked clothing, and placed bandages on his bruises and cuts. A beaker of spiced wine, the like of which he had never drunk before, sent a thrill of reinvigorated life through his veins. When he came back upon the deck he found Cæsar — pale, yet, as ever, active and untiring — still conversing with the captain of the vessel. The

Imperator had a bandage drawn across his forehead, but otherwise he seemed none the worse for his recent danger. The galley, under a swinging oar, was pulling back across the "Great Harbour" to the palace quay. The battle was over; four hundred good Roman lives had been lost, but the disaster had not entailed any serious compromise of Cæsar's position. There was no need of continuing at the Pharos, and it was well to assure the anxious garrison at the palace-fortress that their general was safe and sound.

Drusus, as the one thing natural under the circumstances, went to the captain of his rescuers to express his obligation and gratitude.

"This is Quintus Livius Drusus," said Cæsar, good-naturedly, already at his ease, to the strange commander, "who serves on my staff. In saving him I owe you a debt, O Demetrius, in addition to my own rescue."

The stranger caught Drusus by both hands.

"Are you indeed the son of Sextus Drusus of Præneste?" he questioned with eagerness.

"Assuredly, my good sir," replied the young Roman, a bit confused at the other's impetuosity.

"And did your father never tell you of a certain Demetrius, a Greek, who was his friend?"

"He did; this Demetrius was cast into prison and condemned by Pompeius; my father secured his escape;" and Drusus hesitated. His mind had worked rapidly, and he could jump at a conclusion.

"Say it out, your excellency," pressed the seaman.

"He became a pirate, though my father did not blame him overmuch."

"*Eu!*" interrupted Cæsar, as if to prevent a moment of awkwardness. "Before King Minos's days nothing was more

honourable. I have known some excellent men who were
pirates."

But Demetrius had, in true Eastern fashion, fallen on his
knees and kissed the feet of Drusus.

"The son of my preserver! I have saved him! Praises to
Mithras!"

After this, there was no longer any constraint on the part
of rescuers or rescued. And that evening, when all were safe
behind the palace walls, Cæsar called the pirate chief into the
hall where he had been banqueting with Cleopatra, Fabia, and
Cornelia, and his favourite officers, and asked for an account
of his life. A strange enough story it was Demetrius had to
tell, though Cornelia had heard it before; of two voyages to
wealthy Taprobane,[1] one as far as the Golden Chersonesos,[2]
almost to the Silk Land, Serica, of voyages out beyond the
Pillars of Hercules into the Sea of Darkness, — everywhere
that keel of ship had ploughed within the memory of man.

"And the men that drove you to freebooting?" asked Cæsar,
when the company had ceased applauding this recital, which
the sailor set forth with a spontaneous elegance that made it
charming.

"I have said that they were Lucius Domitius, whom the
gods have rewarded, and a certain Greek."

"The Greek's name was —"

"Kyrios," said Demetrius, his fine features contracting with
pain and disgust, "I do not willingly mention his name. He
has done me so great a wrong, that I only breathe his name
with a curse. Must you know who it was that took my child,
my Daphne, — though proof I have not against him, but only
the warnings of an angry heart?"

"But he was —" pressed Cæsar.

[1] Ceylon. [2] Malay Peninsula

"Menon." And as he spoke he hissed the words between his teeth. "He is one knave among ten thousand. Why burden your excellency with remembering him?"

So the conversation went on, and Cæsar told how he had been taken prisoner, when a young man, by pirates near Rhodes, and how he had been kept captive by them on a little isle while his ransom was coming.

"Ah!" interrupted Demetrius, "I have heard the whole tale from one of my men who was there. You, kyrios, behaved like a prince. You bade your captors take fifty talents instead of twenty, as they asked, and wrote verses and declaimed to your guards all the time you were awaiting the money, and joined in all their sports; howbeit, you kept telling them that you would crucify them all for the matter."

"*Hem!*" laughed Cæsar. "Didn't I make good the threat?"

"You did with all save this man, who got away," was his unflinching answer. "Although in mercy you strangled all your captors before you had them put on the crosses."

"*Hei!*" quoth the Imperator. "I should have spared them to give me criticism of those verses now."

"Kyrios," rejoined Demetrius, "the man who survived assures me that the verses at least were wretched, though your excellency was a very good wrestler."

"*Euge!* Bravo!" cried Cæsar, and all the company joined in. "I must take a few of your men back to Rome, for we need critics for our rough Latin versifiers."

Drusus, as soon as the laugh passed away, arose, and addressed his chief:—

"Imperator," he said, "Agias this morning dragged from off the mole with him into the water one of the most dangerous men in the councils of our enemies. I mean, as you know,

Pratinas the Greek. He is now in the palace prison, but every one is aware that, so long as he so much as lives, we are hardly safe. What shall be done?"

Cæsar frowned.

"This is hardly a basilica for a trial," he replied, "but *'inter arma silent leges.'* Tell the centurions on guard to bring him here. I imagine we must grant him the form of an examination."

Drusus went out to give the necessary orders.

"You did not see Agias's prisoner?" asked Cornelia of Demetrius, who was now an old friend.

"I did not," answered the pirate prince, pouring down the contents of a prodigious beaker at a single draught. "A very desperate man, I imagine. But it is hard for me to blame any one so long as he fights openly. Still," he added, with a laugh, "I mustn't express such sentiments, now that his excellency has given me this." And he tossed over to Cornelia a little roll, tiny but precious, for it was a general pardon, in the name of the Republic, for all past offences, by land or sea, against the peace. *"Babai!"* continued Demetrius, lolling back his great length on the couch, "who would have imagined that I, just returning from a mere voyage to Delos to get rid of some slaves, should save the lives of my cousin, my benefactor's son, and Cæsar himself, and become once more an honest man. Gods! gods! avert the misfortunes that come from too much good fortune!"

"Was Agias badly wounded?" asked Cornelia, with some concern.

"Oh," replied his cousin, "he will do well. If his precious captive had thrust his dagger a bit deeper, we might have a sorry time explaining it all to that pretty little girl — Artemisia he calls her — whom he dotes upon. By the bye," continued Demetrius, as entirely at his ease in the company as though he had been one of the world's high-born and mighty, "can your ladyship tell me where Artemisia is just now? She was a very attractive child."

"Assuredly," said Cornelia. "She is here in the palace, very anxious, I doubt not, about Agias. Come, I will send for her. You shall tell her all about his escape."

Demetrius appeared pleased, and Cornelia whispered to a serving-lad, who immediately went out.

The tramp of heavy feet sounded on the mosaics outside the banqueting room; the tapestry over the doorway was thrust aside, and in the dim lamplight — for it had long been dark — two rigid soldiers in armour could be seen, standing at attention. Drusus stepped past them, and saluted.

"The prisoner is here, Imperator," he said.

"Bring him in," replied Cæsar, laying down his wine-cup.

The curtain swayed again, and the rest of a decuria of troops entered. In their centre was a figure whose manacles were clinking ominously. In the uncertain light it was only possible to see that the prisoner was bent and shivering with fright. The general shrugged his shoulders in disgust.

"This is the sort of creature, Drusus," quoth he, derisively, "that is so dangerous that we must despatch him at once? *Phui!* Let him stand forth. I suppose he can still speak?"

Pratinas made a pitiable picture. The scuffle and wetting had done little benefit to his clothes; his armour the pirates had long since appropriated; his hair, rather long through affection, hung in disorder around his neck. He had shaved off his "philosopher's" beard, and his smooth cheeks showed ugly scratches. He was as pale as white linen, and quaking like a blade of grass in the wind, the very antithesis of the splendid Ares of the fight on the mole.

"Your name is Pratinas?" began Cæsar, with the snappish energy of a man who discharges a disagreeable formality.

"Yes, despotes," began the other, meekly; but as he did so he raised his head, and the rays of one of the great candelabra fell full on his face. In a twinkling a shout, or rather a scream, had broken from Demetrius. The pirate had leaped from his couch, and, with straining frame and dilated eyes, sprang between the prisoner and his judge.

"Menon!" The word smote on the captive like the missile of a catapult. He reeled back, almost to falling; his eyes closed involuntarily. His face had been pale before, now it was swollen, as with the sight of a horror.

"Demetrius!" and at this counter exclamation, the cornered man burst into a howl of animal fear. And well he might, for Demetrius had sprung upon him as a tiger upon an antelope. One of the guards indiscreetly interposed, and a stroke of the pirate's fist sent the soldier sprawling. Demetrius caught his victim around the body, and crushed the wretched man in beneath his grasp. The pseudo-Pratinas did not cry out twice. He had no breath. Demetrius tore him off of his feet and shook him in mid-air.

"Daphne! Daphne!" thundered the awful pirate; "speak— or by the infernal gods—"

"Put him down!" shouted Cæsar and Drusus. They were almost appealing to an unchained lion roaring over his prey. Drusus caught one of Demetrius's arms, and with all his strength tore it from its grasp.

"The man cannot say a word! you are choking him," he cried in the pirate's ear.

Demetrius relaxed his mighty grip. Pratinas, for so we still call him, leaned back against one of the soldiers, panting and gasping. Drusus took his assailant by the arm, and led him back to a seat. Cæsar sat waiting until the prisoner could speak.

"Pratinas," said the Imperator, sternly, "as you hope for an easy death or a hard one, tell this man the truth about his daughter."

Pratinas drew himself together by a mighty effort. For an instant he was the former easy, elegant, versatile Hellene. When he answered it was with the ring of triumph and defiance.

"Imperator, it would be easy to tell a lie, for there is no means of proof at hand. This man," with a derisive glance at his enemy, "says that I know something about his daughter. Doubtless, though, since he has pursued for recent years so noble an avocation, it were more grateful if he thanked me for caring for the deserted girl. Well, I kept her until she was sufficiently old, and then — for I was at the time quite poor — disposed of her to a dealer at Antioch, who was planning to take a slave caravan to Seleucia. My good friend probably will find his daughter in some Parthian harem, unless —"

Cornelia had arisen and was whispering to Drusus; the latter turned and held the raging pirate in his seat. Pratinas had made of every word a venomed arrow, and each and all struck home. The workings of Demetrius's face were frightful, the beads of agony stood on his brows, — doubtless he had always feared nothing less, — the certainty was awful. Cornelia looked upon him half-anxious, yet serene and smiling. Drusus, too, seemed composed and expectant. The Imperator gazed straight before him, his eyes searching the prisoner through and through, and under the glance the Greek again showed signs of fear and nervousness.

The curtain at the opposite end of the hall rustled, Cornelia rose and walked to the doorway, and returned, leading Artemisia by the hand. The girl was dressed in a pure white chiton; her thick hair was bound back with a white fillet, but in the midst of its mass shone a single golden crescent studded with little gems. She came with shy steps and downcast eyes — abashed before so many strangers; and, as she came, all gazed at her in admiration, not as upon the bright beauty of a rose, but the perfect sweetness of a modest lily. Cornelia led her on, until they stood before the prisoner.

"Artemisia," said Cornelia, in a low voice, "have you ever seen this man before?"

Artemisia raised her eyes, and, as they lit on Pratinas, there was in them a gleam of wonder, then of fear, and she shrank back in dread, so that Cornelia threw her arm about her to comfort her.

"*A! A!*" and the girl began to cry. "Has he found me? Will he take me? Pity! mercy! Pratinas!"

But no one had paid her any more attention. It was Cæsar who had sprung from his seat.

"Wretch!" and his terrible eyes burned into Pratinas's guilty breast, so that he writhed, and held down his head, and began to mutter words inaudible. "Can you tell the truth to save yourself the most horrible tortures human wit can devise?"

But Pratinas had nothing to say.

Again Demetrius leaped upon him. The pirate was a frantic animal. His fingers moved as though they were claws to pluck the truth from the offender's heart. He hissed his question between teeth that ground together in frenzy.

"How did you get her? Where from? When?"

Pratinas choked for utterance.

"Artemisia! Daphne! Yours! I lost her! Ran away at Rome!"

The words shook out of him like water from a well-filled

flask. Demetrius relaxed his hold. A whole flood of conflict-ing emotions was displayed upon his manly face. He turned to Artemisia.

"*Makaira!* dearest! don't you know me?" he cried, holding outstretched his mighty arms.

"I am afraid!" sobbed poor Artemisia in dismay.

"Come!" It was Cornelia who spoke; and, with the daughter crying softly on one arm, and the father dragged along in a confused state of ecstasy on the other, she led them both out of the room.

Pratinas was on his knees before Cæsar. The Hellene was again eloquent — eloquent as never before. In the hour of extremity his sophistry and his rhetoric did not leave him. His antitheses, epigrams, well-rounded maxims, figures of speech, never were at a better command. For a time, charmed by the flow of his own language, he gathered strength and confidence, and launched out into bolder flights of subtly wrought rhetoric. He excused, explained away each fault, vivified and magnified a hundred non-existent virtues, reared a splendid word-fabric in praise of clemency. To what end? Before him sat Cæsar, and Drusus, and a dozen Romans more, who, with cold, unmoved Italian faces, listened to his artificial eloquence, and gave no sign of pity. And as he went on, the sense of his hopeless position overcame the wretched man, and his skill began to leave him. He became thick and confused of speech; his periods tripped; his thought moved backward. Then his supple tongue failed him utterly, and, in cries and incoherent groans, he pleaded for the right to exist.

"Man," said the Imperator, when the storm of prayers and moans was over, "you conspired against Quintus Drusus, my friend. You failed — that is forgiven. You conspired, I have cause to believe. against Pompeius, my enemy, but a Roman

— that is unproved, and therefore forgiven. You conspired with Pothinus against me — that was an offence touching me alone, and so that, too, may be forgiven. But to the prayers of a father you had wronged, you answered so that you might gloat over his pain. Therefore you shall die and not live. Take him away, guards, and strike off his head, for his body is too vile to nail to any cross."

The face of the Greek was livid. He raised his manacled hands, and strained at the irons in sheer despair. The soldiers caught him roughly to hale him away.

"Mercy! kyrios! kyrios!" he shrieked. "Spare me the torments of Hades! The Furies will pursue me forever! Pity! Mercy!"

Cornelia had reëntered the room, and saw this last scene.

"When my uncle and Ahenobarbus were nigh their deaths," she said stingingly, "this man observed that often, in times of mortal peril, skeptics call on the gods."

"The rule is proved," said Cæsar, casting a cynical smile after the soldiers with their victim. "All men need gods, either to worship when they live, or to dread when they die."

CHAPTER XXV

CALM AFTER STORM

I

LIKE all human things, the war ended. The Alexandrians might rage and dash their numbers against the palace walls. Ganymed and young Ptolemæus, who had gone out to him, pressed the siege, but all in vain. And help came to the hard-pressed Romans at last. Mithridates, a faithful vassal king, advanced his army over Syria, and came down into the Delta, sweeping all before him. Then Cæsar effected a junction with the forces of his ally, and there was one pitched battle on the banks of the Nile, where Ptolemæus was defeated, and drowned in his flight. Less than a month later Alexandria capitulated, and saw the hated consular insignia again within her gates. There was work to do in Egypt, and Cæsar — just named dictator at Rome and consul for five years — devoted himself to the task of reform and reorganization. Cleopatra was to be set back upon her throne, and her younger brother, another Ptolemæus, was to be her colleague. So out of war came peace, and the great Imperator gave laws to yet another kingdom.

But before Cæsar sailed away to chastise Pharnaces of Pontus, and close up his work in the East, ere returning to break down the stand of the desperate Pompeians in Africa, there was joy and high festival in the palace of Alexandria;

and all the noble and great of the capital were at the feast, — the wedding feast of Cornelia and the favourite staff officer of the Imperator. The soft warm air of the Egyptian springtime blew over the festoons of flowers and over the carpets of blossoms; never before was the music more sweet and joyous. And overhead hung the great light-laden dome of the glowing azure, where the storks were drifting northward with the northward march of the sun.

And they sang the bridal hymns, both Greek and Latin, and cried "Hymen" and "Talasio"; and when evening came,

> "The torches tossed their tresses of flame,"

as said the marriage song of Catullus; and underneath the yellow veil of the bride gleamed forth the great diamond necklace, the gift of Cleopatra, which once had been the joy of some Persian princess before the Greeks took the hoard at Persepolis.

Agias was there; and Cleomenes and his daughters; and Demetrius, with Artemisia, the most beautiful of girls, — as Cornelia was the fairest of women, — clinging fondly to her father's side. So there was joy that day and night at the Alexandrian palace. And on the next morning the fleet trireme was ready which Demetrius had provided to bear Drusus and Cornelia and Fabia back to Italy. Many were the partings at the royal quay, and Agias wept when he said farewell to his late patron and patroness; but he had some comfort, for his cousin (who had arranged with Cleomenes that, since his freebooting days were happily over, the two should join in a partnership for the India trade) had made him a promise to be fulfilled in due course of time — for Artemisia was still very young.

"You are no Ichomachus, Xenophon's perfect wife-educa

2 K

tor," the ex-pirate had said to his importunate cousin; "wait a few years."

And Agias was fain to be content, with this hope before him.

There were other partings than his; but at last the adieus were over, and all save Cæsar went back upon the quay. The Imperator alone tarried on the poop of the vessel for an instant. His features were half wistful as he held Drusus by the hand, but his eyes were kindly as ever to the young man.

"Ah, amice!" he said, "we who play at philosophy may not know all the time that there are gods, but at all times we know that there is the most godlike of divine attributes — love undefiled. Therefore let us hope, for we see little, and the cosmos is past finding out."

He sprang back on to the quay. The musicians on the bow struck up with pipe and lyre; the friends on the pier flung aboard the last garlands of rose and lily and scented thyme; the rowers bent to their task; the one hundred and seventy blades — pumiced white — smote the yellow waves of the harbour, and the ship sped away. Cornelia, Fabia, and Drusus stood on the poop gazing toward the receding quay. Long after they had ceased to recognize forms and faces they stared backward, until the pier itself was a speck, and the great buildings of the city grew dim. Then they passed the Pharos, and the land dwindled more and more into a narrow, dark ribbon betwixt blue water and bluer sky. The long swells of the open sea caught the trireme, and she rode gallantly over them — while the music still played, and her hardy crew, pirates no longer, but pardoned men, — seamen, employees of the honest merchant Demetrius, — sent the good ship bounding faster and faster, as they pressed their strength against the springing oars. Higher and higher rose the column of foam around the cutwater; louder and louder sang the foam under the stern, as they swept it past. The distant land faded to a thread, to a line, was gone; and to north and south and east and west were but the water and the cloudless ether. Fabia, Cornelia, and Drusus said little for a long time. Their eyes wandered, sometimes, over the track of the foam, and in their minds they saw again the water-birds plashing among lotus plants, and heard the ancient Egyptian litanies softly chanted behind the propylons of a temple built by some king two thousand years departed. But oftener their eyes ran ahead over the prow, and they walked again across the Forum of the city of their fathers, and drove across the Latin plainland, and spoke their own dear, sonorous, yet half-polished native tongue.

At last came evening; the sun sank lower and lower; now his broad red disk hung over the crest of the western waves; now it touched them; now it was gone, and only the lines of dying fire streamed behind him — the last runners in his chariot train. Up from the cabin below came the voice of the ship's steward, "Would their excellencies take any refreshment?" But they did not go at once. They watched the fire grow dimmer and dimmer, the pure light change to red gold, the red gold to crimson, and the crimson sink away.

"Ah, carissima!" cried Drusus, "would that when the orbs of our lives go down to their setting, they might go down like the sunlight, more beautiful in each act of the very dying, as they approach the final goal!"

"Yes, surely," replied Cornelia, touching her hands upon his head; "but who knows but that Catullus the poet is wrong when he says the sun of life will never rise save once; who knows but that, if our sun set in beauty, it will rise again in grandeur even more?"

"My children," said Fabia, gently, "the future lies in the knowledge of the gods; but out of the present we must shape our own future."

"No, delectissima," replied her nephew, "to do that we are all too weak; except it be true, as Aratus the poet has said, 'that we men are also the offspring of gods,' in which case Heaven itself must stoop to give us aid."

But Cornelia's eyes had wandered down into the foam, still gleaming as snow in the failing light.

"Ah!" she said, "the ages are long; if there be gods, their days are our lifetimes, and we but see a little and know not what to think. But to live a noble life will always be the fairest thing, whether death be an unending sleep or the threshold to Pindar's Elysium."

And what more of grave wisdom might have dropped from her lips none may relate, for her husband had shaken off the spell, and laughed aloud in the joy of his strong life and buoyant hopes. Then they all three laughed, and thought no more of sober things. They went down into the cabin just as the last bars of light flickered out in the west, and only the starlight broke the darkness that spread out over the face of the sea.

II

Drusus, as he himself had predicted, never wrote a great treatise on philosophy, and never drew up a cosmology that set at rest all the problems of the universe; nor did Cornelia become a Latin Sappho or Corinna, and her wise lore never went further than to make her friends afraid to affect a shammed learning in her presence. But they both did the tasks that fell to them better because they had "tasted the well of Parnassus" and "walked in the grove with the sages." And Drusus, through an active life, played an honourable part as a soldier and a statesman: with his beloved Imperator in the battles of Thapsus and Munda, when the last of the oligarchs were beaten down; then, after the great crime of murder, with his friend Marcus Antonius; and then, when Cleopatra's evil star lured both her and Antonius to their ruin, he turned to the only man whose wisdom and firmness promised safety to the state —and he joined himself to the rising fortunes of Octavius, the great Augustus, and fought with him to the end, until there was no longer a foreign or civil enemy, and the "Pax Romana" gave quiet to a subject world.

So Drusus had share with Mæcenas and Agrippa and the other imperial statesmen in shaping the fabric of the mighty Roman Empire. Not in his day did he or Cornelia know that it was wrong to buy slaves like cattle, or to harbour an implacable hate. They were but pagans. To them the truth was but seen in a glass darkly; enough if they lived up to such truth as was vouchsafed. But in their children's day the brightness arose in the East, and spread westward, and ever westward, until the Capitoline Jupiter was nigh forgotten, the glories of the Roman eagles became a tradition, the splendour of the imperial city a dream. For there came to the world a better Deity, a diviner glory, a more heavenly city. The greater grew out of the less. Out of the world-fabric prepared by Julius Cæsar grew the fabric of the Christian Church, and out of the Christian Church shall rise a yet nobler spiritual edifice when the stars have all grown cold.

THE END

Lindner

Morgan Park -
Claude
September
Lena Eggleston
1250

Guitar lesson - Madeline

Ibadai - Nigeria
Mama give house Travis
Horse, Photography, dating, Guitar
6500 - 3000 - R

- for short-bread and food is
  not enough

Walter chaphear for Mr. Arnold
Walter - 35
Ruth - 30
Beneatha - 30
Mama - 70
Travis - 100 - 11
Bobo waited 6 hrs. for Willie
Springfield for liquor = license